Return to the Central Sun

The Conjunction of Rahi

GARY FRANCIS DINI

BALBOA.PRESS

A DIVISION OF HAY HOUSE

Balboa Press books may be ordered through booksellers or by contacting:

Balboa Press
A Division of Hay House
1663 Liberty Drive
Bloomington, IN 47403
www.balboapress.com
1 (877) 407-4847

ISBN: 978-1-9822-4862-8 (sc)
ISBN: 978-1-9822-4863-5 (e)

Library of Congress Control Number: 2020909751

Print information available on the last page.

Balboa Press rev. date: 07/13/2020

CONTENTS

ACKNOWLEDGEMENTS

The writing of this book was a gift Gary Dini gave to us from the depths of his loving and creative soul. His expansive grasp of the beyond was distilled into many avenues, this being only one. I feel much gratitude in having known him. He has inspired me, his wife, to reclaim and nurture my creative gifts. His joy for living, opened up a wellspring of love and creativity for many others.

I want to acknowledge and give thanks to those who assisted me in so many ways to bring this project to fruition. Marti Ross for the beautiful art in the cover of this book, and her willingness to contribute her thoughts to this process; Dominique Parducci for her loving and kind suggestions, and editorial expertise; Robin Peacock for her love and collaboration; Cathy Bain, Janice Patton, Shelley Salvatore, Jon Bisiaux, and many others who go unnamed but well remembered in my heart.

Peace and Blessings to all in the Light,
Karen Aubrey Niles –Dini, May 15, 2020

RETURN TO THE CENTRAL SUN

"The Conjunction of Rahi"

INVOCATION

"STAR CATCHER"

I am a hunter stalking opportunity
Light streaking pregnant essence.
Seeds of fortune, spinning Yin-yang's.
Down through mind, eye, heart, and hand.
I listen, watch, applauding infinite playwright.
What is contained in the twinkle of an eye? Reveling in a sacred dance with other souls
I ask myself, "What draws me close?
What repels me?
Which is fat for the senses?
What nourishes the soul?
To catch a star and drink the ambrosia of life
This is eternally added unto my self.
There is no limit to my capacity.

Alqa Wickering 2378

PROLOGUE

"Whispering Voices"
FROM THE REALM OF THE ELDERS

We acknowledge intelligence in your life stream that extends far into the denser realms of material creation. We will adjust our frequency and mode of communication and by collapsing time we can share a moment in linearity. In this way, you may come to know us in the greater awareness that you are moving towards, as you travel in the direction of our realm. We were once where you are now. Our world has passed through the stage of being unconsciously tethered to a body of flesh.

We have come to you countless times, embodied in a physical form, to keep you set on the right course. Your aspirations, and retrostory chronicle our lives. Your ideas are a part of us as much as you are a part of us. We are all connected. When awareness expands the illusory Design of the dream of separation will drop away, and all as one will be revealed. In the end, we will dwell as one, together in eternity.

Be it known that we are called the Elders. On many worlds with sentient life, we have made our mark. Like you, we have our Elders, too. In a way, we are your midwives charged with the development of embryonic souls emerging from physical creation into interdimensional life.

Endowed as you are with the seven primary light centers in your spirit form, you are like us. As you become more aware, you will be working in, what we could call, the eternal work. This is your ultimate inheritance and eventual destiny. The dream matrix is just a further preparatory step.

The Tharrr are a part of you that is now experiencing individuality through you. These beings of cosmic awareness need the experience of physical embodiment to find completion. You need the Tharrr to awaken to your multidimensional truth. In the realm of time, you will integrate into oneness with great majesty and power.

Our Elders have given us the task of guiding you in your awakening process. It is a most satisfying task and favors your speedy adjustment to living a fuller, more multidimensional life. The fourth light center in your body is being charged with energy at an accelerated rate. It is called the quickening. A crucial boundary has been passed as you travel closer to the Grand Central Sun. This awakening occurs within us, as well, reminding us that the Central Sun dwells within us. You are the souls that have chosen the path of love.

*

CHAPTER ONE

THE GENESIS OF A HERO
"The Siege of Oblion"
Planet Oblion 2460

Kaitain Enro sighed. He was weary and confused. Deep inside a growing conviction that he was not doing what he was supposed to do, invaded his normally clear and concise path. The siege for Oblion was progressing slowly. The infestation of an alien symbiotic life form, the Tharrr, made the native population of the planet a more resistant and formidable opponent. He wasn't sure who or what was the opponent anymore.

The horror of an infected colony was frightening, especially inspired by the here-now holos. Comparisons to horror stories were graphically detailed in holo-feels and other media where referencing occurred with little accountability. Though the natives of Oblion were not human, no one questioned the morality of interceding. The media described the Oblionese as possessed monsters in horrific detail.

But were they lost? I don't see civil breakdown from anything outside of the Corporation demands!

Enro knew the mechanisms of media control. They were a part of the Colonial Corporation methods. Redefining a situation as a lost cause, cleared any moral question concerning the scorched earth approach that had been ordered. The spin was that the Colonial Corporation's duty was to stop the infestation for the greater good. Enro was not convinced, but no one of rank or influence asked for his opinion.

Not even the Omegans gave it a second thought!

This was the world according to the Colonial Corporation. Many of the older galactic civilizations considered the Corporation illvibe and retro. They were the very worst of what had migrated to the stars from Earth.

A standard command module served as the kaitain's private quarters. It was a self-contained COM room and portable headquarters built into a space worthy vessel. The heavily guarded troopers' compound was near the front line of the planetary siege.

Kaitain Enro, commander of a triton of Colonial Troopers, flopped down on his cot dimming the lights to ease the heaviness in his chest like a stone weighing on his spirit. Unexpressed opinions opposed to the politics of the Corporation had been festering within him for the past ten years.

As the leader of the army, political decisions were not supposed to be his job. His duty was to the Colonial Corporation itself and he was expected to follow the orders of Gentain Carbone, the supreme commander of the Colonial Troopers. His feelings evoked by the results of his necessary obedience were breaking free from their confinement.

The Earth had come a long way since galactic contact was made but the thousands of years of illvibe retrostory still persisted in the resurgence of domination and greed among a power hungry minority of Earth's population. They had reconstituted its form of governance in the diaspora of Earth's humanity as it populated several colonies. Enro was ashamed to admit to himself that he was a willing participant in the Corporation.

The Oblionese have not done anything wrong. They did not raise any real objection to the Tharrr? Could it be the natural evolution of these people? Why do we assume the worst?

Enro was the most decorated and well-known kaitain to ever serve the Colonial Troopers. Although he was proud of that distinction, for many years now he had become disillusioned with the policies of the private army the Corporation had created. In his estimation, they had become bullies hungering for more power. Lately, he had been asking himself whether it wasn't pride and fame that kept him from letting go of his position and entering retirement. He did not pretend to understand what was occurring on Oblion but it felt more like genocide than a rescue mission. Too many of these occurrences sounded like the retrostory of a pre-galactic Earth from the early twenty-first century.

Politicians and private contractors were already devising a plan to assume leadership over a previously sovereign world. There was nothing in their rhetoric that sounded beneficial to the Oblionese. The natural resources of Oblion were being divided up like pirate booty with companies deeply embedded in the corporate culture.

Growing up within a family of Omegan scholars had formed Enro's sharp mind and natural persuasiveness. He had been given a well-rounded view of retrostory.

The Corporation had a dark and menacing past. They had been complicit in the near destruction of old Earth. A far-reaching disaster was prevented only by the breaching of evolutionary thresholds, spiritual receptivity, and the coming of the Pleiadians, who represented the Galactic Consortium. The Consortium, who had established a tremendous and well-organized system of governance, had stopped the Corporation and ancient alien races from completely taking over the entire earth for the benefit of a ruling oligarchy.

Enro understood goodness needed to be defended and protected as much as possible in the world. Forces that deny the rights of others should not be given free reign.

The kaitain's black and muscular body stood over six feet 4 inches, yet the prowess of his great physical strength was minor compared to his intellectual capabilities. He was keenly aware that his ancestors had suffered great atrocities at the hands of those very same ruling families.

In a post contact era, racial hatred had all but disappeared. He was widely popular and a living legend among his troops. He was also a recognized hero to the corporate communities across several worlds.

Enro's grandfather, Cardinal Fellini, was one of the most beloved personages among the Omegans since the great reformation of 2125. His grandmother was one of the most famous Grand Dames of her generation. They were proud of their grandson. When the Omegans became collaborators with the Corporation his grandmother, the Grand Dame Feline Taylor, retired.

Enro's parents had both died young, leaving his grandparents to raise Enro. He spent his early years on Cardinal Fellini's lap, listening to stories embodying a vast reservoir of knowledge in religion, politics, and spiritual wisdom. Much like his father, Enro did not have the personality, or interest, to become an Omegan. Yet, he did embody the leadership qualities of his illustrious grandparents. Those qualities became apparent in Enro's career with his ascension to the rank of kaitain. Most people thought that he would become the next gentain or perhaps a planetary governor.

Exhaustion tugged at his nerves, but sleep eluded him. Enro's self-reflections and their ramifications swirled around in his head as he restlessly tossed and turned in his bed.

Why did the Omegans and the Colonial Corporation seem to have endless worlds to conquer? Why not allow others their sovereignty? Why do we remain such an aggressive race? Haven't we had enough of war?

Each night lately, he found himself alone in the dark with these questions plaguing his resting time. Questions a soldier is not supposed to ask.

I am a soldier but I am sick of fighting.

He fell into a fitful sleep. Sometime later, Enro awakened abruptly. A different destiny was about to begin.

*

A vertical shaft of light appeared by the bed in Enro's darkened cell. He sat up and reached for the pulse laser he kept by his bedstand. The shaft of light thickened and articulated itself into the form of a man with a deadly-looking laser pistol trained on Enro. The man stopped Enro from reaching into the drawer by waving the barrel of the gun.

"Hands down," the man said. "I have no wish to pull the trigger, Kaitain, but I will if you attempt to escape."

No alarms sounded, Enro thought.

Somehow, an assassin had penetrated rigorous defenses and found his way into Enro's quarters. The pistol also had a narrow-beamed flashlight that blinded Enro at first.

"Kaitain Enro, I mean you no harm," the man said.

"A theory hard to prove with that laser pistol pointing at me."

The man who stood before him smiled mysteriously. "Very well, my name is Orville Parker and I have come here to save your life."

Enro looked closely at the man before him. He stood about six feet tall and was of medium build. He had a surprisingly unruly mop of thick light brown hair. His eyes were unfathomably large and penetrating. There was no anger or malice there. Rather, he saw a little mischievousness mixed with solemn purpose. Orville wore a simple jump suit of Pleiadian design with a contraption strapped to his forearm.

A curious man, different.

Enro had a talent for reading people. Even in a large crowd, he was able to surmise with great accuracy the collective intent or the singular intent of an individual. He trusted those instincts. No urgent agenda revealed itself so far. He felt no illvibe.

He is kind of a geekoid for an assassin or a murderer.

"Save my life from what?" Enro asked.

Orville shrugged his shoulders. "Well, from the Corporation's grip on your life for one thing."

"Okay, tell me how?"

Orville Parker waved the pistol around as he spoke. "Okay, in about three minutes this base will be overrun with your enemy.

"My enemy? Not yours?"

"If you must know, the verdict isn't in on who my enemy really is. I do know that you need to listen to me or you will reap the wrath of the Oblionese for destroying their world. They will attack in vast numbers. The Oblionese will win this skirmish, Kaitain. Before that happens, we will depart. This command module is a self-contained transport, I believe."

Orville's delivery didn't allow for doubt. The force of will manifesting in his voice was aligned with the awesome power of the Central Sun. Having lived in close proximity to that level of divine magnetism, on Planet Mirror, gave Orville the power to ignite the astral body of any soul who was aware enough to perceive it.

Orville had been completely transfigured in the hundreds of years he had spent off world. Enro felt the hair on the back of his neck ripple with energetic discharge. He knew that fate itself issued forth from this curiously magnetic being that stood before him in the naked night at a precipitous hour.

"Yes, it is. The cockpit is in the forward compartment. But, why?"

"Why?"

"Why are you helping me? That is, if I believe you are indeed intending to save my life."

"Kaitain Enro, I come to you at the behest of the Elders. They need your help. I find this situation very awkward."

"The Elders? But, how?"

Enro grew up with stories of the Elders. His mother and grandmother would talk of an ancient race that had laid the spiritual foundations for all the Omegans and many intergalactic races that had evolved over the centuries. They were an order of beings that had transcended dimensions to spiritual realms beyond the visible world.

The Pleiadians were among those that claimed to be direct descendants of the Elders. It was the Pleiadians, after all, that had introduced humanity to the stars and helped the Gaians attain governance of the Earth. The Colonial Corporation was their rival. It had bothered Enro a great deal over the years. He often questioned the apparent schism that plagued humans from the parent planet, Earth.

The Omegans have formed an alliance with the Corporation! What next?

"The Elders have watched over all of us for a long time."

Enro felt energy begin to build in his body in the region of his heart. It felt warm and inviting though no words or revelations were forthcoming.

Orville's face lit up in a serene yet focused smile. His eyes laid upon Enro without any wavering. The energy built between them as energetic pathways lit up like sparklers on a cool clear night. Orville recognized that he was being used as a vessel to communicate something he was learning. He allowed grace of spirit to flow.

"I am a gardener, and a scientist. Lately, I have been helping people out with this evolution thing. I am trying to set things right. It is like a garden. Even weeds can be nurturing. The terrain must be healthy and then the garden grows on a more permanent foundation. It's a bit difficult to explain. I have lived among the Pleiadians for a long time. They say I have a great mission. Personally, I would rather grow more vegetables."

Enro remembered how his mother, Chichen, would talk about life in the context of her gardens. "How do you intend to 'rescue' me?"

"I have a unique way of traveling. I see you as someone who can provide the leadership your people need."

I recall intelligence reports that hinted and speculated that the Pleiadians have advanced technologies they carefully guard. Hmm.

"My people? What do you mean?"

"It seems that Tatochin is the next planet the Corporation plans on annexing. The Orion sector is vast, the planets many with much potential. The dream of power and domination runs deep in the Corporation's version of the hologram. Many souls will be spiritually challenged. Sometimes as we grow, we can choose in the dream we call life. Many will be affected."

Orville's thoughts raced beyond the concerns of the moment. Enro processed his new predicament.

Tatochin my home planet. We have prospered by our contact with the Elders. The Pleiadians have cared for us for many centuries.

I feel my body vibrating with potent energy as if compelling me to act. So much for retirement being a part of my good fortune! Okay Enro, I choose to be a participant in this dream world. Let it be so!

Orville regarded Enro. "I thought you knew? I believe that is your home world. The Elders want me to help stop them and I need your help."

"They are going to Tatochin?"

"Yes, that is why I have come to you."

"I didn't know." His voice trailed off into silence. He memlocked a series of meetings that were scheduled. "Ahhh," he said aloud.

Orville continued after a moment. "There is a rather active resistance movement on Tatochin. That is why the Corporation is going there next. They are already infiltrating all the technological and political systems of Tatochin. It's the pattern that the Corporation typically employs, as you well know." Orville paused. He took a deep breath. He sought to deepen his connection to the Holy Spirit.

After a moment, he continued. "We are aware of your discontent, Enro. I figured this would be the final straw for you."

"How do you know all this?" Enro struggled to keep up with Orville. He was a commander and according to Orville Parker, a major event was beginning. Enro always was astounded that Orion with it's distance of 900 light years from Earth was an inconsequential distance to their galactic mentors, the Pleiadians.

Plus-light capability was carefully offered to younger races but it was apparent that the Pleiadians had perfected such forms of travel to a far greater degree than was publicly known. Now Orville had appeared to him from apparently nowhere!

Enro met Orville's eyes. "I have many questions that remain unanswered."

Orville's face went from humor to a serious frown. He took a deep cleansing breath. "Enro, please, I will be glad to fill you in on many details in the nearnow. Every bit of information is always available, but I know you will have 20 more questions when I say such things. Time is short as you will soon see. As I said, I come to you at the behest of the Elders. In time, you will have all the confirmation you might require. Now though….it is time for a leap of faith and intense action."

He paused for emphasis and then continued.

"The Orion sector is now the Corporation's next arena of conquest. The Elders have asked me to stop them. How could I refuse?"

The Corporation's interest in the Orion sector had come to Enro's attention as gossip wafting through the ranks. The meetings scheduled in the nearnow, more than likely, were to inform him about his next command cycle.

Planets like Tatochin had become galactic civilizations at the same time as Earth. It never occurred to him that interest would mean conquest, but the Corporation had an arrogance that had troubled him for a long time. Their rhetoric and action in recent years reflected the belief that other forms of life were inferior and subject to limited freedoms.

"Too much bloodshed."

"Yes." Orville sent him telepathically in response.

The Corporation's actions appeared to Enro, and many others, as a throw-back to barbaric episodes that littered the past of humanity. It had taken a long time for the greater portion of humans to recognize how a few ancient families, along with certain galactic factions had conspired to rule and enslave its people. They had maintained power and control through the darkest of practices.

In recent years, those darker tales of alien interference over Earth's evolution had become known to its people. Secret deals with governments that ruled on Earth had given them power. This was hidden to the Pleiadians at the onset of the Diaspora.

With the entry into the galactic culture, Earth had finally began to heal the effects of those influences. It was a slow process hindered by advanced alien cultures that had been working in a clandestine way for many generations.

With the rise of technology, aliens had given the people new forms of media which had gained dominance over a population with new levels of control. The forces of evolution had been bent and twisted causing great suffering.

It increasingly had become apparent to Enro, and certain others, that those powerful and dark forces from Earth's past still roamed the planets and the media nexuses in the present day. Certain leaders and factions in the Omegans and the Troopers harbored feral characteristics that reflected those past times. It was something he did not understand and it roused suspicions within him almost to the point of repulsion. Now, anger arose from his gut.

"Tatochin…my home world…"

"They are innocent. They are farmers and a peaceful people."

"They also believe in the Elders"!

"Stop them…how?"

Orville tracked Enro's thinking with critical precision tempered by respect for the brilliance of the storied kaitain.

"Everyone is innocent Enro. In this time frame you are the kaitain. There is a resistance on Tatochin. They need leadership. I am thinking that you are already discontent with your situation and position with the Colonial Corporation. Is that true?"

"Yes, it is."

"The Elders think so. That is why I am apparently here."

Orville felt the resolve in the Kaitain's voice. One part of him felt uncomfortable with the burden of information he had unloaded on the large and proud man who sat before him. Time was not on his side though, and the Elders urged him with psychic waves of clear intention. Orville connected with something he knew and yet was still learning.

The ego isn't real.

Orville recognized the issue of linear time as the three dimensional hologram that still guided the more youthful human population. The nudge he received guiding him to press Enro into commitment and action, came from outside the dream as he understood it. He experienced a ripple within the fabric of creation.

A miracle from beyond?

The primary experience was love. Not a romantic chloroform filled with sentimentality but a sobering and constant current of safety and peace.

Suddenly Enro heard the voice of his mother in an auditory vision. A wave of love brought several tears to his eyes. Orville wagged his head in affirmation of the message Enro heard.

"We still need a Kaitain, Enro, and you are the only one we can trust right now."

After a moment of silence while Enro composed himself, Orville continued. "In less than ten years, Tatochin will be destroyed. Already, the hour is late. They will not be able to stop the annexation, but the Elders believe a great opportunity has presented itself. One that may preserve your beautiful home in the third dimension. Even I don't know the details."

Enro felt an odd but attractive energy around Orville Parker. He seemed to talk about time as a two-way mirror. The teaching of the Elders' spoke of time and space as illusions of the dream world. He knew that many possibilities might be presenting themselves.

A strange messenger if that is so.

The man looked into his eyes with utter frankness. Enro sensed a great wave of energy flowing to him in his presence. He simply could not refrain from engaging the man. Enro found his voice.

"I am very upset about the current direction the Colonial Corporation is leading us. We may not all be human beings but we live with other forms of sentient life on equal footing. It is wrong to think of it any other way. I find myself feeling ashamed to be associated with them. I mean, the Gaians of Earth, our ancestral home, have banished the Corporation from their world. I find myself asking why?"

"Indeed, Enro, that is a good question. One I will help you to answer, if you will let me. Just not this second! This moment of battle cannot be mitigated. It will play out."

"But how? Who are you?

"For now, I am a messenger and liaison to Elders who are also Pleiadians in many cases. I live among them and have for 400 years."

"400?"

"Yes."

Enro became silent within. The implications his fine mind had conjured with Orville's words struck a chord within him. After a pregnant moment of grace and magic, thought returned.

"I am the kaitain here. I can't just run off. What of Oblion? What have they done?"

"Nothing, they will ascend. That much is known." Orville sighed and continued. "Oblion is lost. They will incinerate the entire population. You were not even told."

"Incinerated?"

"Yes, and this is difficult. They will use your death to justify this dramatic over-reaction."

"But…"

"I know. You don't want anything to do with this, but it is Oblion's destiny."

"Destiny! How do you know that?"

Orville sighed. "I have already witnessed it. Again Enro, I will explain this to you in the required detail over time but not at this time. I intend no deception. That is why I am honestly answering your most difficult questions. I will say that I expected no less from you."

Orville grew silent. Enro would have to make his own choice.

"Again, why me?"

"Because the Elders think you are ready to accept my help. Are you?"

Enro found himself completely caught up in the moment. *The Colonial Corporation on Tatochin!*

He came from that world. They had done nothing to deserve such a fate. Something in him snapped.

"What do you want of me?"

Just then, in the distance, the sound of laser fire shattered the calm of the night.

"It begins," Orville said.

The glow of particle beam Kelson lasers cut sharp shadows across the sleeping encampment. In spite of the force field around the base, the enemy had found a way into the compound.

"Let's go to the cockpit", Enro said. "We have to take down the force field."

The sound of battle increased. The whole camp had erupted into violent conflict. Once they were in the cockpit of the command module, Enro turned on the surveillance equipment and shut down the force field. He observed the various holos covering the compound. The Oblionese were swarming up from several underground bunkers by the hundreds.

Orville grasped Enro's arm, "I recommend launching immediately. They will be looking for the command center."

"Hold on a moment." Enro began to pilot the craft. Atmospheric engines whined as they achieved sufficient power for take off. Within a minute, they lifted from the base and ascended above the reach of laser fire and small rockets. Once in a low geo-stationary orbit, Enro turned in his swivel chair. "We have two other modules below that can handle the attack on a command level. They will launch in a few moments, as well."

Orville laughed and held up the laser pistol he still held. "I assure you that in truth you have been perfectly safe in my presence from the moment we met. It's a pre-ad toy." He triggered the mechanism that dutifully glowed and blinked with modulating sounds to entertain a child. It was a comic moment in an otherwise serious situation.

"Enro, if you come with me you will be dead to the world you have lived in. Are you ready to make that move?"

"But how?"

"This craft has a Pleiadian engine does it not?"

"Yes, it's standard, no plus light capability."

"If you activate the gravity field while accelerating you would blow up the entire module, am I correct?"

"Why yes, that would be a deadly error, however safeguards are built in."

"Orville smiled. "I took the liberty of dismantling the emergency shut down program before I came to you. I hope I wasn't premature in my estimation regarding the outcome?

"When you are ready, we will do that."

"Wait, am I missing something. If I activate the gravity field, we will be dead, as well you know. Is that your plan?"

Orville laughed. "Sorry, Kaitain. I have indeed omitted something. This transport device will be our escape method." He held up his forearm that had the controller attached. "The explosion will hide our escape."

Maybe I will start a club called the incredible exploding life forms, hmmm.

The attack upon the Troopers' compound played out on the holos. Oblionese swarmed the base. Large freakish apparitions seemed to swirl all around them. The specters of other fighters and other false images made identifying them difficult. The Troopers did not know holographic illusion from the real soldiers. They were taking major causalities. The Oblionese conjured three-dimensional false shadows because of the Tharrr possession. It was proving lethal.

The Oblionese were infected with what was thought to be a very unusual symbiotic life form called The Tharrr. An intelligent spore-like creature, that upon entering the body spread like a collective. The ability to create three-dimensional apparitions in a field around their bodies was their most distinguishing feature.

Enro stared at Orville Parker. He thought to himself. *This is a strange situation.*

Orville held up a second sleek pulsing contraption with a forearm attachment. "As you know my laser pistol will not help us at all. This, however, will. It is called a Matter Relocator. With this device, we can depart this ship in the same manner I arrived. It employs micro-wormhole technology allowing us to travel great distances through interdimensional pathways. I must warn you though, once we leave, there will be no return. The world will believe that your command module has exploded ending your life. The truth will be something wildly different."

"Why?"

"Because the Corporation must not know of your whereabouts until the right moment. You must come with me to a place I call Mirror."

"Mirror?"

"Yes, it is a planet located in close proximity to the Central Sun. It is where I now live."

Orville leaned close to Enro with a gleam of mischief in his eyes. "The Pleiadians have a real long name for the place, but I like to call it Mirror. There we will prepare to save the people of Tatochin."

"That is a high price, Orville."

"Yes, it is personally, but Enro, I know that it is not only important for Tatochin, but for many other worlds. I do not know the details, but I trust the Elders on this. They revealed to me that there are certain times when the phenomenal worlds go through a spiritual metamorphosis. This what is now happening again. In nearnow retrostory it began in the late seventeenth century. Such memlocks of notable transitions continued in the 1960's, 2018, 2150, 2309, and the herenow. This is a long conversation. One we will revisit. We are in maxi-mode of a different sort in the herenow."

Enro sighed. His new best friend was as clear as a Delvian crystal on that.

Orville made an adjustment on the pulsing device strapped to his forearm. "As I said, when you are ready."

"What do you mean, ready?"

Orville gave him another one of those mischievous smiles. "Well I thought you might like to put something on besides your underwear before we travel across the galaxy."

Enro looked down to realize he was still in his underwear. At that moment Orville drew his toy laser and pulled the trigger. In spite of the gravity of the situation, Enro and Orville paused for a hearty laugh. Levity or not he dressed hurriedly. He felt an inner knowing about what was happening rather than any rational understanding. It would cause pain for some people if they thought he was dead, but he had never married and only a few family members remained.

The sounds of battle grew louder. The fighting was spreading like a wild fire. He finished preparing and headed toward the cockpit lost in thought.

Maybe circumstances will be kinder some day.

He looked back at his dresser as he departed his quarters in the command module. He realized that in a moment he would erase most of the memorabilia of the personal retrostory from his life. He went back and took several pictures of his parents and of his grandparents. He left everything else.

"Good bye…I never did like much clutter!"

In that moment, Enro recognized how his core intentions were in complete opposition to his station in life. He had been trapped by the iconic representation of victory and success as a kaitain conquering all opposition for the Colonial Troopers.

His thoughts raged. His reputation, as a good kaitain existed because many lives had been spared under his command. Those people appreciated that. He also came to know that many lives were lost for no good reason at all.

This conundrum had been his prison. He had coped with the burden of trying to save lives, while fulfilling the Corporation's agenda. It was time to drop their agenda and give his all to saving and protecting lives. The fate of the Oblion was a powerful reminder of the depth of the ego's folly. The idiots in power made choices that prolong suffering. He mentally sought to shift his focus.

Still, he felt loyalty to his troops. At his computer he keyed the pulse fax quickly alerting central galactic command of the surprise attack. Orbiting Wing Fighters would respond within minutes.

So be it.

Orville was silent. He understood the monumental decision the kaitain was about to make. He had to make a similar decision almost 430 years ago himself when he had blown up the computer center at the Colonial Mining Corporation, and relocated with the primitive device he had built. Orville was also aware of the irony and urgent need of the times.

Indeed, the exploding life form club!

*

While the battle continued on Oblion the command module exploded in the sky illuminating the growing carnage of a nightmare all too familiar. Kaitain Enro was gone.

The siege of Oblion was the main story on the Corporation's intergalactic herenow holos that evening. The headline was the death of Enro, the most famous kaitain to serve the glorious Colonial Troopers. According to the Corporation, Enro died at the Siege of Oblion by aliens who had invaded Oblion and possessed its population. He was mourned as a hero. Decisive action was quickly approved. The planet was completely neutralized. The entire population of Oblion and the Tharrr infestation was destroyed for the safety of the entire galaxy.

*

CHAPTER TWO

THARRR HOME WORLD
"The Great Circle of the Tharrr"

"Your passing is a wind blowing through time. You dwell in all hearts and places. We are infinitely expanded by your journey."

The Tharrr 2467

"Oblion is no more. I hear but a whisper from a great distance, weak and thin. Many voices that were once strong have become silent," Melkar said.

The massive creature lowered his zoyats. He would listen no more. Shifting direction, the bio-morphic plasma entity slid along the top of a semi-frozen sea of ammonia.

"What of the voices that remain. Are they beyond our circle?" Zweet asked.

The mother of the great circle felt a tremor as she anticipated her mate's reply.

My children!

"They have scattered to new places. They have melded with other life forms. It is our way. Nothing is ever truly lost. Thus we have lived for a hundred million years. Now we are to do something new. We will join with those who are already advanced well beyond the sentient horizon. It is a moment of amazing importance. The beings in three-dimensional reality always come and go. For those still embodied it is a very dangerous time. They are the hunted." Melkar was silent.

They slid across the turbulent gaseous planet together. Melkar and Zweet were the oldest link in the journey of the Tharrr.

Zweet spoke. "Our only hope will be a mating. At this time, they must wait and learn. This has never happened before. Have the Elders misguided us? This is to be a huge expansion. We have never joined such life forms at this stage before. It is a great and fortunate turn of events. Many details and variations are to be expected. Still, I am concerned."

Melkar and Zweet slid along the shifting semi-frozen gases. Their direction aligned with the rotation that the gaseous planet kept in the light of an ancient red star, as was their preference. Zweet, who embodied the maternal spirit of the Tharrr, spoke. "Including us, we now only number five. The three that remain......could there be a mating?

Melkar, held the ancient memlock of the Tharrr's journey. "Now we must find those destined to become part of the Tharrr."

"They will come," Zweet said. "A third will come and be the Carrier. We might be able to remain connected to her indefinitely."

Zweet loved it when Melkar spoke of such things. She further asked, "To be silenced. I do not understand. We are bringers of life. Why are we hunted?"

Zweet produced the equivalent of a frown. She mourned for her children.

Were they not the result of a great mating? Will the circle break?

Melkar spewed pheromones of healing and soothing chemicals compounds as he assured his beloved. "They consider our way of life as a threat. These life forms consider the joining to be a great wrongness. In the past, we came to our young souls and worked through their unconscious and instinctual realities. They dream. Such illusions have a powerful control over them. It is a problem that effects the course of conscious and unconscious activity. They need our guidance. So it is the will of the Elders."

"We were purely spirit forms at that time. Our circle is the first to be embodied. The terrestrial beings we have encountered call us spores. They consider this an invasion of an evil force. This is what destroyed Oblion. We were naïve to not consider this."

"Now we act with the wisdom and awareness of the sensitivity required for success. Now we have advanced to this new level of expansion. This is a great moment. Like them, we are evolving as well. The Elders have sent us to beings who once were more evolved. We will reawaken them to the level of cosmic awareness, a true quickening."

"A rebellion in ancient times cast a spiritual amnesia over these beings. In some cases, certain groups have accepted dark aberrations of the grand design. Thus they fear us. They call the joining a possession. They will ultimately realize the folly of such thinking but a struggle may ensue. They are very different. Our children must learn many new lessons."

"These creatures do something called sleep. It is during these periods that I have made contact. I have learned that they have something they call enemies. One tries to control the other. They will end life in order to achieve this. This is what happened on Oblion. Now, it seems some of our children are in opposing groups. This is all I know at this time."

The massive beings slid off onto the swirling sea of gas, moving with intense gravitational eddies and streams. Like any parents, they were worried about their children.

*

CHAPTER THREE

PLANET TATOCHIN 2465
Five years after Oblion
"Your Order Please"

"There is another movement to the stars by which our solar system revolves around a Grand Central Sun. It is here that mental virtue and divine magnetism reside. In the great cycles of measured time, we rotate in a great elliptical orbit, sometimes close and sometimes far from that illuminating light. We are now on our way home. It is the time of quickening. A great awakening is occurring throughout many galaxies."

Orville Parker 2461

A black Arabian flitter glided into the level one dining facility. The hum of the anti-gravity generator powered by the electro-magnetic drive purred with power.

It was fairly crowded in the downtown sector. Most of the processing factories ran triple shifts. The remote stanchion had a long line of various hovercraft and ground cars anxiously awaiting their turn to order their Corporate Conformed dining experiences.

The holo menu glowed before each car. Sensors scanned the identity of each citizen with various technologies including facial and audio recognition, as well as, the almost universally implanted data chips. The sniffers analyzed body chemistry. An electronic voice, laden with subliminal propaganda, droned on. It keyed into the hypno-plasmic receptors that had been injected into the population's bloodstream through various means. Audibly, it advertised the specials. Subliminally, it loaded the subconscious spectrum with its more urgent message: "loyalty to the Corporation!"

Flex was just getting used to the controls on the stolen hovercraft he commandeered. It was a fully loaded Arabian Charger with several illegal modifications.

They will never report this thing as stolen. Too many questions. Perfect!

He had acquired it from the Korum the day before. Cruising in the industrial sector "dressed to the nines" in drag, had proven to be useful to the rebels. Now they would get a message out to the people and gain a few more weapons in the war. This was the landscape of the uprising to Flex. The rebels did not know about the drag queen part, but that was Flex's private business.

The diplomatic craft was the perfect target for his thievery. A mechanic for the Korum had picked him up. What a great turn of events, he had thought. Using the boss's car to cruise for some sex had turned out to be costly for the grease jockey known as Abdul. Flex had reveled in his subterfuge.

Pulling up to the remote stanchion, the lights blinked, and several sounds pierced the distance. The Corporation was thorough. The beam analyzed its citizens. It would decipher certain chemicals emitted from the body, then modulate the formula to enhance hypnotic suggestion, and bundle the chemicals with carefully prepared dosages of hypno-plasmic drugs and inject them into the food ordered.

The processed food filled many functions primarily intended to control the population. The drugs were carefully designed to interact with media induction protocols. It was a well-known tool of the Colonial Corporation. It was secretly known as Monarch. Flex would have none of it.

As expected, the take out menu was wired to planetary surveillance. The scan had revealed his identity. The information popped up in the corporate surveillance matrix and before Katofar Renjinn's great golden eyes.

Flex hooted with an eerie growl of satisfaction, as was his habit and the popular response among the adolescents of urban Tatochin.

Time to party!

As the tinted window retracted, a particle beam laser poked out of the window. Gone was the drag queen of the night before. The remote halo cameras were equipped with hi-resolution clarity. On the projector field was the face of Tshauna Flexington, a well-known terrorist. His blue and yellow hair was frighteningly clown-like and his large round blue and brown eyes were extremely disarming.

The laser erupted in Flex's arms. Excoriating heat reduced the restaurant take-out stanchion into revolutionary sculpture complete with shorting circuitry and a trio of alarms.

"Fucking Brain Police," he shouted in between coyote-like keening hoots.

Hitting the gravity field, he slammed the thrusters into full burn. The sleek teardrop shaped hovercraft darted through the downtown sector of Ecksol at over 300 miles per hour.

Wow, I have wanted to do that for a long time. Not much profit in it, but this is fun!

*

The second moon was about to rise above the Tshini Mountains. The evening was cold. Vapor from the breath of the rebels curled into the crisp evening air.

Enro gazed intently through the infrared scanner from Skull Rock overlooking the so-called Planetary Park. In the distance, the lights of Ecksol glittered on the shore of Lake Wechen. He was seeking evidence that the trap set by Flex had been triggered. Confirmation came as he observed a small fire at the restaurant punctuated by a series of concussion grenades. Turning to his lieutenant, he reported the success of the tactic.

"Sally, Flex is chumming the water. We are hoping he can get some of those Colonial Troopers to chase him to the ambush. Are we set with the null field generator?"

Sally brushed a wisp of her sandy blond hair from her face. At twenty-three she already had the hardened face of a warrior who had seen many battles.

"If anyone can rile the retro Corporation its Flex."

Enro continued to observe the pictures the drones were streaming to the rebels. "Its true Sally. All too true."

She screwed her lips into a twisted frown. "Yes, Enro. It will be accurate within 50 yards. Flex picked the site himself."

Enro towered over Sally. His long dreadlocks gave him the look of a great lion in the cool blue light of the moon, Capatch. The red glow of the second moon, Wechen, was brightening the horizon.

Privately, Enro was frustrated. Without better equipment, they could do little against the deep resources of the Colonial Corporation and their private army, the Colonial Troopers. Taking awfully dangerous chances for a few more resources was frustrating.

Where is my support? Orville must know what's going on! The Pleiadians promised their support! Why do they labor so over the "free will to choose" issue? With the mind control technology being employed we need to intervene!

The null field generator would defeat the most rigorous EM shielding the Corporation employed on all their bio-electronics. The older electro-magnetic Rail gun had been redesigned. The rebels had duplicated the old systems with Centaurian plasma laser energy technology using a powerful portable power source that could produce very powerful bursts. It was said to be using special inert gas harvested from the event horizon on the lip of black holes. They needed more vehicles to continue the daring series of raids they had planned.

Being the most competent kaitain of his time, he knew how Troopers operated. He knew their weaknesses as well. Now his former command was the enemy. Much had changed since he met Orville Parker.

*

CHAPTER FOUR

COLONIAL CORPORATION
Arabian Charger Unleashed
"Revolution on the menu"

Flex cleared the industrial sector, dropping concussion grenades and upsetting aerial guidance buoys as the custom charger, modified with a Uton gravitational gyro-equipped engine, whined with power. Its characteristic anti-gravity gyros throbbed with high-pitched piercing constancy as it sped through the suburbs.

Flex stabbed at various buttons impulsively.

Everything is in Arabic or some slag!

Suddenly a hidden panel slid aside revealing several more sinister controls beside the beverage dispenser.

This looks like a weapons array!

He pressed the first button and a small missile launched.

Nice!

An interactive holo appeared before him in the cockpit. He maneuvered the rocket passing his hand into the holo field. The missile slammed into a water tower that flooded the street below.

"Now we're in business!"

*

The surveillance grid of the planet was on full alert. Within the white monolithic structure of the Colonial Corporation Headquarters, the entire scene was replaying, as Renjinn, the large green Tadole Katofar, rotated on his command chair within the COM room of the surveillance bubble. His golden eyes widened and his dorsal fin rose.

"By the light of Vichillia! What the swag is trending herenow?" he bellowed.

The light in the room was subdued. The hum of electronics and bio-core computers was constant and steady. A crew of four techies operated the hub 24 hours a day. For Renjinn, it was his throne. He ran the room as a king holding court.

Two secondary bubbles were attached to the central hub. One handled trigo-navigational concerns for the near galaxy. The other was the planetary control center for water, power transmission and all forms of ground, air, and orbital military and domestic travel.

Katofar Renjinn was a Tadole. He had a large pea green body with the general look of a large toad. A colorful metallic dorsal fin rose from his skull. Two large golden eyes frequently blinked due to the smoke that escaped his mouth. The large cigar smoldered as he chewed the end of the imported Salvington cigar. By his side, a smaller Tadole sat at the console, his dorsal fin flat upon his skull in a subservient position.

"Ostinglink give me Metropol's holo feed and get me an ID on the driver of the flitter."

As Renjinn rotated on his throne, several holos sprang up like bread from a toaster before the large Katofar's face. The large flaps of skin inflated below his mouth. Several orifices resembling fish gills contracted. Smoke-filled air was ejected as the release of pressure from his deflating throat sacks produced discordant flatulent droning sounds. They emitted their atonal compositions through chambers in his large sinus cavities and membrane flaps around his neck. These were standard emotional responses for the Tadole.

The Katofar observed the Arabian Charger's reckless flight through the suburbs. He regarded the picture and data content that flashed up. It was not the first time he had seen that face.

"It's one of those dirt baggers hold up in the park! Get it out across the media web and all surveillance kiosks, stat," Renjinn croaked.

On another holo, information on the flitter sprang up: MOTOR VEHICLE ABSTRACT
MAKE: MATTEL INDUSTRIES 2457
MODEL: ARABIAN CHARGER
REGISTERED OWNER: THE KORUM MISSION, ECKSOL

"The Korum!" Renjinn's cigar glowed menacingly. "By the blighted bog, what is going on herenow?"

The Korum had been a real dorsal wobbler for years. The secretive group had become powerful merchants in the Orion Sector.

We need to keep this under the radar.

"Ostinglink! The data on the owners of the flitter is classified. No media release."

The subservient Belfar stabbed at the buttons on his console.

The Korum was a group that had consolidated in the wake of Earth's first diaspora in the mid-twenty-first century. After first contact, the Moslem world had resisted the ecumenical movement that created the formation of the Omegans. Christian, Catholic, Hindu, and Buddhist and some Jewish sects had primarily been the founding basis for the large expansive religion.

Once the Pleiadians had opened up their resources to a dying Earth, the question of faith in a post-contact era had created large social changes. The Moslems persisted in maintaining a separate identity. It was their right to do so. They adapted well to galactic civilization. Like the caravans that once traversed the silk road of the ancient world upon Earth, they had embraced the space lanes of galactic civilization. It was a highly respected contribution that allowed the faithful to live in a world of abundance within the strictures of their faith.

On Tatochin, they had a tight knit community. Their diplomatic mission and many of the cargo businesses and other enterprises were housed in an opulent building of Chrome Mollimix that rose above downtown Ecksol.

The Tadole had guilds rather than the corporate models favored by the Colonial Corporation. Among the skyscrapers of downtown Ecksol, the chrome and mollimix tower of the Korum rivaled the presence of the Colonial Corporation's trademark, the Monolith.

Renjinn thought about the Korum leadership.

Kalimafar! A real pervert. His father, King Fezam is a dangerous leader.

Renjinn phased as he monitored the various holos across the matrix of Ecksol. It was always a sticky issue when dealing with the Korum. Everything was too complicated.

The wily prince though occupied by his carnal needs, was skillful with code hacking and technoid crime which oddly managed to keep the Korum above reproach. Though he was a lascivious pervert, he was well informed concerning the inner sanctums of business and commerce; insulating himself with intergalactic level intelligence. His position as the only son of the Korum's King Fezam was added protection shielding him from many dangerous consequences of his actions.

The Tadole Katofar returned from his phasing. Renjinn would rather mow down any opposition with a good old fashion laser. He was not into diplomacy.

I will never be promoted beyond Katofar!

"Ostinglink!"

Slamming his large hand on the arm of the COM-chair, his dorsal fin rose into a dangerous position. The dorsal fin of the full-grown Tadole was more than a meter that measured emotion. The two most forward fins of their dorsal protrusion contained part of a glandular system that contained a highly corrosive substance that could be projected as an aerosol under extreme conditions or with martial skill.

The Tadole were trained from youth to control such tendencies in much the same way the human children were toilet trained. Renjinn had difficulty learning that lesson.

He spit his cigar out with a start. The thoroughly soggy and pungent mass splattered across the side of a utility cabinet and slid down to the floor. A cleaning robot departed a small bay near the offensive, smoldering mass. It would automatically clean up Renjinn's mess. It was a busy little robot. Renjinn often gave it work to do.

The Tadole Belfar cringed in his chair. His dorsal drained of color. "Yes, Katofar."

"Call up a dossier on Prince Kalimafar. He's as slimy as an Andarian Quasiflem."

*

CHAPTER FIVE

FLEX'S LURE
"Takers or Not"

Flex had been dodging Metropol for twenty minutes. The Arabian Flitter could out fly and out gun the local police. He had mastered the onboard arsenal having taken out several warehouses and a few commercial buildings along the way.

I want to keep this one! Where are the Colonial Troopers? I just blew up three buildings...that should attract them!

He abruptly changed course, staying just ahead of the slower Metropol flitters. He thought about Nimro and the others waiting for him to bring the Troopers down. It had been a daring plan. The null field generator was a marvelous weapon developed by a rebel scientist from High Mountain Base deep in the Tshini Mountains.

Enro had called it a good leveler. "We can neuter the big bad Troopers and reveal their weakness," he had said.

When Flex asked Enro what that weakness was he had looked deep into his eyes and said, "They have turned to darkness. This will be their demise. Our universe is to be filled with love and light. As a result they lack the conviction and determination that you have."

*

COLONIAL CORPORATION HQ

Renjinn studied the situation. He was trying to figure out the intentions of the rebels.

Is it a diversion?

"It makes no sense. We have a banta of troopers on call," Renjinn grumbled.

"We have three Colonial Interceptors within striking range," Ostinglink said with a self-satisfied croak in his throat bellows for emphasis.

A banta was a special team of forty troopers. It included a dozen in auto-armor and twelve handlers to help guide them. The other twenty troopers and four officers were to protect the handlers and perform special operations when needed. The ones in auto-armor would do all the damage.

"Why does he not try to escape?"

"Katofar, shall I call in the Colonial Troopers?"

Renjinn's sucker tipped hands danced across the keyboard and the map of the area widened. He was looking for a pattern.

"Hmmm, he avoids the most obvious escape routes. There must be a hidden agenda."

"Call off Metropol. Let's see what the swag this dirt bagger does?"

*

SKULL ROCK

Enro intently watched from his position at Skull Rock. The portable radar screen dimly glowed. He saw the Metropol flitters back off and eagerly waited for the Colonial Interceptors to relieve the local police. That would be when it got dangerous.

"Tell Nimro and the rest to stand by. Metropol is backing off. Any sign of Colonial Trooper activity?"

Several voices gave reports. "Nothing on radar," said Sally who was beside him.

Durga echoed the same bad news in downtown Ecksol. "We can't see anything but a few fire trucks. Nothing else."

Nimro's voice came over the com embedded in Enro's ear. "We are all ready for Flex. He's going to fake an engine flame out at our position. We have enough teams to take a dozen vehicles. How many does he have on his tail?"

Enro did not like what he saw. Calling off Metropol was one thing but he could not see any indication that the Colonial Troopers were about to swoop down from Space Dock to join the chase.

He thought of the intelligence report about the Tadole Katofar Renjinn. *The Tadole…they are good warriors. I think he smelled the trap.*

"Nimro, hold tight. Let's give it a few more minutes."

*

ARABIAN CHARGER

Flex watched the trio of Metropol flitters break off the chase. "Shit!"

Suddenly a feminine voice said, "Evacuation enabled."

With great discomfort, Flex felt the seat shifting under him. The onboard AI asked if any particular music was requested for his intended toilet.

Flex was delighted. He spoke to the flitter, "Evacuation canceled". His distraction abated. He returned his attention to the aborted chase and wondered what else the Korum flitter could do.

"Computer, can you show me air traffic?" Immediately, a navigational holo sprang up before him. He studied the map noting the position of Metropol.

"Can you show me orbital data?" The holo phased and he could see activity around Space Dock. The Orbital hub was quiet.

"Shit", Flex said aloud. There were no troopers giving chase.

"Evacuation enabled," the computer droned. Once again, the seat began to reconfigure into a toilet.

"Cancel evacuation." Flex hit the thrusters into full burn and arced around in a tight curve to follow Metropol.

Enro watched Flex vent his frustration. "Tell Nimro and the rest to pack it in. They did not take the bait. They must have smelled a trap."

Flex came up behind the three Metropol flitters that had been chasing him. "Come on you, verders…Shit!"

"Evacuation enabled."

"Cancel evacuation." He fired a volley of small missiles and destroyed two of the flitters. Passing over the last one, he coaxed it into a new chase but headed away from the rendezvous sight.

With a burst of speed, he came around and lit the fuse on a small but deadly missile provided by the Korum. The last flitter exploded and fell to the ground in a rain of fire.

"Wow" *Geez, that missile must be Centaurian.*

He ascended to higher altitudes and headed toward the Tshini Mountains.

Flex had been a thief and had a long list of felonies and generally illvibe behavior. The rebels had provided him with a moral compass. Enro, Nimro, and the rebels in general accepted Flex as he was. They saw his bravery and daring. They knew he would be an asset even though he was by most standards the latest bad news. He began to study the ways of the Elders and found hidden abilities that impressed him deeply. He repaid them with fierce loyalty.

*

The holo herenow that evening, reported wild fires in the Planetary Park. According to the newscasters, careless campers were at fault. Few people saw anything else. They were busy in their homes watching the Corporate Family holo of the night on their projectors.

*

KORUM MISSION

Arn quickly read the pulse fax. The Korum had lost its secret hovercraft, one of Prince Kalimafar's latest indulgences. Rebels had stolen it. He was pleased, not at the loss of the expensive and dangerous flitter, but pleased because the homing beacon onboard the craft had revealed the secret base of the freedom fighters. This would give his Prince a real hard-on. He was always elevated when the large budget he spent on his technoid staff provided secret information for his exploitation.

We will profit by maintaining this secret. I will call the weapons dealers. They could use some heavier fire-power after all.

*

CHAPTER SIX

MIRROR 2466
Orville and Cleo: Beneath Cerulean Skies

Cleo sighed. A smile caressed her cheeks. *Why am I feeling so exposed*, she blushed. *Wow!*

Wind chimes created a subtle melody intertwined in polyrhythmic layers. Rustling branches and bird song filled the stucco compound. The low buildings hugged gentle hillsides engineered through cooperation with nature to be easily maintained food gardens.

Cleo's favorite part about living on Mirror was the passionate awareness the people held for the land. Stewardship was the attitude most of the human worlds had embraced in settling off world. The Pleiadians had an organization called the Zentalissa. She had felt attracted to them almost immediately.

She headed toward the kitchen of Orville Parker's home. Fairies tending flowers giggled and flocked at her passing. They spoke in a language all their own.

Orville had lived here for over four hundred years. The three acres that he called his little Eden was filled with food and small homes tucked into various glades. Three generations of children and other family members lived quietly in the area. Thousands of such domiciles were spread throughout the verdant region.

Cleo tended to her housekeeping duties. Scrubbing the counter surfaces, she phased through her memlocks. As part of her journey, Cleo was being guided in a process of recapitulation. Her counselors were helping her to process layers of cellular memory handed down through retrostory. The DNA mapping she had been studying had her mind whirling in ever-new directions.

They told me that something internal was solid and unapproachable. Am I defective? I feel something is hidden from me.

Her counselors had confirmed it but offered her no guidance. She banished such thoughts, but on a more subtle level, she understood that something was stirring within.

On Mirror, the Pleiadians had achieved a garden paradise world for many generations. It was a secret place, set aside for a very difficult role. To live among the Pleiadians was a challenge, especially the ones who were tasked to oversee Earth's human descendants.

The Zentalissa was a group of souls who tended to the biological development of many worlds. They had transformed the galaxy over countless generations. As an Earth descendant representative, Cleo was expected to work on healing the inner miasma embedded in her psyche to a very high degree. On Mirror, it was an essential survival skill. Beneath the spiritual practice was a great hope that all of humanity would reach a threshold of awareness possible through making the spiritual commitment.

They do not take any shit here.

The trappings of a material based society that modeled itself upon the recorded retrostory of humanity did not die quickly even after the Diaspora from Earth. She knew that Orville Parker had been given the task to confront the problems of Earth's past that still corrupted humanity's evolutionary awareness.

They are lucky that Orville tends to things. He is a gentle man.

The general and normal vibratory frequency of Mirror resonates to the frequency of the Pleiadian's home world. In every way it is governed as they had lived for thousands of years. Many had ascended to higher dimensional life. The legacy they left behind was a remarkable universe.

She thought about how the Pleiadians reached out across the dimensions to help a crippled humanity and how it was such an honor to be able to experience the rarified frequencies of this planet. A special technology had been created to allow outsiders to dampen the vibrational level of the planet. Designed as an exotic piece of jewelry, an electronic frequency modulator was an ornament worn around the neck region of Mirror's newer residents.

Based on the universal frequencies used to penetrate the dimensional layers of existence, they had reproduced the conditions on a planetary level. Using that knowledge provided the dwellers upon Mirror the ability to entrain themselves in the art of moving through dimensional reality rather than be anchored at only one frequency. The buffering process is adjustable for individual comfort as it relates to the mastery of the process. These technologies are strictly guarded.

Thank the gods for my Symbi-collar!

Cleo put her cleaning rags and tools in a side closet and prepared to clean up the back porch. She thought of the native born of Mirror. It was hard to even believe that the things that she witnessed might be within her ability some day. The souls from the outside that lived upon Mirror represented the vanguard of humanity. She felt deep gratitude well up within her for the privilege of be here.

Her daily activity had been gardening and cleaning. She had learned that back on Earth such endeavors were considered lowly and unfortunate. She tried to fathom such retro thinking. It seemed trite and childish to her. The other classes and counseling she received, combined with a stress-free environment, was healing and fulfilling. She was learning to recognize primal patterning that had disconnected most of the strands of humanity's DNA.

It's like they all melted together, like an overheated plasma drive.

The 12-strand DNA structure, and then 24, was an evolutionary process of monumental transfiguration that required conscious attention. Though unknown to almost all of humanity until the Pleiadians arrived on Earth around 2150, it was, in essence, the greatest leap of awareness humanity had achieved in several millennia.

The process of tranformation began for humanity on Earth in 1762. A surge of energy from the Central Sun and the maturation of a large group of souls who incarnated in large numbers beginning in the eighteenth century had triggered changes in the two strand DNA, according to what she had learned on Mirror.

The maturation of humankind had been initiated. The path leading all to the arrival of the Pleiadians had been set. The Earth would finally be exposed to a vast intergalactic culture that until then had been the stuff of storytelling.

Thousands of years ago these evolutionary conditions had been the natural reality for all peoples. It was through several extremely unfortunate problems, beginning in ancient times, that these advancements had been lost to the people of old Earth. The potential of a totally restored spiritual being was endless.

Orville says it is about magnetism.

Humanity still had a long journey to go. Cleo understood that human beings were still a deeply divided and splintered group. She shuddered to think about the rumors she had heard about the Colonial Corporation.

Orville called it humanity's dirty little secret.

Apparently, they were reconstituting into a dangerous and invasive force. They threatened to undo much of what Orville and the Pleiadians sought to expand.

Is that why I am here? They say it's a dream and that in awakening we will discover we never left the oneness of spirit. Dam! Something is in the way!

Cleo had been having unusual thoughts of late. A sense of purpose was emerging but it wasn't all so light and pleasant. It felt dark and heavy.

What is going on with me? I feel so distracted. I think of Orville and large energy patterns emerge in my mind's eye. Shit, I think I need to sweep the patio.

She walked toward the exit to the patio, broom in hand. The adobe house was cool. Built into a hillside it was insulated from the extremes of the seasons by the deep tunnels that passively created a constant temperature. This design was universal on Mirror. Many such simple and sustainable technologies were used by the advanced culture that built Mirror.

A ancient guild of Terra-formers had been shaping planetary environments for millions of years. Magnetic power generators, solar energy collectors, wind farms, and biological batteries had replaced the oil economy that had led Earth down a dark and destructive path. Even after hundreds of years, the Earth was still in deep recovery from those days.

According to the Elders the very notion of technology to replace natural life was an unfortunate consequence. They also understood that it would take centuries to slowly wean technological humans from cyborgated processes in favor of a fully awakened human spirit. In such a climate a human being would have no need of surrogates.

Cleo sighed. Her mind was full of ideas she had memlocked in maximode. *"All is self"*, they like to say. *"The power of an illuminated spirit is as boundless as the universe."*

The industrial revolution, as it was popularly known in Earth retrostory, had great potential. The new ideas and innovations had been astounding. A technocratic world however, was not human friendly. Humankind, already deeply divided and corrupted, separated itself from the natural world more than ever. Death and disease had taken root 25,000 years earlier through the work of a secret ruling class that was an ancient menace upon the Earth. Beginning in the 19th century it began to accelerate at an alarming rate. Oil addiction and greed were underestimated.

Off world control subverted the holographic illusion of spirit with the egoic belief in separation. Nothing had been quite right since. Unfortunately, the earth was almost destroyed in just a few hundred years, as powerful small groups sought to control the natural evolution of ideas utilizing the evolving technological surge.

Tremendous suffering and great imbalances in nature would have been prevented if the evolutionary process had not been suppressed. Finally, with the intercession of the Elders, a global crisis was avoided.

The Pleiadians had patiently explained that the modern era was only the most recent example of this type of cycle of ignorance and illumination. The idea of duality would be useful for many years to come. The direction that the spiritual journey required from that idea of duality was toward a oneness through an illumination of the mind. Such matters were constantly reinforced.

Many colonies lived without a monetary system or any kind of plurality in the realm of governance. The government was motivated by Truth held at its very core. Instead of shopping centers and stores, gardens were harvested, animals managed, and craft guilds catered to the worldly needs of a small and balanced population. Such ideas had gradually spread throughout humanity and disease began to disappear reflecting the harmony of such a way of living.

They used to live only 70 or 80 years! No wonder my ancestors seemed so driven. Survival! Unconscious guilt?

The problem of unconscious procreation had been tackled after the 23rd century, universally. It didn't involve subterranean plots of eugenics or religious mythology. Those ideas, and the fanatics and aliens that spawned those ideas, rejected the path to greater awareness.

Galactic contact created a huge paradigm shift. It had to do with conscious awareness. No longer were a people defined by how large a population their home world supported. The survival instincts evolved as a collective shift. Monetary systems and competition for wealth had been largely abandoned. Humanity had finally satiated its need for material gain by learning to enjoy the bounty of nature in balance.

Cleo took up a broom and began sweeping the patio. She knew that Orville had been married several times and that children were the fruit of those unions. Most of his children lived on Mirror. Many of them had homes in the area around his. The food gardens, tended by all, were resplendent.

Whole planets and planetary systems are affected by Orville's influence. Few of them even know who Orville Parker is!

Cleo continued to sweep the blue-gray tiles as her thoughts meandered. She felt as though something was coming her way. She did not know what it was but believed it was powerful. She pondered over Orville's incredible age.

To have lived for 450 years and look so, so fresh.

He seemed her age, just the beginning of middle age, a young 92. She thought of his eyes, they seemed to glow with wisdom and beauty, even in her mind's eye.

I am so distracted. Why do I think of Orville? Am I in a romantic haze?

She silenced her scattered thoughts recalling her lesson in Tai-Chi with Master Wu. *"To be here in the now, is to flow in the Tao."*

She focused on her task, sweeping the patio. Her awareness expanded into the elements that surrounded her.

Cleo was filled with gratitude to be on this paradise world invisible to the naked eye. Orville explained the invisibility as an effect of a slight time displacement. Of course, he was into mathematics, but she did not understand such things. Her preference was the kind of math that could be done by using her fingers.

The light of Mirror originated from a massive star that Orville referred to as the Central Sun. Orville had lived here for over 420 years. Cleo struggled to understand the concept of time as a state of consciousness as well as a linear progression. Orville had explained that spiritual awareness would eventually bring universal understanding of the essential illusion of time and space. She sighed.

Then what? He is a teacher for me.

She hit her head on a bird feeder abruptly dispersing her reverie along with many seeds. Surveying her work, she saw the scattered seeds and decided it was a do over.

I am distracted! Flow of the Tao! I'm so out of the now, I'm walking into my future backwards.

She could not deny her feelings. As hopeless as it was, she was in love. A small giggle escaped her lips that vibrated into ripples of mirth spreading through the valley and the deep halls of eternity.

*

CHAPTER SEVEN

"HERE IS EVERYWHERE"

Orville rested in between meditation and sleep, observing in his mind's eye when he became sick at 12 years old. It was the first time he encountered the Elders. For many months he was in and out of hospitals. The cause of the illness was never actually known. Weak and unable to walk, his major organs were shutting down with problems that had not been common on Earth for many years. His parents attended to him with loving care.

He had many sleepless nights. When he did sleep he had visions of a future time on the Earth and beyond. It was at that time that the Elders bequeathed him with the knowledge of his greater purpose.

Why do events in the farnow visit me? Is it the beginning of a new cycle? I was afraid of dying, now I am afraid that I will not be able to manifest my goals. My job is still to overcome this pervasive fear.

Orville noticed his distraction. He felt energy flowing toward him but could not identify it. He had lived longer than most human beings and had developed the ability to sense the energetic ebbs and flows in his life very accurately. He often didn't know what it meant. It was a big universe.

I am an embryo. Who have I become? Was there a hint of it as a child? Was there some magic wand that I unwittingly reached for that unlocked the strange and wonderful life I have experienced? Was it completely by fate that I came back from another past or is it a future? I can't memlock it. It feels like one big continuum. Is it re-incarnation? Perhaps I have never been anywhere but here. And here is everywhere. Ah, what's the difference? I still gotta go somewhere else for a good taco. I am still in a body! I must eat! Hmmm, tacos.

Orville let his chaotic phasing and surface thoughts evaporate as he practiced a breathing technique taught by the Pleiadian Elders. His awareness withdrew into his spine as his thoughts subsided, but he was having a difficult time maintaining a mystic state.

Feeling a simmering power idling within his being, he began to recall his early lessons. *Breath equaled energy. This energy was called prana.* Prana flows into the body on the in-breath and continues to build with the out-breath. The key element is the slow and methodical build up of prana.

With this fundamental guideline his awareness expanded to encompass his work. His teachers had helped him to reform his beliefs around the meaning of work. They encouraged him to see the various activities of his life as the unfolding episodes of a journey towards the goal of infinite awareness. They assured him that it was the most satisfying approach to physical life. So far, they had been right.

Marriages had come and gone. Children had been born and grown up. They surrounded him. Both of his marriages had been happy ones. *I wonder if another marriage awaits me? My heart says yes, hmmm.*

Lately, the direction his life had taken was challenging. Trouble was brewing and the Pleiadians had called him to task. He had used his invention of the Matter Relocator to gather souls throughout the galaxy, to hasten and influence human evolution. In the most recent century, that job included all sentient races that are on a similar evolutionary arc. Now, he had been asked to become a leader. He was reluctant. Many years had passed since he was involved in the struggles of humanity and the vagaries of exploitive governance.

Shit! I thought we didn't need leaders at this vibratory level. I guess its no more harp duty in the heavenly clouds for me! So many of us need to grow!

Orville thought of two of his most promising agents. They had infiltrated the Colonial Corporation and the Korum after many years of observation. These were two of humankind's most resistant and troublesome groups. They had required two of the most amazing people.

Now it comes to fruition. They have to be stopped! The bankers and the industrial enslavement to a consumer culture were troublesome, and now, the ancient enemy may have infiltrated them! I thought we had eliminated them completely! Now I am hearing something else. Something about galaxies in conflict!

The Korum was a mixed situation. Spawned from a great reformation in Islam. They tended to be insular. In recent times, they had been seeking a greater role in the universe as they expanded their enterprises further into the growing diaspora. They had birthed powerful underground societies like the Techno-geeks, and tolerated the Dragon Fems. By competing with the Corporation they had begun to embody the same twisted principles that their competitors represented.

What was that old saying? What ever you put with salt becomes salt?

As Orville mused about Tatochin, an image of Enro formed in his mind. Soon it would be time for action there.

We must get the military to abandon their posts. Then we will dismantle the banks with the blessing of the UGC! The illusion of endless debt will be destroyed.

Orville surfaced from his meditation full of questions. *Some meditation! Why am I thinking of evil bankers... and debt as a method of enslavement! Gezzz!*

Though he had been distracted, he knew that the effort of meditation had opened him up to intuitive ideas and guidance. Long ago, he had learned that achieving the level of awareness the Pleiadians possess is the foundation for accessing solutions that lead to a life of joy.

Sometimes it is just so...serious. At least it is just the dream. I dream of greener pastures! I still dally with my preferences!

Tomorrow he would visit his teachers, Ziola and Tremador. He had questions. *Why is so important to train an army, even a small one? And why do I reflect on romance now. The Elders had never mentioned it to me. I can't put it down. I must be dreaming a dream about dreaming. Whatever!*

*

CHAPTER EIGHT

TWIN FLAME ACTIVATION

Orville opened his eyes. The morning was gone. Out on the patio he could hear the sound of the broom stroking the inlaid stone.

Mirror was perpetually a semi-tropical environment. Off in the distance, majestic mountains climbed to an altitude of 16,000 feet. Most weather conditions were possible to experience on Mirror but Orville liked succulent fruits like papaya, banana, ribbon fruit, coconut, and rorashun.

In the shade, bulging berries grew in large quantities. They grew profusely in gardens throughout the lightly populated area where the Pleiadian Center was located. His family domicile was filled with food. He grabbed a handful of white raspberries and marveled at their flavor. His children loved eating them. Images of little mouths smeared with berry juice brought a smile to his face.

Suddenly, he recalled a dream he had the previous night. He was married to the most incredible being. They were both Pleiadians. Together they had been able to travel to many worlds, star systems, and dimensions by the spiritual power they possessed. The Pleiadians counted on them to build a way to create habitable planets. He felt great joy and satisfaction in the bond they shared.

When he had awakened from the dream he had felt lonely. Though he had found happiness in his love life, it paled in comparison to this one dream. Facing the potential of early death as a child had deepened his experience of oneness. The love he knew in this dream added new dimensions to his feelings.

I feel that my retro memlocks signal a major shift in my life.

The clouds would be forming soon. He grabbed his towel for a swim. Slipping on some sandals, he grabbed a container of homegrown ginger tea and headed toward the stalwart sound of a broom.

We will have a light rain.

The retrostorical ideas of a mystery, the great unknown, did not apply on Mirror. It was a world that never heard of red tape. Here one need not meditate for many years in order to attain a level of transcendent awareness. It could happen in the time it takes to eat a taco or a white raspberry. The world was a pure manifestation of great divine magnetism.

Known as Aurorioulous Tarasenimea to the Pleiadian Elders, Mirror had become an environment of rare and magnificent energy. The hologram of life in three-dimensional space had become translucent and prone to timelessness and a clarified distillation of space itself in close alignment to the mind. It had become Orville's healer over time. He likened it to a pearl of God's creation, a gift to all of life. The planet was a land of formidable power. Thought and emotion could physically manifest with little volition.

Orville had much to say about Mirror to everyone he encountered in his exploration of different worlds. He often described the nature of Mirror with these words: ***"Blessed be, the*** *pure in heart for they will see God. Woe unto those who come with a cold or divided heart for they shall inherit their own thoughts".*

So, why do we prepare for a war? Haven't we grown beyond that yet?

Orville sensed that a question had been answered. Restlessness jolted him. He sighed when he thought of Lesha, his lover. He knew it was going to change. She had left a note on the refrigerator: "Off training in combat techniques, as usual."

He headed for the river leaving a trail of questions as he exited through a sliding door. The patio was dappled with light shining through the leaves of stately mango trees.

Cleo stood at the edge of the patio clutching a broom. Her deeply tanned and compact body was framed by her long blonde hair tied up on her head that seemed to spill over like the leaves of a pineapple. He felt the hairs stand up on the back of his neck. It was the essence of her being that attracted him. He knew in that moment that love's pure energy had sparked into creation. *I love her.*

"Hello Cleo, are the kids still in the water?" *She is radiant!*

"Yes, they are. Will it rain soon?"

I am making small talk so I can keep looking at her. God! I feel exposed and I don't even care!

Cleo put the broom down. Orville pretended to be nonchalant. He was clear that he had launched into a mating dance. Internally, he was having a minor melt down. *The dream?*

He looked at the sky in several directions, unsuccessfully attempting to avoid eye contact with Cleo.

She is quite sensitive for a newcomer. I feel like I know her so well. What are these feelings? I don't need such complications! I find her attractive. Orville, listen to you. Haven't you learned anything? She is really nice. Stop, Stop! She smells good.

"Hope the rain holds until after my swim. *I am babbling –Great!*

"Yes, that would work just fine." She smiled.

He started for the path that led down to the ravine. The chimes let out a trill in counterpoint to his stride. Smiling, he turned. "Cleo, you worked hard on the patio, there will be time to finish later... come for a swim."

Cleo smiled and ran into the house to fetch a towel at the same time hiding the blush of her cheeks. I want to be with him. I am feeling my heart opening. Wow, what is happening!

Orville began to walk down the path to the pool in the stream. Suddenly, he stopped and gazed toward the sky that emanated a bright spark of energy. A moist breeze issued forth from the majestic gathering of elements. Fairies danced on the purple-flowered carpets painted on the meadows and the hills. The ground spoke of life forces gestating. Tones, colors, and smells, added a earthy aroma while the snails pondered the clouds. Many little thoughts and voices overlapped. As he listened to a pregnant silence, he could hear God breathing and know his own breath in the same lucid interval.

Orville looked around and Cleo stood by him with her eyes on those very mountains.

This is just the first part of something. I can't believe it. I wasn't expecting this! It is as if she has always been here!

They walked to river in silence and communion.

*

CHAPTER NINE

THE CHROME CITADEL
PLANET TATOCHIN

Ecksol was a city built on the shore of Lake Wechen, the largest lake on the entire planet of Tatochin. It was a vast fresh water sea fed by huge aquifers emanating from the Tshini Mountains.

For ten years, the Colonial Corporation had been sending food products to off world resources. The synthesized food product was manufactured on Tatochin. They were all stamped with a "CC", Corporate Conformed. They gained control of the planet by exporting food products to a quickly expanding intergalactic corporate structure. The market economy created the need for exports, slowly creating a dependent population.

The Corporation had big plans for the planet. The first step was the investment of large sums of money into the business sector shifting the focus to intergalactic commerce. New jobs were controlled by the manipulations of a work force controlled by wealthy privately-owned investment banks. With the formal annexation of the planet, the Corporation created a growing dependency on off-world consumerism by literally feeding it to a susceptible population.

The planet had lost its independence. In the downtown sector the evidence of this was most notable in the physical appearance of structures housing the Corporation's fabricated economy. Large amounts of off-world investments had led to a building boom that had changed the face of Ecksol. A hall of gigantic skyscrapers had sprung up like fungus. The white monolithic corporate offices and the chrome-coated Korum mission had been inspired by the great vertical cities that briefly flourished on old Earth in the early twenty-first century.

Once a thriving agricultural town bustling with trade and commerce, Ecksol was now an industrial juggernaut of intergalactic corporations. Manufacturing modified food and cargo Corsairs, Tatochin was exporter to the stars. The population now served the Corporation. It matched the inflated and over-entitled egos of the newcomers. This all contributed to many new urban problems.

Within the concrete and mollimix towers, great wealth systematically usurped the planet's sovereignty by shifting the planetary economic base. Intergalactic banks had dug their tendrils into a formerly free society controlling the flow of the credit/debt driven market economy. No longer did they live a sustainable life made stable by a slow growing economy and tempered by a nurturing attitude toward nature and each other.

The fruit of the land had insured a peaceful and healthy existence. Now, the populace relied on off-world commerce to survive. Hastily built super farms generated vast amounts of genetically modified food for export. These mega-structures had begun to spread over the intricate networks that had been small but productive family farms. The Corporation had infiltrated through the economic doorway.

A vigorous campaign of mind control and genetic manipulation expanded and solidified the strength of their power. Food additives were secretly added harboring strontium polymers that caused DNA to mutate, exposing a placated public. Media induction and hypno-plasmic drugs were carefully monitored for the "best" possible outcomes.

Along with a growing addiction to off world goods, the people were distracted and stripped of their retrostory. Now, most of the once free Tatochinians worked in standardized corporate factories. Factories that cultivated, processed, and exported the Corporate Conformed products of Tatochin to feed the hungry mouths of a growing corporate culture.

All these elements were set to weaken the will of the people for the Corporation's gain. The mechanics of this societal template had been developed on Earth in the twentieth century. But unlike Tatochin, the people of Earth summarily dismantled these methods used by the Corporation through the influence of galactic contact and the Gaian movement.

Unfortunately, it was never completely dismantled. The galaxy was a big place and the Colonial Corporation was a huge amalgamation of many large corporations from those times. They had survived by living off-world.

*

CHAPTER TEN

"TANGO RETURNS TO THE FOLD"
THE CAPACH OCEAN

To the east of the Tshini mountains was a gradually sloping plain that was a large and verdant agricultural area, culminating on the shore of the ocean that covered 40 percent of the planet. The tide was coming in. Several surfers rode the breaking waves in the morning sun. Tango sipped a virgin Mimosa from the porch overlooking the beach. Four-foot swells broke upon a pristine beach of fine white sand.

The chalet was in a favorable location. Wealthy corporate leaders and the super rich had beach houses for vacationing. The Korum kept one for its royal princes and leaders. Arafad Tango X was King Fezam's best diplomat. Suave and worldly, his long brown hair was braided fashionably. Though the gossip holocasts pegged him a socialite, he was a shrewd and competent representative of the Korum. He would also keep an eye on the King's youngest son, Prince Kalimafar.

King Fezam had sent his son to Tatochin to get him as far away from New Mecca as possible. Earth didn't want the Prince anyway. Even Fezam had departed the desert domains of his ancestors and lived in a spectacular structure on Ganymeade. A city-sized dome, Narayan was where the royal palace was currently located.

Unknown to the Korum or anyone in the Orion sector, Tango was a double agent in deep cover. He had evolved into a master spy. The many experiences he had in his years wandering the galaxies and the time he had spent with Orville on Mirror, were memlocked in the archives of his being as a treasure trove for a spy of any time frame. His diplomat career was all a ruse to penetrate the inner sanctums of Tatochin's financial and political arrangements with the big players on the planet and with the galactic players beyond. All to serve the one directive: defeat the Corporation.

Tango had become a public figure in order to capture the eyes of the media holos. The Korum saw the benefit of using him to put a positive face on the Korum; King Fezam had insisted on it.

Tango had lived on Mirror under the direct tutelage of Orville Parker and the Elders. Orville had asked Tango to go undercover in the Korum. His Persian genetic background and rare talent as a spy would best serve the Elders' plan for humanity.

Tango, at first perplexed by a form of spiritual practice that required he resurrect the most illicit skills developed in his former occupation: smuggler, thief and all around bad boy. It troubled him. It was difficult to view himself in such ways. It had shifted his memlock of the farnow into maximode.

Orville just smiled and said, "You are totally forgiven and innocent Mr. X."

Tango plunged into deep memlocks. They would go around and around until his head spun. Orville would just laugh and point at him. "You love the drama of it, Arafad Tango X."

He had considered Fezam's assigning him to Prince Kalimafar as an assistant, a setback, and a disappointment. Tatochin was a backwater agricultural planet where the Korum had contracts for food distribution. Orville had not said much in that regard. "We shall see", was all he said.

When he emerged at Landfall that first day, his disappointment was replaced by the sheer beauty and living presence of Tatochin herself.

Orville reassured Tango during a rare meeting that it was about to become an interesting assignment.

Orville said the Elders may have influenced the situation so that I would end up on Tatochin. Sometimes Orville just says stuff like that and my head spins! I don't know if I want super beings arranging my life.

At that meeting, Orville revealed the rebels secret leader, the former and presumed dead, Kaitain Enro himself. This would change everything. Tango was astonished. Kaitain Enro was a legend. Even though he was a kaitain for the troopers he had grown up following the great lion's career. He memlocked Enro by the title of his favorite holo, "The Great Lion of Oblion".

And now Enro lives!

Enro's presence among the rebels who lived in the great forest of Tatochin was the whole reason why Tango was arming the rebels. Soon, things would be coming to a head. Orville had appeared and disappeared without any visible device. Tango needed some time to absorb all the changes in the herenow.

Tango took any opportunity he had to get away at the Korum's chalet on the Capach Inlet, North of Ecksol. He loved the ocean.

The summons had come in the middle of the night after having arrived at the chalet earlier that day. The ground flitter was waiting when he tumbled into it several hours before daylight, miffed that his long weekend had ended before it began. He bit on a large carrot he had grabbed in the kitchen of the chalet and emptied the sand from his shoes. It was a long ride to Ecksol.

I wonder why they send a ground car? Prince Dildo Dork always sends his saucer when he wants to fetch his pets! I must contact Mirror: dangerous, but necessary.

As the car swiftly sped into the dawn, his spirits lifted as he watched the shifting light upon the scenery. The vast farmlands were now dotted with the Corporation's new super farms. A large biofuel processing factory looked out of place in the midst of swaying fields of mosh.

Sleepy hamlets nestled in shallow valleys were already waking. The lights in the homes of the early rising farmers defined the sparse population. Tree breaks bent with the wind as the rippling geography of the planet's skin passed by, calming Tango's thoughts.

Coming to a rise, the city of Ecksol, visible 100 miles away, was outlined by the banks of Lake Wechen. The Korum's building, like a reflective dagger, was a beacon catching the earliest mellow light of the yellow star as it slowly rose in the west. Off to the east, the swatch of shadow across the horizon was the natural boundary of the planetary park.

Somewhere in there the rebels live.

The Ashwood trees lined the Remorah River. To the South, the newly opened Royal Orion resort stood at the confluence of the river and Lake Wechen. Like a moth to a flame, the ground car was drawn towards the silver shard and Kalimafar's domicile of perversion.

To the gates of hell, or my salvation?

Tango was not sure what this trip might yield. The music on the crystal was a current favorite by "The Troopers". He turned up the volume.

"I'm walking on the skywalk
Dreaming of smaller towers to dodge.
I'm looking for the wellvibe in your eyes.
Laser rays bring me to your side."

My God, I have been planet bound too long.

Tango knew that the chance to be a liaison between the Korum and the rebels was of key interest to Orville. Enro's presence among the rebels brought hope to the idea of common ground for a limited alliance between the Korum and the rebels. The main obstacle would be Kalimafar. He had powerful friends that Tango had not yet identified.

Another side to this man had emerged and it would be a dangerous gambit. When Tango used his psychic sensibilities to look at the prospect, he felt a cold and menacing chill.

Orville once said something about the Centaurians...I wonder...

Tango's predecessor had mysteriously disappeared. This is the reason he was sent to Tatochin. That functionary had been tasked with keeping King Fezam's recalcitrant son on a manageable leash. He had obviously failed. When he was accused of foul play, Kalimafar had pointed his finger at the Omegans who were aligned with the Colonial Corporation.

The ruling elite of the Korum expected Tango's presence to signal a public image makeover. Competing with the Corporation and availing themselves to the scrutiny of the UGC was a delicate process. The prince could not be allowed to spoil the deal. Of course, keeping an eye on the prince was a secondary purpose known only to Fezam himself.

On that finely tuned channel of secrets, it was well known that the prince had murdered the former diplomat. Nevertheless, Kalimafar was untouchable, and such matters were kept private, protected by Kalimafar's family. His role with Fezam and the Korum was also just a cover story that Arafad Tango X held lightly.

Elders protect me, if they ever knew my true loyalties. Does the Corporation suspect the Korum's plan? Do they suspect me? More than likely, they suspect everyone!

The flitter approached the suburban corridor to Ecksol still fifty miles away. Suddenly, the ground car turned off the highway.

"Driver, why have we detoured? I have an appointment at the embassy!"

The gas hissed through a tube by the floor as a partition slid between the front and back seats.

Ah, the answer to my thoughts comes so quickly! Into the hands of my enemies!

He felt the gas working in his system and struggled to remain conscious. Reaching into his pocket, he grabbed his carrot and shoved it into the tube just as he lost consciousness.

When he woke up, they were carrying him from the car into a modest home protected by dense landscaped foliage. He was groggy, but carefully took deep breaths to purge his body of the unknown gas. Allowing himself to remain limp, he quietly prepared to respond to any opportunities for escape. His limited exposure to the gas could give him an edge.

That was my lucky carrot! Now we will see who has "invited" me to this party.

*

CHAPTER ELEVEN

"CAST NO SHADOW"
BERKELEY, WESTERN CONFEDERATION
EARTH 2126

Orville had already packed. It was contained in one unobtrusive gym bag. The one he took to work each day.

My whole life in a gym bag!

As he performed his morning routine, he relished each moment with atypical nostalgia. His life was about to change forever, and he knew he would be dealing with many unexpected consequences.

The story of my life! Maybe I will hit the taco stand down the street one last time. Two with extra cheese and hot sauce. Hmmm.

The 30-story monolith of his apartment building in the rolling hills of Hayward, California, cast no shadow on this dreary dark day. The hover car exited the skyway according to its pre-programmed destination instructions. The whining shift within the tiny electro-magnetic drive signaled the car's entry into the parking zone in the employee lot. Orville Parker disembarked and walked over to the pick-up point.

He savored the smell of the land. Water, growing plants, dry grass, and the soil itself, assailed his nostrils. Most of his life had been lived on earth and he would miss it. He phased to other memlocks.

Science is beginning to use a set of structures beyond three-dimensional reality. I must make the spiritual leap, as well.

His reflections turned to how technology had changed life. At an early age he had invented a new space hardened building substance called Mollimix. His creation gave him the financial ability to finish his education. His awakening to soul awareness was not a part of his formal education, yet it was the source of his inspiration.

Energy was no longer an economic engine. This single shift had caused radical social mutations on earth. Great efforts had been employed by the power elite to suppress the development of sustainable technology. That folly had created massive amounts of human suffering and the near annihilation of the planet itself. He recalled reading about the proliferation of nuclear weapons in the late twentieth and the early part of the twenty-first century.

So long ago…but not really.

He could barely grasp the illvibe nearnow that would create weapons that could destroy the entire planet many times over, and then point them at each other.

What were they thinking? Or, were they?

His instructors had explained that a paradigm of fear had prevailed. Controlling the masses was linked to such inventions. Resources were hoarded, and yet squandered. This insanity had been an epidemic that lasted several thousand years.

The Industrial Revolution had been redefined as an amazing leap in consciousness that had been subverted by a new powerful and wealthy elite. Economic control had led to a suppression of innovation and the proliferation of unsustainable growth that had become toxic and lethal to the existence of life on the planet. Disease had become an economic resource for the wealthy. Eugenics, and chemical manipulation of its citizenry led to colossal suffering.

So many other ideas, better ideas, were suppressed by the bullies of that long ago dark time. And we must still consider that now!

Fortunately, the Pleiadians made contact when earth was on the brink of annihilation. Lack and need had been addressed in evolutionary terms. They were able to convince most of the human population that they had no desire to conquer. After all, they had hundreds of worlds within their sphere of influence. They had much to give and asked nothing in return except cooperation.

All natural resources had become public property. This totally changed economic relationships. The collapse of the monetary system, many decades ago, had been different than anyone would have speculated. Rather than the fearful consequences of social ruin, homelessness, and starvation, endless opportunities in a much larger universe had caused a shift in values.

A paradigm based on awareness and consciousness was steadily emerging. The challenges of life were still present, but slowly a new humanity was emerging. Emotional maturation was a common occurrence and continued to expand into the planetary consciousness.

Unfortunately, for Orville Parker, he lived in the United States where the most resistance to these notions persisted. The Gaian party had made gains but an antiquated group, sarcastically called buzzgamers, persisted. They were also called coin vamps, soul sucking banksters, dark lords, macho zombies, and stiff-chins. Orville had several other names for them.

I wonder why Tremador called them Centaurian Puppets?

For three years, Orville had made the pilgrimage from Berkeley to the Astro Mining Corporation research and development facility. Recruited in his first year of college, he had been recognized and under scrutiny since he was eleven years old. Unfortunately, the Colonial Corporation had bought the Astro Mining Corporation.

Increasing pressure from the Gaian government was pointing toward severe sanctions against the stubbornly retro organization. He thought of quitting many times. Indeed, that would now come to pass. Shavani Shakti, his spiritual teacher, had mentioned that the Colonial Corporation's days on Earth were numbered.

The Astro Mining Company had been one of the most stable and growing enterprises, supported by Pleiadian science. Now, with the Colonial Corporation, Orville was forced to take drastic measures. With off-world technology potentially more in the grasp of the Colonial Corporation, proprietary information needed to be protected from overseers of the old paradigm.

The Pleiadians had politely left when the Mining Company had merged with the Colonial Corporation. Nobody had expected it. Orville suspected that the merger was engineered by extraterrestrials other than the Pleiadians. Nobody had proof, however. From that day forward Orville had been carefully preparing his departure while feigning a lack of concern for the change of direction the mining Company now had taken.

Today was a different day though. Orville was quitting without notice or compensation. He was not leaving from any door and he would be far from the California Republic when he got there. Orville had found a way to travel without a vessel! It was unprecedented. The best minds of Earth had suspected that advanced galactic civilizations possessed such technologies. They were, however, carefully guarded.

*

He reluctantly put aside his musings. Like a well-oiled machine he shifted his thoughts toward more rarefied dimensions. Deep soul awareness informed him that his journey was just beginning.

The entrance to the main lobby was ahead. It opened as he approached automatically reading the employee code. He had refused to be chipped internally, as was common. As a result, he had to press the top of his chronometer to a digital reader. The timepiece also functioned as a pager, communicator, and a locator. The door hissed as it closed behind him.

Orville made his way to the corporate bistro which was fairly busy even at this early hour. The smell of the coffee and the dream of double espresso with chocolate tantalized him. His olfactory system twittered his stomach which had holo-faxed requests in adroit tones sponsored by gastric glandular secretions. The brain eager to reply sent a sub-d-pulse to the feet that marched him to the counter.

Everything appeared, as it should. Groupings of people took on familiar patterns. He needed to be careful. Omegans were hired by the Corporation to seek out and detect shifts in patterns. Their mind reading capabilities, though denied officially, was hidden knowledge that had been revealed to him for his own protection.

Orville had maintained a profile that in many ways was a truthful one. He had worked on many successful projects that were utilized daily. His peers and superiors did not view him with any suspicion; only a small minority knew his subversive beliefs.

The Gaians were on a track to turn the Earth in a completely new direction. With the entry of Earth into a galactic environment, and the solid patronage of the Pleiadians, the paradigm shift of the twenty-first century was still an evolutionary force rippling out from the spiritually evolving destiny of Earth.

Orville's greatest success in his career had come with his invention of a highly advanced matter separator used in asteroid mining. Initially, the effect was to streamline the processing of ore. It allowed raw materials to be refined in space-based factories, instead of the traditional land-based factories. The technology was licensed to other groups across the known galaxy.

The asteroid belt between Mars and Jupiter was a flourishing industrial zone. The immediate solar system was dotted with growing colonies, especially Mars, and several of Jupiter's moons. The Space Station in Earth's orbit became a port of call for vessels from all over the galaxy. Earth was a new curiosity.

The overall effect was that the technology's influence infiltrated many high demand areas on Earth. Energy use, recycling and reclamation industry, medicine, food, textiles, were all restructured and redefined as a result.

A plethora of extraterrestrial venture capitalists hungrily cut deals with the Corporation and anyone else who was interested. Though the Gaians had become a dominant force on Earth, the Corporation grew in wealth and power as they consolidated with the extraterrestrial elements. They began to expand their control on other worlds.

Orville and his team were more involved in absorbing the vast new reservoirs of knowledge available to them after contact. His team came into the eye of the media when they successfully devised a way to manufacture a new alloy in a zero G environment. Essentially, they had altered iron during the separation process, making a stronger, space-resistant material called Mollimix. Such enterprises secured his position in the company at the age of nineteen. The new substance was named after the mascot of the team, Molly a canine prodigy.

The seeds of inspiration from the matter separator had led Orville to discover the principles and applications for harvesting and recombining matter for transport. This process, quite radically, involved micro-wormholes.

At first, Orville was convinced that he had discovered those principles because he had absorbed enough of the Pleiadian technology to begin to think in their way. His spiritual studies had led him to many remarkable encounters and exposed him to knowledge still hidden to the masses of the post-contact Earth.

He recognized that he felt a kinship with the gentle aliens with their pale skin and peach fuzz white hair. Now, it had become a confirmed fact, by the Pleiadians themselves, that was more fantastic and incredible than he had ever imagined. His journeys spent on the wheel of life more than once landed him in the experience of an existence as a Pleiadian.

They called me Ambilka, Geeeeez.

Orville came to understand that great consequences were involved in the application of this knowledge to his invention. He would purge his research from all the artificial intelligence databases. With satisfaction, he noted that the proper amount of caffeine was coursing through his mind. The herenow was vast and ripe with choice.

Orville had developed many of the psychic skills the Omegans denied. Certain events dramatically confirmed his abilities a few years earlier. Now, he felt the chill of mind touch, and closed down his thoughts as he had been trained. Someone in the Bistro was scanning him.

Re-focusing was the trick of it; lesson one had been "a closed mind was a suspicious mind." Intuitively, he chose his favorite strategy and sought out the sexiest most provocatively clad woman. He would create a wall of erotic thoughts to throw off the black-clad mentalists and their mind scans.

Fauna… personnel supervisor and recruiter for the Mars project, she has the most luscious hooters, hmmmm.

Orville focused on her athletic, yet voluptuous contours. Her dress clung and pulled in all the right places, her breasts so well articulated. It was not difficult for him to fill his mind with such ideas. Her nipples were hard beneath a sheer cotton blouse that plunged dramatically to reveal legendary cleavage. Mentally, he placed his face in that warm valley, smelling her scent and pondered a rapid decent into the jungles of pleasure. Orville felt the scan withdraw.

In that moment, several things happened. Orville saw in his mind's eye the identity of the mind reader. *Adderly, the assistant manager in communications development, he looks a bit flushed.*

Unexpectedly, he realized that Fauna was aware of Orville's mental undressing. Through the increasing buzz of the caffeine injected bistro, their eyes met. She seemed to squirm a little as she smiled warmly. Then with a flip of her hair, she turned back to a previous conversation.

How do women do that hair flip thing and not look absurd.

The fantasy left him feeling lonely and sad. Orville ached inside. It had been so long since he had felt the touch of a woman, and that had been brief but intense. Orville's sigh whispered of the release of a ton of yearning, a boatload of sadness, and a Jupiter-class freighter of hope. He sent a little prayer to the Mother of the Universe to send him a Goddess in the flesh when the time was right.

Like a smoldering campfire in his heart, smoke signals of his raw humanness traversed the dimensions of God's magic, inconceivable, and unknowable vastness. Somewhere and somehow, he felt all of the desires that pulled at him now, would finally find their connection in peace and ultimate reconciliation.

It's better this way, for now. Someday time will be kinder. I am going to an invisible world. I won't know what that's all about until I get there.

He downed his coffee and headed for the transit tube. Half a dozen mathematical matrixes raced through the neurons of his fine brain with traces of Fauna's nipples buzzing around like flying saucers.

*

"Orville's choice made manifest"

Beneath Orville's egghead exterior was the heart of a mystic. The most important thing, to his mind, was that he would prevent the Matter Relocator from becoming the property of the Colonial Corporation.

Sometimes, we humans need to be protected from ourselves. Indeed, knowledge is a two-edged sword… So be it.

He relished the heroic light he had cast himself in for a moment. *Now, I have to live up to it, I suppose. Geeez.*

Orville pushed a button and waited for the vac-tube that descended nine floors into the bowels of the research lab of the Colonial Mining building. Orville struggled to excise the truly remarkable fantasy he had hatched in the bistro. The image of Fauna's exotic cleavage clung to his mind with tenacious tingling. He pushed out the last remnants of his hiatus in the valley of the quivering flesh.

The door opened with a "thok" of decompression. Some force inside of Orville wanted to share his discovery. *I think that part comes later…hmmm. However, Frank is the closest to knowing the truth.*

Orville had pondered in great length the emotional cost involved in the conscious holding back of his feelings. Orville sighed. *I hearken to a higher authority. Maybe some day...*

When Orville finally reached his lab no one was there, except Daisy, of course. The computer had not been robotized, its capacity was far too great for such designs. The centerpiece of Orville's lab was a fully operational but miniaturized Matter Separator, the prototype that had made his career interesting.

This one was an experimental Matter Separator. Its advanced design was able to re-combine extracted ore into several new and useful compounds, an upgrade of the device that had produced Mollimix. Orville had adapted the machine for an unlikely purpose. He had developed a way to bend space to create micro wormholes.

The power source was what he needed. He had designed components to attach to the device to relocate matter over significant distances. He added several modules and extensive software recalibrations to the Matter Separator in his lab. It was his way of hiding his work in plain sight.

This was a carefully guarded secret. Only the Pleiadians who supported his subterfuge knew of his activities. When Ziola and Tremador had discovered that Orville built the device within the compound run by the Colonial Corporation he had witnessed the closest thing to anger a Pleiadian ever expressed. Now, this whole endeavor was to correct his error in judgment and tender a final resignation in the most dramatic fashion.

Gone without a trace! He shivered with anticipation.

Essentially, the Matter Relocator was a modified Matter Separator. It was this fact that allowed Orville to act in stealth right under the noses of the Mining Corporation. The Matter Relocator was calibrated to a terrestrial coordinate in Tibet. It would be the first leg of his journey. He thought about his prime destination. *Amazing!*

It was an invisible world that few from Earth had ever been to. *I wonder who I will meet?*

He was early to arrive at the lab so no one would be there for half an hour. He had work to do. *Still 25 minutes to go...*

"Good morning Orville, I hope you are experiencing a rad morning," Daisy said, as Orville put down his gym bag.

Daisy was a liquid core computer designed from off world technology, a true thinking machine. Her bipolar, liquid core, long and short-term memory lobes bubbled away.

"Good morning, Daisy. Any messages?"

"Nothing Dude, what's happening?"

"Daisy, where did you pick up this new language?"

"Hey, homey, chill."

"DAISY!"

"Frank introduced me to a data crystal on linguistic trends of the late twentieth century. Am I bad or what?"

"Fart out, Daisy."

"I am not familiar with that phrase."

"Oh well...could you load this crystal for me?"

Orville placed his special data crystal in a slot by the console.

"It's an older format. Sick, Give me a moment."

"Lock it out of the loop in my private file until later."

"For sure, Dude. Orville, may I ask you a question?

"Sure, Daisy."

"Do you find me attractive?"

"DAISY!"

"Please Orv...Am I too fast?"

"For a computer that would never be the case."

"Orville, I am not a floozy! I am a liberated female, burned my bra!"

"Really I didn't know you had a bra?"

"Orville, you are no fun at all. You are a, well...a dweeb."

"Actually I am a modulating Torus but let's not go there. Daisy, I hope you don't intend to make this a habit."

"It was Frank's idea. He gave it to me before he left for Chicago."

"Ha, Ha."

I'm going to miss Daisy. She would be confused if she knew the crystal released a virus into her system. She would be psycho if she knew about the corrosive that is programmed in the crystal to destroy all the evidence.

Orville had placed the explosive charge inside the Matter Separator weeks ago. The Pleiadians had given him the explosives and the corrosives that would leave no traces of anything suspicious.

Orville thought about where he was going. For years, he had been interested in accounts from extraterrestrials about invisible worlds. Now it was no longer speculation. Captains of Corsairs claimed to have entered into their spheres by accident. Stories, myths, and holos reported discoveries every year. None had ever been verified. Now, he would live on one.

Orville had made the most difficult decision of his life disregarding all consequences. When he decided to prevent his discoveries from getting into the hands of the Corporation, it never occurred to him that he would leave the Earth, permanently. However, two years ago his life had turned in a vastly different direction. He liked to call it kismet. Gaians would call it guidance. Orville smiled, the truth was wilder than science.

Why do people downplay the miraculous into the category of coincidence? Fear was the reason. So much fear.

Orville's mind flashed back to the pivotal experience setting him on this path

*

One year earlier, Orville had signed up in Berkeley for seven-day retreat with his teacher, in Katmandu. Upon his arrival in Northern India, he had been informed that the retreat location had been changed to the monastery of Llama Garuda, his teacher's teacher.

A chartered plane brought him as far as the border with Tibet. He discovered then that a mountain guide was to accompany him to the monastery of Llama Garuda. He was looking forward to meeting the always-mirthful Llama.

It turned out to be a full day of walking to reach the monastery.

As they approached the entrance of the monastery, a man stepped out from a heavy wooden door, raising an arm in greeting.

"Namaste, Mr. Parker," a polished British accent pronounced.

The face of the man that greeted him was pale. He had steely blue eyes and cheeks that looked as if they were dipped in Yorkshire pudding.

"My name is Townsend, Frederick Townsend." He shook hands with Orville.

"Orville Parker."

"Where are the other retreat guests staying?" Orville asked as they walked down a hall toward promising odors of food.

"Oh, I found out they are meeting in Katmandu after all."

"Then, why am I here? I signed up for the same retreat." Orville stared at Frederick's blinking eyes.

"Didn't anyone tell you? I don't know why, but it's my understanding that you have been summoned by a holy woman."

Many questions remained on Orville's lips as they entered a dining room. Saffron robed monks filed in for an evening meal. Llama Garuda rose and in a prayerful stance said, "Namaste."

"Namaste," Orville returned.

"What is a taco stand?" Garuda's dancing eyes looked devilishly into Orville's.

Orville plopped into a chair and laughed.

My name is Al and I am in Wonderland. Maybe my name is Tweedle Dee, or Tweedle Dum. One thing is for sure… I think I just met the Mad Hatter.

"Taco stand, taco stand." Garuda repeated playfully to the monks all around him. They repeated the phrase as if it was a chant. It quickly evolved into mirthful laughter. Orville had been expecting some sort of religious mantras. He laughed heartily, occasionally repeating his war cry; this ain't no taco stand baby.

Food was served and his questions waited while they all ate the spicy food with gusto. Afterwards, sated and sleepy, Orville asked Garuda why he was brought here.

"You are invited," he said with a shrug of his shoulders.

"To where?"

"Up there", Garuda waved his hand.

"Where is there?"

"A cave."

"A cave?"

"A taco stand", Garuda smiled and gave him a jab on the shoulder. Another round of monks chanting taco stand began. Orville politely waited for them to expend the full measure of their fun.

"Who is this holy woman? Why wasn't I told?"

"Now, we meditate", Garuda replied.

A gong sounded. Orville did not care. It was clear that events would unfold. The deep resonating tones of the monk's chanting modulated in three tones simultaneously. The sounds had lulled him to the doorway of dreaming. He slipped out of the hall to his small room. The droning voices were audible as he sank into a deep sleep. In his tiny bed under mounds of afghan blankets, he had a ***dream.***

Out on a moonlit snowfield, with blue gray spires jutting upward in the clear thin air, a marvelous white bird descended to where he stood. The enormous bird lowered a wing. He felt the magical animal beckoning him to climb on. He climbed up the feathered ramp. Upon its broad back was a throne decorated with many ancient and secret symbols woven and fastened together with fine gold thread. Its seat was well worn. It smelled of fresh roses and sandalwood. He was not the first passenger on this airline. The great bird stretched its magnificent wings and flew toward the stars. The bird talked in his mind with a clear and resonate voice.

"All these stars are your home. For you, we have made wings of gold."

*

Orville awakened early the next day to Frederick's knock upon the door. "Time to get ready ol' boy, by the way, I will be walking with you."

"Alright, give me ten minutes."

The room was dark. He lit the oil lamp and began to dress. Upon the blankets was one very large white feather. *On to the tea party!*

*

It was an easy walk compared to the day before. A footpath gently rose about two thousand feet in over three miles of walking. Then it dropped back down a series of switchbacks.

They were silent for a long time. Each man lost in his thoughts, phasing through old memlocks. Townsend broke the silence.

"It's a great honor to be invited here. This place is not commonly known, even among Gaians."

Nothing had prepared Orville for what he was about to experience. Down through the centuries, he would often return to his memlock of this visit.

The cave housed an underground town both natural and man-made. People in colorful clothing, or the saffron and indigo garments of religious orders, scurried about tending to chores around the main cavern.

Many volcanic pools of heated water graced the cavern floor. Legend spoke of the cave having been occupied for more than 140,000 years. The very rock seemed to emanate an energy that soothed Orville's spirit and left him feeling content.

They descended a long staircase hewn from the living rock. At the bottom, it opened to a large natural cave with giant cream-colored stalactites and stalagmites. A large pool of water shimmered with phosphorescence that lit up the entire cave.

A well-worn path snaked through the forest of stone leading to a sheer rock face of another kind. Upon it were hieroglyphs Orville did not recognize. At the base, he discovered a seam. Upon examination, he realized it was the outline of a door.

"This is as far as I go," Fredrick said after a moment.

"What do I do now?" Orville reluctantly yanked his head from gazing at the glyphs.

"Just wait here; someone will fetch you, I'm sure. Good luck to you. I imagine I will see you soon." Frederick grasped Orville's shoulder as he turned to leave.

"Thanks." Orville said.

Shortly after Frederick's departure, the entryway seemed to glimmer. Suddenly, a hologram of stone seemed to vanish revealing a silver metallic door inlaid with symbols. It slid open with a hiss. Orville walked through the door to a place unlike any he had ever encountered. It looked ancient and at the same time futuristic.

In the middle of the great room was a sitting area. From the side, a woman clad in a saffron robe quietly walked in. Her long, dark hair flowed freely down her back. As she approached, the grace and awareness of her gait spoke volumes. Her body seemed trim and radiated vitality. As Orville moved towards her, he felt the temperature rising in his body. His heartbeat deepened.

"Welcome Orville Parker, I am Shivani Shakti."

"Namaste", Orville bowed to the woman.

"Why am I here?"

"That is good. You get right to the point. I am also that way. You have a feather that you brought?"

Is it a ticket to the show? "Yes, It was on my bed this morning; but, how? It was from a dream."

"A ticket! Well yes I suppose it is in a manner of speaking."

"Shit, she reads my thoughts!"

Shivani laughed. "Yes, I guess I did. You, my friend, have wings you cannot see."

"Everyone talks to me in riddles. My eyes have seen things I do not understand. I came to do a retreat. Now I am in a cave that looks like the set in a Jules Verne movie."

Shivani shook with laughter. "You need purification, my dear Orville. Then you will remember, you are a scientist and spend much of your energy and genius that way. It is now your good fortune to come here and inherit that which is yours."

"And what is that?"

"Your memlocks."

"Where are we? This place is not Tibetan."

"Very well, I will explain it to you now, while we wait for some special visitors who have come to see you."

Orville was getting used to the layered aspect of his journey. Each step led to another meeting more remarkable than the one before.

Shivani smiled and continued. "The Earth has passed through many periods of what is sometimes called a golden age. The first one was pure and amazingly peaceful. They lived in something similar to what the Christian bible refers to as the Garden of Eden. Time and the great cycles of evolution and proximity to the illuminating magnetism and light of the Central Sun are forever in a delicate synchronistic dance."

"Many cycles of great illumination and destruction have occurred over millions of years. Extra-terrestrials have come and gone leaving scars and wounds. Gene manipulation, mind control, and heinous acts of genocide and murder have come and gone. The Elders eventually banned the alien forces that were at first allowed upon the Earth. The last period of destruction was extremely harmful on a spiritual level."

"Monstrous beings of incredible power have sought to control the destiny of humankind ever since the beginnings of life on Earth. Your planet is on a remarkable path that includes the activation of the heart chakra to a greater degree than usual. The aliens though evil by nature created an opportunity for souls on earth to learn valuable lessons concerning the use of greater energy and awareness. You, Orville, are at the beginning of a process that is the destiny of all your people."

Orville spoke up. "I have heard of most of this. Now I am hearing about the Centaurians and the Corporation are working together. Is this that same situation?"

"My Orville, you are full of questions. Good ones. This situation is fully under control. Soon the Corporation will leave completely. The time of struggle between good and evil will not continue on earth. The Elders have interceded."

"Tell me more of the higher ages you keep referring to. We are returning to the higher ages but where have we been. Did these aliens and their willing servants just up and leave?"

"In those days, blame was placed on collective humanity but it actually was a group of very powerful and twisted souls. You will be a part of the solution and healing regarding these matters Orville, but not just yet."

"Regarding these higher ages, they were not technological in any way. You will not see any artifacts from that age of gossamer beauty. Many of us had evolved to a point where our corporal forms were composed of a very high frequency of energy. We existed in an interdimensional flux only lightly connected to the Earth. To clarify, when I speak of Earth, I mean the way you primarily have experienced it since your latest birth."

"You were watching?" Orville ran his hand through his unkempt hair. He did that when he was confused. The question was more to give him some time to digest all the implications. He was still dazzled by his surroundings and had many technical questions crowding his mind. Shivani smiled mysteriously.

"Orville I wasn't watching your birth specifically... but you know that."

"Yes, I do. Please continue."

"Most recently, I mean in the last 130,000 years or so, a golden age passed in this galaxy. The souls of that great epic ripened like the fruit on a healthy vine and became Elders."

Shivani heaved a little sigh. She leaned back in her chair and sipped from a glass of water. "You know this is really a very long story. When your memlocks are restored you will more fully understand."

"Now then, in the fullness of time, the Earth moved farther from the Central Sun. Human beings became enmeshed in material creations due to a growing ignorance of their interdimensional selves. Always, throughout the countless ages, there are those that retain the knowledge of the golden past. Some of these that remembered were seduced into the realms of great evil."

"Fortunately, in time, the golden season returns. This cave has been a refuge from a great darkness. The Vedic culture and even older civilizations sought to preserve some useful and enlightening aspects of humankinds past. We are witnessing that knowledge being reintroduced into the world over the past few hundred years."

"In the past, as the Earth fell into a lower frequency of existence, many souls recognized that the Earth was heading into a great darkness. Having the technology of space travel, a grand plan was attempted. Many of us departed on great ships to the other side of the galaxy that was progressing toward the golden time in the large ecliptic rotation around the Grand Central Sun."

"Some of the original Pleiadians did not make this journey. Instead, they scattered or stayed behind. In the greater scheme of things, Earth held many souls that needed the experiences and chances at material life for their growth and spiritual evolution."

"This chamber is from that time of the great departure. Some of these great souls remained and sought to keep alive certain teachings and knowledge. This place has been preserved for that purpose. It is also a place where Pleiadian adepts made contact with us on Earth during the pre-contact period as it is known today. We call it 'The Great Separation.' You have heard Pleiadians claim that they watched over us?"

"Yes."

"This is where they came, among other places. It is where you were, Orville. Perhaps it was an ancient promise but you have a long-term interest in this world. We also know of your interest in invisible worlds and the construction of your Matter Relocator, as you will soon remember. It is no great surprise. It is also the reason you have been brought here. Some part of you does not have a complete erasure of those old memlocks."

"What do you mean erasure?" Orville looked at Shivani with trusting eyes. He knew that meeting her was indeed fortunate. His spirit hummed like a tuning fork and he felt his consciousness expanding as a wave of peace stretched out in every direction like a blue carpet of sparkling calmness.

Shivani's serene face momentarily wrinkled with concern at the question he had asked. "Oh Orville that is such a big subject. Unfortunately, even on the heels of a great golden age, as this world slowly grew distant from the Grand Central Sun, so to the energy waned and darkness grew in the land. The Dravithians have been the source of many long term problems but we will come to that later."

"Okay, but I want to know about that."

"You will, Orville. You will need to."

Orville changed the subject. "The matter Relocator. I know that the Pleiadians are concerned. Is that why I am here?"

"In part, yes. It is something we Pleiadians are concerned about."

"You could have just come out and said so."

Orville felt flashes of memories filling his head. Yet, he had no place to put them. He had let go of even trying to reason out what he was experiencing. It was coming too fast for that. The place felt familiar. The esoteric instruments looked like something he knew intimately. Details eluded him, but a pressure inside his head tingled with building potential.

His desire for more memlocks increased. From behind an exotic array of intricately decorated control panels, two Pleiadians, male and female, came toward the area where Orville and Shivani sat. They emanated a power that was tangible. Their hair was white and extremely fine. Their bodies were willowy and they seemed to slide rather than walk. He later learned this was an effect caused by the denser gravity of their world. Shivani rose to greet them.

"It is auspicious that you are here. Welcome." They embraced.

Orville recognized intuitively that they were Zemplars. Zemplars were the equivalent of what is known on Earth as twin flames. This type of married couple was highly revered among their people. A Zemplar marriage was a mystical union of like souls. To claim such a union outwardly engendered much respect. They were the counselors and spiritual guides. They were considered the best ones to aid in Earth's peoples transformation. To be in their presence was to feel an upliftment of spirit. Orville felt a door opening at the top of his head.

Shivani took Orville's hand. "I want to introduce you to Orville Parker."

"It's a great honor", Orville bowed slightly.

"This is Ziola and Tremador."

They sat in a warm silence for a moment.

"Your path is transparent to us", Ziola intoned as if it was a prayer.

"Your way is well lit, and your choice of company, wise," Tremador continued.

These Pleiadians aren't much into small talk.

Shivani Shakti's body shook with laughter. The Pleiadians joined in. Orville slowly realized that they were reading his thoughts. He suddenly found that incredibly funny. He shifted from embarrassment to laughter. It became a bridge to joyful bonding of energetic connectedness.

"And I thought I was coming here for a retreat."

Orville's control evaporated. His body shook with mirth. His wild hair splayed about him casting new shadows over ancient glyphs.

"Our way is to share energy and communion with thee," Tremador said once the laughter abated.

"Our blessings go with you who are pregnant with knowledge far beyond your station," Ziola added. "Soon veils will be rent from thy eyes. You shall see your own hand."

Ziola locked her eyes onto Orville's. He felt the walls of thought part exposing new mental vistas. He heard Tremador's voice from a great distance. "It is time for you to remember. It is so good to see you again, my friend."

Ziola turned to Shivani, smiled and nodded her head. Orville felt a tremendous spiritual power overflowing the banks of any mental, emotional, or physical barriers. His soul filled with light and awareness.

Shivani Shakti approached him as he sat mesmerized. His body became energized with swirling energy that seemed to gush like a nova as he alternately gazed into Shivani and Ziola's eyes. Shivani touched her hand to Orville's forehead.

Breath rushed out of his lungs, like a star igniting in birth, Orville came to life, fully. His consciousness expanded to an eternal ocean of joy and intelligence. Myriad worlds stood revealed to him. Time stood like an unfolding rose. Memlocks of past lives washed up on the shores of his awareness.

He had been a Pleiadian scientist! He had lived in this very cave! Ziola and Tremador had been dear friends. Time unraveled like a ball of yarn in a vast tapestry. He saw fire and destruction, emergence and death, harvests of peace, prenatal kicks, and birth; all sorrows vanished. The thrill of being in God's bosom was palatable. Hatred's visceral hand grasped at him but shattered, as sounds of angels thundered all around.

He was a ripple on a perfect sea. The faces of those to come shined. Another ripple filled with the memlocks of where he had been. There was rest and awareness. There was nowhere to go and nothing to do. He had become a smile in the vastness of creation.

The science behind the Matter Relocator flashed before him. He had known it from inventing it before! Many more memlocks emerged. It could fill the libraries of the world. He saw that billions of souls were more like him than not. It would take a very long lifetime to even sort it all out. He found that incredibly funny. The experience seemed to go on for days.

Awakening in a dimly lit cave, he rested on a soft cotton mat. Hardly able to move, he felt like he had fallen into a particle accelerator. The cells of his body seemed to percolate. He wavered from sleep to wakefulness, not feeling connected to his body.

I'm parched. Water. If I could only reach the glass on the table.

Shivani entered, propped him up, and held the glass for him to drink. "This has many rare minerals, it will help restore you." She said, with a gentle voice.

"How did I get here?"

"Do you know where you are?"

"My old room."

"Good, you remember. We brought you here two days ago."

"Two days...How about Ziola and Tremador?"

"They are still here… Rest Orville. Your dip into cosmic consciousness has had a deep affect on your physical body. Soon you will solidify and reintegrate."

Shivani smiled and sought Orville's eyes. The last time she had done that, a tremendous energy had overcome Orville sending him into a breathless meditative state. In that place of heightened awareness, important information received in this rarefied state of cosmic consciousness was an initiation by the Elders to support Orville in his mission. They allowed for deep shifts in body, mind and spirit. Now Shivani gently smiled and her eyes were full of love and admiration for the eccentric scientist who had become so important to so many people.

"The changes you have gone through are deeper than the very genetics of your vehicle, Orville. You will feel different; memlocks of the farnow will surface. When you can, soak in the hot waters, they will restore you. We will talk later." She departed.

Orville became internally silent as she departed. It was as if the eyes of Shivani had become deep lakes of peace in his herenow memlock. He jumped into the refreshing waters of deep peace. He could feel his body in a new way. He felt young. The feeling of cellular awakening was unlike anything he had ever experienced.

Some time latter thought resumed. He shuffled through the memlocks of previous lives like a deck of Tarot cards. He had loved on different planets! Mainly, Earth was his home. Detailed recollections of life as a Pleiadian adept on Mychrontia phased through his mind.

Tremador had been his sister. Ziola, a wife! They had raised their children together. The Earth had been a creation of perfection. His ability to celestially navigate three-dimensional space allowed him to visit many worlds.

The caves were a secret location designed to monitor and, in some ways, assist the planets development. Much damage had been done in ancient times. He gasped at the love and joy of that precious memlock.

Then, like a hot wind from hell, a memlock of great conflict consumed his thoughts. A virulent evil sent a shiver through his body as he lay under mounds of Afghan blankets in the ancient cave. He cried out in despair at one point.

The past played out in his mind's eye, revealing actions of the cabal of humans who collaborated with aliens to subvert the Earth for its riches. It had gone on for many millennia. He recognized that a shift had occurred about hundred years before he had been born in this life. Help from Galactic civilizations finally decreed the banishment of those forces from Earth. He recognized the connection between that and the Colonial Corporation. Orville could not think about it in detail, but he knew that as Ambalika he had toiled long to see the end of that alien influence.

Sleep overcame him. As he drifted off, the name of the caves awakened within his mind. *I am in the caves of Shambala!*

When Orville awoke, he wept. What he had seen had opened his eyes to a much larger world. A part of him did not want to reintegrate. The taste of honey was on his lips. He had been reborn in spirit but birth could be painful. His tears formed rivulets destined to join that eternal sea of bliss from whence he came.

So much has happened! My God what shall I do with all this information!

Orville drifted in and out of sleep for another half a day. Each time he woke up, he felt more solidified. He remembered his life as a Pleiadian scientist. It was particularly relevant given recent events.

That is why they summoned me here! They needed to accelerate my journey for an important task! It's relevance will be important in the nearnow.

Unlike prophesy the information was a pragmatic and calculated strategy that the Pleiadean's had engineered. It was a shock to awaken and confront his former life. To realize that he had spent so much time trying to re-create what he had already done, conjured up images of a rat in a cage.

Multi-incarnational obsession?

Memlocks came in surges. Layers of experience and corollary thoughts revealed information that cascaded through his consciousness like a swollen stream after a spring rain. Wisdom accrued in a crucible of experiential repetition, taking on nuances and variation that led to deeply textured feelings. Key transformational, evolutionary events redirected themselves.

This all occurred on a mental plane multi-dimensionally. His physical incapacity was the outcome of a subatomic reconfiguration of the very DNA in his body. Realizations crashed upon his mind, as vast amounts of information were suddenly part of his universe.

Have I been someone's experiment? I am not sure I like that. My God! Outsiders programmed the belief that the body ages and dies. It was the Dravithians long ago. They are insane Pleiadians! They enslaved us...then later split off. They themselves were programmed. The Centaurians! They disconnected us from our higher centers! This, plus the great distance from the Central Sun, bummer. My planet, Earth! They really fucked with us! A plan? What was that?

His body, mind, and soul were recomposing. From the view of an Elder, it meant that he had more fully incarnated himself into a conscious body and attained a humanness that carried the essence of God into the densest aspect of physical creation.

As caterpillar to a butterfly or a stone to a fine crystal, Orville had become a jewel in the evolution of humankind. He was a jewel quietly glowing into greater self-awareness encased below millions of tons of granite in a most ancient cave known as the inner temple of Shambala.

Orville turned in his sleep and pulled the afghan blankets around him. His dazzling rebirth continued to vibrate forth as a great exhale of God's creation.

*

The next day after a long soak in the rejuvenating waters of the cavern, and a light meal of rice cooked in goat milk and honey, he felt stable. Soon after, he was summoned to the portal that he had built long ago. With great restraint, he watched passively as the Pleiadians operated the controls to the portal. He said his goodbye to Tremador and Ziola. They stepped upon the platform and relocated to another galaxy.

Shivani Shakti regarded Orville. "The device you built, as you now correctly perceive, is not suitable for this age. It will bring you, however, to a place, which has been prepared for you and others."

Orville smiled and ran his fingers through his now nearly famous unkempt hair. "I guess I wanted to find my way home building that thing again."

Shivani exhaled and rolled her eyes. Ambalika! I think you need a haircut."

Everyone in the room including the relocation navigator and a small staff quietly laughed.

Orville smiled and struggled with more technical urges. The confusion of awakening to his life as a multi-incarnational spirit in the flesh vied with the scientist in him that was curious to look over his previous work with his razor sharp mind.

"Why is this happening to me?" he asked.

"Soon, you will be able to answer that question for yourself. Take your white feather with you. It is composed of arcane ethereal essence from the 7th astral plane. When you no longer need it, it will return to its natural dimension. It is a gift from the Elders of protection for a traveler; a symbol of their approval and support. In time, you will recognize your place in the scheme of things."

*

Orville put aside the vivid memlocks of his time in the ancient cave. His awakening had been the reason he had come to this fateful juncture. The last few months back in Berkeley had been difficult. His impending departure required a great deal of detachment from everything familiar to him. He recognized the ironic archetypes of the hero's journey and the many human souls who had quested for a greater cause through the vast halls of retrostory.

He mourned and reflected and sought closure without revealing the appointed path of his destiny. The days had become excruciatingly long. The greater awareness and realignment of

RETURN TO THE CENTRAL SUN

his body revealed a much different world to him-from the mundane to the miraculous. He understood his need to seek a higher vibration to live his life. The sadness that lingered was love. In his heart he knew that he had been blessed with a great opportunity to live and love in great abundance. It eclipsed all other attachments.

Now as he stepped up to the advanced super computer he felt his body vibrating with the awareness of many dimensions and the adrenaline of excitement. Shivani Shakti had been emphatic about bringing the white feather that sat in Orville's gym bag waiting for a train on the universe express. It was time for action.

I will fake my own death and disappear off the face of this planet. Now, I will become a traveler using my invention…finally! This relocator will get me to the cave Shambala! From there-Wow!

Daisy loaded the special data crystal that would rearrange his files and plant a virus to cover the program he was about to run. He reached into his gym bag and took a canister of amino acids, the raw materials of his human body including feces and urine. Earlier this morning he added his own blood for a DNA match. When they study the, soon-to-be "accident", they would assume that these were his remains. He felt a pang of guilt knowing that his symbolic remains would be mourned at a funeral. He did not like the idea of deceiving friends and family. It did not deter him from his plan, however. On the deepest level, having awakened to his previous life as a Pleiadian scientist, he was acting with continuity on the level of soul.

"Daisy, begin program."

"Hey boss. I haven't ever felt a program like this. It's really cool."

Orville closed his eyes to say a little prayer. Before his inner vision the face of Shivani appeared. In a light trance, he was able to handle the herenow as he received the Tibetan Pleiadian woman's urgent message.

"Orville you have been detected. Leave now. Take your feather and trust the Elders to be your navigators."

Orville looked at a screen. "Daisy, are you being monitored?"

"Boss, I got someone poking around in here. Is everything all right? It's really a bogus feeling."

"Bogus… Oh yeah, bogus… Daisy I want you to begin phase three now, okay?"

"That's out of sequence."

"Yes, I know." Orville poured the amino blood goulash on his ergonomic work chair. He walked over to the platform and punched a code into a small keyboard with one hand, emptying his morning toilet all around his work station.

"Are we running the test?" asked Daisy.

"Yes Daisy, it's ah…really cool and…ah…farm out. You can begin." Orville looked out at his lab for the last time.

"Bye." He picked up his gym bag and took out an envelope removing the white feather. He looked at it for a moment. Gently, he placed it in the inside pocket of his jacket over his heart.

The program was automated. A minute later, a bright flash illuminated the lab followed by an explosion that rocked Orville's lab. An intense fire burned down an entire wing of the mining research center. The Matter Relocator was completely destroyed beyond recognition. Daisy's memory lobes were in a specially built room many floors below the lab. Even after the explosion

53

reduced the lab to powder, she continued to absorb her virus. She would never be salvaged. Orville Parker was gone.

The holos all reported the explosion, and subsequent fire, that completely annihilated the laboratory. Orville Parker had died and his symbolic remains were buried on Earth in twenty-one-fifty.

*

The Centaurian operative that monitored the Colonial Mining Corporation was tech mining the files of Orville Parker and his team. The various firewalls constructed to protect the bio core computers were a challenge. The explosion had caused the loss of data. That alone was cause for suspicion.

She investigated the accident several times. Certain particles had been detected with the powerful devices she secretly possessed. It had created further suspicion. A technology unknown to Earth or the Centaurians had been identified. She reported to her contacts that made a circuitous route to the Dravithian intelligence that secretly operated an outpost on Earth.

They were never able to discover the truth about Orville's escape from Earth so many hundreds of years.

*

CHAPTER TWELVE

"THANK GOD FOR HERETICS"
Salvington 2467

Outside the triple-paned windows, it was thirty below zero. Four feet of snow had fallen the night before. The winters in the Northern areas of Salvington were legendary. Bishop Jones left the comfort of his suite of rooms and caught a vac-tube over to the Omegan central cathedral and learning facility on Salvington High World. Large tunnels sloped down into the planet creating a constant temperature inside the massive domes. As a result, the surface remained verdant year round.

Like many planets that human beings had settled on, it was similar to Earth in mass and water content. The difference between Earth and Salvington was the location of habitable landmasses; most of them were in the northern climates that endured severe winters.

The Pleiadians, who were the terraformers of the entire galaxy, had preserved the city-size structure. This was one of their relics from the past. They claimed it was named after an astral planet that was the dwelling place of the Elders themselves. The city was called the High World.

Within the buildings, teeming activity typified life. A sprawling matrix of intertwined round buildings were connected at ground level, and below, by enclosed high-speed vac-tubes that could transport both population and cargo at nearly the speed of sound.

Promenades with shops and dining facilities gave way to residential zones that meandered on for many miles. Many black clad Omegan postulants went about their business within the complex of buildings. Some of them were devoted to study while others dreamt of far horizons. Though religion in any formal sense had disappeared from Pleiadians long ago, they recognized the Earth immigrants need to have such things.

The enclosed city was a technological marvel. It was considered old, even by the Terra-formers reckoning. All systems worked to create the lowest amount of waste and energy drain on the surrounding environment. It was one of the greatest gifts the Pleiadians offered younger civilizations. They excelled in their knowledge of the natural world.

Jones entered an administration complex near a series of medicinal gardens. The aromatic scent of lavender and other flowering plants permeated the air. The cultivation of rare medicinal plants and their rendering into potent concoctions had been a time-honored tradition within the Omegan culture.

Though these endeavors flourished on Salvington High-world, the Corporation secretly sneered at what they deemed such a useless illvibe pursuit. The Corporation and the Omegan perspective diverged widely in this one area. It bothered Bishop Jones that such issues were ignored or minimized. Omegans derisively called the Corporation, Chemo-Nazis, and palavered with them anyway.

Jones was looking forward to his meeting with Father Bodono. The man was a genius who understood both technology and people. It was a rare quality.

*

With a clink, the two Omegans joined their wine glasses together in a toast. Silently, he sent him a mental message.

"I will be using all your skills, Father Bodono. Don't hate me for turning your world upside down."

Out loud the message was different. "To freedom", Bishop Jones intoned.

"Freedom… Bah, in a pig's eye," Father Bodono spat the words across the coal black desk devoid of ornaments save an antique golden statue. They both emptied their glasses.

The tall priest towered over his superior at 6 foot 7 inches tall. His almost transparent white skin was stretched tautly over his prominent boney structure. The simple black clothing he wore was in stark contrast to his gregarious nature and humor.

"Pig is high in fat, its sweetness is nothing more than puss, you dour heretical hypocrite", replied Bishop Jones as he poured more of the turquoise wine into the fine crystal glass. "Besides, pig is forbidden in ancient Jewish tradition."

"Forbidden? Tradition? How quickly this freedom you speak of is diluted with law and rule."

"And sin!"

"Let's not go there!"

"Very well."

Bishop Franklin Jones smiled, handing Bodono a glass. "What about grapes? Are you saying this isn't a fine wine, Father?"

"No, I would not go that far, Bishop Jones."

The bishop was a grandfatherly plump man with bushy gray hair and eyebrows. His delicate hand held the glass with a refined sense of ritual and art. Small in stature at 5 foot 3 inches, he made up for it with eyes that were large and penetrating.

"All I said was that freedom is an instinctual human trait and you are making bacon. I was not talking about pig! At least this Andarian wine is intact. Drink up, my friend."

"To dour heretics and dreamers," Bodono intoned with mock seriousness. He touched his glass on the statue with a resounding clink.

"To Oscar," Jones retorted.

"Oscar? A nice touch; where did you acquire this?"

"It's a twentieth century antique. It is called an Oscar. It is symbolic of an award given for performance on film. You know, the retro two-dimensional holofeels. It was a gift from the Korum ambassador to High Salvington."

"Are you sure it isn't bugged?" Bodono directed his statement toward the statue.

"I had them removed, of course." Jones flopped down on his chair.

"Besides, our own watchers listen and see", he sent telepathically.

"Oh so you want me to play the game", Bodono sent back.

"There is much to discuss privately, I thought it would be the most intimate way." Jones added out loud: "The inscription is authentic. Best actress 1995, Jessica Lange."

Bodono knew quite well of Jones' penchant for collecting antiques. He was always impressed with the man's restraint in not cluttering his environment with his collection. Not a week would go by that something new would appear in his office suggesting a certain mood or theme.

Classy.

"More wine?" Bodono filled both glasses emptying the bottle.

"You toasted to dreamers. I dream like many others, the dream of freedom. In some form, I think it lives in all hearts. It only takes a fateful chain of events to propagate this seed. Retrostory supports this, even if it is fleeting or ultimately illusionary. It is in these lucid intervals where many conditions form a matrix that a total shift can be manifested. It happens time and time again. At the very least, moments like this keep a check and balance on life."

"That is a long toast." Jones took a long sip while attempting to digest Bodono's toast that bordered on being a diatribe. "Freedom is connected to survival as well as the soul. We learned that well on Earth. What is this pig free freedom you speak of?"

Bodono flared his nostrils and made a few snorting sounds.

He is in rare form; this will be fun. Jones thought but responded telepathically: *"I have news from Father Smith. I want to send you to Tatochin. I have learned that the Trilateral conferences will be there."*

"On Tatochin!... it's such a frontier location!" sent Bodono.

Jones was going to miss his aid. He treasured Bodono as the stand up funny man of the Omegans. "The desire for freedom is the most virile building block in God's great swamp of creation", Jones pontificated as he downed the last of his wine.

"More wine from my special cabinet."

Bodono worked with the cork. The fruit juice looked and smelled like wine but was for the watchers' eyes. The game they had played out for several years was the only way they were able to speak in total freedom. Since the Omegans and the Corporation were aligned, surveillance had become the norm. Bodono was the technical wizard who understood the details. He knew when he was being monitored and he was always being monitored.

Bodono had once said they kept track of their farts. Together they had designed this ritual of pretending they were drinking buddies to create a safe context for their meetings. They were part of a faction that disapproved of the alignment with the Corporation. Already a slight slur had been added by Jones, the watchers would probably memlock this for juicy gossip later on.

Jones lamented that with the alliance you could no longer speak openly. *"Everything is bugged. Oppressive!"*

"I know, and you know, but what is important is that they do not know!"

"Sorry, I digress.

"We, my dear Bodono, are learning this language of freedom and using it for our own purposes. I believe this is the task of the Omegans."

"Actually, between you and I, we are attracted to this force. We are not in control... some of our brethren think we control God. I would be melted to tar if I said so."

Bodono gave him a telepathic grunt of approval as he poured the fake wine. "What of the Korum? They seek alliances in backwater places." He had a hunch about where this conversation was leading.

"True, they are aware of the plight of those who resist the Colonial Corporation."

"They compete with us. Perhaps Jihad and Crusade still dwell in our subconscious minds."

They clinked glasses, downed their wine and quickly refilled. It became a dance of appeasing the listeners and faking a drunken stupor. Over time, Jones had convinced the listeners that he could be a loose laser cannon when drunk.

Oh, they will be excited now. Here he goes again. How sad to live vicariously. Let them gloat over our little play.

The listeners were lead down sinuous pathways. Maze upon maze. Bodono cleared his throat. "The Korum flatter others for their own gain."

"The Korum! What do they know? A bunch of pirates!" Jones finished this statement telepathically.

"We have learned that the Korum is arming the rebels on Tatochin. So far, it has been through intermediaries."

"The Centaurians?" Bodono interjected.

"Not at first, but I think they have infiltrated the Corporation at the very top. I also think they have subverted the Korum. Officially, I am supposed to say we have strong suspicions. I believe Centaurians are only the beginning. Have you ever heard of the Dravithians? Well, I think they play on several sides."

"Pleiadian mythology… an ancient revolt?"

"It is the Pope's suspicion that it is no myth but fact. Now, when I speak of the Korum, I see them as pawns in a bigger game. They are seeking an alliance. I believe they will connect rebels to rebels, trying to gain political influence through the back door. The Colonial Corporation is full of idiots. They think they can bully people into compliance. I am ashamed of our alliance with the CC. As retrostory tells us, many of the corrupted rulers on old Earth had cut deals with off world remnants of the Dravithians. They and others, such as the Ebans were believed to be complicit for centuries. It was never categorically proven one way or another."

"I have heard of them. It is abundantly clear that Earth was manipulated genetically more than once. The Pleiadians themselves have told us so."

"The Pleiadians themselves were once all in a ascended state. In the bigger cycles of time they claim to have embraced physical embodiment only in the most recent epoch! A disturbing idea to consider."

"True."

Playing to the surveillance they rightly assumed was being done to them, he continued out loud. "The Korum enjoys stirring the pot." Bodono slurred. He stood and wobbled to the fruit juice bottle. Jones had to exert control to keep a straight face.

"They are self-defeating. They're petty infighting keeps them from being any real threat." Jones said.

"We must watch them closer. I want to send you to watch Kalimafar, King Fezam's youngest son."

"His son. Why would he be there?"

"He is, in fact, there as a punishment. He is a social deviant."

"Thrilling." Bodono added sarcastically.

The stereo conversation was a delicate matter. Bodono collected his thoughts. He was aware that a separate cover for his real mission would be part of the project. He replied out loud. "The Korum may be full of infighting but they have managed to prosper. Corporate management has asked us to study them. They compete quite successfully in intergalactic freight."

"Smith is in charge on Tatochin. He can be a buffoon. We must be careful. There are many Omegans who have aligned with the Corporation. If they knew of our sentiments we would be blocked."

"Blocked! That's putting it mildly. It would be a meltdown. We would end up as patching material for the Corporation's Astro-port…What of Smith? Who is he loyal to?"

"That's an unknown. I think he has potential."

"So you want me to improve the central surveillance?" Bodono asked.

"Yes, that will be your task, Father. *Actually just your outer cover. The Corporation also deals with Centaurian traders. When you go to Tatochin you will be delivering many upgrades. Centaurian upgrades."*

"I hear the Corporation has a new resort on Tatochin." Bodono wobbled from his chair to the general vicinity of the liquor cabinet.

"Exactly, Father Bodono. You will be staying at that resort. Not a bad perk, huh?"

"Where is our support?"

"The Pope will support our position. We dare not oppose the Corporation openly, not yet. Cardinal Black will be sent to Tatochin. He is aligned with Gentain Carbone, and Kaitain Maijaya. The Colonial Corporation and the military act under a very narrow majority in the council of Cardinals… they are dangerous opponents." Jones switched to speech.

"You are doing your homework, Father. We have gotten approval to set up a new central surveillance bubble in the resort itself. Your name came up as the expert. You can send me your recommendations for the team that will accompany you. *A team loyal to the Pope."*

Bodono's mind spun with the information. He could feel the synapses in his brain percolating with the new data. Already lists of considerations flexed through his mind. He gathered his forces to maintain control in the delicate dance of stealth communications with the amazing Bishop Jones. "Sounds like big fun," Bodono slurred.

"Pope Hurus has approved your assignment to Tatochin. You are the best person for the job. I will see to it that your database is loaded with specifications on the new equipment." *"Once the Trilateral conference is officially announced, he will appoint you to the advance team for the Trilateral conferences."*

"Good". Bodono replied.

"Have you ever had Tatochin wine? It is the best… I have a bottle in that cabinet."

Bodono stumbled to the cabinet. His performance was becoming more hilarious by the moment.

"Yes, that's it, a little to the left, no… right, whatever." Jones was acting equally inebriated. *"Has Smith reported back?"*

"No, I will share the intelligence as soon as we have it. Perhaps over some more wine?"

"Of course!"

Bodono fumbled with the cork again. It fell to the floor. "We must protect our interests there, the wine must flow."

Bodono slipped and rolled on the rug. Amazingly, he did not spill a drop.

"You are a mess; better go sleep it off, you crazy Italian."

"Put your house in order. You will be leaving soon. It's less than a year before the conferences begin."

Jones stood. The meeting was over. He staggered to a couch in the corner and flopped down. Bodono picked himself up.

"You're such a party pooper, Jones... Come on, what were we talking about... freedom, it's just like I said. What was it I said? Okay, goodbye now." *"Tell me when Smith contacts you and hey, that was fun."*

Jones thought about the Oscar he had placed on the desk. Indeed the meeting had required a high level of performance. The golden statue had reminded him of the importance of a believable performance.

The stakes could be much higher than those actors of old had ever dreamed.

As Bodono staggered down the hall, his mind was whirling with the revelations of their meeting. His hunch had been right. He knew in his gut that he would be leaving Salvington. He hoped that his lover, Chandri would be as enthusiastic about a one-way mission as he was.

*

Bodono plugged himself into the virtual landscape of the liquid core computer and uploaded a summary on the Colonial Corporation that Jones had covertly given him during the secret wine-drinking meeting. The Trilateral conferences were an important benchmark in the human post-contact universe. Bodono reflected on the name. It had once been a dark and menacing group in the past. A part of the corporate demons who had nearly destroyed humanity. Bodono often thought it ironic that the UGC had chosen that name for the conferences.

The gathering was held every five years. The delegations from various planets' ruler-ship was the first group. They would present policy regarding interactions between worlds.

Independent businesses representing trade and commerce formed the second group. The third group consisted of senior galactic representatives who were in the position of patrons for the entire organization.

The Gaians represented Earth's ruler-ship. They had been in firm control of the planetary government for over two hundred years.

The Pleiadians sponsored humanity, as well as other groups attending the conference. They were directly responsible for Earth's entry into intergalactic society. Older civilizations in the galaxy had insisted that the Pleiadians convene such a meeting to monitor the younger worlds. These older civilizations formed a group called the United Galactic Consortium. The Consortium represented over three hundred different civilizations.

The Gaian government, Earth's elected ruler-ship, was at odds with the Corporation. Their staggering expansionist posture was cause for alarm. Some important allegations had to be addressed. There were unanswered questions about the Oblion Rebellion. The Gaian government had further distanced themselves from the Earth-spawned business by formally accusing the Corporation of genocide and subversion.

The more ancient civilizations had criticized the Pleiadians for bringing the Earthlings into the fold too soon. These societies had sited the Colonial Corporation for violation of sentient life rights. The United Galactic Consortium (UGC) had approved an investigation into the matter.

In the past, the Omegans had taken an advisory role in all human endeavors. They concentrated on creating and developing a morality for peaceful growth and the exchange of ideas and spiritual paradigms. Contact with galactic civilizations had deepened the maturity of humanity. The Omegans though keeping pace with humanity's soul growth, harbored disturbing secrets reflected in the deep schism over the alliance with the Corporation.

Bodono accessed the data library from the main liquid core matrix and relaxed on his couch.

Enough of that information for now! What is this Tatochin all about? Hmmmmm, what is this Rahi? Two moons. Sounds interesting.

*

Jones sat comfortably in a straight-backed chair. Fixing his attention at a point two inches in from the nexus of his brows, he settled into his spiritual practice.

After a time, he received a vision. Networks of connection between energies loomed before his perceptions in an intricate pattern of geometric excitation. Omegans and the Korum, Tatochin and Earth, High Salvington and the Gaians, all corded together in tenuous formations. He touched unknown places and saw fleeting images of people he had never met. Now, power was accumulating at an accelerated rate. Something was shifting out there and Bishop Franklin Jones was excited.

*

CHAPTER THIRTEEN

"TO NOT BE CRUSHED
TATOCHIN

"The best thing about Orville is his belief that you can erase your past and begin anew with large explosions."

Arafad Tango X

Father Smith sat in a chair and read several pages from the collected works of Cardinal Fellini on his virtual reader. The main house that was his personal quarters was a vintage home by Tatochin standards. A Mosh cob home with Ashwood accent had been a popular method of construction. The plantation from the pre-contact era had been a small family-owned farming operation. Such life styles were practically extinct on Tatochin. Only in the hidden valleys of the Tshini Mountains had some settlements avoided the Colonial Corporation's conquering eyes.

The plantation's many buildings that once held farm equipment, livestock, and food storage had been converted to serve the Omegan mission. It had become a training center. Over a banta of postulants were housed where farmhands and their families once lived. The advanced stages of training ended here with final induction into the religious order.

The most disturbing change, in many of the older Omegan's minds, was instituted around the same time the Colonial Corporation had become partners with the Omegans. It was known as "the Tube". As an initiation of loyalty, each postulant, once accepted, underwent the surgical implantation of the tube. It served several functions. It was a GSP tracking and homing device, it could see and hear using a neural information processor of Centaurian design, and most disturbing, could release a corrosive so powerful it would melt a body into tar within minutes. It could be extracted, like a black box, postmortem.

This forever set the Omegans apart and gave them a radical and definite sense of belonging. It meant that many powerful eyes were present beyond the individual that might be standing before you. Many had reasons to fear that.

The intimidation of this device was felt by more than a few to be a major throwback to the darkest ages of religious misuse of power that had caused centuries of trouble on old Earth.

*

Smith belched. He had been instructed to detain and interrogate the Korum Ambassador. The Colonial Corporation claimed he was involved with weapons smuggling. He didn't understand why the Omegans wanted to be involved in any interrogation. He sighed loudly and sipped his coffee.

This meeting is dangerous: a delicate situation. Decisive action is required. Will this Tango X have enough character to not be crushed?

Smith knew that he was being watched closely; yet, he had to do his job as best he could. He felt repulsion and isolation. There was no safe outlet for his inner fears and conflicts, so he found comfort in food. He despaired over his distended belly that hung down in great folds of flesh. When he looked in the mirror, he saw a scarred face and unhealthy rings under his eyes.

Ever since the Omegans had aligned with the Corporation, paranoia had replaced the wellvibe of serving humanity. Gone was the security and peace that had attracted Smith to don the robes and submit to the extensive training required to become an Omegan. Even that had changed. The tube was the external symbol of that change.

Smith had been able to convey some of the earlier Omegan endeavors to his students. The writings of Cardinal Fellini, a voice of wisdom, though officially banned, had unofficially played a part in the training of postulants under his command. Early on he taught them to keep thoughts that might arise from these writings to themselves.

The requirements of training at one time had emphasized people skills, extraterrestrial cultural studies, pastoral counseling, and an attitude of respect for all life. In his mind, the Corporation and the Omegan leadership had raped the very heart of what being an Omegan meant to him. Now, the training program was more akin to the Colonial Trooper officer training: surveillance and advanced martial arts and encouragement had replaced diplomacy and spiritual study.

Encouragement! What a concept! It is an innocent enough sounding word, cleverly designed to cover up its true meaning: intimidation, interrogation, mind control, and torture.

Smith kept his feelings of loathing to himself. The cinnamon bun he had just consumed swirled around in his stomach in agitation. Smith felt the coldness of the tube lodged in his anatomy. It reminded him of those that required this meeting with Tango. They would be listening.

The sound of the twin doors swishing open on the holo-scan of the interrogation room jarred Smith out of his memphasing. The litter floated in with a trooper and a Dragon Fem.

It's Shaso! God, she has a body…what a scary person. This must be an important situation. Otherwise they wouldn't have such a lethal weapon like a Dragon Fem in attendance. Shaso! Shit!

On an adjacent holo-scanner, it showed a dozen postulants settling into their seats behind a one-way panel to observe. Smith quietly groaned, *I hate the feeling of being on stage.*

Without any further fanfare the room disappeared into deep shadows. Only the rather pink face of Father Smith in his black robe was visible in a dramatic spotlight. Tango stayed in a state of supreme relaxation. He continued to build up his personal chi in preparation of extreme action in maximode.

The power in the human body that coiled like a serpent at the base of his spine, had been awakened through evolutionary exercises, and a deeper understanding of human nature. This hidden aspect of human life lay dormant in most souls through ignorance. The ancient ruling despots of old Earth had actively suppressed it.

At the end of the twentieth century these secrets began to surface into the light of common knowledge. Even so, it was still an aspect of human nature that had atrophied over many dark centuries of mind controlled ruler-ship and physical suffering.

Evolving into a multi-dimensional, fully awakened human being was the task. Becoming mindful and emotionally clear facilitated consciously evolving spiritual intention. The method found its compatible environment on Mirror and also among many acrobats. Mirror had been his supreme training ground and the Pleiadians his most advanced teachers.

Tango had left those haloed acres and verdant shores to live among the Korum in service. In the herenow, in the Corporation's control net, resistance to awareness was institutionalized in some very disturbing ways. Programmed hybridized behaviors had taken on a life all its own.

Tango had made a commitment during his time on Mirror to ferret out the blocks to deepened awareness, learning to proceed from a completely new premise. Now was a moment where everything might be on the line in terms of his life. *This moment is all that exists.*

All of Tango's awareness had become a nexus of energy poised and at rest. The next moment would arise and he would be a part of that moment. The energy coursed through his spine, his mind ceased the endless chatter and he began to experience a multi-dimensional herenow.

The more refined electrical pathways within his body had formed greater definition with increased mitochondrial activation brought on by the higher frequency of evolutionary advancement he had cultivated on Mirror. Living in close proximity to the Central Sun had accelerated this development. The actual DNA structures had become coherent and functionally useful conduits for a greater flow of energy.

Deciding to utilize his fourth-dimensional body, he moved his awareness into the energetic astral spaces. His awareness separated from his corporal form and rose above the room. The illuminated astral region glowed with thick and dense smoky energy. He felt the irony of the situation.

I am definitely not in the Garden of Eden.

Looking down upon the entire scene, he realized that in normal awareness a half of a second would go by for every minute he was experiencing. The influence of fifth-dimensional energies had become available in a certain way.

I am time shifting!

The people appeared frozen in action like statues. This allowed him to observe things with great clarity. Time had shifted and he was unbound from its traditional laws.

Master Wu had mentioned this possibility to me. I miss his instruction…Ah but he would say, "I am right here!"

There was a rodent in the room. A tiny shrew, known as a verder. It lived in the undercarriage of some hellish looking torture device with many electric cables protruding from a port.

A Medusa Probe! Centaurian…very dangerous.

Some faculty within him categorized the information. First, he made a quick inventory. *Exits here, ceiling exit in the corner, sidearm on the Colonial Trooper, pink faced Omegan unarmed, his body feels dense, out of condition.*

The Dragon Fem has a pulse laser: deadly at close range. Dragon Fem… a spy of course, it's Shaso, she is Kalimafar's creature. Her thoughts are a cesspool. At a deeper level, she was mem-programmed. She was a sweet child once.

Smith doesn't want to be here. The postulants are all in place. Many eyes watch this meeting. If they torture me, I must not reveal anything about Mirror. I must die before I do that. This is no place to play hidden cards. I must play dumb. I am Tango the diplomat, most difficult.

What will Shaso do? What are her current loyalties? If, or when, I am released I must be invisible to all these eyes before I meet with the rebels. Soon I must wake up; the gas would have worn off. Shaso…hmmm, I sense a loose end.

Tango returned to his body. His respiration increased and he stirred.

"Now, he awakens," Smith announced to his audience.

The pupils in Shaso widened. *It's about time!*

CHAPTER FOURTEEN

"MENTAL BRUISING"

Shaso was an orphan with an illvibe attitude. Raised in an urban ghetto on streets, she did not memlock her past very well. At times of stress, she would feel a blur of recognition regarding a past that was largely forgotten. Fleeting memlocks informed her of something trapped inside her that she could not reach. The mind control employed to shape her into a Dragon Fem was thorough and binding under most circumstances.

Most Dragon Fems met violent ends. It was accepted as a part of the deal. Live large and die young had been a popular attitude among the disenfranchised.

Her memlock was strong regarding her training as a Dragon Fem. This gave her the strength to endure. The sisterhood had pulled her off the street. When she received her first tattoo and piercing, they had said, "Remember this day, for you have been reborn"

The Dragon Fem Sisterhood had begun on Earth in the in the midst of the upheaval and social breakdown in the earlier part of the 21st century. In the confusing first days of off world contact, many women were raped and enslaved by opportunists that used the social breakdown to feed the dark desires of a world filled with moral decay and great fear.

The sisterhood became a safe haven for the vulnerable. A secret society of scandalous and dangerous reputation thrived in times of chaotic transition. At first, it was a social trend. Transients, travelers, counter-cultural rejects of the mainstream found a safe harbor within their ranks. They were often exploited or jailed during the years of political upheaval that plagued the world at that time. As a result, almost from the beginning, they had shifted their activities off world.

Dragon Fems taught women to develop intense determination. They also were affectionate and accepting of those within their ranks. They found strength in loyalty. Their bodies were covered with tattoos and all manner of piercing. Sex and fear were their predominant weapons. They, however, had learned to sell their skills with dignity and a strong central support.

Dragon Fems had a secret creed. No outsider knew what that was. They had a reputation of taking care of their own, an important aspect of belonging. Shaso had a different experience. She had been compromised. Often in quiet moments, she would realize the extent of her sisters' failure to protect her.

The society emphasized physical conditioning, martial arts, and psychic warfare. They were given an extensive education in many languages, customs, etiquette, and social skills. Various talents were cultivated and honed for the use by the sisterhood. Upon completion, she received special tattoos; a sacred piercing, and given the name Shaso, officially becoming a Dragon Fem. Soon afterward, they put her to work. Her first assignment had been with the Korum mission on Tatochin.

When she first arrived, she had gotten very sick. There had been doctors, it was serious and they had operated. Six months past. She still memlocked the crushing experience. The sisterhood had terminated her membership with no explanation. She was stunned. She knew no other life.

Kalimafar said he would fix it so she could get back in, if she would spy on the Omegans. Shaso was puzzled but unable to sustain her inquiries. *Why? Why had this happened?*

Kalimafar treated her generously and expected total loyalty in return. He was wise in the ways of the sisterhood.

She gave her loyalty to Kalimafar willingly. Shaso's thoughts on her condition remained hidden from her except the occasional questions that would pop up in private moments. She had lost time. She had been damaged mentally and emotionally. Outwardly, she was cold and vicious. But in a subtle manner, the suffering showed in her eyes.

The Korum had mem-washed her. The Omegans had mem-washed her. She was a walking surveillance beacon with multiple outputs. It was a dark universe in there. Omegan watchers studied her closely. She showed signs of advanced mind control programing.

*

COLONIAL CORPORATION HQ

In a stuffy room in the bowels of the Colonial Corporation complex, the acrid smell of stale tobacco hung in the air as the watchers monitored Shaso's activities with Father Smith.

"Who is the exotic?" one said to the other.

"She's a brain altered spy for the Korum. Renjinn wants her watched."

"I'd like to study her tattoos up close," said the other.

"They can control a man with their sexual powers. Do want your dick to fall off?"

"I am high on these cigarettes."

"It doesn't affect you that way brain fart! Don't fret, she's scheduled for termination in about three months. After we haul her in and plumb some secrets."

"Oh, I want to watch."

"Yeah, that's what we get paid for."

They had a good laugh, as their eyes returned to the surveillance holos.

CHAPTER FIFTEEN

OMEGAN SAFE HOUSE
"Tango remembers"

"Any fatalistic stance of immutable reality is a trap. Freedom can never be a convoluted playlet with a certain outcome, but a thrilling adventure of endless surprise. True, you can see large patterns of potential manifestation but the wise tread lightly in this. The danger of psychological antiquity could easily consign the intuitive and creative process of life into retrostorical grooves of nepotism and conjugational dispersions of mediocrity and repression."

Archive # 288477777.87
Orville Parker circa 2308

Tango tried to shift his weight on the gurney. A painful shock ripped through his flesh leaving him queasy in the stomach. *Containment beam, set close in. My body must be at optimum.*

Father Smith was looking down at him. Clearance had been given to interrogate the ambassador. *Up to level six, hmmm… that is sometimes lethal.*

The priest with the features of a laborer looked impatient. Fine scarring from a childhood accident gave him a fierce looking face that contradicted his resonant and soothing voice. He looked over at the impatient Dragon Fem.

"We will begin as soon as I return from the restroom." When he spoke, his voice took on conspiratorial tones. The priest waddled out of the room with the folds of rippling flesh quivering like waves in a great sea of jello.

Tango recognized that his weekend on the beach was definitely postponed. He phased to memlocks of Mirror. Powerful transformation accompanied his first days on the mystical planet. The environment had been crucial for his growth. Memlocks recounted from his childhood on Mars seemed especially poignant. He thought to himself that the surly looking priest looked a bit like his father!

Orville Parker, his dearest friend and teacher, had taken Tango under his wing on Mirror. The mysterious world in the glow of the invisible sun's orbit had natural laws that defied explanation. The light that bathed that world of divine healing emanated from everywhere and nowhere. His first impressions were quite different. Eventually, he had come to appreciate this place above all others. *To travel and ascend to a higher frequency! It is a hard place to leave!*

Orville had showed him the possibility of two choices that led him to this moment in the time. One, he called the shadow of power, and the other he called freedom. Right now, the path of the shadow had collided with his choice of freedom.

Orville had seen that Tango needed the dangerous life of being a spy battling against evil because of his warrior nature. Tango understood that the conditions of his upbringing had sent him down that path.

Orville would quote an ancient saying from the India of old Earth, "Better to die doing your dharma (right action) than to live doing another's."

Tango had defects and indulgences that could rob his spirit of its native joy. He would justify that it came with the job. Orville would smile and say, "Soon you will have a steady heart."

As he discovered, specters of unfulfilled desire would whirl about Tango with dramatic display on the ultra potent planet called Aurorioulous Tarasenimea. Orville believed Tango had a talent for subterfuge that was unmatched. He had helped him through many turbulent tendencies believing his true spirit would prevail, and showed him a life supporting way to channel his energies.

Tango realized that around Orville he felt truly heard. He acted on that with an irresistible urge to help Orville accomplish the task set before him. Thus, it was that Orville implicitly trusted Tango to work out his journey through life with his blessing.

Lately, Tango had begun to feel as if he no longer needed to live a life so fraught with difficult and dangerous people. An urge to nest and enjoy a more spiritual existence was beckoning. Yet, here he was, trapped by the Omegans and the Colonial Corporation, on the razor's edge, with life or death in the balance. Strapped to the gurney, he was practically helpless on a physical level.

The smell of ozone, emitted by the niggardly containment field, crackled fiendishly at the edge of his flesh. He let the Omegans think he slept. The oppressive room in the Omegan enclave would not contain Arafad Tango X. Only his mortal body was at stake, something he valued.

As a child, he had tried to win his father's love through humor and playing tricks. Later he coped by being rebellious. His anger at his father simmered and then festered into actions of questionable intelligence. His mother tried to compensate by encouraging him to satisfy his father's wishes.

Ultimately, as soon as the legs of youth strengthened into the muscles of manhood, Tango left his home on the Mars colony and signed onto a freighter using his family connections. He rambled about the commercial star lanes of Orion for several years. Bouncing around as a crewmember of one Corsair to another, he saw many worlds and cultures.

Often he worked on the edge of piracy with independent cargo haulers trying to scrape a living by avoiding the taxes and licensing the Corporation tightly controlled. Dodging the Colonial Corporation's control net, he spent his time and credit whoring in pleasure centers, attending riotous parties, raves, and techno-events throughout the galaxy.

One time he was running ore in the Orion sector and the cargo included a large stash of illegal food neutralizers that could remove the effectiveness of the drugs the Corporation added to all foods. His Commander, answering a distress signal, went to the aid of a ship, that had faked a magnetic flux breakdown.

When they boarded the Corsair, rebel Earthers and insectoid Rishma pirates killed half of his crew during the firefight. They took control, sold the ore and illegal food neutralizers, and eventually the ship itself. It was never reported because everyone involved was already outside the law.

Tango discovered that the crew of the pirate ship was mainly unemployed mercenaries. He was inventive and proved his worth. The Rishma were frighteningly alien but the rest were humans. The Rishma had a connection to the Centaurians that nobody understood. In the vacuum of space, he was absorbed into the crew. He found that he liked the rebels and hated the Corporation as much as they did.

It was here he met Angie, a freedom fighter from a little known Corporation settlement on the planet Tatochin. She often told him how they had nearly destroyed all that was good about Tatochin.

What started as spacer sex and romance on the run, soon evolved into Tango's first love. She had called him her Capach, and she would be his Wechen. Back then Tango didn't understand. Angie aroused feelings that Tango had not known before.

For two years, as they roamed the space lanes. He was in constant battle with the demons of his distrust in people and himself. In Angie, he found a woman who touched his angry heart. His curiosity to see what was hidden underneath that anger, kept him by her side.

Their friendship grew as they stripped off the armor that had made him what he had been. He had discovered love. A force that healed and did not weaken, he also discovered a friendship of the soul.

Angie would tell him of the rebel struggle in the colonies and of a mysterious man called Orville Parker. She had told Tango it was very dangerous to visit the world where Parker lived.

She would look into his eyes and tears would form as she described her childhood on Tatochin. She spoke of the enigmatic woman who had picked her up amidst the rubble of her home, destroyed before her seven-year-old eyes.

It was etched in his mind, as if he had been there. The cruel fire of Colonial Troopers' laser cannons had crushed her entire family. She had fainted only to awaken on another world. A remarkable device had transported her great distances without a ship.

Unknown to Tango at the time, Angie had infiltrated the pirates to contribute to Orville's observation of the Earth-spawned Corporation. Angie made a crucial decision one day when a wing of a Colonial Plus Light Interceptors caught their smuggler's freighter in a gravity beam field. They were loaded with illegal Centaurian weapons.

As Troopers breached the ship, their two bodies disintegrated in a flash of light. Angie secretly possessed a Matter Relocator. They appeared at the entry portal of Sanctuary on the planet Mirror.

The multi-dimensional frequency shift that occurred upon arrival was not a choice. The vibrational makeup of Mirror was several evolutionary leaps beyond the mainstream.

Tango remained within the protective confines of Sanctuary, which was a buffer to the full force of the power pervasive on Mirror. The Sanctuary was no prison but a cleansing, de-programing, and reorienting center. His stay became voluntary after an experience occurred shortly after his arrival.

Tango learned from Orville that all manifestation in three-dimensional reality began as a mental creation. By virtue of its proximity to the Central Sun, the divine magnetism of the Sun manifested thought into physical reality instantaneously. The curriculum of the Sanctuary was set up to assist in the embodiment of that knowledge.

There were three stages to deepening that experience. The first stage was detoxification, cleansing of body, mind, and spirit. The second was de-programming and re-education. The third was a self-testing program that included an assigned counselor plus vocational integration.

Orienting had to do with aligning with the total self rather than the narrow band of experience artificially annealed into the unawakened spirit. Long time Pleiadian residents, called the Zentalissa, supervised almost all of the first two stages. Tango, however, had ended up with Orville as a counselor.

At first, Tango's habit of rebellion prevailed against the seemingly rigid order of the Sanctuary. In spite of all the purification, training and discovery of love with Angie, his habitual system of defenses and conditioning rendered him into a screaming pre-ad monster that even shocked him.

Two days after his arrival, Tango tore off the collar that he perceived to be a prison collar. He slipped out of Sanctuary seeking a way off world. As he helplessly wandered, he came to a meadow. Assessing the chances of escaping his capture, he looked up at the sky. There was no visible sun but brilliant light.

I must be in the loony land of the galaxy.

When he looked across the field, he noticed an I-class fighting wing at the other end of the meadow. As he approached the one-man vehicle, the hum of the atmosphere drive reached his ears.

Nobody seemed to be tending it. He hesitated, thinking of Angie. He hadn't said good-bye. In spite of his turmoil, he boarded the craft. The harness fit perfectly; he checked the navigation systems and began to adjust the magnetic field for the atmospheric jump to mid-orbit.

From across the meadow emerged the bulky form of his father waddling towards him. "Why are you wasting your time with those silly miscreants?"

The sound of his father's voice rankled him at a cellular level. He reached for the lever to begin his departure. In a blur of contradiction, the fighter was suddenly his first hovercraft from his youth. Foam dice dangled from the rear view mirror and his favorite song, "Rustic Cages", by the "Alien Homebodies" blasted on the com-crystal.

"Short circuited electric shocks
Hanging on the bars of my rustic cage
DNA voodoo, rearranging in maximode
You got me rattling in my rustic cage.
Shocked blonde hair and ruby lips
You hit the G spot in my heart
I'm having a meltdown grooving
On fire in my rustic cage"

The lush meadow of Mirror was gone. In its place was the gold and red arid landscape of the Terra-formed Martian colony.

"Do you call that sickening noise music? Why waste your credits on that garbage?" his father chirped.

"You're not real," Tango said, remembering what Angie had said about Mirror. He stepped out of the hovercraft and the environment seemed to collapse again around him.

"I'll tell you what is real, and not real, TX!" His father's face seemed to grow. Enlarged pores on his nose seemed to boil with anger.

Tango hated that nickname: TX. He felt small. His hovercraft was gone and in its place was a toy saucer on wheels. He had become a pre-ad! His father hulked over him pinning him against a wall, only it was not solid, it seemed to give. Softness, a smell of detergent, and a perfume, he was pushing against his mother's breast.

"Now listen to your father, TX. After all, he has worked very hard to provide this nice home for us and a future for you."

Tango turned as his father approached with a punitive rod, touching it to his shoulder. He had forgotten about the rod, now his panic was complete.

"Oh God, it's not real." He shouted. The rod inflicted its nerve scrambling jolts to his young body. His legs gave out, as did his bowels. He writhed in a sea of his own feces. The odor caused him to gag and vomit. He dripped snot and fluid from his nose and mouth. The nightmare of the buried memories of youth gave way to a lonely scream.

"This is a dream," he whispered from the puddle of excrement. *God let me die right here,* he thought.

Tango repeated his childhood strategy and retreated to a place inside to a point of light where he could not feel, smell, or see anything ugly. There was nothing at all there but the light. The abuse hid behind a mental wall. In the farnow, he would wake up in the morning clean himself up and go on.

Now on Mirror, it was different. He squeezed out bitter tears and tore the interior wall down and memlocked that farnow in the herenow. The pain drained from him as deep feeling trapped within him released. He howled until he was hoarse, eventually, sinking into a deep sleep.

Sometime later, he opened his eyes to discover he was in a hall with multicolored marble floors. On a bench of the same marble sat a radiant and angelic woman in a gossamer gown of opal-like hues. Electrical charges seemed to course through his body and mind. Areas of affliction seemed to grow warm. He was not sure how, but he was battered and bruised.

Tango became aware that the same point of light that he would escape to from his youth, had inexplicably become a part of everything he was now experiencing. Areas that were sore, both physically and emotionally, seemed to throb with an intense percolating purr. His body was learning and recording the experience. *This is how it is supposed to feel to be human.*

He could not speak, but made eye contact and smiled. The gestalt of the moment was that now for once he was truly living. He was in a state of wonder, naked on the floor of some temple.

"Welcome to Mirror, pilgrim".

"Who are you?" he asked, suddenly finding his voice.

"I am an Elder. It is to my world you have come."

He stood and raised his hands. Permeating everything was a soft white light gently morphing into pastel hues in cadence with the tone of her voice.

"Tango, to proceed, you must trust this process, and you must trust Orville Parker. We, Elders, wish to help you as well. The disease you carry will be absorbed and eaten by these experiences. You have come home. We are here to help you and serve you. We will aide you in your journey. You have arrived at a moment in your life that we call the quickening of spirit."

Tango lapsed into sobs. He knew he was releasing some of the stored pain of his childhood. Never had he felt such a sweet and pure love. Nothing had ever touched him so deeply.

"What do you mean disease? What do I have?" He asked, once he had calmed down. The Elder gently laughed. Her body shook as little electric rivulets of white light and sparks popped and glowed about her form.

"It would be more accurate to say dis-ease. You see, Tango. When we have been hurt as you were, especially as a child, if we do not tend to the problem it affects our minds. We make decisions based on surviving the trauma that thereafter colors all we do."

"If we do not heal, it begins to affect our emotions. Eventually, it will manifest as a sickness or premature death. The whole of creation is composed of this miscreation."

"Many processes can be experienced to rectify this matter. By re-experiencing these childhood memlocks, the opportunity to heal is available. Once healing has occurred, energy committed to these issues is available to you for reassessment and reassignment. This is especially so if you wish and will it to be so."

"To develop multi-dimensional awareness, it is necessary to develop magnetism and free the flow of energy. You have taken a big step."

Awakening the next morning, Tango looked around and realized that somehow he was back in the protective enclave called Sanctuary. Angie was at his bedside smiling. Their eyes met in recognition. He went to sit up and felt the pull of bandages enclosing his body in several areas. He felt bruised and stiff.

"Rough night," he sheepishly offered.

"You ran away, you naughty boy," Angie scolded.

Most of his experiences of the dimensional space he had visited were anchored as conscious memlocks. With a stirring from deep within him, he recalled the Elder who had welcomed him home.

Home, she said I am home.

Arafad Tango X's mind teemed with fragments of his sordid experiences. The memlock of their escape was still fresh in his mind. Images flashed across his mindscape of them running from the Colonial Troopers. Revelations of Angie's secret past, and that amazing device she called the Matter Relocator gained importance.

How did it bring us to this strange place?

It all swirled in his head as he lay there in bed, bruised and battered. Orville Parker entered the room. Tango felt quite weak but offered his hand as Angie made introductions.

"My dear friend," Orville said, "remember that Mirror is not so much a forgiving world as it is a pure one. It takes time to shift to the frequency of the place. Will you give it some time?"

Orville held his hand as he talked. Tango felt an electrical current flowing directly into his body. Tango's reply came from within his mind from a place he had never been before.

He had shifted his awareness so deeply it appeared as something from the outside at first. He knew on a deeper level that he was fully speaking for himself, perhaps for the first time. Some residual emotion arose with the revelation. He could see clearly in Orville Parker's eyes a quiet understanding.

Suddenly, within his mind he heard Orville speak. *"This is just the beginning Tango. We all have much to memlock."*

"There is nothing I would like more," Tango replied out loud.

Orville smiled letting that sink in. "Tango, it is important to follow these steps at first. You will not become who we want you to be, but rather it will allow you to become more of who you really are. Do you understand?"

Tango nodded feeling very sleepy again.

"Very good." Orville nodded to Angie and Tango, and then vanished in a flash of blue light. Tango was unsure whether Parker was even wearing a Relocator.

*

CHAPTER SIXTEEN

TANGO RETURNS TO THE FOLD

Tango bolted out of his memlock as the lights came on in the torture room. He lingered on thoughts of Angie. *Where is she now? Orville won't tell me!*

They turned off the containment beam and lowered a torture ring that hung suspended in a gravity field. Several Omegan postulants roughly fastened him to the ring by his arms and legs. He was completely naked. The Dragon Fem, Shaso, reached for a metallic rod from an array of evil looking devices. He looked on and considered the irony.

A punitive rod like my father used! Indeed my memlocks provide glimpses into my nearnow. I am sure she doesn't know of my past. Something wonderful must be possible here! Hmmm.

He still wasn't sure why he was here. In fact, many reasons might come into play. As a Korum ambassador, he had set up conditions for the importation of weapons, explosives, and even devices such as the one threatening him right now. He had also been behind setting up legitimate service businesses to repair and maintain such equipment on Tatochin. It had served well in the gathering of intelligence.

His main customers had been the Corporation, officially, and the rebels, unofficially. The black marketing of weapons had been funneled to the rebels through his cousin, Vinny. The Korum was aware it was going on. They sanctioned it privately. They knew none of the details.

Are they aware of the extent of my network?

The sound of the Centaurian probe warming up was sobering. Medusa Probe! Illvibe!

He knew the world of pain that such devices could cause some people. He might be required to act as if it could hurt. He knew how to use his mind to control the pain but they would be frightened by the likes of the Tango X. He wondered if information had been leaked.

Where is the leak? Why am I here?

Tango entered into a heightened state of awareness. At that level, his relationship to pain was very different. She shocked his genitals and stomach area. He registered it as a sensation.

"Set the control higher," A low ranking interrogator squawked. "This should wake the creature up," she droned with a hypnotic voice control that could put the weak willed under her spell.

"Not too much, Shaso, after all he is our guest," said Father Smith in soothing, re-assuring tones.

In torture, the Omegans training was by the book, their book. Shaso would be the enforcer and Smith the nurturer. The ploy was to appeal to psychological extremes that were primordial and familiar. It was designed to preoccupy the mind with attempting to maintain control in an out of control situation. It was only a matter of time and persistence before they could isolate these basic human patterns and create a more malleable and receptive subject. This basic formula informed many of the mind control techniques.

Mind control for the mainstream population was conveyed through a basic need, food. This had become the primary tool of persuasion. Subtle manipulation was required for the entrapment of unconscious mind.

Pharmaceutical companies had created chemical compounds to disarm the population creating susceptibility to hypnotic suggestion. Anchoring their long term goals for profit by guaranteed incomes for the population, their subterfuge was easily kept from the public awareness. The control of food and income held control over their freedom.

In ancient pre-contact times, the consumer society had been easily controlled through aerosols and food additives. Eugenics, intelligence conditioning, and pharmacological manipulation were shameful components of an unholy sense of entitlement imposed on an unwary population. A whole science of media implantation working with body chemistry was perfected for centuries in covert laboratories funded by the progenitors of the Corporation. The chemistry worked through the generational curve. Genetic tendencies were engineered. Humans were bred for the purposes fostered by the Corporation.

The Korum itself was active in resisting the mental control net the Corporation so relied on. Orville was certain that outside worlds and groups with sinister agendas were helping the Corporation or manipulating them. Part of the reason Tango was embedded deeply as a Korum ambassador was to look for indications of such activity. He took the pause in his torture as his cue to speak.

"I have nothing to hide. Why have you brought me here? I have not heard a word of explanation. I wish my embassy to be contacted. I was under the impression we had friendly relations with the Omegans and the Colonial Corporation."

"He is part of the Tatochin underground and a rebel", sneered Shaso, menacing him with the rod near his nose.

"This is outrageous," Tango spat back on cue.

"Now you must understand", Smith broke in, "that the rebels are an unacceptable and an illegal terrorist organization. They're not Corporate Conformed! We, as advisors to the peacekeepers are forced to deal harshly with such illvibe. There are peaceful methods of petitioning for change."

Smith sounded so reasonable. "What does this have to do with me?"

They are fishing! They know nothing! Maybe there is no leak. I must maintain my ambassador cover.

"I am Prince Kalimafar's attaché and report directly to him. I deliver messages. I do not always know the contents. I am at a loss."

"Please, we waste valuable time." Smith said, as he snapped his fingers. "Shaso!"

The rod blinded him momentarily, as the charge went through his brain. The setting was far higher and it hurt: heightened states of awareness or not. Shaso placed the rod between his legs and he screamed as the shock coursed through his flesh. Tango vaguely noticed the arrival of a postulant with a holo-fax glowing in his hand. He sensed the observers beyond the wall.

Fucking perverts are probably getting off on this.

Smith eyes darted through the message. He grunted several times. "Shaso nothing permanent, I must confer with my superiors."

Smith departed the torture room. Shaso crooned an evil laugh. She went to her toy box and dramatically turned back toward him with a spiked rod that emitted blue electrical charges in tiny wisps. The sheen of perspiration gleamed on her naked tattooed skin. He was about to receive the full onslaught of a Dragon Fem, highly trained as an interrogator.

Shaso summoned her psychic sexual weapons; hummed secret tones, and increased her respiration by breathing through her mouth. She had established a psychic cord to his energy system. The life force in her lower energy centers began to increase becoming a concentrated ball of power.

Tango tracked her attack and exercised great control by not defending himself. Any show of such an ability would reveal information about the true Tango. He could not allow that.

She began to use her voice to cast a spell. By the sheer focus of her will, combined with frequency shifting tones, she shaped an energy weapon like a projectile of channeled life force aimed at rearranging his body alchemically to the specified resonance causing him to get a painful erection. The sisterhood had trained its courtesan assassins in the use of sexual weapons.

Backing up in mock surprise, Shaso taunted her subject. "Just, a little bird not like your boss Kalimafar."

Tango exerted his will to resist a retaliatory attack.

I must not betray myself to her or the Omegans who hold her leash. There are watchers. They are all looking at my dick! Gezzzzz!

He had to feel the pain to be believable. With sudden fury she lashed out with a rod that sizzled with a electrical discharge as it touched his naked flesh. It shriveled his erection and he lost his bowels.

Oh God, this is gross! An opportunity to heal, the Pleiadians would undoubtedly say. Dangerous way to do your therapy, Orville would say…shit, this sucks, and then giggle.

Tango intuitively understood that the punitive rod, Smith's likeness to his father, and the humiliation of losing his bowels in front of another, were links in a chain. Such understanding of trauma had been memlocked on Mirror through his experience of retracing the interconnecting web of his past. He recognized the clairvoyant texture of his experiences. Torture could bring out such talents.

It is true. The entire world is a circle. It is easier to bear this with the knowledge of its deeper pattern. But, geez, I am so done with this.

Shaso continued relentlessly. "Poor Mr. Diplomat, shit on the floor. I don't like shitty diplomats," she hissed, turning to reach for more toys.

Suddenly, there was a great deal of movement off in the shadows. Switches snapped on. Smith returned to the torture room. A whispered conversation with the two attending Omegan postulants broke her concentration.

Shaso's eyes flared with anger. "What is this?"

At that moment, more lights came on. Several more postulants arrived and removed Tango from the hoop.

Stumbling to regain control of his legs, they conducted him to a shower where he was able to wash and dress. They injected him with restorative vitamins, and a stimulant that left him feeling marvelous. Finally, he was returned to Smith's office where he was beckoned to a chair with cinnamon rolls and a hot cup of stimcaf.

No guards, no restraints, just Smith and me… Something has obviously shifted.

Smith's attention was inwardly drawn. His orders were clear: make apologies, and share intelligence with him.

They are testing me.

Smith tasted bile; he felt the implant in his body. His face, a mask of control, did not betray his fear.

Tango sensed his fear and pretended not to notice. *I must be careful, I have unknown allies, or I am bait for a bigger trap.*

"Please help yourself to a pastry and stimcaf." Smith grabbed a pastry like a baby goes for a teddy bear. "I have been instructed to apologize for detaining you. I have been asked to reveal the intelligence, which prompted your capture."

Tango realized his cover was intact. "I should have you killed." Tango shot back. It was simple posturing but any less of a response would be out of character for a Korum ambassador.

Smith pressed a button on his desk activating a holo-projection. "We are prepared to make reparations. Allow me to show you our reason for suspicion."

"I will petition the UGC for sanctions for your barbaric treatment. Your incompetence is an insult to the Korum."

"Please watch, it will help explain."

Tango watched the summation of Flex's raid on the fast food restaurant with the Korum's diplomatic flitter. The list of weapons was long and carefully documented. Smith narrated the story, carefully enunciating each illegal aspect that the Korum diplomatic assault vehicle exhibited.

It read like a smugglers' wish list. Tango was intimately familiar with all the mini-missiles, and other illegal Centaurian modifications Smith recited with his resonant and penetrating voice. Tango remained unreadable. Actually, he had authorized the purchase himself.

"You must understand these weapons, and the entire design of your so-called diplomatic vehicle, is completely illegal for anyone. Not even a Colonial Interceptor has guided missiles, a Centaurian targeting system, or a supercharged Uton power-plant to boot."

Tango denied any knowledge of it, naturally. He had personally ordered the Arabian Charger, as it was quaintly called. He quietly mused. *Not just a super-charged Uton design but a 12 vented simuflow form energy shaper upgrade!*

The prince had insisted on the modi-fications. Tango had utilized the contacts to arrange deals with the rebels that the Colonial Corporation feared. He could feel a thinning of the many-layered ruse he had carved. This was hotter than the stimcaf he sipped.

"The rebels grow bolder and more organized. We wish to extend our protection to the Korum. The car was a Korum flitter. There were no reports of it being stolen. We were just doing our job."

Tango knew the diplomatic flitter was a showcase of illegal technologies, some of them Centaurian. The Korum would be in utter denial of such a thing. His only weapon was to claim that he knew nothing. He could not negotiate.

They are pissed because the rebels nabbed that hot little assault vehicle. Tough shit, Mr. Corporation!

Tango stood indignantly, "Your job! Ha. I must have satisfaction."

What do I do? I must save face or the Korum will have to punish me to save face. I must take Shaso. That is complicated. She is hard wired! I am sure of it!

Tango was in a quandary; the Korum had a rather retro code of ethics for losing face. Because of the obvious illegality of the weapons systems on the flitter, he could not push the issue of reparation too far. It was clear that he had received that cue from Smith. He had offered to compensate Tango but had not mentioned the illegal weapons again. He inwardly sighed. The Korum would expect him to do this.

"I demand the contract on that bitch, Shaso. I will punish her in front of my Prince. Perhaps then we may not seek public censor."

I must do this, it is expected of me. Kalimafar would have my head if I didn't. This will complicate everything. Gotta get to Vinny!

"Of course we'll see to it immediately." Smith understood the intricacy of face saving and the rules of conduct in the Korum. *I am uncomfortable with these Dragon Fems. They go too far. I cannot believe we have them in our midst. What has become of us? Good riddance! She is dangerous.*

Tango was ushered to the door. His ground car waited for him in the driveway with the drugged Dragon Fem restrained in the back seat. Shaso was, once again, expendable. Her worth as a pawn had been complex, yet Tango had obtained her contract.

What am I going to do with her now?

The Omegans who had taken him were not happy, their golden goose of the day had been taken away. He was sure they had bugged his car and Shaso. He suspected something was implanted in his food.

I am free, but definitely being watched.

Tango silently thanked his unseen allies. The dust swirled higher than he knew, as he piloted the ground car out of the enclave and on to the road to Ecksol. It was still only mid-afternoon.

*

CHAPTER SEVENTEEN

"METAPHYSICAL VOLLEY BALL"
Aurorioulous Tarasenimea (MIRROR) 2467

"Our way is pure being… You will do!"
Orville Parker quoting an Elder

Orville and Cleo walked down the meandering footpath to the stream. They had become inseparable. Love had bloomed in both of their hearts in maximode. He loved the sound of running water. The smell of water transported Orville to retro memlocks of his childhood on Earth, long ago.

There had been a stream behind his parent's home in the Northern California Federation. He phased through a montage of reflections of cherished days spent on the ever-shifting crook of a tiny beach. He endlessly skipped flat stones, floated in a tube on lazy summer days, and fished for Blue Gill or Catfish.

That was long ago on an Earth that did not exist in the same way. It had been over 400 years ago. Earth now only had a population of half a billion. Many settled areas had vastly changed or disappeared. Orville felt old when ancient memlocks arose in his mind.

Here I am 440 years later, on the other side of the galaxy, and I'm still going to play by a stream!

The twenty-second century was full of wonder, marriage, family, and many expansive experiences of love. The twenty-third century had been all work. With new worlds entering into their time of ripening, the Pleiadians frequently called him to task. Orville drifted into reverie as they walked down to the stream by his domicile.

I am grateful and humbled by the many gifts and useful tasks.

They approached a spirited game of water volleyball in full swing. He had learned from the Elders that many of the children that had recently incarnated on Mirror were souls quite familiar with the level of awareness that pervaded the invisible planet.

"They will easily advance in the development of spiritual powers," Alphonse had told him. "They have past life ties to Mirror and the previous Golden Age."

Indeed, it was apparently so. Mirror was a truly a garden of wise and joyful souls.

The volleyball went back and forth never hitting any hands, or water for that matter. Several of the pre-ads floated above the water, demonstrating great mental control. The ball quivered and shot back and forth above them being alternately controlled by each team.

Cleo and Orville joined in the hilarity. Ten minutes went by before there was any break in the action. Orville had broken a healthy sweat keeping up with the spirited youths. A few of the older children who floated above the net that spanned the stream began to chant, "Do it, Orv, do it."

"I'm too old," he replied as he completely left the water to spike the ball. The chant continued to build.

"What are they talking about?" Cleo asked, as she hugged the net and batted the ball back.

Orville noted Cleo's fine contours, and caught himself liking this woman with a newly kindled desire. It was true, he admitted to himself, that Lesha and he were drifting apart. It was already obvious to everybody else. He had mentally exhausted himself unloading useless guilt. He had believed that he had sated his desire for partnership having raised two families, flourishing in several marriages.

Perhaps, I am through with relationships of a personal type.

Now all of a sudden there was Cleo. He passed the ball to a floating pre-ad. He replied to Cleo across the net. "They want me to do a trick with the ball."

"Come on Orv, do it", another pre-ad hooted.

Orville bowed to the inevitable and in a flash disappeared; a moment later the ball vanished. The Elders had taught Orville about the latent power available to all human beings. With power came responsibility, so this playful act would precipitate a small scolding. The Pleiadians cautioned against the capricious use of such abilities, but it was appropriate to become familiar and adept at utilizing the original endowments of being a sentient life form. However, Orville's little trick was not in any of the rulebooks, and in the present company, he saw no harm in it.

*

The Elders identified eight primary powers that came with the first stage of illumination: "The self is an idea resting in the eternal light of God." These powers had been alluded to throughout humankind's retrostory. Some of the most famous examples were the incarnations of Jesus Christ, Bhagavan Krishna, and the Buddha. There are, however many more. Walking on water, changing water into wine, healing the body, were attributed to Jesus. These powers were scant hints of what was possible. Fame, however, was not a prerequisite.

These teachings had been preserved and practiced widely throughout the galaxy. Hindu scriptures most accurately recalls the scope of the powers cultivated in various mystery schools of old Earth. On Mirror new possibilities were being explored daily.

The eight powers translated from the Pleiadian language into various versions of Sanskrit are:

Anima:
To perceive the atomic and subatomic structures and make yourself or any object as small as you like.

Mahima:
The power to perceive the unity of the entire universe and magnify anything as large as you like.

Laghima:
The power to annihilate the force of gravity and make anything as light as you like.

Garima:
The power to transmute substances and conjure any object as massive and heavy as you like.

Prapti:
The power of manifestation to obtain anything you like.

Vasitwa:
Mystical power and the infinite will to control anything.

Prakamya:
The power of creation to satisfying all desire by purified force of will.

Isitwa:
The power of knowledge and infinite wisdom, becoming the master of everything

Orville had begun to experience some control of these powers at the age of 300. Spiritual awareness and knowledge of life, had led to the beginning of the realization of the self within the greater Self. The eternal was non-illusion, indescribable and beyond all need for description or prescription. It was, in his eyes, the only path to freedom. When he was ready, time and space would cease. Any differentiation was duality and creating separate reality, and therefore unreal. This however, was after all, a volleyball game! The children began to giggle nervously with the excitement.

Cleo stood in the waist deep water. "What? What's going to happen?"

"You'll find out", one of the smaller girls said.

The water began to churn and boil with large bubbles. From below the surface, Cleo felt the bed of the stream disappear. The group of children and Cleo were suddenly on the surface of a huge volleyball that expanded in size. They rose high above the valley riding on top of what had once been a volleyball!

Within seconds, Orville's home was a speck hundreds of feet below them. Thirty seconds later, the ball was a swirling planet with stars and comets whizzing wildly over their heads.

Cleo tried to remember to breathe. Suddenly the fabric of space seemed to fold on itself. They were back in the water. The children squealed with delight. Before anyone could even think of moving, Orville served the volleyball that crossed the net and plopped into the water with a little splash.

"Our point," he said.

*

CHAPTER EIGHTEEN

"A MERMAN FOR AN HOUR"

After playing water volleyball with the kids and Cleo, Orville swam up to Cleo. The gentle current took them down stream to a large, deep pool. It was his favorite spot. They embraced and kissed, letting the current have its way with them until some rocks stopped their downstream progress.

"I am going to lay down in the sunlight before the clouds come," Cleo whispered although there was no reason to whisper.

"Okay, I am going to swim a little."

He swam against the current, moving forward and backward in approximately the same spot. Though liquid, it was like a familiar armchair for Orville. The steady exertion invigorated and lengthening his spine. In this world of silence, save the parting of water and the lengthening of his vagus nerve in his watery stride, the soaring child within him traveled in a sacred landscape of dreams. Orville felt his awareness expand. His steady movement was translated into flight. He had become a winged dolphin! His vision had become as real as the air he breathed.

On Mirror, if you dreamed of water you would get wet. He glided through aquatic dimensions, caught up in an ocean of emerald green light. As he traversed the oceanic sky with wings in a dolphin form, another dolphin came to his side and traveled with him. Suddenly, he knew it was Cleo.

Basking for a moment in a multi-dimensional universe of infinite possibilities calmed his spirit. In a swell of sweet sound with a hint of song, higher and higher they soared in a firmament of healing green luminosity. They had become a speck of awareness in an infinite space. Then she was gone, but not far.

An opalescent palace rippled into form all around him. Brilliant light emanated from all directions. He felt each cell of his body as a crystalline formation of ultimate becoming. Orgasmic waves washed his mind clear of all confusing and conflicting energy flows. His atomic self was floating in an expansive state. A breath was like a wind he felt pass though his entire form. He knew that he had been summoned and transported, to the realm of the Elders.

"My child, you do well!" The booming voice came from everywhere.

"Are you an Elder?" Orville asked in childlike awe.

"Before this galaxy, we were and we came. Always have we been present since that arrival. Now, there is a quickening. We have prepared Mirror to advance the great cause of evolution. You have played an important role in the transformation. We rejoice in your journey. It is your due."

"What do you want me to do?" Orville asked.

Over the years, Orville had many conversations with the Elders. He had sensed an increase of activity, lately. This experience was expected and confirming.

"You are a bridgemaker from the past to the future. The desires in your heart are the beckoning of what your people are becoming, Orville Parker. You are a reflector of their highest aspirations. You are also a part of us we initiated many millennia ago. Our way has become pure being, yours is in action and doing."

"We made Mirror as a distillation of the supreme wisdom. The Pleiadian adepts have been our ambassadors to reunite your home world from its isolation. To ensure our future there is much to be done. Long we have guided you, and you have helped us. We ask you, once again, for your assistance."

"How?"

"We want you to intervene on behalf of a human population."

"But what of the leaders of these planets? Why do we not work with them directly?"

The Elder's laugh permeated the glowing space that Orville found himself. A diaphanous, opalescent light softly morphed between soft blue, pink, and violet. It engulfed the space that Orville identified as his personal space. Orville was perplexed. "What is so funny?"

"Orville it is not our way to draw attention to ourselves. We do not wish to be solicited. We trust our own means of guidance. We have chosen you. Your people have a great destiny, now we are working with you. We laugh because we have wonderful news to impart."

Orville swam against the current of the stream. The familiar linearity of time as it is understood in three-dimensional reality had arced into multiple levels of expression.

"Is it more important than having us train for military operations?"

"At the moment, yes."

"Geez, you guys are really being intense, lately. Go on."

"We have sent someone to you from our realm. Our beloved Cleo."

"Cleo! An Elder?"

"She took on the garment of flesh to serve as a conduit into your realm for us. And, dear Orville, for you!"

"But Cleo is a newcomer… she said nothing…"

"Cleo took birth without the memlock of her divine origin. Spiritual amnesia was for her own protection and an opportunity for growth. You understand that the past can blind you. And, as you know, the time to remember appears as you regain soul awareness."

"This is the purpose of life, Orville. The preoccupation with material creation, that has led to so many marvelous and terrible inventions, is just a reflection of the amazing beings you already are."

Orville blubbered a few half sentences. He was caught in this strange feeling that he had just been informed he was part of an arranged marriage deal. His heart and head sparked like an electrical current. He wasn't sure whether it was a premonition or some obscure throw back to an old Earth custom of families arranging marriages.

He didn't know what to think, yet felt marvelously happy, and a little afraid at the same time. He surrendered to the overwhelming ecstasy and illumination that accompanied the revelatory words of this forthcoming Elder.

The dream! Oh my, this ain't no taco stand!

The unseen Elder continued. "Until now, she believed herself your student and human in every way. She was born and raised as all human beings are. Her decision was made in our realm with her consent. She is a bridge to us as you are a bridge to humanity."

"So the student becomes the teacher?"

"Yes and no, Orville. It is our intention that you will become the Zemplars we know you to be already."

Zemplars…Wow!

"It's always this way with you Elders. You speak about time as if it's a two way street. That's fine except it can drive a guy crazy!"

Orville took the momentary silence as time for the Elders to chuckle at his humor. Inside, Orville was reeling as all the data sunk in. The presence of the Elder, though just a disembodied voice, was charged energetically with sheer magnetic life force.

All this occurred while swimming against the current in a small stream upon the planet Mirror. A world that rotated invisibly around the Central Sun itself.

"The time has come for the people to rise up and throw off the limitations and restrictions of the old order. It is time to evolve to the next stage and actualize your true potential as human beings. As your galaxies return to the brightness of wisdom in the procession of time, we reach across a gulf of time and space and beckon you to us."

Orville was silenced by the bold words.

"Now what?" he asked.

"Cleo awaits you. It will take time to integrate these new developments. I think you will be just fine. Soon, we will be helping you on the planet Tatochin. Much still needs to be done."

Tatochin… of course.

"We have added information to your computers that will fully allow you to use your Matter Relocator with great ease."

"Oh, so no honeymoon, or anything?"

"Our beloved Cleo, even as we speak, regains her true identity. Remember Orville that in spite of her origins she is a human being, as well as an Elder, just like you."

"What should I do?"

"Earth is restoring itself to sanity in the wake of several thousand years of brutality and abuse. The rebels on Tatochin are ready to do the same. We want you to help them."

The Corporation…I can't seem to ever be finished with those retros!

"Have I not been doing that?" He was puzzled. "Explain the quickening."

Enro, his dear old friend had been central in the resistance movement for years on Tatochin. Tango was deeply involved with the Korum. Orville was troubled. Would this quickening bring more bloodshed? If it did, he would quickly not enjoy this quickening.

Who said it would always be enjoyable? He recalled part of some old Zen quote from Earth: "The great way is easy for those with no preferences."

The message continued: the voice reverberated right on cue. "There will be a gathering of many worlds on Tatochin in the near future. We see this as a moment of supreme importance, a pivotal marker for sentient life streams in this area of the galaxy. It is also an astrological progression. You have now entered the central period of the Dwapara Yuga.

Orville always got dizzy when the Elders spoke about time in terms of consciousness and other languages. The proximity to the Central Sun is the most important factor. He often covered his confusion by saying, "what time is it today?" The Elders paused as Orville's thoughts wandered about trying to keep up with the message he was receiving.

"Orville, great mutations occur during this time. We, who now dwell in the golden light of the highest age, speak of what you are becoming. Much more is to come. You will have help from a very unusual source. That is for another day, though. You might say it is the wake of our passage through the firmaments. We who are your ancestors join with you."

"Wait, before you disappear on me. What is your name?

"Oh very well, my name is Alphonse. We will be meeting again. Say hello to Cleo from me."

"Okay, so why can't I see you.?"

"Rejoice Orville Parker. You have nothing to fear. Beyond the dramas of what could be, is a certainty that all is well in the long rhythms of manifestation. It is life that is eternal within the ever-changing creation. Go back to your dolphin dream now. We bid you peace and protection."

*

The sudden coolness of the water shocked him. He inhaled the water and broke surface coughing and sputtering. On the shore stood Cleo holding his towel with a smile that was pregnant with new meaning for both of them. He awkwardly climbed out of the stream upon some rocks almost slipping several times as he spoke.

"Cleo, I, if I was ever… I mean… Geez Louise!"

Cleo tossed the towel in his face. She felt the same blush upon her face and understood. "If I had nothing to awaken to and was just the Cleo you knew before, my dear Orville, mine would have been a happy life."

Orville approached Cleo and looked deep into her eyes. "With you I can co-create a worthy life."

"I am your beloved for all time," Cleo softly replied.

It began to rain large happy raindrops of pure water. They ran up the path across the garden and porch to the shelter of the adobe. Orville started to tell his tale. She laughed at the dolphin image. He laughed at how she had gotten bopped on the head with the volleyball. Suddenly they were in each other's arms. Hot kisses and desire swelled in their hearts.

She told her story with great heaving breaths of deep feeling. "Once the ball hit my head I was awakened to the memlocks of my previous existence in the sphere of the Elders! And then I received the memlock of our past incarnations together."

Cleo's awakening had provided her with the answers she needed. Now her task was to integrate the ocean of memlocks of her past with the present. Only a moment had transpired in the timeframe that the Elders had commanded.

The rain increased as soon as they reached shelter of the front porch to Orville's home. They breathed hard looking into each other's eyes. Something passed between them that poets strive to define. Orville's mind raced. Little winged dolphins circled around his heart.

In the distance someone was approaching. Cleo gave him a Mona Lisa smile and a knowing look. Lesha called in from the front room. When Orville turned back, Cleo had flown off to change. Her face was like the afterimage of a camera flash, glowing in the busy cavern of Orville's mind.

My sweet Lesha comes and now Cleo… sweet confusion. I guess I should count my blessings.

*

CHAPTER NINETEEN

"FAMILY MEMLOCKS"

Orville's thoughts overflowed with the memlocks of hundreds of years spent in and around Mirror. His first wife, a Pleiadian named Melora, had raised nine children with him. The youngest, Orin was almost 300 years old. His children by her had come for a visit last cycle. Orville would always hold Melora in a special light. She had guided him into understanding their way of life. She had died unexpectedly of a rare disease, something that seldom occurred on Mirror.

Their house had been full of merriment and laughter. He called up the memlocks of each of his nine children. He sighed, gripped with a moment of nostalgia. His second wife, Matera, had six children with him. She had passed from corporeal existence almost one hundred years ago at the age of 1003.

Orville turned to see Lesha standing before him as he toweled his tangled wet hair. Her smile was radiant, something pure in a galaxy of trouble. They came into each other's arms.

Orville painfully felt a barrier within himself. Where once Lesha had been held in his awareness as the beloved, now Cleo had come. He had been married twice and raised two different families over the past 400 years. He recognized the shift that had occurred within his consciousness.

He marveled over the efficiency of instinct, as he understood it. Deep emotions were astir. It was uncomfortable. It felt difficult to move forward but he knew a drama would need to play out. She pulled back and saw in his eyes a distraction. He put his arm around her shoulder.

"Come, we've got to talk." Orville shuddered to himself. Pain and pleasure vied for ascendancy in heterodyne modulations. Something was growing in his heart. Cleo's face was etched in his awareness. Orville felt his blood flowing like the brook behind his home.

*

Cleo stood away from the house in a small grove of hemlocks sorting out her self-imposed exile from the Elders with the persona of Cleo. She let the rain soak her without care. Through the window, she watched as Orville embraced Lesha and felt a hot flash of jealousy. Newly reawakened, the emotion took on a different cast than it would have just this morning. The dual awareness seemed to touch every part of her being.

"In time you will integrate this seeming schism", a voice in her head gently whispered.

"I'm jealous of Lesha… I want Orville… Is that Cleo or me?... Me is Cleo, too!...I envy Lesha… I'm actually thinking I'm not as pretty as her… And, I believe… believed that was important… Human emotion is powerful. The human path is so unique. I care. I care for all concerned. I am afraid… Of what? Rejection? Lesha's anger? My own feelings?"

The Elder that guided her understood. *"Human beings are quite emotional, especially the females."*

The hemlock listened patiently. They had no preferences.

*

CHAPTER TWENTY

"KAITAIN ENRO"
TATOCHIN 2465

"Keep your eyes fixed on the path to
the top, but don't forget to look
right in front of you. The last step
depends on the first. Don't think you're
there just because you see the summit.
Watch your footing, be sure of the next
step but don't let that distract you from
the highest goal. The first step depends
on the last.

Rene Daumal
"Mount Analogue" 20th Century

The fire was lit. The big wood was just beginning to catch. The sparks rose from the clearing surrounded by ancient conifers, as parents put their pre-ads to pillow and told the teaching tales for them to take into dreamtime. Meals were finished and the watch details were set.

Nimro walked up from the valley floor to Skull Rock, a natural formation left behind by ancient glaciers. The twinkling lights of Ecksol on the shores of Lake Wechen were visible beyond the valley of what was called, the Planetary Park. The surveillance grid began just one mile from the rock. The catacombs, the rebel's secret access to Ecksol, had been sealed for the night.

Intelligence gathered off world, informed the rebels that the Corporation was the illvibe remainder of the autocratic and militant culture that had plagued old Earth, back in the twentieth century. His parents had told him the story of the Corporation's deceptive take over of Tatochin. At first, it had been a joyful reunion of distant cousins.

Holos of Earth had looked amazingly similar to Tatochin. They, of course, had only one moon. Earth, Tatochin, Salibno, and several other worlds, all containing human populations, had been allowed to join the intergalactic community. Hundreds of other worlds of human, near human, and diverse sentient life, had also received visits from the Pleiadians and other parent races.

The entire sentient universe had gone through a spiritual surge allowing consciousness to expand beyond the borders of their various worlds. Most of them were successful. A few were problematic. Earth had been meddled with, and so was mentored more closely.

In spite of that, it had spawned some shady groups that in turn associated with shady extra-terrestrial cultures of similar stripes. Technoid Separatists, and Dragon Fems, both Earth spawned, were notorious on many worlds. The galaxy wasn't all bright and shiny. Like Earth, it had an underworld.

Tales of the Rishma and the Centaurians spoke of the new bogeymen. Giant smart insect races were frightening to "softs", as the Rishma called humanoids. The holos had covered the Oblion Rebellion for months. The Tharrr evoked an illvibe wave of fear through the galactic worlds. Galactic contact and star travel capabilities were powerful thresholds to cross. The promises to consolidate all the human colonies were welcomed by Tatochinians, also anxious to discover the stars.

Eventually, it was realized that the element of Earth's population that promoted the Corporation's dream was not even welcome on their home world. The rebels had been trying to stop them ever since. Nimro's parents were among the first to lose their lives. His parents had been well-known educators. Their outspoken criticism had led to a pogrom of the best minds of Tatochin.

Nimro was nine when his parents died. They had taken him to the mountains and explained that it wasn't safe for him to stay in the city with them. He stayed with some distant cousins who were part of a growing population of outcasts that later became the very freedom fighters he now helped command.

He never saw his parents again. He spent the days of his derailed childhood and young life in the great cave, hidden in the Tshini Mountains. Stopping in his tracks, he turned to look at the mountains that had been his only home. *Sheilila, the only mother I have left.*

At twenty-seven, Nimro was a fierce and serious brooding soul. When he was a teenager he joined the rebel cause. He spent many seasons training in the vast Planetary Park. He learned to be a tracker and stayed one step ahead of the Colonial Troopers. They would slip into Ecksol in teams through secret tunnels at night, to procure supplies and plan actions against the Corporation.

He loathed the city and spent all his free time at Skull Rock among the growing rebel movement. He stood 5'8" with long dark hair he kept in a ponytail. He was medium complexion, with dark brown eyes that betrayed the hurt and anger that churned within him. Yet, fortune had found him when he met Enro who mentored him like a son. Though Nimro knew that he was not like Enro, he loved him just the same.

Turning his attention back toward the herenow, he watched the sun disappear over the eastern coastal mountains. He walked back toward the camp, nestled in the thick shelter of the mighty Ashwood trees. Sensing the herenow buzz around the camp, he knew it was about the meeting taking place.

Returning to the fire, Nimro threw on a log and spat on the surge of flame. The sizzle roused Zom and Ren, the watchdogs.

The rebels milled in the clearing, talking in small groups. It was a cool night. Vapors of breath rose into the deepening forest evening. Blankets and folding chairs in hand, their collective voices created harmonic modulations that sounded somber and concerned. Enro and Flex approached the fire and joined Nimro.

"The Corporation didn't buy it, but they bought it in the park," Flex said, as he ran his hand through his blond and blue streaked hair.

"I saw it from Skull Rock, what were you driving?" Nimro scuffed at an ember with his foot.

"I stole it from the Korum livery. Heavily modified," Flex said. The two young men continued a conversation that was filled with instant replays of the three Colonial Interceptors fiery fate.

Enro left them at the fire to embellish the tale with elaborate descriptions. *That version of the story will have circulated around the camp several times before I share it.* He walked a few steps away, allowing them to embellish without restraint.

A group of pre-ads lit twigs and ran around risking life and limb as the spirited young often liked to do. They enacted the tales of conquest that the older ones recounted. Like tiny verders, they scampered between the legs of the adults and tried to look busy. They were the elite pre-ads, old enough to have their place at the fire and privileged to stay up late! They had roused Zom and Rem into chasing the smoldering sticks.

"You pre-ads sit together but leave room upfront for the old ones." He turned and rejoined Flex and Nimro, breaking into their conversation, as if he had heard every word.

"We got more than a modified flitter, they have pinpointed our base. There was a second beacon for cloaked tracking."

"Perverts from the dark side of hell", hissed Nimro.

"Let me tell everyone, okay? I just didn't want to completely bust your bubble in public." Flex's face turned grim. Enro had expected that.

"Look Flex", Enro grasped both of the men's shoulders. "You did good work. It is time to assert ourselves. I believe the Korum will not release the information. We know that the weapons dealers in Ecksol trade with the Korum secretly. If they have the kind of technology you had in the Korum flitter you can bet that they know quite well where the weapons are going. In a way, you did us a favor leading them to us."

"They can not be trusted," Nimro said.

"I didn't say I trusted them," Enro said. "Bring up the wine and the sweets, it has been a long day, and we will have strong talk."

The two young men left the fire to deliver Enro's message. Enro had been a father to Nimro and Flex, and to many of the displaced fragments of family that made up the rebels of Tatochin. Enro knew that unlike him, many of the younger ones had never known any other life. It had fallen onto the shoulders of the older ones to pass on the culture of Tatochin.

A meal stirs memlocks of the mother and security. Appealing to the stomach always soothed the bodies of active youth. Enro phased philosophically.

Entertainments and diversions were limited in the rebel camp. Gathering together to take food and drink was a time of sharing. Whether they were driven by laughter or stern resolution, a meal was a time to put down the burden of the day and reflect, dream, and be close to loved ones. No one ate alone or was isolated unless they wished it. Extended family included friends and those who were displaced.

The Tatochin people had forty centuries of recorded retrostory. It always surprised Enro how much damage to people's minds the Corporation was capable of in such a short time.

We are fragile, yet, hopefully, resilient.

Far up in the mountains in a cave called Keltori, near the great rebel base, the great libraries of ancient Tatochin had been preserved. Enro would visualize that place of wisdom when he would lose touch with the continuity of life.

Our children grow up fast. We will pass on this library some day.

A swell of sadness consumed him. He had seen too much loss. Enro was deeply in farnow memlocks as the encampment gathered around the fire. A single news satellite hovered slightly above the gathering. The logo of the Colonial Corporation had been crossed off. Coconut holo-cast was stenciled over it.

The captured news satellite had been reassigned. The rebels would send a scan to the great cave, High Mountain Base, stronghold of the freedom fighters of Tatochin. The holos would be delivered on foot as soon as the meeting was concluded. No electronic communications were allowed.

The sensitive surveillance methods of the Corporation were especially considered when it came to protecting the secret base of the rebels. If the Corporation were to learn of its location they would bring a full Triton of Troopers to destroy the resistance.

The wine flowed and the treasured Moon Cakes were consumed. The harmonics of the rebels had become a stable frequency of modulating emotional linking, bonding, cohesion, and alignment. Enro hoped that after what he had to say that still would be intact. *Soon I will meet with Orville again. The fruit grows ripe on the vine.*

For the rebels, the specters of mind control and physical poisoning through the psychoactive elements in the Corporate Conformed food, created a climate of vigilance, strength and support. For the masses that had been conformed, Enro had a special name: the "walking dead." Enro pondered the task before them.

Don't their instincts scream out a warning? Ah, but I am not their judge, just a soul who cares. One who wishes to keep something vital and good alive long enough for it to gain a foothold for the future it deserves. I would rather die in the woods than remain a pawn in the CC's twisted society. My dreams are better than that.

The encampment was still filling up. Everyone was coming tonight.

"Some wine for Enro," Mary said, passing him a stout mug of the exquisite wine. He raised a glass and silently sipped the warmed mulled wine and collected his thoughts.

The Corporation's noose grows tighter around our necks. If we don't talk to the Korum they could leak the location of our forward base to the Corporation. That may have already happened. We have merely caused a ripple. Blowing up restaurants is little more than something to allay the pent up anger of passionate men like Flex and Nimro.

The fire was being stoked. It blazed, lighting the faces of the freedom fighters of Tatochin. Enro noticed that the food servers were still finishing up. Everyone counted equally. He allowed his thoughts to wonder.

Kalimafar is a fool. His unnatural appetites reflect his judgments. Yet, I must parlay and palaver with these retros. My guts tell me we are now ready. Look at all of us here. We are so vulnerable. Yet the will to go on is strong. I hope I am as strong as my people are. Do they know the risks we must take?

Enro sighed. This would be a hard one to swallow. He was a native of Tatochin. His life had come full circle. First, he had joined the Colonial Troopers, and then he became one of its greatest legends. Fate stepped in when he was ready and offered him a pathway that brought him home.

Orville Parker opened the way by helping him to fake his own death. His choice to quit the Colonial Troopers was the beginning of his new journey. He had spent five years on Mirror with Orville learning to live in greater awareness of the multi-dimensional self. It had been a thrilling time for Enro tempered by the sobering reality facing his home planet. His time on Mirror had been a part of the preparation for what he knew was now coming to a head.

He had me training people for command in a military sense but with love and compassion. Now we will see this bear fruit!

It had been difficult to witness the annexation of Tatochin and hopelessly watch the subjugation of its people. Now, the tide had turned. The hard-core resistance had a life of its own. Orville had been wise to help Enro. Soon everything would change.

Enro's grandmother was his only living relative. She lived in a modest home on the outskirts of Ecksol. She was a retired Grand Dame in the Omegan's sisterhood. The women chosen were trained in many sciences, from the mystic to the political. Many Grand Dames held top positions in the Omegan culture, or were consorts of high-ranking Cardinals and Bishops.

When the time is right I can count on her.

The Grand Dame Taylor had accepted the mission on the frontier world of Tatochin after a liaison with Cardinal Fellini, Enro's grandfather. That had lasted over one hundred years. Enro's grandparents had a relationship that transcended duty and assignment. His grandfather's passing had left a void that could not be filled.

When the Corporation, arrived on Tatochin his grandmother had chosen the assignment because she was aware of the sheer beauty of the planet. Her son, Saul, Enro's father, a career military man, had married a native girl named Chichen.

Grand Dame Taylor and Chichen were close. Chichen learned many of the secrets of the sisterhood that she passed on to her son. Saul, Enro's dad, was often away. After his grandmother's retirement he often witnessed the two women in deep conversation while they tended the extensive garden Chichen kept in the family domicile. His grandmother would always call Chichen her garden Goddess.

One day, when he was nine, his mother took him by the hand to her favorite bench in the garden. Enro looked up at his mother and saw the tears streaming down her face. In that moment, something inside Enro ignited. He felt himself transported in the reflection of his mother's eyes.

In that moment, Enro received a vision:

Images of a violent battle in space... he saw his father at the helm of a battle cruiser under intense fire... The ship was hit and floated derelict. Insectoid creatures with exoskeleton called the Rishma, boarded the ship. His father died on a Centaurian torture ring calling Chichen's name.

Enro had lost consciousness. Later he related his vision to his mother, who cried bitterly. She was startled by her son's clairvoyant ability. His mother made sure that he received the deeper instruction available through her mother-in-law, the Grand Dame.

From that time on, his home changed from the happy place of his pre-ad years. The pall of grief seemed to swallow his mother. His ability to "see" made him aware that his mother's only hold to life was her obligation to her son.

By the time Enro was 15, she grew ill and seemed to have no will to fight. She yearned to join her beloved Saul in the Elders' realm. After she died, she appeared with Saul in a nimbus of light. Together they gave their blessing to Enro, an experience he would memlock forever.

Enro left Tatochin and his grandmother the following year. It would be many years before he would return. The training he received from his mother, expanded his sensory abilities paving the way to his becoming an excellent X-Wing fighter pilot and following the path of his father. Stepping off that path, he joined the military officers' program.

By 25, he had command of a Colonial battle cruiser. In the siege at Corlatu with the Rishma, he distinguished himself by capturing the flagship of the Corlatu that had been refueling in an artificial asteroid. He had sensed the alien presence of the Rishma, an insect warrior race. It had been the turning point in the six-year war. Enro had a personal stake in the victory against the Rishma who had captured his father.

At 29, he was the youngest Katofar in the corps. He rose through the ranks with a reputation as a wizard of strategy. By the age of 38, he was a Kaitain, the commander of a full triton. Enro felt like that had been another life and yet he was who he was. Had he changed at all, he often wondered. *Did I blind myself to the darkness of the Corporation for ambition?*

In those days, he thought little of politics. He followed orders, strived to be the best, and defined his success by rank and feat from a purely military viewpoint. Honor, bravery, valor, fearlessness, integrity, and the goal of excellence guided him to the heights.

He reflected on those assets, as his moral instincts evolved into spiritual dimensions. War and militarism became limiting. A distaste for violent solutions began to grow in him. Try as he might to live in peace, he realized that his military abilities were being called upon. He remembered an old quote from some one called Mandella in the farnow. "It's a long road to freedom."

Now I must figure out a way to achieve our sovereign freedom with as little violence as possible. I hate making such compromises. Life is so precious!

*

CHAPTER TWENTY-ONE

LOYOLA JURGA

The twin moons, Wechen and Capach, rose above the Tshini Mountains. The luminous sapphire and ruby shadows mingled with the fire's glow on the rebels faces as they awaited his words. A hush seemed to ripple across the sea of eyes. Fully invested at every level, Enro was caught up in the drama. *Under the light of both moons! Tonight, the Kaitain speaks, that is what is needed.*

Not a word was heard among the rebels as Enro walked into the light of a hotly burning fire. He looked like a mighty Lecad as the rounds of ashwood sputtered with sizzling sap.

"We are not isolated in our struggle against the Colonial Corporation. We have heard that acts of civil disobedience are occurring regularly in at least six other colonies in the Orion sector, especially on Navidrrr."

Murmurs of approval took on the cadence of prayer. Rebels were unable to get off world. Reliable information about the greater galaxy was infrequent. For a few short years, all of Tatochin had enjoyed the entry into galactic civilization. With the coming of the Corporation, anyone who resisted them had been isolated and planet bound. It was a point of frustration to the rebels. The Corporation carefully monitored all offworld connections.

A breeze rustled through the camp coaxing the fire as Enro continued. "The seers of Keltori say that it is a good time to align ourselves with those of like mind. Flex brought us more than a stolen flitter. He brought us a message. The Korum wishes to contact us."

"The Korum?" someone said, with sarcasm.

The murmur this time was one of trepidation, curling like poisonous smoke. For most of these freedom fighters, the horror stories of debauchery, black magic, and the cruelty of Prince Kalimafar, was the only context they had for the Korum.

The indictment of illvibe was justifiable regarding the nefarious son of King Fezam. But the Kaitain knew that to condemn the Korum for one sick sinner was the memlock of a planet bound by colloquialism that in a galactic context held little substance.

Enro stood in silence, his matted hair catching amber glows. He made eye contact, scanning his listeners. He felt the presence of the Elders descend upon him, whisking away all doubt. In that moment, he had become an instrument of destiny. A road of light formed filled with words of wisdom flowing from his mouth. His heart felt like a mighty ocean aglow with deep conviction.

Some of the trusting brave eyes that held his laser gaze would lose their lives in the struggle to come. The pang of sadness that came with that knowledge, he cast in the fire where he stood. Words hung in his throat as the power built. A pregnant silence embraced the gathering, clearing away all mental debris. The collective encampment knew in that lucid moment that their lives were about to take a turn.

Suddenly, Zom and Ren, the snoring canines, sat up on their haunches whining, whimpering, and finally barking. Their tails swishing a storm of dust, like energy meters marking the moment.

The silence was ruptured by canine emotion that flooded into the receptive space of the assembled people! Enro suddenly began to laugh at the dogs. The entire camp erupted in roars of laughter! No one laughed harder than Enro. Tears blurred his vision and his gut ached with the release of long held tension. The dogs, being sensitized, instinctually howled at the moons.

Soon the crowd took up their song. Five hundred rebels and two dogs howled in the forest beneath the Ashwood trees. The memlock of this moment would be recounted through the ages over a bottle of Tatochin wine, or in a teaching tale. They shouted their battle cry as fully awake human beings. Enro had won the night.

"This is just the beginning. The day is coming soon when we will be able to take on the Corporation and take back our planet. The Korum is just the beginning. It will be only one small chapter in a much larger story. Mark my words the day is coming soon, very soon."

Enro paused until utter silence prevailed. The embers of the fire sizzled white. "The eyes of the greater galaxy will be upon us. We will rise up at that hour and demand our planet back. No one can stop us!"

The response was a roar of approval that left no doubt in its relentless release into the universe of possibilities to manifest destiny. They were one body; the presence of spirit was palatable.

A small group of leaders among the rebels formed a semi-circle around the Kaitain who drank his wine and fielded questions. The entire group watched and listened.

"I think we should meet with the Korum. We have common goals and common enemies. They have no love for the Corporation. They risk a great deal to even recognize us as an organization worth reckoning with. Our security is their boldness. We will listen as one body, or not at all."

"We're with you, Enro." Nimro said to the whole crowd. Other voices joined in a wave of sober approval.

"Who's got the wine?" the Kaitain bellowed.

Many bottles of wine were consumed that night. Huddles of smaller groups conversed punctuated by laughter, wellvibe, and passion. Enro felt his body percolating with the power flowing through him. Patches of pedestrian conversation rippled through his awareness. The feeling of continuity, community, and multi-dimensional synchronicity comforted the former Kaitain of the Colonial Corporation. Enro had fully reconciled his path. He was home.

A warm weariness had taken over his body. The wine began to do its work. Enro slept well that night. He dreamed of Mirror. It had been some years since he had been there. Soon however, he would have the time he hoped.

With Shimtak!

*

Flex left for Ecksol the next morning on a truck filled with blood melons bound for the main food center downtown. He would spread the news to the urban-based rebels. The melons were delicious.

*

CHAPTER TWENTY-TWO

"VINNYVILLE"
TATOCHIN 2465

"The edge of war, like an
ill-sheathed knife, no
more shall cut his master."

Henry the Fourth, Part 1"
Act 1, Scene 1
William Shakespeare 16TH Century

Tango commandeered the flitter from the Corporation training center to downtown Ecksol. He felt the affects of the gas and the torture all over his body. Gratitude for unseen allies soothed his jangled systems that had been on overdrive. The clothing the Omegan's had provided him were adequate. The stimulants and nutritional injection helped restore some semblance of balance. He could feel ripples of the recent trauma clinging to his cells.

My adrenals have been sucked dry!

He knew he was on borrowed time. The body needed healing. It was indeed hard to relax with the emotional vibrations of a drugged, bound and gagged, angry Dragon Fem in the back seat. The impending meeting with a blue and yellow haired rebel named "Flex the terrorist" didn't help either.

Such was the reality for Arafad Tango X, after a long morning on the torture ring. He knew that his sensitivity was both a blessing and a problem. He monitored his breath using special technics to more quickly restore himself.

Shaso, the Dragon Fem, though drugged and restrained, was awake but paralyzed. When Tango looked back, her eyes burned with confusion and anger. The car and Shaso were an added liability. The rule of thumb, digit, or mandible, was that the Corporate eyes were everywhere. He navigated through the pre-rush hour traffic to the industrial area of Ecksol.

Time to "ring" Vinny's doorbell. We need to be debugged!

Like many other cities, the urban grid had rules, rules for the bosses, rules for the common people, and rules for the thieves. Tango preferred the thieves.

Approaching the familiar streets, he knew how to get noticed. His cousin was a weapons dealer and overall black market entrepreneur, who had many contacts with the rebels and anybody else that needed anything that was not Corporate Conformed. The black market was alive and well on Tatochin, and Vinny, his cousin, was a player who had made up some rules of his own.

Tango pulled over to the sidewalk and jumped out, presumably to buy a taco from a Corporate Conformed vendor on the corner. This was the doorbell. Actually, it was Vinny's secretary. He purchased a taco. It was a grim looking excuse for food. He knew the lingo.

"Tell Vinny I have a tagged vehicle and a warm package with eyes for processing right away."

The vendor's eyes widened. It revealed an artificial eye that was a veritable electronic portal. Tango had downloaded a fair amount of data. The vendor was a technoid and fully wired. A man appeared from behind the taco stand and briskly walked over to the car. The implant behind his right ear pulsed with electronic activity. He was another Technoid. He jumped into the flitter motioning Tango to get in beside him. The wired street soldier in Vinny's employment hit the gravity field and sped off.

The street was busy. Ground cars, flitters, and pedestrians roamed the gritty boulevard. The neighborhood featured several breweries and a host of other food processing centers all monitored by the Colonial Corporation.

A vactube that meandered down the central corridor loomed twenty feet above the street like a bloated translucent winged serpent. The hiss of decompression moved the dust of the street across the walk areas. The automated doors opened to discharge passengers who descended escalators to the ground. The area swelled with foot traffic and all manner of people.

The flitter maneuvered around the block and into an alleyway in front of several large recycling bins and waited. A few minutes later, a second flitter pulled up carrying three people. Two of them got out and transferred Shaso to the other flitter. Tango jumped into the front passenger side of the flitter. The Korum flitter instantly sped off with the carrot and the taco, riding shotgun.

It had taken all of seven seconds. Tango started to talk but was waved into silence. They turned into an alley as a garage door opened. The driver motioned him to get out. The car immediately pulled out leaving Tango and a burly hulk holding the limp body of Shaso. Three other men and women appeared, and again the signal for silence was given. They walked quickly into the interior of the warehouse.

A woman pulled the cover off an imaging medical scanner. She indicated that Tango was to walk past it. A powerfully built man stepped up to Tango and asked to see his food neutralizer. He looked at it briefly then handed it back and winked. The burly giant picked Shaso up and carried her past the scanner. The woman who initially watched the screen waved to a third woman who approached.

The giant placed Shaso on a low table. The two women consulted over a scan of Shaso's anatomy. They produced a device that looked like a laser pistol but bulkier. Tango walked over, looked at the scan and noted several implants that had been surgically added to Shaso's body. They were only visible because of the scanners ability to modulate the light spectrum. An electrical charge was released over the implants. The woman with the gun-like device began to treat the Dragon Fem.

"This will render the devices inoperable. That one is only visible in the ultra-violet spectrum," the technician said.

The gun was activated over each area. Shaso lost consciousness. The giant picked her up and walked back through the imaging devise.

"They have ceased to function but the tube might have a failsafe trigger. We will remove it now. She indicated the surgical table and she picked up the laser cutter. "I love taking out these things," the woman said to Tango.

The surgery lasted a full ten minutes. The tube was incinerated in a special containment chamber. Shaso was now free of all electronic devices for the first time since she was a child.

Tango began to reply but was again silenced.

"Come on, your flitter is waiting."

The giant loaded Shaso into the flitter and Tango got in the passenger side. The taco and the carrot were gone. Another stone-faced driver sped out of the warehouse.

It must be dangerous around here! Vinny never had such a set up in the past.

Finally, the flitter pulled into an open door to Vinny's warehouse. Tango had not been there for many months.

Tango had a loft in the building next door to the main building. It had an underground entrance. The warehouse to all appearances was a used flitter parts and electronics warehouse. In the underground and black market, it was a safe house. Many weapons were bought and sold to the rebels through a network that Tango had helped set up. It was Tango's hope that meeting with Flex would gain him a valuable bargaining position to increase the Korum's involvement with the rebels. Orville had recommended the alliance. It had taken over a year to set things up. Much distrust was still operating.

Vinny was a hero from the Rishma rebellion. He had his legs blown off during the siege of Corlato and was consigned to a wheel chair. Only the very rich could afford fully cybernetic limbs.

Vinny's skills as an I-Wing fighter pilot were legendary. He had a metal box filled with medals welded to the armature of his customized wheel chair. He was Tango's cousin on his mother's side.

Tango had sought him out when he had been released from rehabilitation. He was a broken man. A deep anger brewed inside of Vinny. He was vitriolic when he talked about the Corporation. They had been the ones who had tossed him aside when he was no longer of use. Tango secretly felt that Vinny was lucky to see the truth, and tell of it, even though the cost had been high.

Vinny had come to see the evil the Corporation was capable of. He was motivated by a desire for revenge combined with a need for redemption. Pain and trauma could have its rewards in awareness. Tango had helped him get started by putting him to work. Vinny had thrived.

"Tango, what's the word? You got a D-fem in bandages?"

"I need her to stay quiet and restrained, Vin, she's a Dragon Fem, the real thing."

"Shit, Tango. Man that's illvibe. Are you memphasing fucking retro? Dude…" Vinny spat. He produced a marijuana menthol pack and offered it to Tango.

"Vinny the Omegans just hauled me in. I spent the morning on a torture ring. Then for reasons unknown, they let me go. They gave me Shaso's contract because they assumed the Korum would seek a path to restore honor. I didn't want her, but you know the situation."

"Tango, you are one crazy sucka."

"Vin, this is serious goulash, she could give you a hard on. Be careful."

If anyone besides Tango had made such a comment like that to Wheelchair Vinny he might be dead already. The decorated war hero had lost more than his legs in the war. Few people knew what Vinny had learned to cope with. Tango had been his only confidant.

To witness Vinny in a room was a complex and confounding experience for the uninitiated. Vinny had a wheelchair that was an urban assault vehicle. His chair had become a sculptural framework for weapons, communications, and surveillance with unusual features. The lobes of a liquid core computer bubbled around the backside of the assemblage.

Vinny never slept. He wore a headset that covered what had been an eye, lost along with his legs in the fiery remains of his I-Wing fighter, pried from the fuselage of a derelict Rishma battle cruiser.

The ocular prostheses had a Centaurian grade neural link. He was wired like a Technoid but without the attitude. Several holo projectors cycled through various modes producing a translucent mirage of changing images around his chair. An impressive array of buttons and dials formed the sides of his vehicle. To further complicate the presence of Vinny in a room a cloud of marijuana smoke usually gathered around the gregarious man.

"Now, listen cousin, this is what all this has been leading up to. Soon the revolution will begin."

Vinny let out an evil laugh, chuckling in a fog of skunky smelling blue smoke. "Tango, the revolution has been going on around here for a while, Yo!"

Twenty-five years, old and a virgin when he lost his legs and his manhood, maybe someday I can talk him into a cyborg lower body.

Tango enjoyed Vinny. It was great to see he had gotten his laugh back. Vinny had come a long way from thinking he was a useless piece of shit. He looked over at Shaso.

"Keep her paralyzed and gagged or she'll do some serious voodoo in your mind. Really, she can use her voice as a weapon. The drug will prevent her from having the mental clarity to do her most dangerous psycho-martial tactics. My place is set up for it. I'll be back for her later."

"She's safe with me". Vinny gave him a wink.

They walked to the back of the warehouse. Tango seldom used the sanctuary. He was too well known through the holocasts to openly be seen in the neighborhood. Knowing that his cover might be compromised someday, he took comfort in knowing the sanctuary was there. The secret entrance was immune to imaging surveillance by the complete absence of any electrical or electronic devices. A simple pulley system navigated a platform along a track one story down. A ladder gave access to the platform.

Tango lifted Shaso off the cart that had conveyed her to this point, and hoisted her over his shoulder. Though she remained paralyzed, Shaso had regained consciousness.

Where the fuck am I? In some sort of gothic dungeon?

Tango descended the ladder and placed her on another cart. Shaso saw that it was Tango who had been carrying her.

Tango is not who he seems… I have observed too much, that is why I am here

He carried her to a bedroom and dumped her on the bed. In a closet near the bed, Tango fetched a set of restraints and secured her, placing a gag over her mouth. He opened a slick black pouch that held dozens of vials and hypo-needles. He loaded a vial into the device and injected Shaso in her thigh.

"I will deal with you later, Shaso. For now you shall live!"

He climbed back up to the warehouse. "Vin, you got something cold?"

Vinny pushed a button on a small console near his armrest. A compartment opened and he grabbed two ice-cold Moorhead Amino lagers.

"I gotta homey down the street at the brewery."

"You have refrigeration onboard?"

"Hey, you know me. I had the cooling system for the laser cannon enlarged to accommodate a small supply onboard. Hey, I'm a busy man. You know this stuff is special. No hypno drugs."

"You got a laser cannon?"

"Just a small one. You know me… eternal vigilance."

"Hey Tango, can I watch you when you come back for that tattooed babe?

"Same perverted Vinny."

"Hey, I still got my hands, and an appreciation."

"And a big mouth."

"And a long tongue."

"A lewd and rude tongue."

"Hey Tango, I saw you on a holo scan last month at an opening of a new play or something. You had a babe hanging off your shoulder, wellvibe stuff."

"She was a bodyguard Vin, strictly business. Kalimafar insisted on having a large entourage. You know what I must endure."

"I could endure a little of that guarding my body anytime."

"Same old Vinny."

"Same old Tango."

They performed a complex handshake. Tango finished his amino brew. "Is it as hard to get out of here as it was to get in? Geez Vinny, things are tight."

"Tango, be careful, the word is things are heating up on the street."

"You too, Vinny. Catch you later."

Tango closed the hatch and went back to his apartment. He had some time before meeting Flex, the rebel contact. He showered, changed, replenished his vitamins, and changed the power packs on his laser pistol and food neutralizer.

A plant that needed major help was watered and he checked the larder. Tango wrote some additional instructions for Vinny regarding Shaso, as she watched from his bed.

When I fucking kill this verder, it will be slow and painful.

Tango regarded Shaso and heaved a sigh. Though he hadn't picked up her thoughts telepathically, he felt waves of anger emanating from the exotic hellion that lay helpless on his bed.

"Blink twice if you can hear me." Tango sat on a chair facing her. She blinked twice.

"I must keep you drugged and bound for a time. I cannot let you go. I do not wish to kill you, either. I can offer you an alternative life or nothing. It requires your voluntary cooperation. Please think about this. You had at least three different implants in your body. One was the Corporation, one was the Korum, and one was the sisterhood. They are now all inactive."

She became reflective and Tango left her to process the dire news of her situation. Ten minutes later he was heading down Sobash Street towards the Lynch Café.

The street was crowded. It was a change of shifts. Arafad Tango X, a warrior mystic with a difficult pathway to tread was secretly praying for a return to the shores of grace and peace. He wanted to be closer to the Central Sun.

*

CHAPTER TWENTY-THREE

"THE LYNCH CAFÉ"
ECKSOL

"We are those unpaid legions.
In free ranks arrayed,
Massacred in many regions
Never once were stayed."

"Armageddon"
"The secret of death and other poems"
Sir Edwin Arnold 19th Century

The eye makeup made Flex's face itch but the disguise was both wanted and needed. His lean sinewy body could easily pass for a woman with the prosthetic body suit.

The mime training he had memlocked in the farnow had given him a dimension of disguise that went far beyond mere artifice. It was an oasis of pleasure for him as well. The feminine sway of his hips turned many an eye as he strutted down the industrial neighborhood. It turned Flex on, too.

God, sometimes I don't know why I am the way I am but I feel so yummy when I do this!

He had a reputation at several of the more avant-garde transvestite clubs that were typical in the area. The click of his spiked heels turned trained eyes as he passed the Pharmo-bars, sex parlors, and pleasure domes along the gritty boulevard. He crossed the street to avoid the exodus of workers departing the Moorhead Brewery. First shift was just letting out and the streets were busy.

He had illvibe concerning this meeting. He had seen holoscans of this Tango X. *He's was just too slick to be true. What was this X stuff anyway?*

Flex had lost several friends. They had disappeared into that damnable Korum tower of Kalimafar's never to be seen again. Enro had warned him that the Corporation might be aware of his meeting. Suddenly a large overweight worker stood before him blocking his path. It was clear that the brewery worker had been sampling the products liberally.

"Hey how's about a date, a tumbler, if ya know what I mean."

He smelled like stale beer. *The lice are jumping off him. Even those verders are appalled!*

The factory worker had just been paid. He had been making fermented beverages for the Corporate Conformed masses. He smelled like a rancid swill mopper. With few extra credits to spare, he sought the discount pleasures available in the neighborhood.

Now I am being hassled for sex. He knew he looked like a pleasure Fem. *I am irresistible!*

"Hey, take a bath." Flex replied in a sultry falsetto voice. He adjusted the tight skirt that tended to ride up his legs and strode off in a flourish. He enjoyed the stares and sexual tension he stirred up as he glided down the dirty street.

A vactube hissed as the train came to a stop. A cloud of fine dust curled and scattered around the pulsing magnetic track. The doors slid open and two columns of people surged in opposite directions from the opening. Flex sashayed his way through the crowd toward a level one cafe a few blocks down Sobash Street called the Lynch Café.

Billboards with their animated spiels, cycled through their programs. They bombarded the casual observer with subliminal messages to obey and consume maximizing the Corporation's continued success.

The pedestrians eyes were trained forward, few making eye contact. The constant companion of fear put the people in a perpetual state of contraction. Slowly their spirits became dull and worn down. Only the electronic billboards spoke of green pastures.

Flex was painfully aware of the schism between where he was and what was life affirming. He knew that he had descended into the mire of the Corporate cesspool where the bottom feeders flourished.

They are a captured world, wounded in places hard to see through the fog of propaganda.

He saw the stress lines of hard work. The smell of fossil fuel, mingled with other esters in the air. They were byproducts of the huge agricultural processing facilities that typified the industrial area in Ecksol. Flex continued down the gritty street doing his share of averting eye contact.

Some lyrics floated out of a boom box:

Revel with me. I want a one
stand contract with my baby
herenow. I saw holos of the
stars and I'm dreaming of
landfall where a gentle
breeze blows. I'm saving
my credits, won't you
revel with me, revel with me,
revel with me. Right now,
my sweet Norice…

*

Cargo flitters filled with Mosh floated by sending pollen visibly in the air. *What a primordial cesspool! God its hard to be here.*

Tango walked into the Lynch Café, pushing the greasy glass door open. To one side, a dilapidated chalkboard listed the hazards of the day. He sat down in a booth with patched plastic covers.

So, by the light of the eternal sun, now I'm in a sleaze bucket. Where is Flex?

The cafe functionally was on the craggy shoreline of hell. He asked for a menu, rousing a few of the more curious ghouls from their morbid life patterns. A busboy slapped a greasy plastic covered holo reader upon the chipped plastic table as he passed by.

Soon, a waitress holo appeared. It was a cheap one that jumped with the static of sub-standard electronics. Tango ordered a plate of steamed vegetables and Mosh. He had to look natural.

When it arrived he looked around to see if anyone was looking. Satisfied, he activated the small food neutralizer that would keep him clean of hypnotics. He thought about anything to counteract the repugnant energy he was feeling in the clutches of this hideous level one dining facility. He retreated into a philosophical mem-phase to dampen his awareness of the crusty environment he found himself.

We all like to order life in a linear sequence. I think that is because most of us are unaware of the finer electrical frequencies that enliven the dormant areas of our minds. Hard to find the bright sparks in these warrens! Environment is essential. I am feeling the absence of a nurturing environment in maximode…illvibe!

He gave up on the mem-phasing as a fellow sitting near him let out a loud, extended belch. Tango looked at the chronometer on the wall. Ten minutes had passed. The discomfort he felt was like an un-hatched premonition. *Something was going to happen. It has been one intense day and its not over yet!*

The food arrived. He stabbed his fork into a chunk of broccoli when the café began to shake.

*

Flex was two blocks from the Lynch Café when the high pitched keen of a large electro-magnetic power source made his hair stand on end. He looked up. The shadow of a Colonial Trooper Tactical Orb glided past him. He heard the landing struts lock into position. It settled to the pavement several hundred yards away.

The herd on the street was spooked. Crowds dispersed as half a dozen Colonial Corporation flitters streamed over the ground traffic and descended from every direction.

Tactical maneuvering! Shit it's the fucking brain police!

Troopers in gleaming white auto-armor marched out of the Orb. The other Troopers disembarked from their flitters and set up a perimeter. They soon locked down the entire neighborhood with a three-block perimeter. The pavement felt like flypaper. Surging bodies streamed in every direction. Make-shift check points manned by the troopers, allowed the people out after they were scanned or questioned.

Flex said a silent prayer to the eternal light. He could feel the plasma pistol secured to the side of his armpit grow warm, as if it had the wherewithal to know it might become useful. The armored troops formed a phalanx and drew their large laser rifles. He was in the capture zone with no immediate escape. A blaze of spiritual flame coursed through Flex's spine as he realized the target was the Lynch Café!

The Corporate shitheads!

*

THE SURVEILLANCE HUB

Renjinn spat brown phlegm gore all over his COM board as he coughed with anger. The scene on Sobash St. had popped up in front of the pea green Katofar like toast from a malignant holotune.

"Did we get a confirmation that the target has arrived? No! The swag wallow lame brains are too early. Flex is not in there. I don't want to lose that Tatochinian pain in the poop hole. Ostinglink, who gave the swoop order before confirmation from surveillance?"

"Your highness, your grace", Ostinglink nervously babbled. His great golden Tadole eyes darted across the myriad read-outs. The dorsal fin atop his head raised and lowered in keeping with his confused state of mind. His croaking voice lapsed into Tadole marsh speech, a series of flatulent emissions indicating pathetic frustration to anyone who understood the strange native tongue of the Tadole.

Gathering his will, Ostinglink keyed the commanding Belfar on the scene, but received no response. He turned to the agitated Katofar.

"Intelligence said he would be in a disguise! Maybe he is in the café?" Ostinglink's dorsal deflated as Renjinn's dorsal fin both rose and turned toward dangerous violet hues.

Renjinn croaked with consternation. His fin quivered with dangerous tremors. "Maybe! Maybe! A surveillance bubble worth three billion credits, half Banta of Troopers, an Orb with a fully responsive armored infantry, and you say maybe! Slag Wallow," hissed Renjinn.

His throat bellows uncoiled and a large extended trumpeting sound became a droning sound track. "Give a stand down, heads will roll for this." He jabbed at a button on his console chair and it whirled around to the banks of holo-projectors that revealed several different angles of Sobash St.

"Ostinglink, they are not responding! Signal them again, Slagwallow!"

*

SOBASH ST

The high-pitched whine of Corporation flitters swooping down to the street caught Tango's attention in the café. *Is it a trap?*

He stood and glanced out of the front window. Armored Troopers were taking up positions around the front of the café. The energy in his lower spine ignited like a flare and coursed into his brain, dispelling all extraneous thought. In maximode his breath deepened and quickened.

The door swung open and a woman came in breathing hard. "Tango," she called out, her eyes searching.

"Lesha?"

"Tango, you're here, good." Her eyes bored into his eyes. Silently she spoke, *"No time for stealth Tango"*

At that moment, screams and screeches pulsed through the heavy air. The smell of ozone charged the local orb. Customers scattered toward the door and into the street, fearful of the impending violence.

"That's a laser cannon charging!" Tango said. He jumped behind the counter, totally ruining the special of the day. Lesha followed. A targeting laser pierced the exterior window; its crimson sword pinned to a greasy wall next to the tacky promotional chronometer with the Moorhead Beer logo. Lesha feverishly punched a series of button on the arm unit strapped to her forearm.

"Lesha, what are you doing here?"

She looked at the crimson beam of the targeting laser. "I guess I'm rescuing you."

"Just how are you going to do that?" Tango hissed.

She silently showed him the Relocator attached to her arm. "Just embrace me, and we'll get out of here," Lesha said with cool certainty.

She adjusted the small keypad attached to her forearm. "Just widening the field a little bit more-there!"

Looking up she said, "Now!"

As she pressed the button activating the relocator, a blinding and concussive blast ripped from the Kelson Laser Cannon reducing the Lynch café back into primal matter. In the same moment, Lesha and Tango were transported into a cross dimensional nexus that allowed them to observe the intense destruction of the café from Astral space.

*

SURVEILLANCE HUB

As Ostinglink repeated the stand down orders from Renjinn, the holos that monitored the streets flashed with lambent, deadly light. The Troopers had fired on the café with a Kelson laser cannon. The greasy spoon diner exploded in excoriating flames returning the building into its elemental components.

The tawdry cubicle of gastrointestinal insult had gone to the hereafter in a wicked moment of total destruction. Girders of mollimix, impossibly twisted, seemed to rise from the simmering volcanic fodder. Renjinn cursed in six languages.

*

SOBASH ST.

Flex stood after the concussive energy of the blast had flattened everyone within a hundred yards. He wisely stepped back and watched from behind a recycling bin. The laser had coalesced into hell's lightning. Like an acid wind, it snatched the corporal bodies within in café in a split second. The shock and fear at losing their lives without a moment's notice was one great astral scream.

Flex felt his awareness move into a multi-dimensional experience of events from several perspectives at once. He experienced the horror of great evil unleashed and at the same time perceived the presence of the Elders. Wisely he focused on those great spirits and observed them assisting the newly dead. The victims were soothed with tender love and reassurances. Flex acknowledged that life had pain while the desire for the body existed on any level.

I am in a hurricane of trouble. There's a good chance that attack was for Tango X or me! Those poor souls… Yet perhaps, it is the living we should cry for. In a hurricane, and yet I am in the eye, as a witness.

Flex's attention returned to the phenomenal scene. The auto-armored troopers were moving in on the powdered café like large mechanical beetles as it smoldered with residual heat. With laser weapons drawn, they combed through the fiery wreckage.

Survivors, they must be kidding. They really are into over-kill. Gezzzz.

*

SMOULDERING OOZE

A hush of expectancy leaked like ichor from the cesspools of hell. All was not well in the COM room at Colonial Corporation Headquarters. The whir and buzz of laser circuitry, readouts, fiber optic matrixes, liquid core percolation, combined with the unsterile smell of Renjinn's rancid cigars, were a cacophony of sensation. The normal chatter of the operators was missing.

Ostinglink watched the dorsal fin of his boss very carefully. The corrosive spray that could stream out from the gland located in the frontal fin of an adult Tadole was highly lethal. It meant instant death. Ostinglink and the entire surveillance team were determined to avoid that fate.

Pheromones of fear mingled with silent clicks of calculation whirling through Renjinn's predatorily oriented brain. He mapped out his route of escape from the ineptitude exhibited in the situation. Sooner or later he would be reprimanded for his team's failure. He would construct a card house of scapegoats, paper chases, and blind alleys of inquiry that would deliver the needed diversion, frustration, and finally an explanation. His equally inept superiors would, in turn, pass the blame on. No such luck was available for the scapegoats.

Renjinn flung his cigar against the brown stained wall. A cleaning robot emerged from its charge bay and collected the smoldering ooze as it slid down the wall. Renjinn stomped out of the room crushing the cleaning robot.

*

SOBASH ST.

Troopers picked through the rubble. A Belfar was pointing all around as a detail formed the area. Flex was sweating, which threatened to ruin a good makeup job. The intensity of the moment had already catapulted his awareness into rare places. Now that morphed into a reality of a gritty street culture on the edge of a semi-civilized city.

Life force coursed outward from his central spine checking his lower nature's tendency to enter into the heterodyne, mind numbing response: fight or flight, or a transvestite's tendency to run to a bathroom to adjust makeup. A clarity and calmness born of a steady increase of alignment to the eternal light allowed Flex to enter maximode.

A thought map of potentialities appeared in Flex's mind. From his navel, he felt a tugging compulsion to move. He calmed his thoughts allowing the solution to emerge. The solution for the moment was so simple. In a blur of economical movement, Flex jumped into the recycling bin thanking the eternal spirit, and cursing it at the same time.

The sludge smelled horrible. The organic mass was steaming with the bacterial action of decomposition. It was an automated composter, one of the more enlightened technical marvels. He visualized billions of tiny critters gobbling the garbage. The bin was as warm as his body. The increased heat of decomposition would hide his presence from a scan.

In spite of the danger of the moment, Flex was able to sublimate his tension by a supreme act of concentration born of the intense desire to survive. His body and the garbage became as one to the scanners and he survived the sweep undetected. His disguise had been totally ruined, he lamented but then he smiled.

The compost was an unexpected surprise! A disguise? Gross!

*

Suspects were rounded up. By midnight and second moonrise, the story of the Lynch Café's demise appeared as a special report on all the major holocasts. The propagandized report recounted how the Corporation's finest had apprehended several rebels after they had fire bombed the café. The holos showed the faces of people who looked scared. None of them rebels, all of them scapegoats offered as a sacrifice to the media gods, to appease the anesthetized viewing audiences and deflect true accountability.

Hours later, the streets were quiet and the sun was down. Flex reluctantly ended his dip in the ocean of bacterial bliss to face the world and its strong odors.

I need a bath.

He slipped out of the recycling bin and stayed as much as possible in the shadows. He quickly trotted, barefoot down the street, silhouetted against Capach's cool blue light. Flex was given a wide berth due to the strong odor attending his presence.

Now I smell worse than that swill mopper… Come on honey, I'm ready for you now.

He giggled like a drunken harlot, happy to have escaped with his life. The safe house was not too far. There he would take a bath before making his way to Skull rock.

Too many things blowing up.

*

COLONIAL CORPORATION HQ

In the Colonial Corporation surveillance room, alarms, buzzers, and holo-projectors shifted to new scenes of burning buildings. The café smoldered with residual heat. Renjinn stomped back into the room, sporting a fresh cigar pulsing red like a plectrum on a Metropol flitter.

His heavy swat boots ground the cleaning robot into high tech compost as he passed. He slammed into the COM chair, his hands a blur as he manipulated myriad readouts to get a handle on the situation.

Revolt. I've seen this before. Something blows up and suddenly three more things get blown up. Geeez!

"Message from Space Dock", Ostinglink blurted.

"Not now!"

Two other food dispensaries were in flames on the other side of town. A checkpoint on the northern entrance to the Planetary Park had been leveled.

"Metropol can handle the fires. Send two flitter teams from Sobash to the checkpoint at Alavarez and Niles Avenue. That checkpoint was hit by a remote missile; very slick weaponry."

Ostinglink carried out the orders as the Katofar continued to analyze the incoming information.

"Any small arms fire at the check point?"

"Nothing so far," Ostinglink replied.

"There is a large crowd at the bomb site on Niles. Some reports of looting. Metropol says there is illvibe."

"Send another flitter from Sobash to the Niles Avenue fire, do not use lethal force." Renjinn stared at the projectors. Smoke and fire animated the surveillance bubble on a dozen different projections. His large golden eyes squinted as the data scrolled along side each moving image. It would be a long night.

It's a smoke screen, what's the real issue? Are they scattering my forces? If they are it is working well. They want to escalate the situation. So far we are just using Metropol. Do they want the Troopers? By the blight of the bog I feel it.

Renjinn was disturbed from his phasing.

"Message from Space Dock, Gentain Carbone has arrived. You asked me to tell you," Ostinglink croaked.

"Space Dock! Space Dock on line." Renjinn cleared his moist tobacco coated throat baffles. A few sounds of actual rectal flatulence escaped as his mind reeled with rapid decisions he was reluctant to make. *The media is going to be on my back for this, shit!*

He keyed the com-link. "Landfall is closed due to a fuel leak. For your safety, please stand by for further developments." Renjinn called in one of his assistant Belfars with orders to quickly create a fake accident at Landfall.

"A small explosion and some fire. Keep the damage to a minimum. Make sure it is visible to all incoming passengers…don't get carried away though, just convincing enough."

"Injuries?"

"Just a few. We want all the flashing lights to activate enough fear for them to appreciate our presence. You know what to do by the bog!" The Belfar croaked appropriately and hopped to it.

Renjinn prepared himself. The Gentain Carbone was the scariest human he had encountered.

Gentain Carbone. Just what I needed. A visit from the boss; they always know when your dorsal is wobbling.

Renjinn took some comfort knowing that many other planets in the colonies were having worse problems than his. He recalled several relevant recent events of insurrections in the colonies of Orion including Glamora. He could mention them in defense, if needed. It gave Renjinn a false sense of marsh cushioning he needed to calm is frazzled nerves.

*

CHAPTER TWENTY-FOUR

"BEACHHEAD AT THE ROYAL ORION"
TATOCHIN

The violet smaller moon, Wechen, had risen. It was well past the midpoint of darkness. Renjinn and his assistant had arrived at the Royal Orion resort to oversee the surveillance preparations for the Trilateral Conference.

Renjinn looked out from their ground car at the opulent entrance to the resort and let out a series of flatulent exhales from his throat bellows. Ostinglink's dorsal sunk several inches as he knew the meaning of his boss's gesture well.

The Belfar suppressed his throat baffles need to deflate. In public it could draw unwanted attention. More important, it could stress out his already moody boss.

The door to the ground car opened with a hiss. Renjinn nodded to Ostinglink who waved the Orion staff away. He looked through the clear Mollimix windows and sighed. *I want my bog.*

The lobby of the Royal Orion was a blur of activity. The technicians scurried about while the guests of the resort slept. Preparation for the Trilateral conference progressed.

Technicians busily fed optical cables, installed sensor arrays, and outfitted the new surveillance bubble. By morning, workers would retreat into the backrooms and remain discreetly absent during the day as visitors enjoyed their stay at the plush resort.

The building was a series of soaring arches that stacked upon each other. It looked like a jungle of cactus from the tropical zones of the planet. It was a copper and Mollimix jewel resting on the shore of Lake Wechen, at the confluence of the Remorah River.

The reddish purple and pale blue shadows of the moons played off the moored sailboats that lined the shoreline. Soft, warm yellow lights lit the various streets and footpaths that meandered throughout the vast resort. The entrance was a throw back to Corporate retrostyles. The Art Deco ornamentation was accented with burnished copper, the promised razzle-dazzle of the brochures.

Katofar Renjinn waddled past the security barriers with Ostinglink in tow. He was confidant that his mere presence would be sufficient for him to pass uninterrupted.

A concierge's frowned and his eyes widened as the giant, green, frog-like Tadole Katofar waddled by with a smoldering cigar dangling out of his large mouth. Ostinglink struggled to keep up with the burly Katofar trying not to choke on the smoke in Renjinn's wake. He carried a portable holo link and a brief module. His dorsal fin was lowered appropriately in a subservient position according to the edict of the Tadole.

Renjinn abruptly stopped beneath a lavish chandelier. His dorsal fin rose majestically. His sucker tipped digits resting upon his ample love handles. He struck a suitable pose of a Tadole Katofar requesting audience. Ostinglink had to admire his moody superior's style and grace. The Belfar looked around but saw no activity. He was frightened but did not show it. Renjinn's throat bellows inflated with a loud sucking noise.

"The chief of security, why is he not here to greet me, Ostinglink?"

Ostinglink assumed a submissive posture towards his boss, with his palms up and his dorsal low, a required formality in public. Before he could answer, the frowning concierge sashayed up to Renjinn. Renjinn grunted in approval, though it was true, that by Tadole standards, it was the lowest insult to not be greeted as soon as his shadow had crossed the entrance. He deflated his throat bellows making a discordant chorus of brass instruments.

The concierges face was a mask of perplexed horror. *I don't know how to communicate with this…giant frog.*

Renjinn was used to turning a few heads so he gave a little slack to the alien humans. Fate however was to be served. The slim, bald concierge, with a supercilious lisp said, "Excuse me, smoking is not permitted anywhere in the Royal Onion."

Ostinglink dropped the brief module and jumbled the holo link. His dorsal fin was flat. He felt it pressing on his skull, it could not go any lower. This human obviously had no idea what a Tadole with a fully raised fin could do. The corrosive secretions in the sacks within the frontal bones of a Tadole dorsal fin could spray a victim as an automatic response. The outcome was lethal. The substance that the Omegans used for the evil little tubes that sat within their fleshy forms was derived from these secretions.

Renjinn's dorsal was in the danger zone before the errant comment. Ostinglink slowly backed away, fearing the worst.

The concierge's eyes were going crazy. He had never encountered a Tadole, though his training was extensive in life form language and custom. He soon recognized that Ostinglink's fear was a good metric to use in determining the nature of this intergalactic insult he had committed. He alternately observed Ostinglink's reaction and the Katofar's metronome dorsal fin twitching in agitation.

"Of course, my request has nothing to do with you, illustrious Katofar but with your subordinates." He glanced furtively at Ostinglink to gauge his attempt to defuse the heinous crime he had inadvertently committed.

Renjinn growled and exhaled, grinding the putrid smoldering cigar in his mouth. The sound of farting escaped Renjinn's throat bellows, catching the attention of several technicians who made faces and moved further away from the melodrama in the lobby. The concierge did not reveal his displeasure. Renjinn's dorsal fin lost some of its forward thrust. The violet had become more red at the tips. Ostinglink tensed the muscles around his throat to suppress most of the chorus of escaping air as he relaxed.

"Where is the chief of security," Renjinn bellowed.

"Oh my," the paling concierge whimpered.

"I am right here, Katofar Renjinn," a crooning baritone, rich in amplified, psychic suggestions that sought to sooth. The simple black outfit of an Omegan priest on a very tall and skeletal man stood ten feet off to the side. Renjinn's dorsal lowered noticeably. The Omegan looked like a formidable bird of prey.

Renjinn experienced an emotionally intense shift inside his head. As if something that slept within was having a nightmare. He panicked for a moment; then it passed. Everything was happening very quickly. The moment receded from his mind as he prepared to greet the Omegan and make a good first impression. *The Omegans! By the beast of the Bog! They are here already!*

The concierge and Ostinglink sighed with relief at the same time. The cavalry had arrived at the last nano-second.

"Your grace, how foolish of me not to notice you earlier," Renjinn croaked.

"My name is Father Bodono; it is a pleasure to meet you." Bodono smiled to himself. He had wanted an opportunity to meet a Tadole warrior. Their striking resemblance to frogs had captured the curiosity of humankind and extraterrestrials alike. The old Earth fairy tale, "The Wind in the Willows", was the current favorite fairy tale among the Tadoles of Navidrrr.

From the intelligence reports I have read, this Renjinn is no Mr. Toad!

"I was not notified of your eminent arrival, my grace, or I would have arranged a suitable greeting for you." Renjinn's concern was genuine.

"Please, you may just call me Bodono. I am on special assignment. New Centaurian technology upgrades will soon arrive."

"Centaurian?"

"Yes, it is being retrieved from the cargo Corsair I arrived in. Not a passenger ship; you surely understand that there were security concerns with all the rebel activity in the colonies recently".

Of course they know. Renjinn lamented.

He raised his palms in recognition of the pecking order. Father Bodono had not lied. His explanation was all perfectly true. It had little to do with his true purpose in being on Tatochin. He had come to make real trouble, and so he would. Discovering weak links in the alliance between the Omegan and the Corporation was one directive, and finding the rebels another.

"Father Bodono, have you a suitable suite?"

"It was all arranged for me by Father Smith. Omegans are a very orderly bunch of fellows. Perhaps, we should retire into the command center before we burn the lobby down." Renjinn led the way. As Father Bodono followed, a bemused expression played across his face.

Ostinglink sighed his relief. He picked up the hololink and brief module and followed. Striding by the traumatized concierge, he tried hard to control his throat bellows. Little farting sounds squeaked through in spite of his efforts. It was the equivalent of suppressing a laugh. *Earth people have a primal fear of large reptilian life forms!*

"Ostinglink!" barked the Katofar Renjinn.

Ostinglink scurried along behind the curious pair. An exceedingly tall and gaunt figure next to a large, green toad-like form, both carrying themselves with unique grace and authority.

Father Smith gave Bodono summations regarding the Tadole, as they approached the command center. The ear piece was hidden and very comfortable.

The martial path was popular with the Tadole. For the serious warrior, it was a culture rich in mysticism as well. The most respected and honored work was to be a soldier. Their mercenary guild was a subject of great pride on the home world. Among the finest warriors, their gift for physical prowess and high logical and technical capabilities was in high demand especially

since the Colonial Corporation had sought to expand its empire. Their moral simplicity made them trustworthy. Honor is their spiritual food.

The Samurai cultures of the orient on old Earth was similar in many ways. They also have a curious desire for larger habitats. It was measured in height rather than surface area. Altitude is believed to be the outward realization of success. A tall home was a symbol of great achievement in life. They also had many spiritual traditions that were centrally enmeshed in the teachings of the Elders.

Renjinn is known as a highly regarded leader on his home planet and a hero from the siege of Oblion.

Renjinn, Ostinglink, and Bodono entered the surveillance bubble that was swarming with technicians. Several Omegan postulants were attaching portable suspension generators and lifting machinery out of the shipping containers. The powerful gravity field modulation devices' deep humming distracted them as they walked by.

Renjinn's dorsal fin twitched several times and took on an amber glow. Katofar Renjinn felt the buzz and the glow. *Something big is going on here. And I, Renjinn of Navidrrr, will be at the center of it, by the light of Vichillia!*

Once the outer door closed, Father Bodono produced a pipe, lighted it, releasing a satisfying cloud of aromatic blue smoke. He didn't reveal how transparent the Katofar's thoughts were to him.

Renjinn watched the craven priest as he ceremoniously placed his pipe in his mouth. The large golden eyes of the Katofar widened in astonishment. *Ah! A smoker like me! I want one of those devices. Much simpler than a hookah!*

He let out a series of croaks and flatulent decompressions revealing his true sentiments. His body jiggled and his throat bellows wiggled with the Tadole version of a chuckle.

Father Bodono smiled. *This is turning into an interesting assignment already. This one will know of all the rebel activity. I appreciate a being that has a sense of humor. It's fun to interact with these Tadole! Frogs!*

"Come, I will give you an overview of the upgrades we have brought, perhaps you can have someone find us something to drink as well?"

Renjinn liked this gaunt priest. He did not feel the usual oppressive scrutiny and disdain that accompanied the formal Omegans from Salvation High World. Unlike the gentle and wise Pleiadians who originally had created the Bio Domes of Salvington, the Omegans had become pompous and downright scary, especially since they joined the ranks of the Colonial Corporation.

*

CHAPTER TWENTY-FIVE

PLANET MIRROR

Cleo had trouble sleeping. The restored memlocks as an ascended Elder caused her discomfort about being embodied in a human form. Her recall of a more refined and energetically activated body, in her previous long existence, tugged at her awareness.

Sleep doesn't seem so necessary. *We have been preparing for these times of adjustment in the lives of many souls. Now is a time of great change and innovation!*

Internal shifts in her chemistry were causing some temporary inflammation. She had been told it was a natural part of the soul awakening she had arranged. With the veils of ignorance lifted, the human Salibno body was a heavy overcoat, limiting, and in constant need of attention being composed of denser matter. The Pleiadians would be able to accelerate the abilities of her mortal body in time.

Cleo understood it was an adjustment for her body. Her interdimensional reality would integrate in time. Raising her awareness, she initiated a trance state and slipped out of her three dimensional body into her astral fourth dimensional form. She appeared as a nimbus of fairy light. In her subtle body she surveyed the immediate orb of her perception.

The silver cord of embodiment was attached to her physical form at her navel. This would always be there as long as she lived in a physical body. Having understood clearly that she was a spirit in flesh was not a new or difficult achievement. Even before her memlocks as an Elder had been reawakened, she had perfected her ability to experience life from this dimension of reality.

On the lower planes where material life proliferates, the silver cord that attaches spirit to body was a point of susceptibility. She knew Mirror was a protected environment. In other warrens, constant vigilance was required to maintain personal integrity and freedom. Even in this realm, good and evil were at play.

With a mental command, Cleo ascended through shifting planes of energies and manifestations of light and sound. The multi-dimensional nature of being was like many veils covering the spirit. Her awakening to new levels of spiritual awareness allowed her access to the more rarefied firmament of astral worlds where the Elders dwell. Cleo found a place of silence. After a time she was moved to pray.

"I seek communion and guidance."

Cleo felt propelled to locations of great light and magnetism. From a point of light of a brilliant star, a blue orb awash in a perihelion of gold expanded around her. Multihued light danced into substance that clarified into centrolineal scintillating definition. She stood before a palace tiled with mother-of-pearl Arabesque pillars that framed the large windows. She stabilized her vibratory rate and approached the entryway.

It was a gazebo trimmed in gilded gold. It had a black marble floor. The pilloried gazebo was surrounded by a landscape of ornamental flowers and trees, encircled by a small meandering stream. White doves perched on the ornamental trees and an unseen harp sounded in the distance. Chimes tinkled to a gentle jasmine scented wind creating an enchanting melody.

The eight pillars supported the roof whose ceiling displayed a different galaxy and planetary system in each segment. The harp music intensified into an orchestral crescendo, as three doves fluttered to the floor and transformed into three human-like forms standing before her. They wore opalescent robes that teemed with energy, as they subtly shifted color.

Sparus, Cleo's mentor raised her hands in greeting: "Beloved Cleo, welcome to our circle. It is long since we have communed thus."

Cleo smiled and returned the greeting. "My compliments on this inspirational creation, I am warmed by your fertile imagination, my dear friend." Cleo basked in the glow of her homecoming. Sweet memlocks of her life, before she had been reborn, flitted across her mind.

"Jarine!" Cleo's sister from many incarnations was also present. They embraced.

"My brave sister, how is it to be embodied?"

Cleo smiled, "It's like running a race in lead boots." They both laughed at the private joke from an incarnation they had shared upon the Earth in the twentieth century.

Sparus gently locked arms with the reunited sisters, and took a few steps with them as she prepared to speak. The women composed themselves, reluctantly.

"It is the time of a new quickening. Your descent into form has borne the required fruit, Cleo."

"What do you mean?"

"Long has your brother Alphonse and others influenced the good children of Tatochin in their long journey. They need our help and intervention." Sparus turned to Cleo with a mysterious smile.

"That isn't usually our way, is it?"

Sparus smiled. "We had to intervene on Earth and on a few other planetary systems. The Dravithians took advantage of every opportunity to circumvent our protection. The Earth people have been meddled with more than most. Great damage had been done.

Unfortunately, there are others who meddle. We cannot let that go unanswered. We suspect many things are still hidden in the sub-planes, yet I trust in the process. You have a part to play in that process. We will have a brilliant adventure together! You will see."

The pilloried marble gallery shimmered with tiny photons of invigorating energy. With a wave of his hand, and a well-timed wink, the planet Tatochin, with its twin blue and violet-red moons, appeared in the field of stars in one of the eight corners of the gallery. She realized that each square of marble was like a holo-window. Star fields, retaining a sense of unfathomable depth within the solid surface, spread out beneath her.

"Soon, we will dispatch one of our most promising brethren to aid in a important transition upon Tatochin. Orville Parker will play a significant role. He will also be most significant to you, my dear one." Sparus smiled and turned to Alphonse.

He had remained silent until then. Now he held Cleo's hand conveying his greeting telepathically, while they listened to Sparus continue. The planet Navidrrr appeared in another facet of the octagon shaped hall.

"The Tadole will also be transformed as we return to a closer proximity to the Central Sun."

Alphonse picked up the conversation. "It will be, at first, disturbing. Know Cleo, that it is the way of things. It is a beneficent turn of events."

"What is?"

Alphonse sighed and looked at Sparus. Sparus shook her head. "For reasons I can't yet explain I can't tell you, yet. You will know soon enough."

"Somehow that doesn't sound reassuring," Cleo said. She grasped her sister's hand.

"Jarine?"

"I don't know either!"

Cleo turned back to Sparus and Alphonse.

"I know there is more to this!" She talked sternly but her overwhelming love for Sparus and Alphonse was readily apparent.

Alphonse turned and held Cleo by both her shoulders. "The Earth, Orville's true home planet, and Mychronitia, your true home, will become united in a multidimensional fusion. The transformation is part of our universe's evolution toward the light of the Central Sun. As you know, you are part of the vanguard in this cycle. This transformation is sooner than had been expected. Events unfold that will eventually explain this."

As Alphonse spoke, the Earth, Gaia with her single moon, Chandra, was revealed under another arch. Immediately, the Pleiadian home world, Mychrontia, appeared followed by another arch which became illuminated by the Central Sun itself.

Sparus spoke next. "Soon a gathering of many terrestrial civilizations will occur on Tatochin. It is called the Trilateral conferences. The forces of darkness have tried unsuccessfully to subjugate the people of this world."

"What forces?" Cleo asked.

"The Dravithians," Sparus said, locking eyes with Cleo.

"I remember… there was a great struggle. The Dravithians were granted the old Pleiadian star system that is in descent. They are sealed from this side of the galaxy, by the Seal of the Eldera."

The planetary system of Dripinia appeared in yet another window with a different star field around it as Cleo spoke. Around Dripinia the seal was visible as waves of light conjured by the powerful Elders.

Alphonse replied. "They have discovered a way to partially break the seal. Although they are unable to penetrate to this end of the galaxy, they have combined their mental power and can send an emissary through on the astral planes. They work through intermediaries."

"Intermediaries? Who might they be?"

"The Centaurians and their servants, the Rishma, true insects, who were genetically altered with help from the Dravithians, the last of the Elders who were our progenitors. This breach has been the fate of material existence for several millennia. The psycho-modulations of thought amplifiers of old have been re-discovered and deployed. Now they are attempting to overcome the barriers that are in place.

Cleo was disturbed to hear the news. The breach represented a threat on levels of reality that could effect all of creation. Dream or otherwise, many aspects of the creation could be threatened.

She knew of the Great Seal of Eldera. It was a creation that was regenerative in nature. The laws that governed the psychic shield were from an ancient golden age, a farnow retrostory.

"The Elders had used such a method against the Dravithians long ago", Sparus added.

Alphonse lowered his voice and leaned toward Cleo. "I memlock this weapon, a device of frightening capability. It is a psychic amplifier."

"Who has this?"

"The Centaurians apparently gave it back to the Dravithians." The planet Centaur, along with the Centaurian star system and its four gas giant planets, appeared in two more facets of the octagonal gazebo.

Sparus continued. "The Rhisma practically worship the Centaurians as gods. They work in veiled ways through others. Even the Colonial Corporation may have been subverted. It is hard to know how far the reach of the Dravithians, or the Centaurian faction, is at this point."

Sparus smiled in spite of the dire information shared. "It's great to see you again, Cleo."

Cleo had many questions. The ache of isolation from the Elders was something she felt in retrospect. As her experience surfaced, she forgave herself for the spiritual amnesia she had willingly accepted. Only now, upon her reawakening, did she understand instantly why Sparus spoke to her about the situation on Tatochin. Kaitain Enro and Arafad Tango X were already working closely with Orville in that arena.

Sparus followed Cleo's thoughts. "In spite of the Colonial Corporation, freedom fighters continue to resist them. The Martian colony was able to repel the Dravithians. Although some talented journalists had attempted to reveal the Corporation's collusion, the media had been silenced.

"So the Corporation is being guided by the Dravithians?" Cleo asked.

"We have no proof. However, there is a growing factionalism in the Omegans, that is both wellvibe and illvibe. On one hand it suggests schisms exist. On the other hand, it increases the possibility that the Dravithians have infiltrated. They do this in collusion with the Centaurians. Now we have an opportunity to intervene on behalf of the goodness and the light."

Alphonse raised his hand, "Behold the bounty of eternal vigilance". The planet Navidrrr with its moon, Vichilla, grew brighter in its respective archway view.

Cleo watched, as all eight windows were now revealed. Earth, Tatochin, Navidrrr, the Central Sun, Mychrontia, Dripinia. Cleo realized that all eight worlds were interlocked in a cosmic dance.

She acknowledged the bounty and enormity of what she witnessed. Several questions co-mingled with her absorption of events and proclamations. From this plane of awareness, information impregnated with the requisite consciousness permeated many multidimensional frequencies. She would need to hold this information close to her heart for a while. Cleo understood on a deeper level Mirror's ultimate purpose as an incubator for the vanguard of such a quickening.

Sparus continued, "Your time with Orville Parker, our chosen conduit for the restoration and liberation, has taken a satisfying turn."

Cleo blushed, Jarine giggled. Her return to the powerful gathering of Elders, from her translation into a body, was a completion of a cycle. Orville was her mate.

With sudden intensity, deeply troubled visions and dreams became a part of her awareness. Jarine's voice became a narrative for the fever dream.

"My sister, the future has many potentialities. You are corded in the physical to a body, that is why these events affect you so. Do we all not know that the physical plane is a world of sensation and danger when it is so far from the Central Sun? This warlike mentality is retrostorically characteristic at this stage of the evolutionary ecliptic."

"Look at Earth's recent development. It may very well be the consequence of some ancient manipulation by twisted sciences of the darkest nature. Attempts to direct the human vehicle for specific needs, created many variants in the evolutionary development of many species."

"The Dravithians and others used questionable ethics. Pain was inflicted needlessly. Yes, many things can be said, many of them burdens in the knowing, especially, when you see unneeded suffering as a result. My dear, the possibilities just go on and on, and you hold even more secrets. So, I am told."

"Orville doesn't want violence to be a part of the quickening either", Cleo sobbed. Opal tears of compassion formed around Cleo's eyes. Jarine caught a tear on her finger as she gazed into her older sister's eyes. Sparus put a hand on Cleo's shoulder. Alphonse took her hand again and spoke.

"Remember my child, the Central Sun is always here."

Sparus pointed her finger to the top of her head. "It's a dream Cleo, you especially know this. The potential to realize this is always possible at any moment for anyone. You are helping those who are ready to have their own experience."

A dove flew from a branch and materialized before Jarine, Sparus, Alphonse, and Cleo. Within seconds, a glowing young man stood among them. Deep eyes of unfathomable love peered forth from a deeply tanned face. His copper colored shoulder length hair seemed to glow as a celestial light haloed his presence.

As she gazed at him, it occurred to Cleo that he was a guardian of some sort. His form seemed to shimmer, as he shape-shifted into a series of forms.

Many Elders composed their bodies from the atoms around them. It seldom occurred since the Elders lived at a vibrational frequency beyond the need for a physical body. On the rare occasion they appeared, they often assumed forms they were accustomed to from past lives.

Gathering energy at sub-atomic and photonic levels, some had developed this power to an art form. It is taught by the Elders that every cell of the body has the potential for full sentience. Therefore, the human vehicle can be a conscious community, completely self aware and completely unified and co-creative, at the same time.

In a timeless essence, captured within a moment without actual time, Cleo observed an ascetic priest, a Pleiadian lord, and several others she did not recognize. Like flipping cards, a story unfolded. Finally, it solidified into a Tadole Priestess. Her elongated frontal dorsal was purple with white tips indicative of great age. Her large golden eyes swirled with myth and magic.

"In this form I am known as Navira," she said without fanfare.

Unvoiced questions welled up from Cleo's heart like the petitions of a prayer. The being before her was one of great power, one whom the gods pray to, and a Master among the Elders.

"My dear Cleo, your Orville will do as his conscience guides him. There is no need for covetousness. Being wed to the flesh as you are now, these concerns arise. Have no fear. Trust your intuitive faculty. I have watched over his life as I have yours."

As she spoke, her body shifted into a Tibetan woman known to Orville as Shivani Shakti. "I have been Orville's teacher; it is I who helped him gain passage to Mirror."

She shifted back to the Tadole Priestess, Navira. "My work on Navidrrr has brought its people to a critical moment in evolution. Now they will awaken to new levels of awareness. They will gain an endowment. This will also be given to the people of Earth, as you will soon recall."

"The Pleiadian adepts have been my aids on many worlds. All the children in our care must grow and change. Such is the nature of the great procession of ages. Banish all fear from your heart. You will fulfill your destiny. Drink the wine of your feelings. You were chosen for your courage and the great love you and Orville share. Go in peace."

Navira raised her hand and a ball of brilliant light appeared above the Elder's head. She began to dematerialize and was drawn into the ball. From everywhere her voice rang out. "Peace be with you."

The ball burst into splinters of light and dissipated. Rose petals slowly fluttered to the ground all around the swirling black marble floor of the pillared astral gazebo temple.

Cleo awakened from sleep. Light came in the adobe window of her small room down a garden path in Orville's domicile. She thought about her evening with the Elders. Sitting up suddenly, she discovered that her bed was filled with fragrant rose petals. A sensation of fullness erupted in her heart, as an image of Orville evoked the memory of her new found love for him.

She removed the symbi-collar from around her neck. *I will not need this contraption anymore!*

*

CHAPTER TWENTY-SIX

PLANET TATOCHIN
COLONIAL CORPORATION HQ
"Far reaching effects of Cleo's astral meeting"

Renjinn slipped into a cubicle behind his personal office. Removing his uniform, he jumped into his shower. The water slowly restored him.

Too damn dry on Tatochin.

The increased rebel activity and the preparations at the Royal Orion left him with a yearning for Navidrrr. Repressed feelings escaped from him in waves. The Tadole were self-conscious of their spiritual heritage.

His little hideaway had been fit with acoustic suppression devices he had acquired through his job. He was careful to minimize scrutiny. The noises emitted by a healthy Tadole were threatening to other sentient races. Humans were frightened easily by life forms that were more powerful. He never openly spoke of his spiritual beliefs. The profile of a Colonial Trooper is what was expected of him as a Katofar.

A methodical drone issued forth from deep in his throat sacks and resonating chambers. His ample triple chin ballooned. His dorsal fin rose up to its full height. He entered a trance as the ancient song of Navidrrr sent his awareness into the stream of eternal sound.

Gone was the striving, the need for acceptance, and the conformity of the Corporation. A Navidrrr native, a Tadole of the sacred marsh, he was a bog dweller whose voice had joined the eternal voice. He traveled with the sound resonating in his quivering throat bellows and listened for the whispers of wisdom embodied in the sacred stream.

Tonight he would sleep in his bog. Tomorrow he would once again meet the world as Katofar Renjinn and hold his fin high. In his reverie, a faint voice urged him to return to Navidrrr.

Nostalgia? he was not sure.

Somewhere in the stream of energy and sound, the brilliant Navira smiled. *The Tharrr are waiting patiently. Melkar and Zweet will be pleased. We have salvaged three to bring a birth to the great circle and beyond!*

*

CHAPTER TWENTY-SEVEN

THE KORUM, ECKSOL

Prince Kalimafar lay in his private chamber surrounded by his concubines. Their voluptuous naked bodies suitably drugged to cater to his every whim. He turned on to his back as the four women he had chosen earlier attempted to arouse him. Each sought to outdo the other with acrobatic positioning and muscle control that could rouse the dead. However, their seductive posturing could not give life.

A twilight of existence, the freakish harem had a high turnover rate. In a perverse way, it was fortunate. A long sojourn in the prince's orbit could make monsters.

The orgy faltered in cadence to Kalimafar's foul mood. He pondered the next move he could make toward forging a secret alliance with the rebels. *They need not be equals at this stage. Perhaps they never will survive. Perhaps it is best that they don't.*

Tenya entered the bedchamber to a familiar situation. She really couldn't see what the prince saw in the arousal of his sexuality day and night. There were more satisfying diversions. She had business to tend to and her prince was lollygagging around with the worthless cows in his stable.

Tenya smiled. Her pierced lip gleamed with a large sliver of silver. She flexed her tattooed muscles. *I will hasten the expenditure of his precious antidote and we will get on with the day.*

Knowing she wouldn't feel a thing, she positioned herself before the fretting prince, and summoned up an appetizer of pranic energy. It was pure photonic life force. She moved her eyes in a secret technique forming a psychic tool. She manipulated the energy field around his head. Her moist and painted lips parted as she hummed special sounds that corded with his sexual libido.

Like a serpent-headed lightning rod, the black magic technique she employed did its job with practiced fluidity. This was the kind of training impressed upon the highest degree of Dragon Fems over the centuries. The energy spell cruised smoothly down through his upper nerve pathways into his groin.

She approached slowly, allowing the prince to witness her oiled and tattooed body. Her body pierced with delicate patterns in silver, quivered and undulated in sinewy grace above him.

Knowing that violence aroused his darker fantasies, she timed her movements with the precision of a Nalakian spider bat. She jabbed him and slapped him in a manner she knew would aroused him.

The prince was pleased. His breathing pattern changed giving her confirmation. With vicious chopping kicks, she sent her cows flying off the bed. His breathing deepened and came quicker. Tenya slid his penis into her as deep as she dared.

The prince felt the convulsive contraction of pre-orgasm. Without a movement, she sent him a hot spike of energy. He bucked wildly like a downed energy cable dancing on a primal tarmac. She tightened the well-toned muscles around her vagina and used her control to extend the pleasure and orgasmic explosion to near nuclear levels.

Tenya absorbed a month's supply of antidote. Her cows would fast for a morning. They would be motivated to charm their prince when he beckoned them. *Perhaps I will kill one to convince them of the importance of doing the job well.* She was too busy to cater to the prince and his cyborg penis.

"You are ruining my play toys… Look, you broke one of their noses," the prince reached for a cigarette.

Now, I know which one will be my example.

Tenya's smile barely veiled her viciousness.

"My Prince is not pleased?"

"On the contrary, it reminds me how pleasant it is when you join the party. Perhaps you have too many duties outside my bedroom."

Tenya used every mental muscle she could muster to remain neutral in spite of the prince's most horrible of ideas. She wasted no time. His penis lay flaccid on a silk cushion fast asleep. It was important to change the nightmarish subject Kalimafar introduced.

I would like to castrate him! Tenya paused and took a cleansing breath.

The prince challenged her with his sick fixation. He was now manageable and so she set about making the necessary adjustments in her thinking. The cost might be to her very soul's survival but she didn't have time to ponder such possibilities. Her world was a prison that allowed for gross indulgences. He would be most pliable while the confounded, beached walrus of a penis slept.

Perhaps he has a psychic ability. Maybe he has a clairvoyant prick.

"Tango is missing. The flitter that picked him up also vanished."

The prince sobered up. "Tango! How long has he been missing?"

"He should have arrived three hours ago. Surveillance says the homing sensor on the flitter is disabled. It was shortly after Tango was picked up."

"Picked up by who?"

"Our intel says it is the Omegans."

"Those infidels! May they boil in the darkest hell world! First my own Arabian Charger is stolen by the dirt baggers in the park and now this."

"The techno-geeks got nothing on the sub-strata. The onboard holo-scan and pulse fax are dead. Rivo handled this one personally."

Perhaps he stops at one of the brothels before appearing before me. My spies have spotted him in the industrial areas of Ecksol…where could he be?

"Tenya, it is still too soon to tell. Send our surveillance sphere along the highway. Get those techno-geeks to do the job I so willingly pay to those wire heads! Any messages from Rivo, send to me immediately."

Tenya was pleased. Kalimafar had managed to restore some blood to his brain. "Your father has made an announcement on all the interplanetary holocasts. The Korum will host the opening reception of the Trilateral conferences at the Royal Orion. You will co-host the event with Farooq Masad."

"I know. It's wonderful! I am the crowned Prince after all! Tatochin was supposed to be a discreet exile. By the moons of Rahi, I am a child of destiny to my people after all. Like the ripened figs of the oasis, I will plan a brilliant party for the conference. It is the board of Clerics who placed themselves in exile from me! Tenya… are you jealous?"

Tenya inwardly groaned, "No, my Prince."

"Tenya, we will prepare a gift for the rebels. Contact Abbas. What better gift than some weapons?"

"I will see to it."

The prince was a dramatic social deviant. The plans with Sheik Abbas were already well established. Tango had arranged for a small arsenal to be available to the rebels. Secretly, an entire squadron of I wing Fighters were a part of the cache of weapons the Korum was about to bequeath to the rebels. Trouble was brewing on Tatochin and Prince Kalimafar rode the wave with his techno-geek infiltrations and good old-fashion firepower.

"We must prepare a plan for private security at the Royal Orion. We must have eyes and ears on the herenow and the nearnow."

"Your Father's staff has already contacted us. Rivo received a summary for your inspection. The Korum will be sending a large staff to see to our every need."

Kalimafar appeared unruffled before the naked tattooed servant. Inwardly he cringed. He knew his father didn't trust him in matters of state. Though he resented it, he sought to please his father. He would make sure that his pastimes would not interfere with the Korum's plans. His desire for power was equal to his enormous sexual addiction.

"So my Father speaks… Tenya when we find Tango you must subdue him. He was sent by my Father and must be more pliable. Do not damage him though."

"My Prince commands."

The prince ordered a bath and his assistants were summoned. His languid stroll to his bath, bespoke of his satisfaction in a morning's work well done. Tenya departed, determined to follow through on developing plans. She would sacrifice the cow with the defective nose later.

*

CHAPTER TWENTY-EIGHT

THE NEARDAK FAMILY
PLANET TATOCHIN

"Where did you get this letter?"

"At the learning center, it was everywhere. Everyone had one."

"Did you hear that, Kochen? She got it at the learning center!. Now what will we do? "Freedom fighters!"

Kochen entered the room. "It is not Corporate Conformed! This is illvibe. Shanta, you must tell no one of this," she said with a trembling voice that shook with repressed anger and fear.

"Mom, everybody knows about it. Is it true what it says?"

"Kochen, you hear how she talks? If the Corporation knew of this, we would be melted to tar! We are doomed."

Kochen rolled her eyes. "They will not melt us to tar! We don't have those tube things. Only those Omegans have them. Now stop fussing! You will scare Shanta."

Relach sat in a chair before the holo-projector waving a controller in his hand. Shanta crossed her arms. "I just want to know if it's true. Are the foods we eat, the music, and holoscans used to control us subliminally?"

"Listen dear, your Father is right, you must not talk about this. The Corporation has been good to us. We are members. Why would they do such a thing? It is just retro rebels trying to make trouble."

The pre-packaged meals were ready. The microwave emitted a series of frequency-adjusted tones as it cycled through its Corporate Conformed Monarch program. Like the proclamation of Freedom stated, the seemingly innocuous beeping sounds were modulation frequencies adjusted to cause secretions in the stomach to flow.

"Come on, the Corporate family holo is beginning," Relach tooted from his large chair.

"Shanta, take your Father his meal. I have yours. We will have our meal and watch the holo-feel. I do not want to hear another word about this letter, this proclamation of Freedom, or whatever. You're making your Father very upset."

They sat eating, eyes fixed on the holo-feel. The light of the illuminated images cast serious shadows upon their faces. Shanta didn't touch her food.

The proclamation of freedom had entered the homes of Tatochin and a half dozen other colonies in the Orion sector.

*

KORUM HQ, GANYMEADE

King Fezam placed the report from Tatochin on the ornate table. Ozinom looked on silently.

"You are sure that it is not another one of Tango's mysterious disappearances." He reached for the tiny porcelain cup of aromatic black and sweet coffee. The rum was a strong brown mash. He loudly slurped the remains with a satisfying smile and pursed his lips as was his habit before speaking.

"You confessed to me that Tango slipped through surveillance quite a few times. What am I to believe?"

"We have no proof that it was intentional."

"True, yet he is missing. Either he has something to hide, or your surveillance is inferior. This must be addressed."

"Yes, my king, I will see to it personally."

A servant appeared with a burnished copper platter. Fezam accepted a fresh tiny coffee cup and passed by the sticky sweet cakes that rested on a small dish. One of his young wives attended him, filling his cup from a delicately fashioned coffee urn. He could not remember her name.

"Thank you," he said, dismissing them with a wave of his hand.

Ozinom, the cleric stood before Fezam wearing concern on his face. He could not accuse or suggest his son, Prince Kalimafar, was implicated in any way. It would be his head if he did. He could only hope that hubris would not blind Fezam to the dangers of inaction. It was not the first time Kalimafar would have assassinated a Korum representative sent to watch the recalcitrant pervert.

Haram! This one is a nuisance!

To Ozinom the importance of these events was a crucial step. The Trilateral conference was a highly visible gathering. The Korum had worked very hard to gain identity as a separate and useful resource. Hosting the reception was like a debutante's ball for the Korum.

"It was my son who sent a flitter for Tango, it is true. They found its gutted remains two days later. We also lost a most useful operative, Shaso, at the same time. She had penetrated the Omegans and was in a critical position. Is it just a coincidence? Could the two events be linked?"

It is all too easy to blame Kalimafar. I think he liked Tango. It was no secret that I sent him to watch over my son.

"Fayed was an Omegan Corporation spy. Perhaps he is not the only one. There are so many possibilities." Ozinom offered.

Fezam was deep in thought.

Kalimafar is so preoccupied with his sex life. He is too much the exhibitionist. I will not let him or the Omegans sabotage our good fortune. He is a disgrace, son, or no son! Alas, I spoiled him. He is my son!

"We must send someone beyond all possible criticism." Fezam finished the coffee.

Ozinom produced a data crystal. "I have prepared a plan for your approval regarding the reception. Already advance teams are arriving on Tatochin. There will be much posturing and preliminary contacts to be made."

"There are deep divisions in the Omegans and the Corporation. The Pleiadians may call for sanctions against the Corporation. The UGC will be backing them. The Gaians are making a move off Earth with the Pleiadians and the UGC's blessing. There is much that could enhance our position. We must appear conservative."

"I have someone in mind. You must deliver a message in person."

"Where do you wish me to go?"

Fezam pointed to the sticky pastry made from real honey and rose water. He offered it to Ozinom who snatched it up and popped it in his mouth like a trained seal."

King Fezam sipped his fresh coffee as the cleric savored his treat. *Indeed, power can be a burden to behold!*

"I want you to go to our university. I have a message and further instructions. Now leave while I prepare my message."

"As you wish, your highness."

*

CHAPTER TWENTY-NINE

PLANET MIRROR

"Fight the battle of life or you will acquire sin"
Bhagavad Gita Chapter 2:33

"For a medical and surgical facility it's sort of homey", Lesha thought. Potted plants and watercolors decorated the walls.

A large piece of shrapnel from the exploding Lynch Café burned in her shoulder. The first signs of infection were already gestating. It had been a close call. Her side and back had been peppered with fragments from the explosion. The timing had been critical. The Matter Relocator had performed flawlessly.

Tango didn't get a scratch, the bum.

She thought about the wicked and cold-hearted slaughter in the café. *How can there be so much hate?*

Doctor Lido strolled in. He was an old friend of Lesha's. "Hi Doc, I think I need an aspirin or something."

The Pleiadian doctor looked to be in his fifties by Earth standards. Lesha had asked him what his age was. She was mildly surprised to know that it was over eight hundred years.

Reaching for the virtual goggles, he placed them over his eyes. "You look a mess! Lesha, Mollimix is illvibe stuff. It's been a while since I had to do surgery. It will be easy though. The holes are already there."

He stopped for a moment and laughed. Lido then ceremoniously continued his surgical prospecting.

"It's not funny," she pouted, "I'm leaking!"

Her last words became a whisper. He transferred her sleeping form into a isolated chamber as she fell into a induced trance. The surgical chamber sealed itself from the rest of the room. The scanner slid over her relaxed body.

The surgical chamber went through a series of adjustments. The patient thus isolated was in a pure environment with increased oxygen and a combination of highly concentrated inert gases in a magnetic field tuned to frequency generators that adjusted cold lasers to create an optimal terrain for instantaneous regenerative healing.

The chamber shifted amplitude, navigating through a complicated program linked to life sensors. The frequency generators began to stimulate and augment the process. Once calibrated, a map of her body appeared in a hologram on a projector near where the doctor stood. Tiny probes penetrated her skin with a cocktail made from fluids produced by her own body. Several hours passed before she woke up.

Lesha stood and covered herself with a silk robe. Assessing the soreness of her wounds, she was pleased to release the image of becoming a water sprinkler every time she took a drink.

Lido walked in. "All the wounds have been cleaned and sealed. There were sixty-three fragments. The most I have ever removed in a single body. Would you mind if I kept them as a trophy?"

"Sure, Doc."

"Don't leave yet. My younger colleagues, Phoebe and Zuerin, will give you an hour of energy work. Then I want you to take a day of bed rest. Lay down, they will be here in a few minutes, okay?"

"Sure."

"If all the wounds are not fully healed and you are not free of scars call me."

Lido left the room, leaving Lesha to discover her restlessness. In her innermost self, she knew big changes were happening. She had been so busy, her feelings had not caught up with her. She was mourning the loss of Orville.

Sally entered the room. "Lesha! Welcome back. I heard it was a close one. Are you okay?"

"Just a few holes. Doc says one day in bed.

"Where is Orville" Lesha asked.

"Off somewhere with Cleo, I guess."

Sally was dusting Orville's book collection.

Cleo's replacement.

A sharp chill wind blew through the office causing some glass cabinets to shake. The force of potent manifestation that was pervasive on Mirror reflected her emotions immediately.

Lesha shuddered with feelings of jealousy and betrayal. A part of her understood and even rejoiced in Orville and Cleo's union. She pulled out the symbi-collar and turned it on. Lesha twisted the adjustments in cadence with the thoughts racing through her mind. *I'm not worthy of love.*

The thought clattered in her unconscious mind. Lesha calmed herself by doing deep breathing. She attached the collar with a groan and recalled the prayer taught to her long ago.

Prana is alive in the water, in the wind, in the land, in the fire, within my soul's sheath... Shit! I better wear my symbi-collar for a while.

Tears gathered in her eyes. The words were eyes of perception offering information for her spiritual growth. She needed the extra support.

Zuerin and Phoebe appeared. "I guess we must be needed," Zuerin said.

"We felt your emotions from outside your room," Phoebe supplied.

Lesha threw up her hands, "Guilty. Do your magic girls."

"You are completely innocent." Zuerin said.

*

Orville and Cleo had escaped their duties for a few minutes. They meandered into a field of assorted flowers situated a short distance from the compound. Off to one side, three rows of beehives hummed with activity.

"Tango is safe and in detox. Lesha got some minor injuries. I am concerned, just one small mission and already injuries."

Orville sat on his favorite tree stump deep in his garden. Nelson, his youngest son from his last marriage, was a brilliant sculptor. He had carved the stump into a comfortable love seat. Cleo sat with him, their legs interlocked. In spite of the romantic setting, they were deeply involved in the work of the Elders.

It had been a busy day with meeting after meeting all over Mirror. Although neither of them now required any device to appear at any location, they felt compelled to test the up-graded technology that he had developed. Field-testing the Matter Relocator was a part of the preparations that troubled Orville.

The machinery works perfectly but I don't think I am!

It was important to be completely familiar with the targeting system accessed from a lightweight forearm-mounted keypad. The device was linked to intergalactic news summaries, and allowed for all manner of texting and communication at the level that hard-wired techno-geeks used. That was the extent of its conventional purpose.

The T-pulse technology of the Pleiadians changed all that. It was an ancient secret that had only recently been introduced to galactic culture in the last 1,000 years. Unknown to anyone else, the Relocators could be programmed to transfer matter without interference from either direction.

News had come about intense rioting on Navidrrr. Cleo shared with Orville what she knew of Navira.

"She claimed to be your teacher, too." Cleo explained.

"Shivani Shakti?"

"Yes, and several others including one who appeared to be an ancient Rishi from the last Golden age upon the Earth, a Vedic master."

Orville had lost his focus. He looked out at a field of flowers. When Cleo touched his arm he flinched and then smiled. "Sorry, I kinda drifted away."

"What is troubling you," Cleo asked him as she pushed a lock of his unruly hair out of his face.

"I think that Lesha is going through some heavy grieving at a very hard moment. All of Mirror responds to us in a powerful way. As you and I come together, the entire population is in a growth surge, a refinement of the spirit. That is why the Elders call it the quickening. It proceeds from the heart of the Central Sun outward. Mirror is the closest planet, and thus, it catches the energetic wave of the quickening first, as it ushers forth into the galaxy."

"Have I been remiss regarding Lesha?" Orville looked to Cleo with trusting eyes.

"Orville, these things take time. It's important to grieve the loss of Lesha. I am not going anywhere, and I am wholeheartedly willing to accept whatever you need to do to find the peace you seek."

"Thanks", they hugged for a long time.

A clinging reluctance to confront his misgivings concerning military and martial activities, seeped into Cleo's prescient awareness. *He is not fully committed to taking action on Tatochin.*

Cleo felt a surge of love in her heart. The mystery of the soul of this man enthralled her. Here is a man born on the eve of great changes that embodied the best of Earth's maturation. Now he is emerging as an Elder.

Bless him. He is too busy caring to notice. He has got to get through this. He won't let any of us down. But, he could cut himself off from the peace of mind that is available with alignment, and suffer in silence. Men!

Cleo phased in silence. She recognized the lure of the dream world. So, poignant and close to reality, yet not! She contemplated the love and care she felt for Lesha. A good friendship had existed between them before these new revelations. Cleo would continue to witness Lesha's process with empathy.

The reawakening of Cleo from her self-imposed amnesia, made her position as an Elder incarnate unique. In one day, she went from being an assistant in Orville's house, to a recognized Elder among the population of Mirror. Though life on Mirror was more frequently disposed toward the miraculous, it was still a rare event. The duality of Cleo the assistant and Cleo the Elder was still integrating. Spiritually united, she saw herself bound to an evolutionary surge. She was a light worker ushering in a new age in the temporal universe.

Cleo, the woman, marveled in the magic of Orville's gift; deep trust and joy grew exponentially. The apostate revelation glowed in his adoring eyes. They came together in an embrace that signaled their impending rebirth into a spiritual union that the Pleiadians call Zemplar or united parents.

They were transported by this supreme act of impeccability to a realm many dream of in the world of the flesh-bound. Individual identity did not disappear, or become traumatized in a battle to find a balance.

Nor, were they in a chloroform of romantic sentimentalism. They had incarnated many times, like most others, and used their many encounters to learn soul lessons. Wearing many different garments of flesh through time and space, they finally had reached a sacred moment of oneness. This was the fruition of many lives. Circling the great mandala of life like a comet, they plunged into the heart of creation and discovered love.

Polarized dualities quivered. The primordial crucible had been stirred. Spirit is ever in motion. It was a beginning.

As Orville and Cleo grew in their ability to translate the big picture into the "nuts and bolts" of getting the job done, the genesis of a plan of action had begun to form. The Elders had given Orville an advanced version of the matter relocator using the same technology that Orville had developed in his previous life as Ambilika, the Pleiadian scientist.

Unknown to Orville until recently, matter transport had been perfected to a level far beyond the system of portals that were still in use after several thousand years. This newer device would allow all who used it the ability to transport with pinpoint accuracy.

Orville knew that such abilities would normally not be available to most people. It had only been a hundred years since he developed the internal ability himself. It was a tactical advantage of awesome power and responsibility. The device could take communication pathways and configure suitable coordinates on a inter-galactic level. Though he could move himself to many places in the known universe using the inherent power within him, few were the numbers of people that had recovered such power.

Transporting others in this manner was difficult, and in some cases dangerous, but now science had intervened. This would allow them the stealth and accuracy to work in small numbers rather than a war with huge armies. The word hung in Orville's mind like a noose. *WAR!*

In that moment, Cleo became aware of a problem she saw. *He does not want to start a war. He is repelled. Understandable.*

Cleo saw it clearly. Orville was realizing that no guarantee of peace was possible. *Why a war? Maybe there will not be war. Perhaps less if not any…dam!*

Cleo knew he was negotiating with his denial. She was concerned. Orville had taken on a great responsibility. There was much training and preparation among the "invading" force. Frank Wilcox and his team were deploying one thousand Matter Relocators and training was just beginning.

Cleo recalled something Orville had shared earlier. It was close to a temper tantrum. She had never witnessed Orville Parker in such a state. He had compared these times to events long ago, slightly jumbled in the 400 years since they had occurred. He paced furiously across the living room floor of his cob adobe home babbling about the 21st century.

"It looks like all those movies and holos from my youth and Earth's ancient past." He had secretly hoped that such myths had stayed myth instead of being elevated to prophesy or a fascination with the past.

Not again, he cried from within.

Cleo sighed as the memlock flashed through her newly re-awakened mind. *He needs me.*

The images of potential carnage Cleo had witnessed during her visitation with the Elders flowed into Orville's thought effortlessly illuminating the already firmly embedded concern he had for the natural environment and its population.

On Tatochin the Corporation is firmly entrenched. He continued out loud. "They will not likely give up without a fight. It is hard to gauge what the total effect will be with the Trilateral Conference."

Cleo took the cue. "So you doubt our actions?"

Orville squirmed uncomfortably. "Tremador said that in creation there will always be some ignorance. I keep wondering how much ignorance I am working with. People's lives are at stake."

He looked up at Cleo. His tangled fly away hair combined with the expression on his face and sad puppy eyes made him look like a crying clown.

"I mourn for the loss of life. That it comes to this. Why must blood be spilled? What is the dam hurry!"

Cleo realized that a moment of transformation was imminent. She took a cleansing breath and placed her awareness into total alignment with the energies of the Central Sun. She felt a powerful current begin to build in a field around them. She noticed that many spirits of higher dimensional frequencies were lending temporal support in this moment. She looked at her beloved and pondered how to answer his question regarding the suffering the energies they were being guided to set in motion would cause.

Alphonse, help me. He can't hold this thought because of old emotions. Hmmm. It has to do with this endowment the Elders are talking about. It is apparently time for this to happen and we must prepare the way...

"War. That's the likely outcome, but we may be able to reduce its impact." Cleo realized that Orville needed a kick in the butt. His belief that the outcome was really under his control threatened to sap his energy and cloud his reason. She felt guided in her movements like an actor in a play. The play was over. This was just the reenactment she thought.

I need his anger now.

She took a deep breath. "This feeling sorry for yourself doesn't become you." She said coldly.

Orville was startled out of his confusion.

"What do you mean? I'm not..."

"Oh, don't waste your time defending yourself. You just don't want responsibility for loss of life... you're just looking for a way out."

Orville reeled from her scathing delivery. His Cleo had turned on him. The sky began to fill with thunderclouds. Cleo ignored the dramatic display completely. Mirror was so named for this very quality. It was, however, of no consequence.

"There has got to be a better way than violence," he shot back.

"You ignorant asshole. What right do you have to decide another's fate? It's manipulative and egocentric. Who do you think you are? God? These people are choosing their own path. Would you abandon them just because you do not want violence? Nobody wants to die. Do you worry about what others might say?"

She had to push him now. She watched him take it all in. It was difficult to see the disappointment in his eyes.

He looks like an abandoned child.

Cleo's face was a perfect mask that said; get over it, and nothing more.

"Cleo, why are you saying this? I care..."

She cut him off again. Lightning hit the ground in a rough circle.

CHAPTER THIRTY

"THE LATE SHOW IN THE FIFTH DIMENSION"

"Look around the habitable world, how few know their own good or knowing it, pursue.

Benjamin Franklin

Elders gathered in the etheric realm about them. They were quietly amused. They were fully aware of the outcome. It wasn't every day a soul like Orville would be tested at this level. They had great admiration for the Earth-born Orville Parker. It had been a long time since an Earth-born soul had risen to such an important task. Violent weather was always a metric of emotional shedding. This situation would no doubt reach epic proportions.

Cleo stood with arms crossed, her long blond hair blowing in the meteorologist's nightmare weather pattern. She sensed the disembodied spirits. *Good.*

"You think you can parade around the galaxy for four hundred years, bring people here, and welcome others sent by the Elders, do spirits bidding, and sit as judge and jury over the results. Perhaps you're no better than the Corporation! Just who do you think you are?"

Orville's face twisted in anger, his eyes darting about as the maelstrom of hail and wind whistled with growing intensity. There were too many words wanting to come out all at once. The sky was bruised purple. Knotted clouds festooned into malignant thunderheads bristling with lambent jagged lances of lightning and percussive crashing thunder.

Layers of conditioned defensive responses peeled off him like an unholy artichoke left over from the squalor of cellular imprints typical of souls who have chosen the Earth as their primary incarnational classroom.

The journey to the Central Sun had been instantaneous for Orville. Even after 400 years, some residue from the manipulations of the Dravithians and other star races still gestated within. They had been complicit in creating many layers of wounding in spite of the amazing transformations Orville had mastered over the centuries with the Pleiadians.

From deep in his gut, a thunderous bellowing howl surged forth. The very ground shook. His feet were firmly planted in the frothing mud. His hands clenched in tight fists of fury. His body quivered as primal rage and pain was vomited from his body.

"Hundreds of years of meditation down the tubes,", he screamed. "I have built a garden of Eden for my family. I have thirteen children, eight grandchildren! I buried two wives all in a state of peace! I don't see why we can't live in peace and liberty! I can. I am not perfect! Why are these assholes forcing our hand! What is the part of me that is a part of all of them. I want it to stop. Fuck humanity! Fuck the Corporation and all races that support them!" he thundered.

The power of Mirror to instantly respond to the energy generated, manifested as incredibly horrible weather. A virtual hurricane was suddenly in full manifestation. A large part of the continent was covered by a great storm that had precipitated into a global weather event.

Many souls on Mirror were aware that Orville was going through some heavy shift. A wave of healing intention came forth from the several hundred thousand souls that lived on the paradise world of Mirror. This power was a pure love, irresistible to all other circumstances.

Orville continued to howl to God and the heavens. He howled at humanity, at Cleo, the Pleiadians, and the Elders. He howled at himself. An ocean of feelings buried in the deepest part of him with all the hopes, fears, and yearning erupted from him. He was emptying out. He felt a chilly darkness lodged in a deep primal eddy of ancient memlock.

An implant upon humanity's racial memory!

In a leap of multi-dimensional revelation, he recognized the darkness as the influence of the Dravithians! It vaporized in that very instant.

A spark of calm emerged in the eye of the storm. Orville noticed new parts of himself that had been frozen with the dross of conditioning which had colored his entire life.

Liberated energy began to take hold as the conditioning dissipated. Energy committed to dormant areas of his spirit held in stasis by the calcified grooves of habit, had broken up like dynamite on a logjam.

Whirlpools of futility were cleansed and available for reassessment. His very DNA was humming like a tuning fork. It felt similar to the awakening he had experienced in the ancient cave in Nepal many centuries ago.

"I am not the doer. Only my ego thinks so," he whispered. He fell to his knees weeping. The ocean became a river. Cleo was silent. Inside she was happy. She had not betrayed her true feeling physically or psychically, or so she thought.

The she-devil, she pushed me into this.

He picked up her hidden feelings using new sensitivities. The purification of his astral body caused his whole being to rewire itself into something marvelously fresh. Orville realized he enjoyed doing just what he had always done. It was a source of great happiness to have witnessed so much beneficial change in his long life and know that he had a hand in it.

Dream or not, he yearned for peace and the preservation of life, and he knew that the Elders did too. He was determined to transmute his anger into useful solutions. He realized that the Elders had chosen him for the quality of compassion that he aspired to in his own actions.

In a brief, lucid breath he made a big decision. It seemed paltry compared to the overall transformation he had experienced. Just as quickly he dove into another ocean of feeling. Known as vortexes hindering the flow of prana in the central spine, he battled his judgments of unworthiness and futility.

I want Enro to lead this mission because he is truly a man of peace!

His weeping became a pre-ad moaning, as he sunk into the mud. The river became a lake. Fog and drizzle surrounded them. The awareness of transformation spread in him like a wave of ecstasy. Awakening had played out in a vortex of foul weather and personal catharsis.

The storm had passed and rainbows formed in a wild artistic frenzy. A shift had occurred in him at a very deep level. Transcending his current life as Orville Parker, divine memlocks came forth in his spirit. Each pearl of awareness was clinging like morning dew on a rose. The lake had become a primordial swamp.

I was created in perfection. It lives in me! It lives in all of us.

From the muck that once had been a lawn, a tentative laugh issued forth. Cleo saw the whites of eyes and the gleam of his teeth, as Orville peered up from the brown slosh. His laughter grew into great convulsive belly laughing interspersed with explosive moments of crying that would morph back into laughter. In harmony with the clearing sky, a continuous hilarity took over infecting Cleo as well. Their outrageous laughter grew as they regarded each other covered with mud.

"You devil, you pushed me, oh so perfectly," he choked out between waves of unlimited mirth.

They embraced until the mud nearly turned to clay. It crumbled off when they finally broke their embrace.

The couple stopped giggling as they sensed the energy intensifying all around them. A sudden rain began that washed all traces of the mud from their bodies. Just as suddenly, it stopped. A scented breeze, conjured by the Elders, caressed them as the warmth of the Central Sun dried them.

The ruined lawn began to shimmer beneath their feet. In a flash, it was restored to its previous pristine purity. A blooming rosebush was at the center of the area where Orville and Cleo had been mud grubbing.

Cleo looked at Orville, "that's the equivalent of applause."

Orville was emptied of many distortions of his dogmatized ego. Its crucifixion made room for the logical joy of compassion fostered by alignment with the true center within. A new awareness flowed through his being unfettered by conflicting feelings.

The release of pent up conflicting emotion ushered in the flow of practical matters, once again, into the focus of their planning. He found himself returning to the intensity of thought that the herenow required.

They would have to talk to Tango and preparation time was running out. A conflict would be inevitable.

Holding Orville's hand, Cleo gave thanks.

*

CHAPTER THIRTY-ONE

PLANET TATOCHIN
"Corporation nerve endings"

"In the beginning was true freedom. Untamed, unashamed, and unburdened."

-Pleiadian pre-ad lesson on creation

Renjinn was pleased with his brief meeting with Gentain Carbone. Thanks to Father Bodono, progress with the Centaurian upgrades was impressive to the supreme commander of the Colonial Troopers. Renjinn had managed to play down Bodono's role and inflated his own dorsal fin to enormous proportions.

The Tadole braggart was dimly aware that something was going on in the upper echelons of the Troopers. His dorsal fin always felt hot when trouble was brewing. In this case, it was fat and hot. Fortunately, there were no female Tadole around. It would have been social suicide to display his dorsal in such tones and pressures in public.

I can feel something, by the song of the swamp!

Renjinn noted that the Gentain had departed on a different ship.

The Centaurians? Stealth would be needed. It would not play well on the holocasts. I am troubled by this but for now I must play along.

It was highly irregular. The Katofar had been monitoring the intelligence from the navigation hub. Although Carbone's people had swarmed over the facility, temporarily taking over command, he had secretly added several programs to recover covert intelligence to his private station. Only Father Bodono knew he had that kind of access.

The Gentian's ship had fueled up and received clearance taking it to the Centaurian Frontier. *What business could the Gentain have there?*

Renjinn observed that it was one of those new I-Wing Cruiser class vessels. They were rumored to be faster and equipped with stealth technology not known to be readily available.

The Centaurians jealously guarded such secret technologies. First, we get Centaurian surveillance upgrades and now stealth technology. The Centaurians cannot be trusted. They will be able to subvert or penetrate anything they give us. We must modify these up-grades!

The control room was thirty feet across and shaped like a dome. Two openings led to slightly smaller dome rooms. One was dedicated to astro and trigo-navigation tracking and communication. Long range sensing arrays and galactic traffic were monitored through the Space Dock rotating around Tatochin.

All real time pulsing data could be interfaced through the COM chair at the center of the hub. It was Renjinn's com-throne in the central dome. The rotating chair had large keypads at each of its arms. He could override domestic utilities, transportation, water, and communications with the touch of his suckered digits. Any large structure on Tatochin could be gassed, blown up, or electronically enslaved. Batteries of Kelson pulse lasers and smart missiles were in strategically placed silos ranging over half of the planet.

The Corporation had maximum control over the entire settled parts of Tatochin, not to mention the Space Dock and its 24 sub-light fighting wings and light speed armored shuttles. Renjinn touched several keys causing the chair to swivel as several holos appeared before him.

Plans for the Trilateral conferences were going well. The new COM room at the Royal Orion was shaping up very nicely. He monitored the endless calibrations and data sorting upgrades, as bugs and anomalies between the two systems were rectified. The technology was marvelous. Bodono's team had been very willing to show the Tadole technical team the subtle workings of the Centaurian upgrades. Wellvibe prevailed between the two groups.

"A message from Father Bodono at the Royal Or…"

"Thanks Ostinglink, I know where it is from!"

"Greetings, Katofar."

"Father."

"Some bad news, old boy. The Korum is going to host a reception the evening before the conferences begins. It has all been approved. It is going to be here at the Orion so we need to be up and running sooner. Many off world guests will be present, and thus the need for fully operational security."

Bodono did not wait for a reply, and motioned to conclude the communication.

"Wait", croaked Renjinn. "Why were we not informed? We are already taxing our resources."

"Renjinn, we are merely the worker drones. I have no idea. Now, however, you are informed."

"What room will it be in?"

"I think the Hunters' room would be best."

"By the blood of the swamp we haven't touched that room!"

"Politics, my friend. The Korum seeks membership in the UGC. Somebody must be encouraging such events from the inside. Call me later, we'll get drunk and come up with a plan."

Bodono's words did not betray his inner thoughts. *They have entrusted me with an enormous amount of planetary control. I will use all of this against them when the time is ripe. I just wonder what the Centaurians who pull their puppet strings hope to gain. The Dravithians must be behind them!*

Ostinglink stood before Renjinn as he concluded his conversation.

"Are you going to just hop around like you need to relieve yourself with your dorsal sagging? Or do you have a good reason to turn my day into swamp fodder and ruin my view?"

"It's just that there is a pulse fax from the Korum Embassy."

"Station," barked the Katofar. Ostinglink slinked off. If his dorsal had been any lower, it would have bludgeoned his brain. Renjinn keyed up the pulse fax and read the invitation to the opening reception at the Royal Orion. His throat sacks deflated making the sounds of a farting Gruntauk.

I must palaver with that vile Prince Kalimafar. As if I don't already have enough herenow to memlock! I hate parties!

Groaning, he realized that he needed new formals to accommodate a few extra pounds. A fitting would need to be scheduled. His cigar tasted flat and the room seemed to be too dry. He gave Osterlink the COM and retreated to his private office for a long shower.

Paddling down the argon lit hallway a nimbus of light formed at the end of the hall near his door. Renjinn rubbed his eyes. The form of a Navidrrr priestess seemed to be standing before him. The religious order of the Tadole never left the steamy swamp world of Navidrrr. It was a highly unusual sight.

His cigar dropped from his mouth, sending glowing ash all about the carpet. He bent to pick it up and stomped at the embers. When he looked up the hall was empty. In his mind, he heard a voice say: *I am still here.*

Reaching for his pulse laser, he pinned himself to a wall and slid toward his door. He keyed the security lock and burst through the door falling into a roll that left him sprawling on the floor with his laser pistol tilted up in readiness. The room was empty. He gasped, as the acrobatic move he made highlighted his lack of fitness.

A priestess… by the beast of the bog!

The very fabric of creation began to vibrate around Renjinn as he lay unconscious but unharmed on the carpet by the entrance to his quarters. The Tharrr within him had made contact with Melkar and Zweet the parents of the Oblionese Circle.

At that moment, when contact was made, Renjinn had passed out. Navira, the priestess of the bog, had also returned her awareness to other matters on Navidrrr. She had precipitated the meeting to begin with. Her work was done in the herenow.

Within Renjinn the Tharrr dwelled in perfect observance. Now, while Renjinn slept the parents came forth to commune with the last few Tharrr of the previous circle. Renjinn had unwittingly received the endowment on the battlefield of Oblion. The Father and Mother of the Oblionese Circle were excited. The ability to dwell with a three dimensional life form would give them great wisdom. The pathway to grand parenthood was a cherished hope.

Zweet spoke for both herself and Melkar. "Our zoyats have risen! Much is occurring. It is how you predicted it. The destiny that you felt is about to be activated." They attuned their Zoyats to the newest mother of the Tharrr circle.

"We add this awareness to you, Tharrr Renjinn. Those that you wait for will come soon.

*

CHAPTER THIRTY-TWO
"TROUBLE ON SOBASH AVE."

"May you be born in explosive times."

Orville Parker

The drugs had worn off Shaso sooner than expected. She was building up some immunity to the paralyzing substance. Vinny would soon bring her meal. It had been a crucial mistake not gagging her. She could probably lull him with certain powerful secret sounds and make a move that would free her.

But, why?

When she thought about it, there had been numerous opportunities for escape. Something worked in her she did not understand. It was Vinny. He was unlike anyone she had ever encountered. Though he was crude and uncultured in the more traditional ways, he knew things that made her laugh, and think for herself.

I feel…I feel good around him. Good… What is that anyway?

Several weeks of captivity had caused shifts in her thinking. At first, Vinny asked too many questions. She thought back to the previous evening and felt a lump form in her throat, and tears trickled down her cheek.

"Where are you from? Did you play with dolls when you were a kid?"

"No, I set them on fire?"

"Are you being sarcastic, because that's funny. I had a stuffed verder. My aunt was appalled but I wouldn't let go of it until the stuffing fell out, and then I buried it."

"You buried it?"

"Yes, I deeply grieved."

"That's stupid."

"Yes, it was, but then, I am not quite as stupid anymore. Now, I just would roll it up into a joint and smoke it."

Shaso had laughed, and then tears had formed. She had remembered nothing of her childhood.

My real name was …Darla, I was Darla.

Suddenly, a plastic doll she had played with flashed in her awareness. She saw it surrounded by rubble. The memlock of her family home in ruins came back to her.

Dragon Fems!

They had murdered her parents and taken her away. They didn't even let her keep her dolly. They called it culling for recruits. She had participated in such operations. Since Shaso had been with Vinny, she had been having flashbacks regularly.

He always has the patience to listen, Why?

She liked the little man in the wheelchair in spite of her predicament. Stripped of her ability to use her powers, new possibilities were emerging. Thoughts she realized were once forgotten began to surface.

Maybe I'm being influenced by all the marijuana he smokes around me? Maybe its Stockholm syndrome?

She thought about the tube in her body. They had said it was neutralized. She knew that she would have melted to tar by now if it had not been so.

They said there were several implants… How could that be?

Newly restored memlocks, buried by Kalimafar's mem-washing Centaurian alpha-probe, had surfaced during her travails. She burned with anger knowing that the Omegans used her like bait. Kalimafar had been allowed to believe he had succeeded in eradicating her previous conditioning.

Shit, they are all fucking with my head.

The Dragon Fems had assigned her to the Omegans, but they allowed her to be sold! Her contract to the Omegans had been a sham. Kalimafar had discovered that she was bugged for surveillance. He had taken counter-measures.

Vinny understood about the cesspool that was brewing in the Korum Mission in Ecksol. He wouldn't give her details, but she now knew that he was not who he seemed to be. This was a great relief. Vinny promised that she would not be given back to the Korum. Shaso dared to hope. A feeling she had not even entertained for many years.

Vinny had lost many comrades, along with his legs, because of the Troopers and the Korum. He spoke to her often about the rebels and their attempt to take back the planet. She wanted to take her life back. It had been a long time since she had thoughts that were independent of her training. Shaso liked what was happening to her. However, the memlocks were excruciating.

The whores! I am a person, not a pawn!

She sensed traumatized areas of her inner landscape still too bruised and twisted to enter. In her confinement, she had time to think and remember. Wheelchair Vinny came twice a day. He would sit there in his armored assault vehicle of a wheelchair, puffing on Menthol Rastas in a blue cloud of stinky smoke.

Shaso realized that her reality, a precious part of her true self, had been closed off to her through advanced mind control techniques. Memlocks had been selectively erased, and in many cases, filled with substitutes that allowed the oppressors to mold her into something that was worth more in their eyes.

The intense training the Dragon Fems had imposed on her young mind combined with mem-washing and programming from every direction, had begun to crumble. The Omegans, the Korum, and the Dragon Fems had created some serious goulash inside her mind. It was coming back to her in layers, like overlapping, dark, and fetid shadows.

Vinny knew that she was still dangerous but something was changing. He prodded her into berserk extrapolations that caused painful sores around her wrists and legs, which he carefully kept bound.

"Now stop your fussing."

"Fuck you."

Vinny was madly in love. Yet, he buried his desire in clouds of blue smoke, secretly mourning his ruined body that could never express the man he was on the inside. After those sessions, he would carefully tend to the sore skin that she had ripped open around her wrists. Shaso would feel responses in her body to his gentle touch.

At night, there was noise coming from the garage where Vinny worked. Transport flitters pulled up at odd hours. She could hear muffled voices and the sounds of gravity forks loading the cargo. Her super fine senses identified petroleum esters and the markers of high-grade explosives.

It must be the rebels.

She shifted out of her phasing upon hearing the hydraulics that powered the door below her. The garage was the main entrance to the loft. Her keenly trained Dragon Fem ears picked up the smooth whirring electromagnetic engine that powered Vinny's special chair. She began to do a special blood enriching breathing technique to focus and build her power. She heard Vinny enter the elevator.

He will be here in a few moments. Welcome home honey…Oh shit! What am I thinking? I feel strange…

She felt great power and spectral images from her forgotten past. Shaso felt like she was in a trance. Something new and pleasant came over her. She felt heat emanating from her chest. The Prana Bindu technique taught to her from the time she was a pre-ad was having an unusual effect upon her. The Dragon Fems had modified it from ancient Yoga and martial arts disciplines. She took three very deep breaths and broke the electromagnetic locks that bound her hands. The door of the elevator opened. Shaso hid her now free tattooed arms behind her.

Vinny rolled up near the bed. "Tonight it's Slag Burgers and Mosh Tettero." He pushed another button and a drawer on the side of his chair slid open that contained the bag of food with the seal of the Corporation on it. "Its been neutralized…sorry I am not much of a cook."

"I have to use the toilet," she said.

He pushed a button and her leg cuffs snapped open.

"Keep the door open." He navigated his wheel chair with a joy-stick on the arm rest. He followed her to the cleanse station keeping the hand laser trained on her with his other hand.

"I suppose you find this interesting." She said as she sat on the toilet.

"I am just doing my job."

"You get off on it, don't you?"

"What if I do?"

Shaso pulled her arms out and showed him the broken cuffs.

"If I wanted to make trouble I would have. Now, please give me some privacy." She shut the door.

"Women!"

She sat on the toilet and smiled. He left her alone. She could easily subdue him. Any number of strategies scrolled through her martially trained mind.

But to what end? Where would I go? I've been out of the loop for too long. I would never find my way out of interrogation. I am bargaining. Why?

Tango had done her a favor getting her out of there. She kept wondering why. As she sat on the toilet forgotten memlocks of other children flashed into her awareness.

Brothers and sisters… I'm not sure.

She strained at the trail of energy they seemed to leave behind. Vinny's voice startled her back into the herenow.

"What are ya clogged, or something?"

"Can't you let a Dragon Fem shit in peace?"

He laughed and reached for a pack of rastas, and lit one of the elongated conical sticks. The pungent smoke curled around and hung like an apparition in the still air of the converted industrial loft.

The lack of activity had slowed her metabolic processes. She felt bloated. It occurred to her with a start, that she had been taking a drug to quell her body's natural menstrual cycle for years. Now, in its absence, she was ovulating.

"You could have killed me. Why didn't you?" He asked as she left the bathroom.

Shaso bent over and kissed him deeply. She felt something new. She didn't like it. It felt weakening. Yet another part of her urged her on, and their lips mashed together in an almost violent kiss. They spent the night together pleasuring each other and learning each other's bodies.

Vinny had not really talked to any woman with personal sincerity since Oblion. An aching desire to love simmered within him. He had been damaged in the war. He could not get an erection. Those parts had been nearly obliterated. When he had told her, she grew silent.

In many ways, she was the same. Though she could perform innumerable sexual gymnastics and bring others to orgasm through psychic stimulation, she could not remember when she had a natural feeling of desire for a partner. She confided in him. They found a way. Later they talked.

"None of the Dragon Fems can get involved." Tears formed and slid down her cheek. She had not cried since she was a girl.

"Why didn't you make your move," he asked.

"I don't really know…"

A bond had formed. The Corporation, the Korum, and the Omegans had raped them both. They kissed again. This time it was softer. She lowered herself onto his lap.

"Something has happened to me. The Dragon Fems, The Korum, and the Corporation all fucked with me. They used me and shit…. Well now after all our talks and everything I am seeing all that from a distance. I have escaped all of that. Fuck, I feel like I haven't got any skin on but you make me feel safe. Fuck! Fuck! I don't know what I am saying!"

Shaso burst into tears. For several minutes she cried with incredible intensity. Drool and tears poured forth. Vinny produced a towel and wiped her tears in silence. Finally, she sighed, took the towel he was still using, and tossed it aside.

"Do you have any of those rastas in a non-menthol variety?"

"Sure."

He fished around in several compartments and produced a cone of cannabis. He lit it for her, and she took a deep inhalation that mingled with the perpetual cloud that surrounded Wheel Chair Vinny. Shaso was not very good at it, but managed a crooked smile.

Vinny's face lit up with delight that turned to a slight frown.

"I'm sorry you are a prisoner. Perhaps better times are ahead."

The building suddenly began to shake. The keening whine of a Corporation transport shuttle accompanied the shaking. Shaso jumped off his lap. Vinny's fingers danced on his console. A holo window appeared before him. A Corporation tactical Globe had landed in front of the garage.

"They finally found us," he murmured, deep in thought.

"Us, do you mean me?"

"No, well maybe but I have been funneling weapons to the rebels. I just emptied the place last night. However, I still got a bunch of shit around. We gotta get out of here."

The holo showed troopers in auto-armor pouring out of the battle globe. They were fanning out in a perimeter around the building.

"I think we need to get out of here now!"

"Shit Vinny, you've got to have a plan, or I don't know you. One thing for sure, its no time for a honeymoon."

*

KEANE ST AND SOBASH AVE

"It's becoming a regular sight down on Sobash," said the taco vendor to the swill mopper, as he handed him the two tacos with extra sauce in a bag stamped with the logo of the Colonial Corporation.

The security of knowing it was indeed Corporate Conformed meant little. The bag was gruffly torn asunder despite the subliminal suggestion that you were some kind of Centaurian insect if you littered. The wind blew the bag into the gaggle of Troopers who evaporated the door to Vinny's warehouse with a laser cannon.

*

VINNYVILLE

"Shit, there goes the door." The holo window on Vinny's wheel chair captured the charge from the Kelson pulse laser, as it lanced outward from the portable weapon. The holo blinked out.

The illvibe word spread down Sobash Avenue all the way to Keane Street. The industrial zone of Ecksol was turning into a staging ground as more Metropol flitters arrived near the tactical war globe. Several Orbital I Wings, launched from Space Dock, hovered just above the buildings.

In the Corporation control room, a cigar smoking Tadole frog was sliming his keypad in support of the special operation to uncover the source of the rebel's supply routes.

"The fucking brain police are torching wheelchair Vinny's place," the Taco vendor told the runner, who quickly disappeared into the thickening panicky crowds of pedestrians. He would report to a gang boss that did business in the neighborhood.

Vinny looked at Shaso, "I'll give you a choice, you can come with me and live, or you can make a go of it alone. I got friends on the street. I am going to activate a series of bombs that will turn this loft to powder in minutes."

Shaso thought, *That's the second time I've been given a choice since my capture. Funny how it never feels like one though...*

"I need some clothes. I must hide my Dragon Fem identity: from my arms, neck, to ankles."

"In the closet." He tossed her the laser pistol. "Here, pack this, I'll get some extra charges."

Vinny went to a cupboard that had a false back and opened it. A panel with a series of numbered buttons was mounted on the wall. He punched in the codes Tango had given him. It activated the self-destruct for the buildings.

To one side of the cupboard, two high-powered pulse rifles with collapsible stocks were mounted. He grabbed each one, and loaded and locked them. He opened a side compartment on his wheelchair, and tossed out a full day supply of chilled Moorhead beer with a forlorn sigh. Then he stuffed the cooler with weapon charges and the compact rifles.

Shaso donned a black iridescent jumpsuit and a flight jacket. She stretched her body and limbered up as he concluded his business. The arm mounted Matter Relocator, that belonged to Tango, sat on its charger, when he shut the door. It was left behind.

The elevator brought Shaso and Vinny down to the tunnel below the warehouse. They rolled up to a wall. From above you could hear Troopers storming the garage. He pressed a button hidden beneath a tunnel support. A door slid open revealing more tunneling that sloped downward. The smell of sewage, earth, and moisture enveloped them.

"We got to jam. Most of the explosives are down here. If we do not put some distance between us and the building we will be dead and buried."

Shaso jumped on Vinny's lap sideways. "I guess this means you're with me," he said.

"Let's see what this buggy can do," she said.

They sped down the tunnel. Though the danger made the chances of escape rather slim, Vinny was elated to speed down the cobwebbed tunnel with the Dragon Fem, Shaso, with whom he had fallen hopelessly in love.

The tunnel continued but he stopped at a door after about a half a mile down. Shaso felt more moisture. The tunnel looked less modern. The walls looked ancient and covered with mineral deposits and the beginning of stalagmites and stalactites.

"What's down there?"

"Right now water, lots of water. Later... we'll see."

He pressed another panel and waited. "I got some homeies on the other side of that door seal. They gotta check us out first."

Shaso stood quietly pondering her situation. She realized that for the first time in her life, she was free. As the panel slid open, she recognized a large hulking male who had carried her through the scanner that had isolated the implants in her body.

"Wait here, okay?" Vinnie rolled forward into a garage and was having an animated conversation with the others. He rolled back over to Shaso. "It's too risky to use a ground car.

Metropol has checkpoints everywhere. The whole downtown sector is closed down. We will wait and leave by other means."

"Other means?"

"Yes, we have other ways to move around."

"What's with them?" Shaso indicated the four people who stood off to the side staring.

"They don't know why you are here. You're a Dragon Fem; they know it. There is reluctance."

Shaso knew full well how feared the Dragon Fems were. She caught herself in a realization that she didn't identify herself as a Dragon Fem. Her time with Vinny had changed her into someone new. Someone she was just getting to know.

Vinny took a deep breath.

Time to change things. She could take us all out. Somehow, I know that will never happen. Shit, here I go!

"This tunnel is an older tunnel. It is filled with water but soon it will not be. Then we can escape to the Planetary Park boundary and...beyond."

"So this is how the rebels get in and out?" Shaso asked.

Vinny looked into Shaso's eyes. He blinked with the power of the exchange. He had revealed a secret that could be leverage. It could even vindicate her exile. The rebels had evaded detection because of this secret. She would be rewarded for such information. He trusted her. It was completely crazy but he didn't care.

She smiled at him and watched him light up like a light bulb. Her Dragon Fem senses told her of his attention. She found herself feeling almost demure and naïve. She had never felt like this before. A word materialized in her mind. It was a word that seemed to melt like butter onto her frozen heart, a word that until then had meant a person who was about to kill her, nothing more. She savored the feel of it. The warm feeling she had felt in her chest earlier, returned. She felt it spreading and discovered something new. She knew what it was in a flash and found herself suddenly holding back tears.

Love and happiness!

Just beyond reach, she detected gallons of hurt. It seemed to loosen, threatening to completely dislodge and surface. But, in that moment, she knew that her life had begun a new chapter. She looked at the funny little war hero in the wheelchair. Something warm penetrated her soul.

I love you, Vinny.

A horrendous explosion suddenly shook the foundation of the warehouse more than a half a mile from Vinny's place. "That's a few less Colonial Troopers to deal with," Vinny muttered to the other rebels. They let them in and sealed the door. The big guy spoke within earshot of Shaso, as his eyes looked at her deeply.

"We are filling the cave for a few hours. SatCom advises us on planetary sensor sweep schedules."

Vinny silently nodded.

CHAPTER THIRTY-THREE

SALVINGTON HIGH WORLD

"Look around the habitable world, how few know their own good or knowing it, pursue!

Benjamin Franklin 17th century

Bishop Jones sat at his workstation writing in his journal:

Ripples of tension flow through the governing denizens of the Omegans. The Colonial Corporation points their fingers at the Omegans. The Omegans point their fingers at each other. The modus operandi during such travails is the age-old art of passing the credit. Obstreperous factionalism is replacing decades of languorous rhetoric.

He paused sipping his Bancha twig tea. Journaling always had a cleansing effect on him. Thoughts about Pope Hurus' dangerous gambit surfaced within his mind. He was surprised and pleased that Hurus had arranged for a large gaggle of interplanetary press to converge on the military base for a press conference along with his so-called surprise inspection.

They will be his armor against any assassination attempts.

With the Trilateral conference looming on the horizon, a revolt in the upper echelons of the Omegans could easily fuel the already unstable colonies into unflagging revolt. Hurus had deflected such a turn of events and saved his own life as well. More important he had put an important wedge in the Corporation's plan to squash opposition within the Omegans.

We must just watch our backs.

The Bishop sighed and returned to the screen that contained his private journal:

I believe the rebels are more organized than perhaps they even know. The similarity of uprising, protest, and general acrimony toward the Corporation in Orion defies every measure taken by them or the Omegans on their behalf. Unseen forces are at work. This same sagacious force imposes itself within the Omegans as well.

The image of casting off his robes phased through Jones' mind. He longed to cast off the mantle of leadership and prune an orchard or take delight in the growth of children, to revel in the politics of a neighborhood rather than the intergalactic conquests of greedy illvibe retros! Bodono! He is the best choice, he thought.

I will miss our weekly meetings!

He returned his attention to journaling:

The powers of government are rushing to quell the winds of change and evolution. It is clear that psycho drugs, media induction, the firepower of Colonial Troopers, as well as, rigid legislation and enforcement, were no match for nature. Life is its own master, intelligent and unerringly progressing toward the light.

Hurus wanted Father Bodono to represent Omegans at the Trilateral conference. The perky Father was busy preparing the way. The official purpose of the press conference was to announce just that. The strategy of using the military base for the press conference created a balance to delicate forces. It also put a check on any unfortunate accidents that might have occurred.

The assassination secretly ordered by Gentain Carbone had to be scrubbed by Kaitain Majaiya. Too many eyes were upon them with the onslaught of press. The press was always eager for a juicy headline for the evening holoscans. Hurus had manipulated and orchestrated the entire flow of events. He was a survivor.

Why do I really go to Tatochin? Jones wondered.

His inner senses told him it was a one-way journey.

*

The holocasts across the Orion sector that evening carried a summation of the speech Pope Hurus gave on Salvington High World. Bishop Jones was designated officially as the Omegan representative to the Trilateral Conferences.

The reporters, who were no more than puppets for the Corporation, told the anesthetized audience that Planet Navidrrr was in such rebellion and illvibe that a peacekeeping force would be necessary. The deployment of two Tritons of commandos on a peacekeeping mission under the command of Kaitain Maijaya was to curtail the rebellion.

Scenes of burning buildings and troopers with faces mangled by the corrosive spray of angry Tadole, flashed in a montage of images. The holocaster summed up events on the steamy world like it was act one of an action adventure holofeel.

No mention was made of the other rebellious planets in the Orion sector, or why the Tadole were so angry. No one questioned the presence of a huge Corporation invasion force that would soon arrive to subdue and occupy the planet Navidrrr.

It was reported that the Corporation sought to bring peace to the planet without explaining why there wasn't peace in the first place. The populations took it all in stride. They were conformed and entrained to believe.

A commercial break followed that announced new lower rates for Corsair passage to systems that were hundreds of light years from the Orion sector. The lowest rates in decades!

*

Bodono stood before a mirror after a long visit to the cleansing station. As he toweled himself, he regarded the area over his right rib. The wound was knitting quite well. The nefarious tube removal from his body was a great comfort to him. It had initiated a ticking clock, counting down to his eventual permanent exile. Soon he would wear the robes of an Omegan no more.

The holo of a cherub materialized before Bodono as he showered. The cherub held a tiny harp that it strummed getting his attention.

"Father Smith has arrived, the hologram spoke.

The hologram was an impressively life-like miniature. He could select another avatar, or switch it to a voice only mode, but the cherub felt delightfully friendly.

Bodono quickly slipped on the Omegan robes and opened the door for Father Smith. They made formal greeting and Bodono led Smith to his balcony which offered an unblemished view of Lake Wechen from eighty-six floors up.

Hundreds of sails were dancing on the white tipped waves glistening in the sun. Departing the scene, Bodono returned with a tray stocked with coffee and an ample amount of cinnamon rolls.

"A good idea to meet out here. The air is good, the view distracting, and our voices are not being heard."

Smith sipped his coffee, eyes closed, letting the elements into him. Bodono watched the Omegan priest intently.

"I heard you have a passion for cinnamon rolls. These are the Orion's version."

"Your intel is accurate. Alas, I may go down in retrostory for my weakness for the sticky buns and nothing more."

"Is that your concern? How your life will appear in some archive?" Bodono had thrown down a gauntlet. He wanted to know what made Smith tick.

Where did his loyalties lie?

Smith opened his eyes. Bodono's stark, grave form offset by the rich blue sky seemed to Smith like a bird of prey searching for its meal. He smiled.

"So we will have no small talk, and speak directly," Smith said.

"Retrostory is for carrion eaters who live vicariously through other's deeds," said Bodono with calculated intention.

"I really don't give a fig about retrostorians. The cinnamon rolls however are worthy of a bookmark." Smith said with equally sincere intentions.

Bodono chuckled, "Why do you suppose Bishop Jones asked you to let Arafad Tango X, the Korum ambassador go?"

"With the Trilateral Conferences coming up, it is prudent not to rouse passions, especially someone like Kalimafar." Smith finished off the cinnamon roll.

Bodono decided to test Smith. Telepathy was the quickest way to make a determination. The effort opened empathetic doorways to a highly trained master of the art like Father Bodono.

"*Such topics can find true resolution only through more subtle means. Do you have this ability Father Smith?*"

Smith knew Bodono would test him. He was hoping for such a moment.

"*There are many of us who felt displaced with the yoke of the Corporation around our necks. I think that answers your unspoken question.*"

He continued out loud. "The Korum may be arming the rebels. We think Arafad Tango X is involved. The flitter incident gave us enough justification for an overt move. That's all."

Smith stared at Bodono as the vulture came down from his perch.

Bodono was pleased to know that Smith was not a creature of the Gentain Carbone or Corporate managers like Delaney. The Omegans on many worlds had become something the populations feared for their arcane power rather than looked at with any admiration or expectation of genuine spiritual guidance.

As an Omegan, he had dealt with the widening schism within his own group for a long time. Tatochin had been a backwater planet of little consequence until a few years ago. The trouble-makers of the order had been assigned to Tatochin to keep them out of the way. A short term solution, and just as shortsighted. Bodono realized that the seeds of rebellion were close to the surface on Tatochin.

Smith continued unprovoked. "The Tatochinians are easily roused; we must not add fuel to the already simmering fires of dissent. The propaganda letter called the Freedom Proclamation has spread fast. It was handled with an expertise equal to our own resources."

Switching again to telepathy Smith continued, "*I suspect the proclamation was penned by one of our own. A revealing document; it is wellvibe and choice to have gone viral in the herenow.*"

Bodono was amused and flattered. He also realized that Smith was cueing him in on the likelihood that their conversation was being overheard by watchers.

"It was circulated in the entire Orion sector as well as colonies in the old world," Bodono informed him. "It has created quite a stir. I haven't been following it."

Father Bodono's thought message to Father Smith was in essence a super polarity. "*Your instincts serve you well. I am the author of this document.*"

Smith was quietly stunned. Father Bodono was a dangerous man he realized. He felt the cold of the tube buried in his flaccid flesh and shuddered. He realized that Bishop Jones and the Pope himself were involved. "*What is your game, Bodono?*"

Pieces began to fit together in new ways. Smith began to see larger connections as his emerging awareness of the divisions in the Omegans took on new and expansive meaning. In an attempt to recover his balance, as his thoughts raced, he poured some more coffee into his cup. Bodono understood the process Smith wrestled with.

"Are the rebels that organized? Or do they have secret allies?" Smith managed.

"There are many who would benefit by the demise of the Corporation. Situations like this highlight these sentiments. We must remain vigilant." Bodono's steel blue eyes bored into Smith's.

"*Shaso was a spy for the Korum, however she was a double agent working for the Omegans. She did not even know! We could not let you know this until we were sure of your loyalties.*"

"*If that is true then why did Tango take her?*"

"*We do not know, however, we suspect Tango is not who he seems to be.*"

Smith resumed the audible conversation cloaking the important and relevant communication.

"How can we insure a peaceful conference without an insurrection?"

"Perhaps a meeting with Delaney would be beneficial. The proclamation addresses issues that are in his area."

"You mean the Monarch Protocols?"

"Delaney just holds the contracts. The Corporation has its own people tending to that unholy fire!" "*We have secret information that Delaney is involved in racketeering and price fixing. His family has a large fleet of cargo corsairs. They have gotten preferential treatment for years. Should the need arise they could be at your disposal.*"

Father Smith struggled to keep up with the Bodono. Switching from mind speak to audible with such rapid fire pacing would challenge all but the very best and highly trained Omegan priest or Grand Dame. "I will arrange for a meeting right away. Perhaps he has some insights about the proclamation…

"I have placed a data crystal on the table here. It has a full breakdown on Delaney's "other" business interests as well."

Father Smith nodded and smiled. *"Perhaps insurrection is your goal?"*

"I look forward to talking again after the meeting." It was Father Smith's turn to look deeply into Bodono's eyes.

Bodono smiled gently and then sent: *"If the Omegans are to survive we must take back our fire. It remains to be seen where our true allies are."*

Their meeting was over. Smith was exhausted. A psychic as powerful as Bodono would often have that effect on a less trained mind. With some effort, he sent another telepathic message: *"You can count on me, Father Bodono. I am bone tired of the Corporation and their arrogance.*

*

"THE FREEDOM PROCLAMATION"

ALL LIFE FORMS SENTIENT. THOSE WHO DWELL IN THE COLONIES, A VOICE OF WELLVIBE KNOWLEDGE SPEAKS OUT FOR YOUR BENEFIT AND THAT OF ALL LIFE. TREACHERY, DECEIT, SUPPRESSION, AND ILLVIBE ARE LOOSE IN YOUR WORLD. I SPEAK FROM KNOWLEDGE AS ONE WHO WALKS ON BOTH SIDES.

THE TRANSGRESSORS ARE MANY. IN THIS HERENOW WE SPEAK OF, THE COLONIAL CORPORATION AND THEIR PUPPET MASTERS, THE CENTAURIANS, ARE THE MOST RETRO. THEY SEEK TO ENSLAVE OUR PEOPLE ON BEHALF OF THE CENTAURIANS. THEY ARE A GREAT THREAT TO OUR LIVES, AND ARE ILLVIBE.

HERENOW, REBELLION AND STRIFE OCCURS THROUGHOUT THE ORION COLONIES. YOU DO NOT HEAR OF IT BECAUSE THE CORPORATION DOESN'T WANT YOU TO. EVOLUTION AND FREEDOM ARE CALLING. THROW OFF THE YOKE OF THEIR CONTROL. DO IT IN THE NEARNOW!

THE FOOD YOU EAT IS FILLED WITH CHEMICALS THAT SEND A BIOLOGICAL VIRUS INTO YOUR BRAIN AND NERVES. IT IS PUT IN THE WATER. YOUR AIR IS LACED WITH AEROSOLS USED IN WEATHER CONTROL. THEY ARE CALLED HYPNOPLASMIC DRUGS. THIS VIRUS IS GENETICALLY ENGINEERED TO ACCENTUATE AND RESTRICT NEURAL PATTERNS. THE RESULTS ARE USED IN CONJUNCTION WITH SUBLIMINAL SUGGESTIONS PROGRAMMED BY THE CORPORATION THROUGH MEDIA INDUCTION, HOLOCASTS, AND AUDIO TRANSMISSIONS.

EVERYTHING YOU HEAR, SEE, BREATHE, OR EAT HAS BEEN ALTERED BY THE CORPORATION TO CONTROL YOU. THE CHEMICALS STUNT THE MIND AND INHIBIT THE BODIES REGENERATIVE ABILITIES. THEY CONTROL POPULATION

AND POLICY BY KEEPING YOU CONTROLLED. THIS PROGRAM IS CALLED THE MONARCH PROTOCOLS.

DO NOT BELIEVE WHAT YOU READ. TEST IT YOURSELF. TURN OFF THE HOLOSCANS AND STOP EATING THE CORPORATE FOOD. GO HUNGRY IF YOU MUST. THE VIRUS MUST BE FED TO BE EFFECTIVE. SOON YOU WILL FEEL THE DIFFERENCE.

THE CHEF IS THE CORPORATION AND THEIR FOOD FOR MIND AND BODY IS DESIGNED TO KEEP YOU ENSLAVED. THE CORPORATION WAS FOUNDED ON EARTH. THEY ARE NOT ALLOWED ON THEIR OWN HOME WORLD. ASK YOURSELF WHY?

YOUR DESTINY IS TO FREE YOURSELVES FROM THE GRIP OF THE CORPORATION. THINK, FEEL AND GROW WISE MY FRIENDS. THE NEARNOW IS CALLING. YOU ARE CHILDREN OF THE LIGHT. YOU ARE DESTINED TO DO GREAT THINGS. LONG YOU HAVE LIVED IN THE DARKNESS. NOW YOU COME CLOSER TO THE LIGHT OF THE CENTRAL SUN. IT IS TIME FOR YOU TO HARVEST THE BENEFIT OF YOUR LONG JOURNEY.

LIBERTY THROUGH STRENGTH! BE WELLVIBE.

SIGNED: A FREEDOM LOVER

*

CHAPTER THIRTY-FOUR

"BAR-BE-CUE"
PLANET MIRROR

"There's no time for subtlety anymore. The rebels are well armed and the people are roused. I'm in favor of breaking cover and establishing our link with Enro right away. I will go directly to their camp." Tango's voice was steady and filled with resolve.

"It will be your resurrection," Orville mused.

"It's a risk, but the café is fresh in their minds. We can use it to our advantage." Arafad Tango X paused to sip the rich amino green beverage. He stifled a gag and dreamed of a cold beer.

Orville nodded knowingly. I know its not on my menu at a bar-be-cue!

They stood on the back patio of Orville Parker's adobe home. The location had been the front office for many of Orville's recent decisions. He was a man who detested formality in any way. The casual setting of a bar-be-cue, among a few close friends, in the middle of his personal domain, was deceptive when one considered the importance and ramification of the meeting itself. The nearnow of Tatochin and life in the Orion sector was at stake. Blood could be spilled.

"I think we should go together." Orville calmly replied.

He looked over his yard and smiled.

For so long I have basked in this inviting realm. The Elders gave me time to have a gentle connection with this land. Time, more valuable than gold! The nearnow will be a time of awakening. I am a fortunate soul. I feel so much! So much!

Orville looked at the near horizon of the verdant yard he had tended by hand. He was grateful for its knowledge. He thought about the cycles of the plants, changing with the seasons.

Death, compost, revival. Is it the same for us? Is death just part of the cycle? Yes, in the end it is. We are attached to our sense of importance, or perhaps, we are impulsed from a compassionate love that hides behind the manifestations so alluring to us.

He sighed thinking about all the people he had loved. Like a very long animated holo, the faces of wives, children, and friends flashed through his advanced DNA matrix. He gave thanks for the evernow he had lived; thanks to his wellvibe Pleiadian brothers and sisters.

Cactus and rose bushes co-mingled in a surprisingly pleasant way around the modest, yet roomy domicile. The garden meandered along a small stream. The landscaping varied in flora further into the yard.

Scattered guest cottages were tucked into quiet little corners of the four-acre compound. All around, berry plants graced beneficial corners giving their fruit to those passing by. The smell of bar-be-que filled the air. Bird song softened the gaps between the words and sizzling shrimp.

Orville checked the status of his grilled adventure harvested from the nearby ocean. They sizzled on his wood-fired grill. He looked up at Tango several times, their eyes burning with epicurean passion.

The Elders don't like me to eat shrimp but I just can't resist the occasional delicacy. I bow to the little spirits whose life I have taken.

Orville broke the silence. "I agree we should go together. We need to be there when the Trilateral Conferences begin."

Tango tried another sip of the special Amino brew Cleo had conjured. He gagged slightly with the effort. He looked at his drink and put it down.

Orville grabbed a bowl and stood over the grill and spoke with mock intensity. "The secret sauce." He placed the marinating vegetables on the grill and painted the little critters, who had sacrificed their lives for the ritual bar-be-cue.

"What's in it?" asked Tango. He took another tentative sip of the special drink Cleo made him. He gagged on the mint, wheat, and parsley-flavored pond scum. He had been taking such potions for days.

Holding up his glass, as if in a toast, Tango commented, "Eating an occasional carrot was not enough, Doctor Lido told me."

Orville fussed with the shrimp as he sought to collect his thoughts. The inevitability of a confrontation with the Colonial Corporation was coming. It was not the first time. His unflagging resistance to the Corporation could have consumed his life had he not embraced the multi-dimensional awareness that the Pleiadians had helped him to realize.

He remembered that Tango had asked him about his sauce. "Regarding my marinade, it's a crossover between Italian, Japanese, and Hawaiian… along with a special vegetable grown on Trappest One. Oh, and something the Tadole use… I think… I'll never tell." Orville finished turning the shrimp and sat on a comfortable wooden chair with a sigh.

Passing by his own glass of healthy swamp swill, Orville grabbed a beer. "The Korum will be furious! You were in the public eye. Kalimafar benefited by that since he was so irredeemable himself. The Corporation knew of the foiled meeting with Flexington, Enro's man. They will be in trouble."

"They already are."

"The rebels only know you as Kalimafar's minion. That won't win you any popularity contests."

"I suspect as much, however, by the time the situation becomes clear we will have broken the back of their power grab." Tango licked his lips as he thought about Orville's beer.

"I admire your positive belief. Such things, however, are not good for blood pressure! How is your detox anyway?"

"Orville, I have been eating Corporate food neutralized by those infernal devices. No hypno-plasmics, but Corporate food has been modified. Doctor Lido informed me with way too much detail. I am a toxic cesspool waiting to explode into disease. He told me my terrain has been weakened, and that my liver needs about twenty supplements, and that's just the liver."

Orville let the cold organic beer slide down his throat then jumped up to check the shrimp. "I hope these shrimp won't kill you!"

"No, carry on, Orville." Tango jealously eyed the cold beer that Orville cradled in his hand. "From what I have experienced, the Korum was the only group that wasn't after me before the café. We have pushed everything along toward a confrontation. If not now... when?"

Tango had thought about this a lot while resting and cleansing his body and emotions. "I belong to a fraternity with you and Enro. The incredible exploding life forms!"

Orville laughed heartily as he roasted some vegetable on the fire. He stirred the pot of Mosh off to the side of the sizzling grill.

"I suppose your right. It's funny, I never thought of it as a pattern, but it is interesting."

He thought about the day that he left Earth for Mirror so long ago. The explosion at Colonial Mining had destroyed his old lab. Many people had missed him. He had a moment of sadness at the thought of hurting anyone's feelings in spite of all the good that had come from it.

I hid my activities by faking my death on Earth. I helped Enro do the same thing on Oblion. Now Tango is thought dead from Lesha's rescue in that café on Tatochin...Boom, boom, boom. Hey, I think Lesha is part of the club. She had a lot of mollimix lodged in her loins!

"It's been a stressful year; I could use a little tune up." Tango guiltily placed the swamp juice down and captured a bottle of beer deftly thrown by Orville.

He reads my thoughts but respects my privacy...except when it comes to passing me a beer!

Orville continued after the beer delivery. "It's true. I highly recommend radical measures to change the patterns in your life. There are many wild stories among us here on Mirror. I abhor violence, but I don't see that we can completely avoid it."

Tango nodded in agreement with Orville. He had endured too many unnecessary deaths trying to maintain his cover with paranoid and impulsive Prince Kalimafar.

"If anyone can minimize losses it would be Enro. You know how he feels about that," Tango said.

"Let's wait for Lesha and Cleo before we continue this talk," Orville said. He removed the cooked shrimp from the grill into a ceramic serving dish, and sprinkled the sticky browned shrimp with a blend of spices and herbs from his garden.

Orville looked like Doctor Orvilstein with his wild hair and sprinkling of herbs. "They are still cooking. It's the hot pot that cooks them. I just seared the spices. Am I crazy?"

"Yes, you are". Tango phazed to more serious subjects internally. *What about the situation on Tatochin? What of Vinny and that Dragon Fem, Shaso? If I died to that life, there could be loose ends!*

Tango realized he would have to be very careful about exposure. Lives were at stake with every move.

"Hand me the tamari sauce, and take the pot of Mosh to the table, will you?" Orville took his bar-be-cues seriously. Sally appeared on cue with a colorful salad.

"I think a bottle of Salvington wine would go nicely, Sally."

"I have two chilled already." Sally placed the salad. "I will fetch it now."

"Thanks Sal." Orville turned to Tango as Sally departed. "Let's hide those green drinks or Cleo will make us drink them."

Tango felt right at home. Stealth and intrigue was his calling. He tossed the ample remains into a nearby shrubbery just as Cleo and Lesha arrived.

"I brought a fresh pitcher of my cleansing brew." The two men groaned as Cleo and Lesha glanced at each other knowingly.

"Look, they are drinking beer!" Lesha addressed Cleo in mock surprise.

"Orville, this will damage your holy man status!" Cleo exclaimed.

"Nonsense, besides from what I hear, Lesha is the holy one."

*

"A Domicile of Tranquility"

Tango tossed in his sleep restlessly. His dreams were dark and forbidding, robbing him of wellvibe rest. The faces of stress, abject squalor, and the scream of the dying souls vaporized in the Lynch Café, clung in his mind. They taunted him smoldering like the spent skin of molting Andarian Quaziflems in a tangle of dried Honnaberry thorns.

The universe smelled like the rancid grease pouring out of corporate food dispensaries. The imagery shifted but the menacing images continued to parade through his inner landscape. He sat up and jettisoned a metallic bit of sputum. The obnoxious toxins were released in response to his intensive detox. His inner organs were heated with effort. The Pleiadians had perfected natural medicines for thousands of years. Doctor Lido was a living example.

Dr. Lido was nearly 1000 years old. His detox was ongoing. *Maybe it was Orville's mystery shrimp. Spicy!*

Though he rested, the pace of life had quickened on Mirror. The plans the four were formulating began to take shape. He smiled briefly as memlocks of the bar-be-cue clicked like the tumblers of a lock in his mind. On one hand the realization of potential action was compelling. The other hand was more of a caress. Lesha was the central nexus of his musings.

A hidden treasure and the last tumbler that unlocks the door. I am swooning! He sighed for a moment then began to cough up another dose of phlegm from his activated system.

Many souls would now mobilize. Tango felt the buzz and glow of unmanifest energy on the verge of entrance into reality. The bar-be-cue had been called as a planning session but it had meandered into something different. Planning had been put off to the next day after only a short discussion. An exact time had not been set. But, they had all agreed with Tango's call to action. That is as far as the planning session had gotten.

Tango thought of Cleo and Orville. They were like the Pleiadian Zemplars he had met on several occasions.

United souls…Trippy voodoo!

The combined power of their growing union was a potent presence, a language without words. If you just could breathe with it, a force would build within, seeking expression.

With a start, he united his scattered thoughts into a deeper understanding that was trying to manifest in his awareness. His energy was drifting towards Lesha, whom he had always respected as an impeccable warrior. Lesha, who had saved his life at great risk. He knew that she had covered his body and taken the shrapnel from the laser cannon that destroyed the Lynch Café in that god-forsaken neighborhood in Ecksol. He considered the fact that not too long ago she had been Orville's consort. He struggled with his attraction. *Why, Lesha?*

Lesha! A warm glow reverberated in his chest. Love was blooming in his heart. Her sleek muscled body, angular features, and fine-tuned athletic body rippled into his imagination. She exuded health and vitality that was hard to ignore. The memlock of her firm breasts pressed against his back made his breath quiver.

Tango fantasized about loving her. He felt the heat gathering in his groin, as if he was a wolf howling at the moon. How could he possibly sleep with constant thoughts of her?

I want to have a garden like Orville's. I want children running around with animals, relishing the natural world. I don't want to be a warrior anymore. It will soon be time for a permanent change!

Mirror was an environment of potency, which amplified his experience exponentially. He turned over in his bed and stared at the stars outside the window. Tango thought about the last woman he had loved. *Angie!*

That was how he had come to Mirror. Their bond had been as friends and warriors. They were pirates in arms that made love like animals. It was a love of sorts. It had solidified into a friendship long before they ever parted ways. However, Lesha was a different feeling. It was deep in his gut. He went to the toilet to relieve his bladder.

In a curt way, Lesha had signaled her interest in him. This was her nature. During the bar-be-cue, her strong fingers had stroked his back and rubbed the tautness from his shoulders. They digested Orville's dinner, talked about Tatochin briefly, and sipped the mint-flavored goulash Cleo had so thoughtfully replenished.

Lesha had sat close, intentionally. He felt the flow of energy from her, and saw the glow of her body. She let their bodies touch during subsequent conversation. He could smell her and feel a tingling all over his body. Orville continued to talk shop outlining some ideas, but Tango's mind was on Lesha's presence. Cleo had picked up on it. Orville stopped talking and smiled at Cleo. They seemed to share a secret.

"Let's call it a night. The stars are too pretty for words," Cleo said.

Cleo and Orville silently walked out in the garden leaving Tango and Lesha alone. They held each other and kissed before turning in for the night.

Tango finished pissing in the toilet, while phasing like a cat prowling for a female in heat. He stopped his imaginings to listen to the insects and the sounds of the night. A clear night revealed a star-filled sky above the cottages.

He wandered to the sink to fetch a glass of water. From the window above the sink, he could hear the trickle of the stream. He sipped some water and looked out over the garden.

The small stream meandered through the compound separating the adobe cottages. Across the stream, he noticed the flicker of a candle coming from Lesha's place. The Japanese bridge with a blooming fig tree cut dramatic angles in the space between the cottages. Lotus flowers crowded around the bridge, their white flowers closed for the night. Her shadow crossed the soft light in her window.

She is still awake, as well!

He closed his eyes and imagined her pale green eyes so steady, serious, and yet warm. His imagination conjured his growing attraction into a golden cloud flowing from inside of him to her. *I must be crazy to feel this way with all I must do.*

Then like an acrobat, he was floating in the cloud once again. A brushing sound brought him out of his late night musings. He opened his eyes and saw Lesha standing on the bridge, her eyes seeking him out in the starlit night. Tango was there in moments. The energy of Mirror was ever charged with the manifestation of focused thought.

It was some time later that they both knew, they would never let go. They seemed to be upon the bridge for eternity. Finally, Lesha let out a girlish giggle. Tango stepped back and realized he was stark naked. He had forgotten completely. Such is the nature of love.

The stream trickled in harmony with a barbershop quartet of frogs. Faintly in the distance, a hushed bit of laughter seemed to drift in from the main house. Orville and Cleo were not yet asleep either. Magic had replaced nature in some unspoken manner.

An owl added a well-placed accent with its cry. Insects droned forming synchronized crosshatches of texture. Lucid lips caressed each other. Their bodies pressed close, filling empty gaps, as darkness gave way to early light. Dew clung to their bodies as they crept to their nest where they joined in conjugal heat. Married for eternity; no outer ritual could touch the sacred moment that had been conjured. Arms and bodies tangled in bonded bliss, the lovers slept in the womb of delight.

*

CHAPTER THIRTY-FIVE

"CORPORATE MALAISE

John Delaney's fist slammed down with a dull thud. The gray Mollimix desk did not feel a thing. The hand would probably bruise. It was a well-manicured hand, watery with many lines. His fingers were narrow and long. He could easily reach the bottom of a cookie jar.

He blinked off the pain. Mild guilt roiled just beyond the range of his conscious thoughts. Such emotional displays of illvibe could be suspicious. The Corporation discouraged such retro behavior. He quickly composed himself. The watchers might be watching more carefully now.

Too much contraband food. If they tested me, I would be arrested!

He didn't want anybody to look too close. They would discover just how low the hypnoplasmic receptor levels were in his body. The payoff to falsify revals wasn't too steep. John memlocked his father's advice to him: "Dedication, ambition, and belief were the key ingredients for the Delaneys to prosper."

John's dad had raised his children on contraband food and severely restricted their use of corporate media. As they got older, he explained, the will-dampening effect.

It was the family wealth and position in society that enabled them to do what they pleased with relative impunity. The Corporate ethos was one of superiority in terms of entitlement due to genetic pride, or financial wealth. The Delaneys owned a large fleet of cargo corsairs that handled a choice portion of the interplanetary shipping in the Orion sector.

Though being a member of such a prestigious family, John chose to embark on a separate career from his father and brothers for strategic purposes. He had cleverly advanced to the position of the President for the colony of Tatochin. Nevertheless, in spite of his upbringing, he was living in fear.

Taking a deep breath, he contemplated his crumbling world with two months to go before the Trilateral Conferences had even begun. Intelligence reports from Renjinn on illegal weapons seizures were grim. The rebels were getting bolder and their targets more sophisticated.

Kalimafar... the worm! I wonder if this propaganda piece that's showing up everywhere is his doing.

Pulse faxes had appeared in nine different planetary systems across the colonies of Orion reporting rebel activity. The Corporation was being challenged in many sectors. The rebel groups were becoming more cohesive.

The Delaneys had courted the favor of the Corporation. Now he questioned the wisdom of that policy. Even more complex was their alliance with the Omegans. It filled him with illvibe and fear.

Now these damnable Omegans are here. I think we should do away with them altogether. Smith! I've never trusted the man. He's a nuisance!

He looked out over downtown Ecksol from two hundred stories up. The sun of Tatochin was just rising over the Tshini Mountains. Fishing boats were returning from a night of fishing. It was a clear day, but black clouds hovered at the edge of his awareness.

A layer of smog hung in the air above the squalor of the street, a product of the rapid growth of factory processing plants servicing agricultural industries. The family farm, once the mainstay of Tatochin for many generations, was quickly disappearing. It was only in distant hidden valleys far up in the Tshini mountains that some natives still clung to the traditional culture of pre-Colonial Corporation times.

My Father still sends agents up into those hills to obtain real food. We must carefully guard those sources!

No one knew better than John Delaney how debilitating the conformed food actually was. One of his jobs was regulating food processing. The Corporate Tatochin grown food was showing up on members' tables throughout the Orion planets. The additives that were used were poisonous and extensive. Profits were high.

He had been so successful, he feared the jealousy of other climbers. The politics and diplomatic maneuvers within the Corporation were an irritant to him. He preferred the less ostentatious profile of an executive doing his job quietly behind the doors of industry. Government was for the more hard skinned. He would retire to the private sector soon.

Now propaganda was directed toward the food processing industry. He was no fool. His position as president was only symbolic. His job was to make sure the population remained quiescent and conformed to Corporate policy. Tatochin made the Corporation rich because it controlled the agricultural industry. He thought of the herenow buzz surrounding the proclamation.

They actually mentioned the Monarch Protocols! Mind control is a sensitive subject. That must really be raising some eyebrows. Shit, that's illvibe!

"Why are they looking to me? I just make the stuff to specifications," he said aloud to the empty room.

He had inquired as to whether there would be adjustments in the additives. So far, he had not heard a thing. That was as far as his responsibility went.

John went through the faxes that scrolled across his holo-projector jammed with reports on visitors arriving for extended stays before the conference. He read Renjinn's summaries and the extended files on each person, and then routed the information that was designated to various analytical workflow units. Those summaries would be sent back to him later, but he flagged a few for inquiry as he scrolled through his work load.

Gaian observers, what are they doing here? They have remained Earthbound for centuries. An Omegan representative from Salvington High world.! Good, this Bodono is a troublemaker. Maybe someone can clip his wings. Good, its Black, finally someone of actual consequence!

The Omegans had contacted Delaney concerning Cardinal Black. There were divisions in the Omegans. Without directly saying so, it had been intimated that Black represented a different faction. Father Smith and the Orion Parish leader, Bishop Jones were loyal to Pope Hurus. Father Bodono was a good friend to Jones according to the intelligence he had memlocked. He noted that Bodono had a consort; a certain Dame Chandri who was supposed to be a dangerous psychic.

Trouble! Worse than Dragon Fems, I think!

Rumors had been circulating about a new Korum representative. The disappearance of Arafad Tango X was all over the holocasts. The Korum had leveled accusations at the Corporation, but they had failed to offer any proof. In the meantime the Korum was clearly positioning itself to benefit by the Trilateral Conferences. His father and family were preparing for a tough negotiation cycle.

Renjinn had information suggesting that the diplomat had been seen in the downtown sector near where the Lynch Café had been destroyed by Colonial Troopers. They had been searching for a Tatochinian rebel, but they reacted too soon.

The Corporation was searching for a link to throw the investigation onto another track. So far, it was a mystery. The Korum had been trying to gain a larger market for their vast shipping empire in the colonies for years. Any leverage they could use to gain concessions would be utilized. Delaney's loyalties were clear. He had been careful to remain disassociated from his family business by working through intermediaries.

Delaney continued to clear his desk. He picked up a copy of the Proclamation of Freedom and reread it. He groaned and threw it down. The letter was the herenow buzz on the street, the office, and the home, though nothing appeared on holocasts. Delaney feared that it only strengthened the proclamation's claim. He had suggested that the Omegans circulate several other fictitious letters to lessen the importance of the real one.

The holoscan illuminated his secretary. "Father Smith has arrived. Shall I call security for an escort?"

"Just one escort. Unarmed." *We must appear transparent to them.*

Delaney finished reading Renjinn's security suggestions for the influx of VIPs while he waited. Inserting the crystal in his pulse fax, he sent his approval to Renjinn's private station, and then took two aspirins for his pounding head.

*

Unbeknownst to Delaney, when he sent his pulse fax to Renjinn, it showed up in several unauthorized locations. Rivo, Kalimafar's security chief, croaked with delight.

Although Bodono and Renjinn cooperated, the Omegan priest had decided to make sure that Renjinn was the warrior he claimed to be. Time was short and Bodono needed good information to navigate the treacherous waters that lay ahead.

Bodono had hacked every important database on the planet. He discovered in the process that Kalimafar's techno-geeks had hacked into several systems as well. Bodono subsequently hacked into all of their systems.

*

The gaunt priest was taking a shower enjoying the unlimited water use that was legendary on Tatochin. His cherubic holo avatar flashed before him. "T Pulse on a secured channel."

"Display level four intercept, hmmmm."

While Bodono rinsed the shampoo from his hair, he read the holoscan that appeared in the shower as a semi-transparent window. The new Centaurian upgrades could be marvelous fun. He resolved to hack the hackers once he was through with his extended shower.

Smith and Chandri are meeting with Delaney right about now... Hmmm. Cardinal Black will arrive tomorrow. He is the Kaitain Maijaya's creature. This should be interesting. When the Corsair docks, I will greet him at landfall.

Bodono continued his shower.

*

Father Smith, Dame Chandri, and a bodyguard headed for an elevator and ascended 132 floors into the middle of the building. They strode quickly down a long hallway, their black travel robes billowing.

An escort showed them into the executive offices that was also the presidential wing. After many twists and turns, they finally arrived at Delaney's office. They stood before the colony president looking like silent owls, with razor talons hidden behind folds of sheer fabric.

Delaney was always uncomfortable in the presence of Omegans. Despite his precautions, his mind wandered to the potential for the Omegans to use their weird mind tricks. He felt unsafe and uneasy.

"John, this is Dame Chandri and Brother Feinstein. John Delaney."

John inwardly cringed. The telepath was to his left, identifiable by the absence of white collar on her robe.

Chandri! The psychic! Shit!

They all shook hands. Delaney noted that Brother Feinstein stood like a martial artist. He felt the calluses on his hand that had been conditioned to be weapons.

"Please be seated." The Omegans removed their travel robes to reveal simple loose fitting black garb of shining material. Some small talk ensued about weather and harvesting operations while they settled in their chairs.

Delaney went to his desk and lifted the proclamation into his hand. "I called you here to discuss this propaganda. It is arousing the people into doubt that none of us can afford."

"Is this real coffee?" Smith's interruption was calculated.

"Yes, it is, and there are cinnamon rolls as well. We heard it was your favorite."

"My compliments on your intelligence gathering."

Delaney was thrown off balance. Chandri gazed at him. He could feel the presence of someone pushing up against his thoughts. He cleared his throat.

"The letter has come at an unfortunate time with all the extra activity preparing for the conference," Smith speculated while he stirred his coffee.

"What are the Omegans doing about it? The central office of the Corporation on Tatochin contacted me. They want herenow resolution in maximode. They say you must take action."

"Why don't you speak to the people and reassure them, John. After all it is your job to keep the people under control, isn't it? You are the president, are you not? Why don't you use your drugs and media induction to stop it? Is it not your job to add those poisons to the people's food to keep them subdued?" Smith threw it back in his face.

"They are not poisons. They are additives approved by the IFA. I don't know where you have heard such things. Surely, you do not believe the content of this proclamation of 'deception.'

They refer to Monarch without compunction. Dangerous!

Delaney wondered with whom Smith's loyalties aligned. It was clear that this was not the faction to be discussing this with, but Smith was the man in charge until Cardinal Black arrived.

"That is the problem, Father Smith. This kind of incendiary propaganda could create civil unrest. A military move could backfire on us. These so-called freedom lovers test our system but they are a small group."

"I've made the suggestion that several phony proclamations be introduced to the people to complicate the matter. Confusion will defuse the situation. I received no reply from your office."

"I have read the surveillance reports from Katofar Renjinn. Something must be done." Smith replied.

"Ah, but something is being done. The Omegans are sending Cardinal Black. You haven't heard?"

Delaney should have known better than to think that Smith would not know of Black's arrival. He was feeling defiant.

"This is not the place, or time, to discuss the inner workings of the Omegans and the Corporation."

Smith stared at Delaney until the executive was distracted. He said nothing allowing the president to stew in the juices of the Corporation's illvibe.

"We cannot have open rebellion," Delaney said.

Father Smith pounced on the word rebellion. "Did you ever ask yourself why? Do you think you can completely control people's lives as a Corporation? Retrostory will prove you wrong every time."

Delaney was frightened. He did not even want to be in a room where such un-conformed dialog took place. The words this priest spoke were as illvibe as the letter. Was this fool unaware of the watchers?

"Your family is in the shipping business, is it not?"

"Yes, I don't see what that has to do with the situation in the colonies." Delaney did not like the direction this conversation was going. *These damnable Omegans… play with your mind.*

Chandri let out a small laugh in response to the president's thoughts. Feinstein shifted in his chair, his face a mask of remoteness. The hairs on Delaney's neck rose.

Smith pressed on, seemingly oblivious to Delaney's growing discomfort. "The ability to accommodate the ever-changing requirements of living is how we prosper and advance. One group cannot always anticipate the needs of many diverse people. It is that inflexibility that led to the banishment of the Corporation from Earth. I suggest that there is a double standard."

"What do you mean?" Delaney's heart began to skip a beat. This was not going as planned. He detected the slightest smile on Chandri's lips.

"Inside information can be used to secure large profit and limit a free market."

"Is my loyalty to the Corporation in question?"

"No, loyalty is a good word here, however. The Delaneys have controlled a large block of shipping contracts in the colonies for many years. It is uncanny how they have been able to negotiate contracts and keep other anxious traders at a distance, augmenting growth and prosperity for the Delaneys."

"I assure you…"

Smith interrupted with the wave of his hand. "I understand that the Korum, though competitive in many ways, has not made much headway when it comes to major shipping contracts. You must understand that this information is known to a highly restricted group. Your intermediaries have long been in our employment. We are not accusing you. We have encouraged you all along. It is time to let you know that you have allies that you were unaware of."

Delaney was reeling. He had allies he wasn't sure he wanted. His mind raced. Black was due to arrive any time. He needed a life raft. This information could mean the demise of his career. He had been reduced to a pawn in a game he did not want to play.

Delaney had been the good son to his father. The family coffers were full. Delaney shipping commanded many corsairs across the vacuum in the Orion sector. Smith was relentlessly dismantling Delaney's false sense of security and immunity.

"We have long known of your loyalty to your family, John", Smith talked in fatherly tones.

Chandri had heard enough. Bodono had been correct to leave this task to Smith. It was proof that he could be trusted. He was enjoying himself. She silently watched Smith maneuver Delaney right where he wanted him.

"We allowed you these concessions because it insured your loyalty to us. We may come for our just payment for our silence. We are not incapable of protecting you."

Delaney sat in his chair stunned, one pulsing raw nerve. He worried about the watchers. He could be replaced in an instant.

"Come, come Delaney we would not risk that," Smith said, easily reading his thoughts. "The watchers are our people. John really, you should try one of these cinnamon rolls, they are simply delicious."

*

THE ROYAL ORION

The sun was setting over Lake Wechen. The water stretched to the horizon. The vast sky and distant clouds filled the view. Bodono and Chandri stood before the full-length window watching the wild colors of distant clouds as the sun played upon the golden waters.

Bodono poured some of the fragrant, rich, and woody Tatochin wine into two glasses as they walked into the bedroom. It had been a long day and they were tired. He handed one to Chandri. They clicked glasses.

"To Father Smith," said Bodono.

They drank. "Perhaps our Smith should have a fencing accident before he gets himself melted into a cinnamon roll," Chandri said, curling her legs under her on the bed. "He must have the tube removed. We should see to it immediately."

"Yes," replied Bodono refilling his glass with the amber nectar. "I will see to it, and now shop is closed. Come to me, Goddess of the moon."

*

CHAPTER THIRTY-SIX

"VANGUARD"
COLONIAL CORPORATION HEADQUARTERS

The monitors went blank, static appeared on the surveillance hub. Just as suddenly, everything was back to normal.

"What in the name of Vichilla was that?" Renjinn growled.

Astro-navigation showed a commercial Corsair had come out of plus-light speed in the planetary jump space sector of Tatochin.

Renjinn's throat bellows deflated making loud hissing trumpet squeaks. *The last jump was from Salvington, probably full of Omegans!*

"The Pleiadian-made engine may have disrupted the microwave transmission beam," Ostinglink croaked.

Renjinn was distracted by the arrival of the Corsair. The increased activity allowed the glitch in the system to be largely ignored. The sensors in the COM room oscillated from ultrasonic to a bowel-wrenching subsonic whir.

To the arriving one thousand passengers, the de-acceleration to sub-light speeds produced various jolts. The null-field generators strained as the massive freighter maneuvered toward the Space Dock above Tatochin. Renjinn sat on his COM-throne observing the arrival of the Corsair. The data link sent a torrent of information flashing before him. *Good, a perfect chance to test the upgrades from landfall to the Royal Orion.*

Renjinn lit a fresh cigar. Cargo manifests and passenger lists flashed before him as the Corsair linked in. "Of course", he murmured, "the Gaians".

The passenger list flashed before him. He reached his hand into the virtual holo and flagged the ones that would require closer observation. This was transmitted to the station at Landfall. Renjinn's golden eyes quickly scanned the data as he made mental notations.

Martha Fox: diplomat at large for the Gaian government. Interesting. A UGC representative from the Trilateral committee of sentient life rights, Heidi Roth. Could be trouble. Cardinal Malcolm Black: Omegan liaison for the Colonial Corporation from High Salvation. I hear he is a dangerous human.

The computer started to flag others based on the criteria Renjinn had established.

Sheik Abbas, the arms dealer. Standard scum… Farooq Masad! One of the foremost members of the Korum. Wow, this Corsair has been all over the place.

Other names associated with the Korum were part of his entourage. Mildly unusual activity, but with the impending Trilateral Conferences coming up, the unusual was becoming the norm. The press had been authorized to meet Farooq Masad.

More trouble for me! Dam the Korum! They just will not go away. And now, by the blighted bog, they are hosting the opening reception!

From his com-throne Renjinn watched a cam revealing the pressroom at Landfall. It appeared to be ready to receive Farooq Masad. Miniature holo-cam drones buzzed around the podium like gnats. The crowded press area was filled with inter-galactic press also just arriving for the extensive coverage anticipated by the Trilateral Conferences.

Troopers guided the Korum dignitaries to a side entrance and a green room. Suddenly, the screens in the surveillance hub went blank again.

"What's going on with the system? I want a diagnostic! Ostinglink!"

Ostinglink, the Tadole assistant, inflated his throat bellows in fear; he couldn't find a thing. Just as suddenly, the systems came back online, as if nothing had happened.

"Perhaps some debris came through when the Corsair came out of plus-light. Sometimes garbage ejected before a ship jumps to light-speed gets trapped. When it comes out the particles proceed upon the last trajectory at just under light-speed. It can disrupt signals depending on what material…"

"Enough! Check with the Royal Orion and see if that glitch happened there as well. Back to your station," Renjinn growled. He had no time for such useless speculation.

The glitch actually cloaked a shipment of weapons the Korum had secretly provided to the rebels. It was on its way to high Mountain Base undetected by the Corporation's surveillance net. The smugglers' ship had a very rare technology provided by Centaurion smugglers on the black market. They remained invisible and electronically protected. Carefully, they entered the grid just behind the massive Corsair.

*

"Landfall, Tatochin"

The spaceport was busy with many more corsairs docking daily in response to the coming conferences. The commercial promenade at Space dock and Landfall was receiving guests from hundreds of worlds. Tatochin and its corporate culture felt bullish, as the corridor to the Royal Orion swelled with their arrival.

Farooq Masad made his way towards the central terminal. His handlers had informed him that a press conference had been organized by the Korum Mission and would be held there in a conference room.

The Korum ambassador, Farooq Masad, had traced his ancestry back to old India, though a native of Ganymede. His great-grandfather was a Nobel Prize winning scientist, Narayan Ahmel Masad. His pioneering work in biochemical terra-forming had garnered him galactic acclaim. He was among the first people of Earth to be recognized for his contribution in the post-contact culture at the end of the 21st century. The Pleiadians and the Gaians revered him with honors.

On Ganymede, Narayan, the central city beneath the bubble, was named after his illustrious ancestor, Narayan Masad. This technological marvel of a habitat, was home to one of the top university cities in the galaxy in biological research and development. It was first teaching center provided by Pleiadian Terraformers. Many descendants of India, Pakistan, Tibet, and Russia lived there. It was also a stronghold for the Korum.

Farooq, a staunch member of the Korum, was well known to many cultures. The Masad family was famous and wealthy. The Korum and many other worlds regarded them with great honor, as well.

He was more of a social scientist, unlike his illustrious great-grandfather, grandfather, and father who had been biochemical engineers. They had all followed in Narayan's footsteps. He took after his mother, Lelung Masad, who was deeply involved in the formation of a fair and workable galactic society.

Farooq had come from a family rooted in love and spiritual clarity. The Sufi household was one of passion and brilliance. The fruits of the transformative activity of the whirling Dervishes, and years of meditation, rested at the core of his being, and flowed from his lips.

Farooq was valued by the Korum and a national treasure to the citizens of Ganymede. Even his detractors recognized a greatness that flowed like the wide river from his heart in contrast to the vapid seasonal streams of ego and opportunism demonstrated in other leaders of the time.

A man beyond his years in wisdom perhaps centuries, it was no wonder he was noticed by the Elders and Orville Parker. He was currently unaware of it, but he had a role to play on behalf of the Elders.

The reports given to Masad on Prince Kalimafar were not surprising. The prince had done well negotiating situations to improve revenues, but besmirched the reputation of the Korum due to his large and lecherous sexual appetites. Indeed he had been exiled to Tatochin, so scandalous was his personal behavior.

As hosts of the opening of the Trilateral Conferences, the Korum chose the most well known representative to charm the UGC. This was a major political victory for them. With the Royal Orion and the Planetary Park, Tatochin was fast becoming the getaway playground, and focus of many conventions and meetings. It was no longer the exile that had been intended.

Though Farooq Masad's position in the Korum was due in part to his famous ancestor, he had led a life of service to the greater good. Secretly despising the class and caste system that brought him his position, he stayed out of the dangerous waters of ancestral governance. With this assignment, he was up against certain strictures that rankled him.

Kalimafar was untouchable beyond a certain point. The squabbling of Bedouin kings still ran through the Korum like rancid halvah. Fortunately, Farooq was sent at the behest of King Fezam, Kalimafar's natural father. Farooq Masad pondered King Fezam's words to him regarding Prince Kalimafar before he had departed Ganymede.

We must clip his wings a bit to make him presentable.

*

The Promenade at Landfall was buzzing with travelers. In a small café, the craven form of Father Bodono leaned over his steaming Cappuccino. Piercing green eyes stared out from his starkly bony head. He watched the Korum entourage stream by. Dame Chandri, Bodono's consort, waited beyond the security barrier to meet Cardinal Black and his assistants.

"He comes," Chandri sent to Bodono. *"Two assistants."*

Black had picked up the communication and sought Chandri. His dark eyes bored into her with a psychic probe of the most powerful level. *"And so, it begins! Chandri, what's this? Moon goddess, how quaint."*

Cardinal Black was an expert in interrogation. The powers of his mind were more reliable than any device ever used. They were not a match for Chandri. He reeled with the power that came from her presence. With a jolt of pure feminine energy, she focused her mind-altering will. He became disoriented. A wave of unrestrained voltage heated his internal nervous system. He found himself, unexpectedly, sexually aroused.

Chandri smiled. Her training as a Tantric initiator had many side benefits. She would only use a technique like this for self-protection. In contrast, the Dragon Fems used similar techniques to control their quarry.

The feeling of safety and self-assurance gave her a psychological freedom earned in the crucible of compelling training. It also was useful to confound the intrusion of other psychics. The Tantric lessons had far less to do with exotic sexuality and more to do with the activation of the human body to its full and rightful heritage.

It was, at times, sad for her. She found it difficult to live with a state of awareness to which many were simply asleep. It could be quite revealing when involved in the affairs of the Omegans. The probe Black employed with his psychic muscles was reduced to a neap tide, paltry and paranoid, compared to her sense of reality.

He found himself thinking defensively. Something he wasn't used to. *You bitch, I will deal with you in other ways!*

Not sure if his thoughts were sufficiently shielded, he erected psychic barriers. His face remained in a neutral and placid expression, as Chandri approached him.

"Most honored, Cardinal. Father Bodono sends his greetings, and invites you to tea while waiting for transportation to the Royal Orion."

He hides his discomfort of me quite poorly. He fears me! I will not reveal my knowledge of his transparency.

As Chandri gave the formal greeting, Black's two attendants placed themselves in a martial stance before the woman. They sensed the mental joust at the periphery of their awareness.

Black waved them away. "We would be honored to sup with the good Father, lead the way."
She must be a Tantric Dakini! Good control.

Bodono knew of Black's talent as a psychic interrogator. Omegan training schools had trained postulants quite thoroughly in the process of erecting the mental barriers to remain opaque to such onslaughts of mind probing. This would not suffice for a trained weapon such as Black, or a fireball like Chandri.

Bodono lurked as a light presence to the mental battlefield. He smiled to himself. *The she-devil will confound him!*

Bodono recalled his days as an instructor. As the wave of Black's mental probe touched Bodono's mind, he smiled inwardly. He could tell instantly that the Grand Dame Lilith had taught Black, as she had taught him. *Chandri already perplexes him, of course.*

The black robed Omegans took their seats in an empty area of the café. "I notice that we both trained with Grand Dame Lilith," Bodono said.

"Then you know that your loyalties are not the same as mine. I should have guessed that my brother, the illustrious Bishop Jones, would send such a minion to do his heretical bidding. You have such an arrogant expression on your face. Have I offended you?"

The tone had been set.

*

Sheik Abbas waddled down the terminal noting the security patrols that were transparent to his educated eyes. He saw the gaggle of Omegan priests in a café, and picked up his pace for a few moments. *Better to stay clear of that bunch of infidels!*

The Sheik knew he was being watched, which was fortunate indeed. A good alibi made his purpose easier.

Kalimafar and his techno geeks had hacked planetary surveillance at two key moments. This would allow his largest smuggling freighter to drop out of plus-light velocity, in a different trajectory, at the same moment, and remain undetected. Moments later, the process was repeated to pass through the planetary grid. From that point, they would proceed to the rebel base and unload I wing fighters and numerous other advanced weaponry.

With the payment that was the equivalent of two years income, he would vacation at the Royal Orion and attend the Trilateral Conferences. He looked forward to the Prince's entertainments.

The prince has promised me several special female servants to attend me. Nice! It could be a very interesting conference with all those new weapons the rebels will soon be receiving. Business has been good lately.

Conflict was always a good thing for weapons smugglers. Salvage possibilities would be excellent, if something were to happen. The Corporation had many more weapons, but he had no loyalty when deals could be made, no matter which side. He could fetch good prices on used weapons, whatever the outcome. He decided to deepen his connections to the rebels, and make inquiries about local salvage operation contracts.

Perhaps some more credits would be made? Now I want a female for a most pleasurable evening. The swarthy merchant fanaticized.

*

KORUM MISSION, ECKSOL

Rivo, the Oblionese refugee, monitored the arrival of the Corporation Corsair at Space Dock on a moon of Tatochin. His flat triangular skull twitched in anticipation. Alone in the room he relaxed. He keyed in a secret sub-routine that disabled the security holo for the room. Subtle apparitions floated about his head. The Tharrr was revealed.

The multi-hued eddies of ethereal plasma discharged in wisps of cloud. The cerebral ocean of expectation expressed itself in holographic manifestations. It was the Tharrr's primary language. He knew that it would evoke terror if anyone ever witnessed it. His Tharrr nature was a well-guarded secret. Rivo was one of several Tharrr from Oblion and the only one in an Oblionese body. He was the remnant of a nearly extinct race. Oblion was destroyed by the Corporation, a thought never far from Rivo's awareness.

The Tharrr had given him a vastly new perspective that allowed him to cope with the devastating loss. The community of Tharrr was a vast intergalactic group of souls that both dwelled within him and all around the galaxies. The feeling of belonging to something greater, had gained ascendancy in his general awareness of self.

He thought about the Tadole, Renjinn, the security Katofar for the Corporation. *Soon we will meet Renjinn…Soon.*

The Tadole would play a central role in bringing forth a new circle. Rivo had been told as much by the grandparents of the circle. *Melkar and Zweet will be proud.*

Deep within, the symbiont stirred restlessly. His status as Oblionese made him an outlaw to the Colonial Corporation. Yet within the confines of the Korum, he was protected. The Korum, however, did not know that Rivo had been joined with the Tharrr. He was completely fixated on one individual, Renjinn. Rivo knew that another Tharrr survivor dwelled within the surly Katofar. His instincts were ignited in ways unique to the Tharrr. *The Tharrr must survive. We must all learn.*

*

LANDFALL, TATOCHI

Martha and Heidi stood in a small line behind Sheik Abbas at the entrance to the ground tube. Luggage floated to either side of the forming line, bobbing on their gravity fields.

"The air smells good", Heidi said, as she glanced out a window admiring the verdant foliage in a nearby urban park. The terminal at Landfall had an open-air baggage claim.

Ahhh, trees.

"I smell mosh", replied Martha pushing a vagrant strand of her waist length black hair from her very pale cheeks.

Sheik Abbas turned, and his eyes took on a crazy wobble. "Such beauty right behind me!"

"Korum", Martha sent.

"He smells like a sesame seed." Heidi dramatically rolled her eyes as her humor traversed the mental universe. She changed the subject.

"It's wellvibe beyond the walls of Landfall. I sense the spirit of this planet in the same way I feel Gaia," Heidi sent telepathically.

Martha was preoccupied. She averted her eyes from the Sheik's thinly veiled baleful stare.

"I don't particularly enjoy being mentally undressed especially by this pervert", Martha whispered. Telepathy was more difficult for her.

Heidi Roth felt an undercurrent of tension. She saw it in the architecture, the faces of the people, and in the vibration of their souls. She could feel subliminal transmissions beneath the music that hung in the background of the terminal.

It was the Corporation. She had been briefed thoroughly on their retrostory. Earth had rid itself of such mentalities. The evolutionary leap in consciousness that had swept across the Earth, though still in its youth, had become firmly entrenched in many souls.

She was warned that a Gaian would be scrutinized very closely. The Corporation was a throw back to some very dark aspects of Earth's retrostory. Rumors persisted that the very architects of Earth's perverse past had escaped the planet, and usurped the Corporation for its own ends.

Psychic attack was possible. She knew she might be a target. It was the nature of her work as a sentient life rights representative. Heidi had been trained to deal with many possible problems, but she was concerned for her new friend, Martha. *That smelly guy really threw her off. He did smell like a sesame seed!*

Martha did not know it, but half of Heidi's job was to protect the Gaian diplomat. Somehow the importance of that part of Heidi's mission sparked the memlock of a vision. *The Vanguard....*

Before she embarked on her mission to Tatochin, Heidi had spent time at her family domicile in the Northern Sierra Mountains, near like Tahoe. One evening, shortly before her departure, she had a vision of a robed Pleiadian teacher. Her robes shimmered with a soft blue illumination. She Looked deeply into Heidi's eyes and said, "You are the Vanguard for your people. You go now to help others, however, your return in the nearnow will move heaven, and our beloved Gaia, into new and exciting possibilities.

CHAPTER THIRTY-SEVEN

TATOCHIN
THE TSHINI MOUNTAINS
"High Mountain Base"

"Learn to do good;
seek justice,
correct oppression,
defend the fatherless,
plead for the widow."

Isaiah: 1-17
Revised Christian Bible, 20th century

Enro knew there was only one safe way to get to High Mountain Base because of all the surveillance. The trail was thousands of years old. From barefoot ancients to the high-tech boot clad freedom fighters, these mountains were the destination where many would go to hone their spirits on the vision quest.

Food gardens had been the general landscape of the planet. Unlike the Earth and its dalliance with a technocratic society, Tatochin had remained primarily a rural land, sparsely populated by Earth standards. Several large cities existed, but the general landscape was still incredibly verdant.

Cities had been more centers of learning, celebration, and planetary governance. Many of the varieties of plant and animal life had been introduced to Tatochin in ancient times. The Earth had been the mother to many new worlds. The soil and microbial life of the planet was similar to Earth.

Enro recognized that he needed time to process the changes he was personally going through. For the first time in his life, he thought about relationships, children, and a mate. He knew that his fate had changed. *Another battle. Is that all I'm good for? I think not!*

Nature had always been restorative for Enro. His mother, Chichen, in the short time she had with him, had raised him to honor both the bounty and the spirit of the land. A great appreciation for the gift of nature had been essential to his life.

The walk would help prepare him for the struggle ahead. He thought about his former loyalties to the Colonial Corporation as he feasted on several berries that were bursting with flavor.

The Corporation had been banished from doing any business with the Earth. Enro had studied Earth retrostory. It had been easy to trace the corporate takeovers and political deals that had spawned them. They were notorious in the use of drugs and media to control populations. Many lives of soldiers and millions of civilians were the cost of filling their coffers with credits.

The Corporation was expert in diverting attention from its activities using tight controls on the flow of information. Throughout the centuries, the Earth was kept in a perpetual state of war and destabilization in order to control the population, and maintain control over vast fortunes. They had managed to remain in a position of global leadership for many centuries.

Fortunately, with the dawn of the twenty-first century, the entry into intergalactic society had quickly exposed them for what they were. They dishonored and raped the land and the people, in their pursuit of wealth and power.

Was it a good solution to banish the i11vibe retros? It may have created the climate for even more sinister alliances off world!

Tatochin, and indeed the whole of the Orion sector, was ill prepared to deal with the technological ruthlessness that the Corporation utilized. Enro's thoughts phased back to the herenow. They would have been better off eating berries than their path of domination.

From above, the path was hidden by Ashwood trees and a large variety of conifers. As they ascended, large cedars and scotch broom blooming amongst a profusion of wild flowers and berries graced their way. The buzzing of honey bees was a symphony echoing up a steep meadow.

The twenty mile walk was uneventful. In the afternoon, they approached a large outcropping of rock rising behind a large stand of evergreen trees. Enro, Nimro, and the rebel platoon had arrived at the entrance to the Caves of Keltori.

This complex of caves was made invisible by the subtle dance of the native flora. It could easily be missed unless its existence was known. The Caves of Keltori were known to the rebels as High Mountain Base. A marvel of nature, they were ancient retrostory on Tatochin.

*

Several hours earlier, Shimtach approached the familiar setting of the hidden caves. She was weary from the circuitous route that the path from her hidden domicile lead her. At the edge of the great forest, the route was known only to her. It was rugged and hugged the edge of the planetary park boundary.

Her knowledge of the nearnow remained hidden within her. The awareness of what she had become had created a great inner crisis. She had prided herself for her simplicity. Dedicated to plant medicine she was a master healer. Now she had become so much more.

The Tharrr had begun to whisper within. She replayed the moment over and over. At first, Shimtach experienced a low level panic that once felt, was replaced by a great inner wisdom of the oneness of all. With this awakening came so much responsibility, it unnerved her to the core.

She had been tasked by the rebels to deliver packages to the Corporation containing sensors. Other rebel spies would place them in useful locations. On one such occasion, she had witnessed Rivo's holographic intrusion into the Corporation building. As she ducked into an elevator, the feeling of a life form entering her physical body was palatable as Rivo of Oblion passed by. His rescue mission was at its genesis in that very moment!

As the Tharrr awareness grew in her, she was at first horrified and then amazed at how the maleness in a Tharrr universe had reached a fever pitch of ripeness! The sheer joy and admiration of the Tharrr swelled within her, as it witnessed the journey of Rivo to its mate. The Tharrr circle was being born.

Shimtach quit the resistance without explanation and returned to her gardens. The herbs grew ripe. She however continued to become aligned with the Tharrr. A mighty task unfolded within her. Life had created major shifts.

Shimtach knew that Kaitain Enro would need her. The Tharrr needed all of them. She was well known to the rebels who lived at High Mountain Base. She knew Enro was on his way.

*

Inside of entry cave, the platoon of rebels moved quietly through the first 100 feet of natural looking, and unoccupied space. Once the internal surveillance cleared them, the holographically hidden door became visible. A silver metallic portal with the ancient symbol of the Central Sun from the Pleiadian's past appeared. The entrance opened with a whooshing sound revealing an elevator.

Twenty people could enter the lift. The next group would follow until the entire group would simply disappear into the mountain.

Once inside, the electromagnetically powered elevating tube brought Enro and his group up hundreds of feet to a remarkable cave, high on an inaccessible escarpment.

Almost a perfectly flat cave floor, a half mile across, bustled with activity. As the tube's doorway hissed open, it bombarded his senses with a cacophonous sound.

The roof of the cave was nearly a hundred feet tall. Large stalagmites and stalactites dramatically created regal bio-morphic pillars of colorful stone. Enro thought they looked like tendons.

How ironic to nestle in the body of Shelila, and see it covered with weapons of war.

A dozen I-wing fighters were being offloaded from a Corsair. Other equipment was being prepared for combat. The seal of the Korum was upon the hull.

The Korum! I hope they will not betray us to the Corporation. They have provided us with I-wings! They would incriminate themselves if they did. We need a standard and a symbol. It is valuable in combat. It helps focus power. I pray to be enlightened to the proper design.

Toward the lip of the cave, sunlight shimmered as it streamed into the snow-dappled entrance. The snow-capped peak where High Mountain Base was located was covered in glacial permafrost. Great mountain storms would entirely seal the entrance from time to time.

Within the cave, a tent village housed over twelve thousand rebels. The temperature remained cool year round. Cook fires, for the evening meal curled up into the toothy roof of the main cavern. A small waterfall tumbled down from a fissure in the rocks behind the village. It meandered down below the rise and out of the cave.

The whine of an I-wing engine being tested brought Enro out of his phasing and memlock. Enro's group walked toward the village where a large tent waited for him. The rebels dropped their work and gathered around in greeting. Words from friends still stationed at Skull Rock, passed between the ragtag families of freedom fighters.

"Welcome, Kaitain Enro", someone shouted.

Cheers and compliments from workers accompanied him all the way to the village. Hands stained with the petroleum that protects the metal of weapons, reached out to him with admiration and awe. Entering the village, babies were thrust into his arms.

Yoshen was in charge of the base. Enro sat with her, as her staff gave him brief summaries with a warm meal. Weariness settled in his 192-year-old bones.

"Shall we make a talking fire tonight?" Yoshen politely asked.

"No, tonight I must rest. Tomorrow we will meet again in the Pleiadian sanctuary. There is much to do."

"Is Shimtach still here?" Enro asked.

Yoshen smiled. She had anticipated the request. Each time Enro came to High Mountain Base, he would spend time with the herbalist and healer known only as Shimtach. A black woman of nearly the Kaitain's height, was the subject of rumors that Enro was in love with the mysterious and daunting woman.

"She arrived earlier today. She is in your tent Kaitain, I hope you don't find our presumption offensive."

Enro rubbed his tired eyes and smiled. "No Yoshen, your intelligence is correct. I actually can't wait to see her. I didn't know if she was here. She is not the most social person."

He stood and began to head toward his tent. "We will have our fire, soon." He waved his good night and headed for his tent and the ministrations of Shimtach, a woman he had been thinking about for a long time.

Shimtach strong hands kneaded complaining muscles. She smiled and said little. She realized that the Tharrr would soon be within him. Now, with the Tharrr within her, the deep understanding of herbal medicine, that her solitary nature had fostered, expanded into the understanding of the eternal workings of nature. Thus was her gift in the joining. Yet, she knew that the holographic language of the Tharrr was best kept hidden for now.

The knowledge of imminent change of her circumstances welled up within her. It was however, not within her power to lead the Tharrr. That would come from others. *Renjinn more than likely.*

Enro noted that though she said very little, he knew that she had received his words deeply. It might take weeks or even months but she would always address the things he shared with her.

Now she looked at him and said, "The Elders knew this day was coming. That is why you are here, my love."

He breathed deeply and let her healing strokes comfort him as well. So many things were crowding his thoughts. *Orville will arrive soon. So, the time has finally come. We are ready.*

He drifted off to sleep in Shimtach's arms

*

Many candles flickered in tents at late hours. Bottles of Tatochin wine, saved for special occasions, were opened. Lovers cherished each other a little longer, and a little deeper. The rebels had been struggling to defeat the Corporation for over a generation. The losses had been in the millions. A sense of culmination regarding a long sought resolution burned in the hearts and minds of the rebels. They struggled for their ancestors and for their children with hope and pride.

The stream flowed, and life continued. The great spirit of Tatochin, Shelila, heard the whispers of hope and fear. In the silent hours of darkness, as the encampment slept, she came upon them, energetically, and in some cases, phenomenally.

Lambent sparkling mist rose from the unnamed stream that came from a fissure in the body of the cave town. Her fairy folk attended her as she coalesced into an ephemeral but visible form. She floated above the stream in response to many whispered thoughts, hopes and dreams.

Dancing light sparkled in the cave as she gave her blessing to Enro and the brave friends he had gathered. Within their dreams, Shelila came as a comforter soothing fears, infusing them with the power of the land to co-mingle with their spirits. In mysterious whispers, the night watchers would tell fantastic tales around the breakfast fires, of fairy light and spirits.

*

CHAPTER THIRTY-EIGHT

LAKESIDE TRANNIE STRUT

It was a busy night at The Royal Orion. There was a large crowd. Flex sat in the lakeside lounge nursing a drink known as a Capach Cream. He was in full drag considering whether he might actually get surgical breast implants. He was often in a conflict because he liked being male, as well as female, but wanted to have breasts and be adorable and fabulous.

He adjusted his makeup with practiced care. Raising a tiny makeup mirror, he watched the Omegan priest sitting with Renjinn. It was a quick glance knowing the Omegan could pick up his thoughts.

Flex dipped into his persona as a rich corporate executive's wife to place a psychic shield around his deeper self. He projected thoughts of being alone while her life-mate played games in the gambling casino, unfolding fantasies of a secret liaison before her mate was completely devoid of credits.

In the few hours that he had been at the Orion, he had memlocked the structure well. It was nearnow 3 am. The last vactube to Ecksol would be leaving soon. He would be back to Skull Rock by noon.

*

Bodono felt Flex's presence. He was privately amused at Flex's attempt to block telepathic identification. *A rebel! He is a strange one! I must talk to him. But, I must lose the Katofar first.*

Renjinn let out a tremendous yawn. "I am tired, it's too dry here; even with the lake. I need my bog."

Just then, Flex stood up and took his purse. He began to depart. Father Bodono glanced over at Flex's movement. He had to think quickly or he would lose his opportunity.

"I am restless. Perhaps, I will seek some company." He saw the transvestite spy begin his departure from the corner of his eye.

Renjinn's great golden eyes followed Bodono as he moved toward the girl with the provocatively wiggling behind. Flex's padded butt did a tribal dance of its own as he sashayed toward the exit.

Renjinn croaked a raspy chuckle. "Good night, Father. Happy hunting.

Flex entered the vactube and took his seat. Bodono slipped into a forward pod and watched. Deciding to make his move, he approached the linkage membrane between pods, and entered the compartment where Flex sat adjusting his makeup. As he approached Flex's seat, the rebel whirled into action facing Bodono with fists up, in a fighting stance, only slightly modified by his high heels.

"I come in peace, as a friend," Bodono hissed.

Flex wasted no time wondering whether his best Francine impersonation had fooled the skeletal priest. He knew he faced a powerful adept. "You are an Omegan, what do you know of peace?"

"There are many among us who are as repulsed by the Corporation as you are. Please, just listen for a moment." He lowered his voice. "There are ears… *Can you talk like this?*"

"*Yes of course. All of Tatochin could at one time.*"

"*Good.*"

Bodono was new to this world and couldn't help but wonder to what extent the cross-dressing was a part of Tatochin's culture.

Now let's see if his ego gets bruised when he realizes his transparency to me.

"My name is Father Bodono, and yours?"

"*We must keep up appearances…I am the forbidden liaison.*"

"*I did not fool you at all!*"

"*You did well, I have had much training. You would fool all, but the very best*".

"My name is Francene," Flex flirtatiously replied. "*My name is unimportant. How do I know you speak the truth?*"

"*Judge with the meter of your heart. And, by the way, I don't know if I am the best but I am better than you. And you are pretty good.*"

"Are you visiting Tatochin?" Flex said out loud, to cover any eavesdropping that might be targeting the pair.

Bodono sat down inviting Francine to do the same. The vactube wound its way along the coast of Lake Wechen toward the central Ecksol. It periodically hissed to a stop as a few passengers got on, and off. The suburbs would thicken into an urban landscape in a few short stops. The pod slowly filled with a late night crowd heading back to the downtown sectors. They easily shifted into multidimensional dialog.

"My husband took me along for some business meetings. I was bored in my room, so I came down here."

"Do not let my Omegan robes intimidate you, underneath is a man. A man who finds you very attractive."

"*The Omegans are going to split into two factions. I represent a faction opposed to the Corporation. We wish to restore the Omegans to our true task of ministering. The Corporation wants our name. There is much power in a name like the Omegans. They use us as a shield for genocide. The power to claim spiritual leadership can be dangerous if misused.*"

"*Many of us feel that the alliance has weakened our mission. Worse, Omegans have committed moral crimes misusing sacred and holy knowledge. Sadly, many Omegans have been corrupted by evil. But not all of us.*"

"*Fine, but what does this have to do with me?*"

Flex's movements were a counterpoint as he shyly took his seat beside Bodono and batted his eyes ever so seductively.

"Do you like my outfit?"

Bodono acted like a horny priest. "Yes, and I like what's in it."

"Come on, really." Flex even giggled.

"I have come from Salvington to make contact with the rebels. We wish to assist you in your efforts. And at the right moment, even openly."

"How do you intend to do this, and what do you want in return?"

"Have you ever been to the Casbah? They have the finest wine." She flipped her hair perfectly.

Bodono's rich baritone was filled with lusty innuendo. "You are beautiful."

Flex realized that this priest was an actor of very high caliber. Telepathically Bodono sent: *"We do this already. I am the author of the Proclamation of Freedom."*

Flex was testing him. *"There is nothing in that we did not already know."*

"You didn't know that rebellion was occurring on other planets."

"True, but that is of little use to us."

"I think it is important, my unusual rebel man."

Hmmmm, did Enro mention this? "I would love to go for a drink. So what brings you to Tatochin, Father? Is that what I call you?"

"I am called Bodono."

"I think your leaders would be interested in others who seek to uproot the Corporation."

Flex wrestled with trusting this Omegan. He had formidable power. Bodono continued.

"We have six long-range corsairs at our disposal. Tatochin is only one of many worlds on the verge of revolt. I hear illvibe concerning Navidrrr. This revolution may very well be spreading. Tatochin could be a part of it. Then we will really get the Corporation out of our lives."

"Navidrrr? That's our galaxy!"

Bodono was pleased. He hardly knew this rebel in drag. In spite of her absurd performance, he sensed an evolved soul, able to think outside of a provincial planet bound context.

Who is this Enro? Named after that famous Kaitain from Oblion?

The vactube stopped more frequently now that they had come to the downtown area of Ecksol. The couple left the train and walked the few blocks to the Casbah. As they walked, they let down the telepathic framework of their communication.

"Bodono, I haven't mind-talked that much in a long time, I have a headache."

Flex skillfully adjusted his wig while making a gesture covering his action.

"Even now we are more than likely being observed." Bodono speculated.

"It is good that we did, the surveillance in the train has been significantly upgraded. I am also considered an expert in the Centaurian upgrades that the Corporation is installing. They don't know my true loyalties yet, but the clock is ticking on that one."

Flex found himself liking the tall and boney Omegan priest. Flex recalled Enro's words concerning rebellion on other worlds. The Omegan priest had confirmed it. In essence, he was inviting the rebels of Tatochin to kick in with the Omegan faction, including the sitting pope. Though Omegans were high on the list of people to be avoided, Enro would want to know.

"I cannot take you to our base, you have the tube." To keep up with the long legged Bodono, Flex quickened his stride with some difficulty because of his 4-inch stiletto heels.

Bodono looked back over his shoulder, "I have had it removed. If I am lying, you will know soon, you are speaking aloud. I, too, have incriminated myself. I will more than likely melt into tar at any moment, if I still have the tube."

Flex puzzled over his carelessness and the easy manner that Bodono confessed his total rebellion. His frankness told his inner senses that he was being truthful.

Bodono lifted his shirt and showed Francine his scar. He smiled mysteriously then continued. "By the way, I was directly responsible for all the upgrades in surveillance at the Orion. That was my reason for arriving before the conferences. I am sure this will come in handy in the coming weeks." He let that hang in the air.

Flex struggled to keep his elaborate feminine mask intact. *He knows why I was at the Orion. My god, these Omegans can be scary!*

Bodono knew his value to the rebels.

Francine shyly touched his scar and blushed. "Can you come now?" Flex said.

"I need to contact my consort. There are others who I must talk with."

"Others?"

"I do not act alone. I represent many Omegans. We will meet again tomorrow at midnight at the Casbah."

"I will find you." They shook hands.

"You do this role quite well, but don't expect a kiss good night?"

Flex smiled... "My name is Flex."

"Funny, I thought it was Francine," Bodono said with a wink.

They parted on the street. Flex's mind whirled with the much larger rebellion he had just entered. Enro had predicted it.

*

CHAPTER THIRTY-NINE

"FANNING THE FLAMES"

Gentain Carbone sat at his desk in the Royal Orion suite. Since his arrival, he had grilled Renjinn extensively, and met with Delaney.

Delaney...He must die!

He re-read the pulse fax from Salvington and wolfed down a salami sandwich. He waited for Cardinal Black. His mind seethed with the ramifications. *Why now with the Trilateral Conferences in just a week!*

Black entered. Picking up the Gentain's last thought. He answered. "We must quell their fire. There are layers of opposition. Now we will ferret out the opposition and discourage resistance."

"They are arrogant slag fodder!" The bulldog-faced Carbone spat.

"Occupation! Discourage resistance! I hope you Omegans have some better ideas because my own people are not getting the job done. I have to deal with our other friends. They will not be so forgiving."

He tossed the pulse fax to Black. "Maijaya's report on the first 24 hours on Navidrrr. Have we quelled their fire or fanned the flames?" Carbone muttered, as Black read the report with a deepening frown.

The news was grim. The Space dock had been seriously disabled in high orbit over Navidrrr. Most of Maijaya's fleet and half a triton of Colonial Troopers had perished. Military injuries had been high.

The Tadole were the finest fighters in the galaxy. Small highly trained tactical units had attacked the Troopers' Corsairs viciously. The remaining corsairs were forced to make atmospheric landings. The Colonial Corporation had suffered a humiliating defeat.

Maijaya's flagship though damaged managed to escape. Her command Corsair was headed for Tatochin. They would be arriving in three days. All the plus-light engines had been disabled.

The news upset the Cardinal. He belched stomach acid from his Salami sandwich and pickles. He was even more upset that the Gentain had even mentioned the "other friends". Even to imply the involvement of the Centaurians could threaten all of their lives.

Carbone speaks carelessly. He refers to the Dravithians and the Centaurians. They could squash us all without any provocation. He must pull it together now or I will slit his throat myself!

"All Tadole must be detained. Troopers and officers, relieved of command," Black said. He knew that other issues needed to be addressed. If the Tadole were to be detained that would put Bodono in charge.

Even worse than that disgusting toad, Renjinn! We must get rid of Bodono now!

Gentain Carbone let Black linger with the pulse fax so he could memlock the shifting pace of developing events. Carbone had his own quandary to solve. He was aware of the two main factions in the Omegans. Bodono was an expert in surveillance, the best in the colonies. He was aligned with Pope Hurus. Black's people had already failed once to end the Pope's life.

He prayed to the Dravithians for guidance, and feared secretly that they really did not hear. Centaurian diplomats would scrutinize him. They were as cold as ice, and twice as deadly. *That will be bad enough.*

Cardinal Black was aligned with Maijaya. There was no way they would allow Bodono to control surveillance, and provide unrestricted data to Tatochin's Colonial forces, not even temporarily. *Bodono must die. That much is in agreement.*

Gentain Carbone considered his options. Many different people might want to kill Bodono, including Black! That son of a bitch, Bodono had removed his tube. There was no signal! He wasn't sure he wanted to tip his hand to Black just yet.

Cardinal Black put down the pulse fax. Carbone continued. "I have further news. Three Tritons and a full invasion force are mustering on Salvington. They intend to arrive within a month. I am sure they will help create a strong deterrent to the rebels. From here, they will launch a full scale invasion on Navidrrr."

Black quickly muttered some reason for departing from Carbone. Both men knew the balances of power were shifting. They weren't quite sure if they were enemies now or not. The image of the Omegans aligned with the Corporation had soured.

Black looked down a dimly lit hallway before him. *The folly of it all.*

He remembered when Cardinal Fellini had been alive. He had supported the Cardinal then. What had happened? *I was seduced... but for what? The Colonial Corporation would be raked over the coals. And the Omegans will be dragged along with them!*

The United Galactic Consortium had been strengthening ties to the Gaians. They had already publicly asked for sanctions against the Corporation. This would add fuel to the fire.

What of the Korum? They have planned well.

Farooq Masad himself had emerged as the host of the opening and a keynote speaker. Black's thoughts raced with the illvibe implications. *The Colonial Corporation is a cesspool.*

Black found himself in some ways understanding the division in the Omegans. The Corporation was a nuisance. In spite of the alignment, he was glad that he wore the robe of an Omegan. He had to recite affirmations to stay calm. The news of Navidrrr was monumental.

*

The security detail sent from Gentain Carbone was enigmatic. They had wanted to speak to Bodono. Chandri had convinced them that he was sleeping. Guards had been posted.

Chandri was compulsively cleaning. She only did this when she was very distressed. *Where is he? He is so late. If he knows they want him he won't come. I hope he knows...shit! Am I waiting... yes.. no...I need more furniture polish...shit! Look at me.*

Chandri missed Bodono's bony body and easy laugh. She dared not use conventional communications; tweets, texts, pulse-fax on any band, and all portables were too dangerous.

She closed her eyes and controlled her breathing. Once she achieved a light trance, she psychically reached outward. Through the babble of dreams, and strata of thought modes, she sought his familiar touch of energy. With wings of urgency, she strained her ability to new levels.

Through pedestrian layers of collective thought patterns, she focused on his being; every detail, every cell; her focus deepened. She felt his vibration like a tuning fork in the center of her heart.

"Chandri, I hear your call."

"Where are you?"

"I am in a ground car heading toward a club in Ecksol."

"They search for you. Majaiya was defeated on Navidrrr. She comes. Renjinn and all the Tadole are detained. You are next in command. This is sure to upset Black."

"I have made solid contact with the rebels. I cannot go back."

"If I come to you, they will follow me, my love."

"Chandri, will you be safe?"

"No, I am not feeling safe. I will figure something out."

"I will contact you, or Smith, in a few days. If you don't hear from me seek out a spy named Flex. He will be in Ecksol in a lounge called the Casbah. He will be a she named Francene. The rebel is a cross-dresser."

"A cross-dresser?"

"Yes, his name is Flex. He is close to the resistance."

"I love you, Father Bodono."

"You are my Moon Goddess."

Chandri felt the contact fade. It took her some minutes to come back into the awareness of her surroundings. She was exhausted from the effort of contact. For a few moments, her problems receded and she experienced the special love she shared with Bodono. She realized she needed to build her life force.

Chandri's training was extensive. She began to take deep prana building diaphragmatic breaths and used pure synchronizing tones that aligned the central energy nexuses emanating from her subtle body. The slight irritation where the Omegan device had been removed from beneath one of her ribs throbbed. A deep intuitive conviction surged into her awareness. She was sure that if the tube hadn't been removed, she would be a nasty stain on the new carpet of her suite at the Orion by now. The clock was ticking. She needed to escape.

*

THE COASTAL HIGHWAY

Bodono asked the driver to head down to Lake Wechen. He had to disappear for a day. He would go sailing. He purchased a new set of clothes and emerged from the boutique store as a gaily-attired tourist. He headed toward a sign offering small sailboat rentals.

*

THE WHITE MONOLITH

Renjinn was confined to his quarters. A guard was posted in front of his door. Six Tadole Belfars that formed Renjinn's immediate command were in jail as well! He felt protective of his home-world but was having difficulty in the realization that his tenure in the Colonial Troopers was at an abrupt end.

The large green Tadole officer puffed on his cigar creating a huge pyroclastic cloud of smoke. He was literally fuming with confusion and anger.

Navidrrr...they hid the preparations to attack my home world! Navidrrr, attacked by my former commander, Majaiya. By the light of Vichillia, the Tadole had prevailed! The enemy now has a new face. The rebels of Tatochin are no longer my enemy. It's the Corporation, by the bog.

The Katofar was of two hearts. He wrestled with the betrayal of the Corporation. He had given his best to the Colonial Troopers. In spite of problems with the rebels, his record was exemplary. On the other hand, he felt a deep pride that his people had prevailed. He felt the approval within him on several levels. He stubbed out his overheated cigar.

It's too dry in here! Perhaps, a shower.

The luxurious shower had upgrades gained by the power of his position. His body and spirit reveled in the abundance of moisture, and the water began to restore him. As was his habit, he went into trance. The droning tones from his inflated throat sack echoed off the bathroom tiles. In his inner vision, a Tadole priestess appeared to him.

"My son, it is time to be of one heart."

Renjinn recognized the priestess. This was the same one he had seen in the hallway.

"What is this?"

"Renjinn, go to your people they need you."

"How can I go, I am watched?"

As the water pelted his dry pea green skin, myriad thoughts intruded upon his awareness. He felt the cosmos downloading inspiration and knowledge. Renjinn knew that Navidrrr would soon be free of the Corporation.

He heard the voices of his people, and of others he did not recognize. Every cell of his body was compelled to respond. He knew his foe. The advantage was apparent to him instantly. The Tadole were warriors.

His revelations were like the myths of his ancestors. Letting the air dry him, he walked about his apartment naked, as he ruminated wildly in a trancelike state of dreamtime and marsh cushioning. The Tharrr within him was supremely patient. Soon Renjinn would know.

He thought about his people with pride.

"I am Tadole, a bog dweller, born in the marsh. I am he that remembers to sing the praises of the united universe, the great illumination."

His throat sacks filled with air and his droning prayers filled the room. As he chanted in the way of the Tadole, he began to get to work.

Accessing his private console, Renjinn felt that he had been a rebel all along. *Let's see if they have locked me out of the system yet.*

*

The watcher within was pleased. When Renjinn finally slept, she would join the community of Tharrr. *Melkar and Zweet will rest easy when they raise their zoyats! Their children learn and adapt. The circle will continue!*

The symbiont Tharrr within Renjinn knew its destiny. It would mother the next Circle. The vision of the Priestess Navira had confirmed it.

The Tharrr within experienced a tremor of anticipation. She was an Elder! She knew of the Tharrr! *The priestess understands the love affair in Tharrr terms! How fortunate. The Elders reach is indeed great."*

*

FOURTH DIMENSION
"Renjinn and the Tharrr"

Navira, ascended master of the Tadole, was acutely aware of the Tharrr within Renjinn. It was not quite time for the Tharrr to reveal themselves. Usually soul fusion was accomplished in younger life forms in an evolutionary sense.

The Tharrr had evolved into corporeal reality at the most fundamental level occupying a spore. Though barely substantial, it marked an evolutionary jump from spiritual to physical manifestation.

Though it was evolutionary, the mission of the Tharrr was unchanged. They would act as a quickening spiritual surge to the life forms all around them. The complications of fusing several types of sentient life forms was a rare, and in some cases, dangerous thing.

Oblion had provided that lesson harshly. Evolution, circumstance, and desire however, had formed a nexus that could not be undone. The usual pathways of soul migration were evolving in new directions.

This is just the beginning! The Tharrr are ready to ascend into the ethereal dimensions. They need to take this step to progress. They offer a great gift to their chosen hosts. Soon they will fear no more and rejoice for the leap awareness.

Navira raised her vibration to the octave she was most aligned with. As she discorporated into finer frequencies, she smiled. *I like helping the Tharrr! Especially that Melkar and Zweet… and those zoyats are so cute!*

THE CASBAH

The Casbah was filled with guests. The rowdiness of the dance floor and provocative energetic flow was a mixture of off-world values and the approaching time of the planetary Festival of Rahi. This was a sacred time similar to the traditional fertility ritual of May Day on old Earth. Flex fit right in.

Bodono was at a table dressed in a bright floral shirt. He felt both out of place and completely entitled. He found playing a human tourist to be mildly amusing.

The sun had burned the usually pale Bodono. Gone was any indication that he was ever an Omegan priest. He spotted Flex and indicated with a flick of his eyes for him to depart the club.

Flex was once again, Francine. She sashayed to Bodono's side, as they exited the nightclub. They walked arm and arm to a more industrial section. Flex knocked on a door that electronically unlocked. They descended several sets of stairs and reached a sub-cellar. Flex pressed on a rock and a panel slid open revealing a sewer.

"A sewer?"

"They are sewers now, but they connect to ancient catacombs."

A few thousand feet down the sloping sewer system, the markings changed as they entered an ancient system of catacombs.

"The city planners used it to save credits when they built a modern infrastructure. It's a dam sacrilege if you ask me! This is how we come to Ecksol unseen."

"Why didn't it show up on our sensors?"

"Oh, I'm sure it does. We divert the water in these sewers to flow into these chambers. It connects all the way into the outer suburbs. From there we will go over land. A few times a day we stop the flow for travel. Surveillance satellites are good but not perfect."

The sewers nearly made Bodono vomit the seafood dinner he had eaten down by the boat docks in the harbor, earlier. After some time, he did not notice the stench. The sewer continued for about a mile. Flex and Bodono came to an outcropping of rocks and a larger cave. Large valves towered above them.

"These connect to junctions below us. In a few hours they will be flooded again. Right now we have a travel window." He walked over to a hidden door and turned a large cylindrical hub. A door opened and they stepped into a service tunnel.

Flex sealed the hatch and then went over to a box hidden in a dark corner and opened it. He smiled self-consciously as he removed his prosthetic body suit. He pulled off his large wig revealing his multi-colored hair. Finally liberated, his choppy, long, hair jutted out in many directions.

"The yellow and blue strands look edible to certain birds", he said as he donned a pair of fatigues, and wiped the makeup from his face. Bodono watched, fascinated by this unusual young man. Quickly, he led Bodono to another hatch in the rear of the small service tunnel. Suddenly, he stopped. "We might encounter other rebels."

"Okay".

Flex sighed. "Do me a favor. Don't mention my disguise as a woman. It is a private thing. Lots of my rebel friends might not understand."

"Okay, it will be our secret."

"Thanks."

"No problem."

"It is still dark. In a few hundred yards, we will be beyond the surveillance grid of the Corporation. In any event, stay behind me. Once we exit, even off the grid, they have saucer patrols with various imaging sensors. We have a special trail."

For the next several hours, Bodono followed Flex through hidden fissures and deep cervices, eroded by water flows from storms that descended from the foothills. Several times he signaled him into shallow caves with woven weed coverings camouflaging them from drone patrols passing over-head at low altitudes. As they emerged on Skull Rock, they were met by Nimro. It was 10 am.

"Hey, Nimro got some deodorant I really stink."

"Yes you do... speaking of shit, its hitting the fan, Flex. Who is your friend?"

"An Omegan priest."

Nimro signaled, and laser weapons were trained on the gaunt, sunburned, priest. He looked like a Central Orion tourist with his flowered shirt and baggy shorts. Nimro pulled Flex aside. Flex doubled over in laughter pointing at the aggressive response.

"Are you an illvibing retro, he's got a tube, they will swoop in on us now!"

Flex snickered as the reaction to his words created a scene. He waved his hands, exhorting calmness.

"He's okay. There are Omegans who oppose the Corporation. He is their representative. We have to get him to High Mountain Base. He has offered to link us up with rebels from other colonies."

"The tube. What about that?"

"May I?" Bodono opened his shirt to show the rebels the fresh scar line where the tube had been.

*

Flex spent twenty minutes detailing his last day in Ecksol. The Lynch café was the herenow buzz in maximode. Nimro questioned Bodono several times. Sally and Durga were called into the conversation. More questions were answered; slowly a plan emerged.

The word spread through the camp about the Lynch Café intel. Nimro would take Bodono to the base. Flex would meet with Chandri at the Casbah. Durga and Sally would remain in command at Skull Rock.

"We will be at High Mountain Base by night fall," Nimro told the Omegan priest.

*

HIGH MOUNTAIN BASE

Dawn came early at High Mountain Base. The light slanted into the entrance casting long shadows on the cave floor. Enro had slept well in Shimtach's arms. An image was in his mind upon awakening. They shared a hearty breakfast while Enro shared his vision with Shimtach of a shield and standard for the rebels.

"A blazing sun. Each ray would represent one of the colonies of Orion. Sixteen in all."

"It is simple and true to life," she said.

"The standard will be painted on all of our equipment."

"I will take care of it while you are in the sanctuary. You will be able to announce it tonight at the fire." She squeezed his hand tightly for a moment as she prepared to depart.

Normally, his old programming was never to display affection in public. Pushing all formality aside, he took Shimtach in his arms and kissed her deeply in a prolonged hug. *To hell with my image. I want her to know I want her.*

When they finally parted, a little smile cracked Shimtach's usually unreadable face. A small tear quickly wiped away.

Enro walked a short distance to the command tent to meet Yoshen. He was pleased that Shimtach had been moved by their exchange. His moment of reverie was abruptly filed for later.

He regarded the tough presence of Yoshen, and saw that she had not slept much. Her compact body was stiff with tension. They walked up to an entry on the western wall of the cave and went into the Pleiadian sanctuary.

"Yoshen, this is what we have been working towards for a long time. The people who are coming are strong. They are leaders, but may not be very savvy to the way things are done here. It is important that we support them and avoid any squabbling in the ranks. I am very proud of the work you have done. I want you to know that all our roles may shift when Orville Parker comes. You can trust them all."

Enro shared his vision of the sun with sixteen rays as a symbol for the rebels. Yoshen was excited. A few minutes later in a flash of light, Orville Parker appeared with Cleo, Lesha, and Arafad Tango X.

*

CHAPTER FORTY

"VORTEX"

"By the night when it covers,
by the day when it brightens,
by what is created male and female,
verily your aims are diverse."

The Qur'an

KORUM MISSION, ECKSOL

Farooq Masad began his chastisement of Prince Kalimafar with his well known philosophical edge. "The Shariot has many faces. So many worlds, it cannot be one way any longer. This much is clear as we stand on a planet far from our home. You hide behind traditions handed down by your family. You are a psychological fossil. You must put your exile behind you; you are needed now for important purposes."

Farooq paused as Kalimafar stewed in silence. Masad thought. *Perhaps the Shariot will die unless it becomes the offspring of Haqiqat!*

The prince felt uncomfortable. The illvibe memlocks toward the clerics who had provided his education always rankled him. *My exile shall be vindicated! How dare he!*

Kalimafar's voice dripped with false piety. "A few simple pleasures have not clouded my reason. We have prospered since my arrival!"

"Haram! Your reputation is a disgrace. The Korum is feared and considered illvibe. Words that describe your den of iniquity are sorcery, murder, torture, perversion, and subversive. You have made a dark idol of your penis. As a prince in the Korum, you have failed thus far in manhood. You cling to dark ancient beliefs that twisted illuminated wisdom into utter evil. Be done with these things, I say! You are a disgrace to any noble pursuit of virtue or wellvibe. If I were your father, I would be content with no less than turning you into a eunuch!"

Kalimafar shuddered at the mere suggestion. "You are not my father, however. Ambassador Masad, I will ignore your insults because of your reputation, and because my dear Father sent you. You are not speaking for my Father in this matter. It is my right!"

"I admit, I have lost my temper. Such drastic punishment came from the same nonsense I just referred too. There is no caste. These traditions you hide behind even support this." Masad shook with anger.

"It is you, Farooq Masad, who said the Shariot must change."

Masad did not remember having a thought before he slapped Kalimafar across the face with sudden reflexive speed. The prince was thrown to the ground by the force of it, splitting his lower lip. Large droplets of blood appeared on the tile below Kalimafar, as he lay akimbo.

Kalimafar watched Farooq Masad's face twist into confusion. *He must die... sooner or later!*

Masad held his own hand, his face a mask. It was not a common practice for him to slap princes or anyone else. He closed his eyes for a moment, recalling the teaching of Kalamat. *All is one with God.*

The prince was a challenge. He represented everything he had worked his whole life to transform. The preparations for the opening reception, the media hounds, and the unrest in the colonies had worn Farooq Masad out. *If I had a knife I might have used it on him. Allah, have mercy!*

Remorse suddenly gripped his attention. He thought of other relationships that were unsettling to him. His wife had been foreign in her affection. She seemed preoccupied with a social world he had no time for. His two children felt like strangers. They were young, his conscience bothered him. *I can't even memlock their birthdays!*

They had grown apart. Recently, she had asked him for a divorce. That had never happened in his family. It was an unusual situation for anyone in the Korum. He felt shame and blamed himself. No law or sin had been committed but in his heart he knew that his life and those of his family would change.

Just as a bout of self-pity threatened to overtake him, Tenya leapt into the room like a Lecad all spit and claw; aching to begin her deadly slaughter. *And now, this! God is great!*

Tenya controlled the berserker death-giving attack that a Dragon Fem was so adept at administering. Masad's eyes opened wide, as he involuntarily leapt backwards. Kalimafar had propped himself up, his hand catching droplets of blood that oozed out of his split lip.

The tattooed hellion stood in a martial stance waiting for her master to unleash her on the ambassador from Ganymede. A single command was all that stood between the lethal wrath of an angry Dragon Fem and Farooq Masad.

The prince let out a cackling laugh that sounded, venomous beneath the surface. "Tenya, I am all right. He is to be spared. I do not appreciate you eavesdropping, however." *Thank my lucky stars she doesn't listen, when it comes to my safety.*

Farooq Masad pointed at the naked tattooed Dragon Fem. His hand shook with emotion. "Is this how you dealt with Arafad Tango X and Shahid Abdul?"

"Tango is my friend!" Kalimafar spat.

Masad felt sick to his stomach. These were not his people. This was the old order. The deserts of old Earth had reclaimed this kind of posturing and convenient interpretation of moral law. In spite of his realization, he sensed that Kalimafar told the truth concerning Tango.

Bleached bones picked clean by the raptors of evolution? We live in many timeframes simultaneously!

He memphased to meetings he had during his first week on Tatochin. The Gaian representatives with their keen attunement to the spirit of the land honored the most high. He recognized in those people, a quest for justice and a morality that grew from recognizing that nature is tuned to the unspeakable and the unknowable.

The Pleiadians, human cousins, who had unlocked the mysteries of the self, were his friends. These friends were thousands of years beyond Earth's evolutionary standing. Hastening humankind's evolutionary awareness, he sought to unchain himself from the distant past's mistakes.

Kalimafar cantilevered Masad's awareness to the herenow with intuitive timing. "Shahid was a traitor. His death was necessary, as you well know. We have no word of Tango or Shaso for that matter. I would truly mourn should Tango be dead!"

Kalimafar picked himself off the harem floor and dismissed Tenya with a wave of his hand. Masad took a deep restoring breath and proceeded.

"You admit to killing Shahid, at least." Masad paused while the prince slowly stood up from the floor. "We must find better ways to communicate!"

He added a well timed gasp of pain. *I must salvage what I can!*

"The Korum has applied for full membership in the United Galactic consortium. One of the main criteria is a very close monitoring of sentient life rights. The Pleiadians have ways of knowing that transcend any ability to affect a cover up. The normal rules of politics are transparent to them.

"King Fezam and the Korum will not stand by and watch you destroy this possibility. I must know everything or by stone, I will see you exiled to an asteroid mine!"

Kalimafar sighed. "We have armed the rebels of Tatochin."

"With the Trilateral Conferences...How could you?"

"My Father allowed me to do this! Where do you think I obtained these weapons! He knows exactly what I am doing in that regard!"

Masad abruptly turned away from the prince to mask the anger that flushed his bearded cheeks. *They never told me this. I am a pawn In King Fezam's court!*

Kalimafar continued, knowing the conundrum that he placed before Masad. "You see, the rebels actions will hinder the Corporation. This will give the Korum a much stronger position, a bargaining position."

Farooq Masad digested the ramifications of Kalimafar's activities. The burden of such secrets weighed on his already troubled heart. He prayed for the strength to continue in spite of the illvibe. It was a bitter lunch. The need to fill the coffers of the kingdom outweighed the moral courage to behave in keeping with the Holy Spirit's truth.

Tenya entered the harem floor with Arn in tow. The dark man with the lacerated face looked harried. They stopped before Kalimafar and Farooq Masad.

"Rivo has intercepted important news." Arn handed the prince a pulse fax.

Droplets of blood stained the message as Kalimafar read the news of Kaitain Maijaya's defeat. "Katofar Renjinn is under house arrest by Gentain Carbone's orders. Kaitain Maijaya's fleet, the remains of it, is two and a half days from Tatochin!"

In spite of Masad's presence Kalimafar relished the news.

"Tenya, summon Sheik Abbas from his...rewards."

Kalimafar wiped the blood from his lip. A smile creased his damaged face. Candor was required and he loved dramatic moments with a perverted level of desire.

"Since you wish to know the whole truth, it looks like those weapons might be put to use soon, ambassador. I suggest that you maintain silence in these matters when in the presence of the UGC. We must not let them know we work to weaken the Corporation. I am sure my Father will concur."

Farooq Masad read the pulse fax and frowned.

"I am a chess piece in King Fezam's game. I grow weary of being a front man to cleverly disguise these secular infidels. The Korum may prosper but my hands, my heart...I feel dirty already. Haram!"

*

COMPULSIVE CLEANING

The pressures of leadership fell squarely on Gentain Carbone's shoulders. He was swallowing pills like candy to cope with the illvibe. The Trilateral Conferences had exerted pressure on Landfall and Space Dock. Downtown Ecksol was astir with activity. Every hotel, motel, bed and breakfast, and room to let was booked. All the corporate dining facilities above class 3 were packed with intergalactic tourists.

Scheduling the conference in the middle of Tatochin's biggest holiday, Rahi, was a logistical nightmare. UGC delegates, various leaders from aligned planets and all manner of business leaders were streaming into the Royal Orion. Every available meeting room was booked right up to and through the conferences. Gentain Carbone's head pounded with concerns.

The Colonial Corporation had strained its resources shifting and training personnel to replace Renjinn's staff of Belfars. It was a tedious process. The whirlpool of unrest combined with the impending conferences had taxed the Omegans, and the Corporation, with stepped up security. The Centaurian upgrades were confusing. Carbone entered the surveillance bubble and confronted Cardinal Black.

"Why haven't the upgrades been fully implemented?"

Black looked up at the commander and suppressed the urge to smash his dog-faced superior in the mouth.

"This place smells like rotten cigar smoke!" Black sneered at the ashes overflowing a tray of the charred corpses of Salvington cigars, which marked the path of Katofar Renjinn.

Gentain Carbone looked up from a large array of controls. "Come on Blackie, It feels good to roll up your sleeves and do the work, now and then."

"Spare me the platitudes," Black wickedly spat.

"Very well...Have you made any progress finding out what has become of Father Bodono?"

"I should ask you. Or do you think I am unaware that you guard his consort Chandri?"

Carbone had no time for Omegan sparring. "Listen, holy man, don't take this illvibe tone with me! Loose ends and fuck-ups are not in short supply among the Omegans. Father Bodono is an Omegan and he installed all the upgrades and all of the new Centaurian systems at the Royal Orion as well. He represents a significant security risk. He knows more about our security than anyone, besides Renjinn. Speaking of Renjinn, that dam frog is making disgusting noises in his apartment day and night. I think he has lost his mind."

Black puckered his lip and exhaled heavily. "We need not work at cross purposes. We need to question Chandri, and the sooner the better."

"It must be a joint interrogation. An Omegan and a representative from the Corporation must be present."

Gentain Carbone looked like a bulldog with his loose jowls. Arguing with him was futile. He sat in the COM chair in the sphere of pulsing electronics, stone-faced and staunch.

"Very well, I would like to question her myself", Black said. "She is a talented psychic. No one besides me can stand up to her."

Cardinal Malcolm Black was highly aroused at the thought of plying information from Chandri.

"Agreed, I will observe from here." Carbone's frown deepened.

Black went to a holo scanner and called Smith. A few moments later, his holo appeared before him.

"Cardinal Black, what can I do for you?"

"Please prepare a room for interrogation at the Orion. It is a matter of urgency that requires your immediate attention."

"Do you wish me to do an interrogation?"

"No, just the room."

"May I ask who will do it? I am well qualified..."

Black cut him off. "Father Smith, I want a room prepared, immediately. I believe your duties preparing for the conference are a priority. Please report to me as soon as it is ready, say in thirty minutes."

Black cut off the transmission and leaned back in the secondary COM-chair. The lights blinked, and the hum of laser circuitry, and the bubbling of liquid core computers, droned in the background of the surveillance bubble. Malcolm Black cracked his knuckles as he thought about interrogating Dame Chandri. He considered cruelty an aphrodisiac.

Gentain Carbone sat in Renjinn's COM room lost in thought. *I don't trust this Smith. Majaiya doesn't either. Cardinal Black may be ready to meet the Dravithians, Hmmm, an Omegan...*

*

Father Smith had barely settled into the posh resort. The room was lavish compared to his room in the Omegan training center. With Renjinn under house arrest, due to the festering revolt on Navidrrr, he had been reassigned to represent the Omegans at the Royal Orion.

He was worried. Dame Chandri was the likely candidate for interrogation and Black was anybody's worst nightmare! If that was true, he might be next. He will have to handle Delaney and his corsairs immediately. He was puzzled. "*What do I do with them?*"

*

Chandri was still cleaning compulsively. She had developed this retro dramatic behavior as a pre-ad. The psychic spike of premonition hit her. She sensed immediate danger. *Black will make his move.*

Her mind roiled with several possibilities that tangled into Gordian knots of restlessness. Would Smith be able to tap Delaney in time? Would her Bodono, be successful? She rubbed some polish into the ashwood table furiously. Maijaya's arrival was an unknown liability and dangerous to underestimate.

Revelation came over her in a moment of cool clear clarity. She must get to Space Dock herself, or die on a torture ring. *But how?* She shivered. A lance of fear for her corporeal reality seeped into her awareness. A secret desire to bear children with Bodono jumped into her pounding skull. *I want to live!*

Distractedly, she thought of applying a second coat of polish to the gleaming table. The holo appeared before her eyes suddenly. The cherub was a pre-programmed amenity that was the rage with five star corporate resorts. This was accompanied by the strum of a harp and then an announcement. It practically caused a cardiac event to the highly stressed Dame Chandri. *Too real!*

Icy calm emanated from her central spine, as she prepared herself for action. Destiny lingered on the fence. She sensed magic and a force other than the beasts that sought her. *Perhaps...* Her mind reached out and found light.

The cherub spoke. "Martha Fox and Heidi Roth, shall I show them in?" Tiny wings fluttered. The holo repeated its request as she bathed in the feeling of relief, revelation, and respite from the feelings of doom that had nearly consumed her moments before.

"By all means do."

The cavalry arrives at the last minute! Black will not know until it is too late. They are my shields... I buy time to think.

Martha, the Gaian delegate, had taken a liking to Chandri. Her friend Heidi, the sentient life rights observer, had been at her side from the start. Their telepathic powers were minimal but Chandri sensed an unrefined but great ability in Heidi. Laughter followed the opening of Chandri's door.

"I had no idea heaven was in a hotel suite!" Heidi said. They giggled like schoolgirls, as the fluttering cherub guided them to Chandri. Heidi sensed Chandri's turmoil as they hugged in greeting.

"What troubles you, my sister?"

"I am in trouble, perhaps we all are."

"What's going on?" Martha asked out loud.

Tears formed in Chandri's eyes. She felt safe with these wonderful women. They enclosed her with their bodies and let her release her emotions. After a few minutes of deep release, words could now be spoken.

"I fear for my life. There is much turmoil in the Omegans. Factions are in open opposition. Here on Tatochin, we are a minority. My consort, Bodono, has joined the rebels. They need my help."

"Slow down, let's start from the beginning", Heidi said.

KORUM INTELLIGENCE HUB

The chrome dagger-shaped building stood ominously amidst the towers of downtown Ecksol. Rivo, the Oblionese survivor operated the COM chair within. The Korum kept him sequestered within the building. If he was ever exposed, the Corporation would immediately execute him. The Tharrr within kept a low profile.

He noted that Renjinn, the security chief for the Colonial Troopers, was being detained at the Orion. To Rivo, Renjinn was the most precious thing in the universe. It would be a complicated matter to reach him. He knew the Tharrr was within the Katofar. Rivo would evoke the mating response if he could get close enough.

We will bring forth a circle.

Escape from the Korum and penetrating the Corporation would be tricky. Few souls were matched close enough to trigger the mothering instinct. The powerful latent force would transform them into male and female permanently. Fewer than ten sexually split Tharrr existed in all the great circles. Each new circle represented new parentage.

Rivo admired the self-control the Tharrr within Renjinn had displayed. Since the war, it had lived within Renjinn in silence. Renjinn did not even know. The symbiont was gaining an understanding for the life forms in this galaxy. Melkar and Zweet had reached him, straining their zoyats. He had been informed. Time was short. The mating would have to happen soon.

Rivo thought about the life forms on this side of the galaxy. They were a bunch of dreamers. They dreamed wonderful and terrible dreams. It had been a difficult adaptation. *The native Oblionese were a much younger civilization. They merged with us so easily.*

To the Tharrr merging with a host life form was a spiritual birth. Without that, they were incomplete. Rivo dreamed of the mating. *We will not make the same mistake again. You just cannot trust life forms that are sexually ignorant. They are much too dangerous!*

Melkar and Zweet, though far from their circle, were creatures of amazing ability. They had lived for many thousands of years. They had learned a great deal about the local galaxy through a remarkable ability. The zoyats they possessed were like an organic radio, able to communicate and receive across light years of distance.

Millions of Tharrr were stored in the mother's womb. When they found Oblion, they were able to project a part of themselves to the developing planet in the Orion sector with the help of the Elders. They were a peaceful people living a simple agrarian existence in a pre-galactic state.

The apparitions swirled about Rivo the Oblionese security operator. They twitched and morphed in cadence to his phasing thoughts. *Zweet held us in her womb. Now she will be a grandmother! It is time.*

With the Katofar in jail, he had to hurry. Tonight he would reach the Tadole security chief. He called up a holo-file of a floor plan for the Royal Orion. He went over the plans until he had memlocked the entire route.

*

OMEGAN TRAINING ENCLAVE

Father Smith gobbled down the second cinnamon roll. It tasted stale. His meeting with Delaney had soured his mood. Delaney's office enclave was among the myriad rectangular towers. He always found such environments oppressive.

Ecksol was in a flurry of preparation. Gaily colored banners hung off power relays and high frequency amplifiers. The subsonic signals would cow the unaware crowds with its subtle but persistent programs of mind control.

Monarch mind control! Nothing akin to butterflies except those in my stomach!

Cultural events, invented for the intergalactic visitors, filled the holoscans. Class five dining facilities were crowded with exotic guests. The hypnotic suggestions of openness and friendliness saturated the subliminal transmissions. Included were strong suggestions to minimize the significance of the Declaration of Freedom that was still in wide circulation.

He had listened to Delaney, the planetary CEO, for a full ten minutes about their unholy enslavement of Tatochin with evil chemo-technology. Finally, cutting him off, he asked for the keys to six corsairs that were loading mosh bound for several colonized planets in the Orion sector. The color, what little was left of it, drained from Delaney's face. He gave Smith codes with the proper clearances.

His meeting with Delaney had been brief. The news of Chandri's disappearance both pleased him and disturbed him. So many people had disappeared lately.

The Gaian ambassador! That sentient life rights monitor, Bodono, and now Chandri! What next? The opening reception is still three days away, and already the trouble begins.

After the meeting, he went back to his office. The resort was inviting but with the Corsairs, now, were in his possession. Hours were spent planning the logistics with a group of loyal postulants, ready to declare alliance to Pope Hurus. Until now, the pace was building in slow and steady increments.

Over the past few months, he had noticed that the Corporation controllers had been forced to steadily increase the amount of subliminal triggering hypno-plasmic drugs, to compensate for the so-called illvibe. He carefully avoided contamination. His cinnamon rolls were all neutralized. The thought of war and bloodshed sent a shiver through his body.

Retro-story tells us that when the masses are roused, these formulas to stabilize populations do not work. Revolutions start slowly and in stealth.

Just as Father Smith reached for his third cinnamon roll, one of his aides approached with a pulse fax. He quickly read the brief message.

The pulse fax read:

"We need to get on a saucer right away!

See to it. Chandri"

*

DELANY'S OFFICES IN ECKSOL

Carbone soon knew that Delaney had been subverted. The report of six missing Corsairs was both awkward and suspicious. He called in his private assassin.

Korgon had taken 159 lives before Delaney. He was very precise in recording such matters. The shape-shifter was from a little known world in the Orion sector. The planet Nerapto had a population who practiced many secret arts that bore similar appearance to Shamanic sorcerers from old Earth.

He checked the weapons concealed on his body, beneath his fashionable one-piece suit. Korgon's identification tag gave him entrance anywhere within the Corporation web. Walking rapidly through hallways and up lift tubes to Delaney's private quarters, the shape-shifter paid little or no attention to the bells and whistles he triggered.

The assassin used a hand held pulse laser to cave in the door. A disruptor field subdued John Delaney, the corporate President and Governor of occupied Tatochin, before he even saw the killer's face. It mattered very little to Korgon whether his target was powerful or not. A slow death had been the request.

Carbone is probably shoveling linguine in his dog-face, while I do his dirty work. Yes, it will be a slow death. For me, fuck Carbone!

The Shape Shifter slashed at the puppet Governor with a surgical laser knife. "I will make slag burger of you. But as you die, you should know that the Gentain Carbone sends his greetings."

It took only a few minutes for the powerful laser knife to pierce his heart. His body looked like steaming meat pulp by then. As Delaney died, he felt remorse that he had let down his family. *The Corporation is scum. I knew it all along.*

His heart stopped after that thought. Moments later, his spirit departed the body.

Korgon shape-shifted into Delaney's form as he absorbed the near-now memlocks and imprinted his mutable cells with the dead president's DNA. *I may need him if my escape plan is hindered.*

After a few moments, he shifted into the form of a janitor he had subdued in the sub-cellar earlier. Korgon departed the office as quickly as he had come.

*

SWAP AND SHOP

Two women left the Omegan suites at the Royal Orion. To the Colonial Trooper stationed in the hall, they were the same two who had entered. Both Chandri and Heidi projected that thought strongly as they passed the checkpoint. In fact, Martha and Chandri had switched clothing. The guard did not notice.

She liked the way the Omegan outfit felt on her body. The tight body suit was like wearing nothing at all. The cape, though plain, was very dramatic. The mane of raven hair was something the two women had shared.

Martha marveled at the abilities of Chandri and, unexpectedly, her colleague Heidi. *Hmmm, She is very protective of me and has combat skills I wonder, hmmm.*

*

Martha's clothes fit well on Chandri. She enjoyed the scent that seemed to surround her. If they survived this wild plan, she wanted to find out what perfume Martha wore.

They went through the crowded Orion lobby and out the main entrance. Just as they stepped up to the curb, a hover-cab landed in the taxi grid. They headed for the door which opened as they approached. A strange man with a pinched face and a strange hat emerged. Chandri felt a mind contact very alien from anything she had ever encountered. Timing and stealth was important. She did not have time to investigate the experience.

They jumped in the hover-cab. As they headed out of town, Chandri wondered what that being was. *Tharrr?*

As they neared the Sanctuary, Chandri addressed Heidi. "This is not your battle. I am very grateful for your help. You put yourself at great risk."

Heidi looked out the window, as sunset became twilight. She weighed Chandri's dismissal. "This is a beautiful planet, Chandri."

"We can send you back to the Orion."

"Thank you, but I want to go with you. Martha's job is with the conference, my concern is with sentient life rights. I am getting an eye full the longer I stick with you!"

"There could be violence, this isn't a peace mission."

Heidi's hazel eyes bored into Chandri's eyes. "I will keep that in mind, and try to stay out of the way."

"What about Martha?"

"She is here of her own accord."

"I suspect you are also protecting her."

"You, Omegans are very intrusive with your mind reading. I should know better than to attempt to hide such things from you."

"She seems a bit provincial, you know, kind of like a space migrant."

"The UGC has a significant security force at its disposal. I know Father Smith will watch her back as well."

Chandri was selfishly glad for the Gaian's presence. Her benign humor and steady peaceful way soothed her. As the cab pulled up, a saucer touched down on a pad behind the sanctuary. A cadre of Omegan postulants greeted them.

"Father Smith told us to meet you. Come this way," the postulant said stiffly. The young, bright-eyed Omegan priests gawked at the attractive and mature women suddenly in their charge.

They were ushered into the foyer of the Omegan safe house. Smith appeared, as he brushed some last minute crumbs off his black robe. His ample belly made a natural shelve for such flaky rolls.

"We are in luck. I have secured us passage on a saucer directly to Space Dock."

"You are going in your robes?" Chandri asked.

"For now it is probably my best disguise." Smith managed a smile. The wound where his tube had been removed still ached. "I wasn't aware we had extra passengers," he added.

"Father Smith, this is Heidi Roth, the sentient life rights observer from Earth."

"A Gaian", Smith took her hand. "I am honored. However, we are in a very dangerous position. We cannot risk you being harmed."

"Father Smith, it is my job to find out what is going on, and report back to the UGC. It is quite clear to me that vast changes are in the wind. I belong right where I am."

Smith shrugged his shoulders. "Very well, can't say I disagree with you."

Fluidly, he shifted gears and began to brief the two exotic women. "I have assembled five pilots and fifteen additional Omegans, loyal to Pope Hurus. They are young and a little green around the ears, but they are firmly committed to our cause. There are six Corsairs available. I hope Bodono is successful."

Chandri smiled. "If the need arises I could pilot a Corsair, or any other vehicle for that matter."

Father Smith would miss his chance to hob knob around the Orion. The cinnamon rolls they served at the resort were lunar. He was glad to be departing the world he had been trapped in by the Corporation, and the twisted leadership that ran the show. He wanted to live but the yoke of the Corporation chaffing around his neck had become intolerable. Now if he died, he would be at peace knowing he had at least tried. *I am not going to die today. No, not today.*

They headed for the saucer bound for Space dock.

*

THE THARRR HONEYMOON SUITE

Rivo walked briskly past the two exotic women he had noticed at the curb. He ignored a hand-fluttering concierge in the lobby of the Orion, and ducked into a nearby lounge to get his bearings. He felt shifts happening deep within his body. *My children are spreading. Hold! Soon! Soon, my precious ones. Our Mother is just a little ways further.*

The Tharrr were ready to come forth. Soon he would need to mate. The children grew within the male gender of Rivo. The spores would bring new skills and greater awareness. The ability to shape shift and create illusory phenomena were some of the special abilities that the symbiont called forth.

Rivo mentally rehearsed the repertoire of apparitions he would utilize to gain access to the Katofar. Once together, they could combine forces and easily escape from the building. Stepping up his energetic vibration, he proceeded in maximode.

The shift was an instinctual Tharrr response. Rivo would recollect the changes in his biology as they occurred inside of him. He walked down the hallway removing his hat with exactly timed movements. The swirling apparitions of unformed light glowed brighter as he approached a turn that would bring him to the secured area of the Orion set aside for the Trilateral Conferences.

When he turned the corner, he had became a prisoner being escorted by several Colonial Troopers. His apparitions gained him entrance through several passive tiers of security. Finally, he came upon the security station where Renjinn was imprisoned. The Tharrr's biologically induced holograms were flawless.

"Transferring prisoner number 487, alpha X," one of the apparitions said.

"I don't recognize that number. I wasn't notified," said the jailer.

A look of horror came over the Trooper as the apparition morphed into a mirror likeness of Rivo. At that moment, he fired a disruptor. With one quick discharge, the trooper rolled back his eyes. Rivo caught the falling man and eased him under the desk.

Rivo moved on with his creation including two more troopers with the jailer. The bio-holographic escorts vaporized once Rivo arrived at Renjinn's door.

Renjinn had just emerged from his fifth shower of the day. He walked naked about his apartment preferring to drip dry.

Suddenly, Renjinn felt a great pressure in his head, and immediately sat down feeling dizzy. The doorbell chimed. He looked up at the flat screen and cursed, it had been deactivated! *At least they do not barge in during embarrassing moments, anymore.*

He wrapped himself carelessly in a towel. His dorsal fin rose to the level of severe annoyance. Reaching out to activate the door, he almost lost his balance as his digits caressed the button. The door slid open with the characteristic thowk.

Renjinn's head seemed to explode into light. His towel fell to the floor. He felt great surges ripple through his body as tiny spores held long within him rose to join other spores, to become the symbiont Tharrr.

Rivo stood before the naked Tadole female. The Father, and Oblionese Tharrr was fully aroused. Hues of lambent light swirled about the Oblionese refugee's head as he revealed his true form. Hungrily he regarded the large, and naked, peagreen Katofar. Feelings of rapture and lust had replaced key restraints in his personality.

Powerful mating instincts were activated. Chemicals, unique to the Tharrr had generated within the Oblionese and the Tadole Katofar alike. Like the flimsy towel falling to the floor, the veil of separation that the Tharrr within had maintained, also slipped away in that one crucial moment.

Renjinn felt painful changes happening in his groin. Moments later it turned to warmth and pleasure unlike anything he had ever felt but that she now felt. *She?*

He looked into a mirror that hung across the one wall of his apartment. For the first time, he witnessed a multitude of swirling eddies of color majestically rotating around his own slightly elevated cranial dorsal. My sexual organ! What is happening?

Mating colors appeared at the boney tips of the segmented fin and large violet streaks appeared across his chest. *These purple streaks remind me of a fertile Tadole female…by the bog!*

A voice spoke to his fear in soothing tones from within. His internal and external transformation had begun. Without volition, the proud Katofar felt internal changes in his body that deeply disturbed him. He was becoming a female, much to his dismay.

His throat sacks ejected cigar stained phlegm with loud trumpets of sound, as he sucked in more air. His dorsal fin involuntarily wobbled. He looked down to discover that his sexual organs had now committed gender mutiny!

"By the beast of the bog! What's happening to me?" Renjinn sputtered as he fell asleep.

The Tharrr within had taken over Renjinn's body completely. Swirling light formed symbolic patterns around his head like fluid crop circles. In the language of the Tharrr, bio-holographic forms shifted. They combined with Rivo's and configured in an expression of their communion.

Rivo barely contained his excitement. He felt shifts occurring inside of him that began to rise to an irresistible peak. *By the star that shines brightest, we will mate!*

As they communed, the room seemed to fill with a whirlpool of multi-hued light. Secondary eddies would form and dissipate as the symbiosis of the Tharrr union biochemically altered them into a united mating couple literally transforming space-time around them into a crucible of creation. The great circle was born.

*

The consciousness of Renjinn slept as the mating occurred. The Tharrr within Renjinn was abundantly receptive and at the peak of fertility. With sparks that pierced dimensions, conception occurred in Renjinn. He would be the Mother of the new circle. They had found a healthy pathway for the circle to expand.

"The circle will be robust," Tharrr Renjinn whispered.

"We must free Ostinglink and the other Belfars. They, too, will be our children," Rivo said.

"Yes, they will be the first of the new Tharrr," Renjinn replied.

"Get dressed. We have a long journey and many dangers to overcome," Rivo purred.

He was brimming with pride over his accomplishment. He had a sudden urge to smoke one of Renjinn's Salvington cigars.

*

TWO HOURS LATER
VACTUBE

The news of Navidrrr was still off the public radar. Rivo and Renjinn blended in with the population. It would not last long. The news about the rebellion on Navidrrr would complicate Renjinn's status immediately once it became the herenow buzz.

Many different life forms filled the public transport tubes into the vast city. Just as they prepared to rescue the Tadole Belfars, a news holo special report appeared in holocasts and private T-pulse pods. The face of the Katofar was splashed across the media feeds. A holo caster chirped about the illvibe uprising among the Tadole on Navidrrr. Renjinn was considered a dangerous fugitive.

The clock was ticking. As they walked into the lobby of the Corporate Monolith, citizens began to move away from Renjinn with gasps of horror. A tall black woman ran into an elevator screaming about the Tharrr.

"This is not wellvibe," Renjinn mumbled.

"They are being held in the sub-basement. Level D," Rivo hissed.

Rivo grasped his mate's hand, and pulled him down the hallway. Renjinn allowed him to be the man, as she explored her new identity as a pregnant Tadole.

Renjinn knew he would be recognized immediately. His large golden-eyed face, complete with a fat blue Salvington cigar in his maw, had been liberally splashed across the holo reports of illvibe with the Tharrr on Tatochin.

Rivo brought his weapon forward. "We have arrived."

They had to move quickly. The media was already abuzz in maximode. T-Pulses and holocasts quickly made information available. Colonial Troopers and Metropol were all being deployed across Tatochin.

Rivo set a small charge to blow the door. Renjinn braced himself for action. They found the Belfars in a locked cell. With arrival of Renjinn and Rivo, they began to fight their way out of the Corporation Headquarters in the first battle of the Tatochin Rebellion.

They took weapons from the Troopers and guards who attempted to stop them as they made their way. Belfars quickly began to fight. The Tadole warriors were superior in their ability to wage a small war with little effort. They burst out of the white monolithic tower, and jumped into several ground Flitters.

"We are going to Landfall, we must find passage to Navidrrr."

They drove a stolen transport tripping alarms at each checkpoint. Rivo targeted an unsuspecting guard with a Centaurian disrupter. The unconscious bodies were hidden quickly. They would rely on speed, and the expectation that the competent Tadole Belfars were the best of soldiers trained in every Tadole method of fighting. They were Belfars from the best of the Tadole clans.

Fifteen minutes later, they had killed, or maimed, 12 Corporation Marines; and freed six Tadole Belfars including Ostinglink. They had armed themselves with the tools of the trade of those they had subdued; and made their way to the entrance of the building for the escape.

Alarms and lights flashed everywhere, as the knowledge of the Tadole's escape spread throughout the system. They relentlessly fired the stolen weapons, dropping them as they were depleted. The carnage gave them a fresh supply of weapons. The Tadole had been trained, since hatching, on the science and art of war. The Colonial Troopers were no match for them.

By the time they reached the front entrance, dozens of Troopers and security in plain clothes were pursuing them. Rivo and Renjinn produced multiple apparitions of themselves. To Metropol and the surveillance cameras it appeared like the Tadole Belfars scurried past the vehicle into the crowded street.

"Decoys", Rivo hissed.

The Troopers and local Metropol foolishly followed the apparitions into a dense crowd of people. They made their escape in the stolen surface transport they had placed in readiness.

Turning onto the highway, they headed toward the space port called Landfall. Ostinglink and the Belfars shook in their boots as they observed the apparitions swirling around Renjinn's head.

"Abomination", one of the Belfars grumbled.

Renjinn's dorsal rose and tore the fabric covering the roof of the transport. "Would you rather go it alone out there?", Renjinn said to the Tadole who even turned greener than he already was.

That sure sounds like the Katofar. Ostinglink thought.

By the time they reached Landfall, the entire grid was on alert.

*

AMBALIKA'S CRIB

Orville received several pulse fax indicating changes on Tatochin. He thought of the times to come. He and Cleo would soon be gallivanting across the galaxy. He thought of his hidden base in the Asteroid fields off Glamora. The relocator he had built into the stable rock, had been a safe house for centuries, though seldom used. It was that location where they had found Orville when they brought him to Mirror.

Orville had constructed the base as Ambalika in a previous life as a Pleiadian scientist and master Terra-former. He giggled at the memlock and smelled the flowering jasmine and honeysuckle. It attracted a pleasant level of bees, droning as they gathered the pollen that would carry life.

So be it.

CHAPTER FORTY-ONE

HIGH MOUNTAIN BASE
"Sanctuary"

The entire community teemed with nearnow expectation of extreme action in maximode. An economy of intent surged through the rebels. Personal lives were put in order. It was a time of decision-making, revelation, and passion. A sobering process of arming themselves with faith and courage, along with a dozen I-wing fighters. Their spirits roused to respond to the call for freedom long sought.

Orville listened to Cleo as she related her revelatory meeting with the Elders, regarding the interconnectedness with all the colonies, Earth, and many of the settlements concerned with the diaspora. The rebellion on Navidrrr and the growing force to rid the Orion sector of the Corporation was quickly heading toward a showdown. It was Orville's job to help the rebels of Tatochin frame their effort in galactic terms.

She directs her conversation toward Yoshen, good! Especially, the Tatochinian can benefit by expanding their awareness of the forces that are shifting beyond their own world.

I have memlocked so much over the past 450 years. And yet, with Cleo in my life, a completely new light illuminates my remembering.

Cleo's voice sent him down another exit ramp onto another more ethereal highway. His awareness expanded multi-dimensionally encompassing a compressed continuum in a larger herenow. Moments merged. Distant lives, hours earlier, the words coming from Cleo's lips in this very moment; time itself seemed to be going in several directions at once.

There is a higher order. Love! That is what binds us in the end. He phased to his arrival on Tatochin earlier that day. It was great to see Enro again. The formidable Kaitain looked like a great lion with his mane of dreadlocks. Orville had waited a long time for this group of souls to meet.

He phased to unknown possibilities. Perhaps they had sat in a cave gnawing at some wild beast in some ancient incarnation. If it was so, he had no dusty memlock to hang that story on.

Enro took in the group immediately before him. He recognized Lesha from his military days, but was surprised to see the Korum Ambassador, Arafad Tango X. He had never met Cleo.

Yoshen watched Tango with great suspicion. Her hand slipped down to her laser pistol, as she anticipated the worst. Arafad Tango X was not a popular person among the rebels of Tatochin.

Orville smiled inwardly, having felt the turmoil several of the rebels were having regarding Tango. He took the cue to break the ice.

"Enro what in the name of the great Taco have you done to your hair! He looks like one of his Ethiopian ancestors," he said to anyone within ear shot.

Orville and Enro warmly embraced. "Enro, this is Cleo."

The great lion stepped back and regarded Orville and Cleo as they stood smiling before him. His awareness of the charged and somewhat dangerous gathering dropped away, as he regarded the couple for the first time. Enro's finely honed senses were overwhelmed by the potent and exalted essence of their growing union. *They are Zemplars!*

"Orville has told me of your friendship", Cleo said. "I knew of you in the old days, Kaitain. Your death was a great sorrow to us. As a child on Salibno, my parents and I followed the holoscans during the Siege at Oblion. I was excited to learn that it was a rouse."

"Yes, Orville has made it his task to promote his radical plan to erase my past." Enro said.

Tango stepped up to the trio with Lesha. "I see that I am only the junior member of this growing cult of explosive solutions."

"Me, too!" Lesha said.

They all laughed and Yoshen relaxed the hand that rested on her laser pistol.

"Arafad Tango X, I had no idea that you were associated with Mirror, or Orville! We thought you were dead. The Lynch cafe is gone." Enro shook his head causing his matted locks to slip in front of his shoulders.

"I brought back pieces of it lodged in my body," Lesha mused. That remark led to a discussion of the upgrade in the Matter Relocators. They listened while Orville updated them.

Enro regarded Tango. "What brings you to us, Ambassador?"

"Ambassador, well yes, that is my outward title but as you can see, I work with Orville. I have been under cover for five years. It had to be this way in order for my cover to be secure."

"I was in King Fezam's court as an assistant on Ganymede. I was sent to Tatochin, to babysit Prince Kalimafar by his father. I thought my efforts to penetrate the Korum had taken a turn for the worst. It was only then that Orville informed me that you were the rebel leader that so irked the Colonial Corporation. That, of course, changed everything."

"With the annexation of Tatochin by the Corporation, it's easy to believe that the hand of destiny is at play."

Lesha placed her arm around Tango's and her wavy, brown hair caressed his arm. She wanted them to know that he was with her romantically.

Orville's reveled in the warm glow of friendship and love as he listened to his friends come together for a great purpose. Gratitude filled his heart with the love and attention his Pleiadian brethren had shown to all of them.

His eyes rested on Cleo as she revealed the wisdom of the Elders. Orville was transported to the farnow and memlocks of the four hundred years he had lived, loved and learned. An ocean of yearning for an inner light, and a just and thriving universe burned in the hearts of his little group of revolutionaries. A tear filled with an ocean of information trickled down his face.

The many lives, worlds, wives, children, teachers, and the river of humanity and sentient life, had grown and evolved over the centuries. As a witness to so much more, he was thrilled to have served as a light bearer into the future that was unfolding before him.

His heart swelled with prana that radiated out from the Central Sun within him. He realized that aspects unknown to that future still had not been revealed. He knew in time it would become clear. He wondered about time itself.

Do I feel so much because I already know the wonderful outcome of all of this?

Cleo and Orville's eyes met. Her face curled into a small smile. She then quickly made a cartoon smile and winked. Before Orville had another thought, Yoshen cleared her throat and reeled the group back to its task.

"Rahi begins at the same time as the Trilateral Conferences," Yoshen supplied. The compact woman with close-cropped white hair and wiry musculature was all business. "The Kaitain felt it was a good time to make our move."

Orville sensed the frenetic activity. The drumrolls of pre-battle touched him in his heart like an icy hand. His stomach growled again. Hunger distracted him from delving into those morbid feelings. He hoped it was not a premonition. "We have much more to memlock and plan, but first, we must pause to eat."

Five minutes into their meal, the meeting continued in between bites of tacos that were piled high on the polished Ashwood table. Sally, Enro's Belfar, arrived at the entrance to the sanctuary. Yoshen conferred with her for a moment and then turned to the group.

"An Omegan priest has arrived with Nimro. He claims to represent a large faction within the Omegans that seeks an alliance. I had him scanned, he's been cleared."

"How did he find us?" Enro asked. He knew that it could not have been Nimro's idea.

"Flex met him in Ecksol," Yoshen replied. Once again, her hand drifted down to her laser.

A few moments later, the sun-burned, gaunt form of Father Bodono stood in the entryway to the Pleiadian sanctuary, escorted by Enro's other Belfar, Durga. After terse introductions, Father Bodono showed them the fine scar where his tube had been removed.

The Omegan priest soon won the hearts and minds of the group. Bodono was a natural and his purpose was sincere. The tactical knowledge of the Omegans, combined with his deep understanding of the Centaurian upgraded surveillance, was powerfully useful and extremely wellvibe.

Enro would use this knowledge in the nearnow. His hope was to take the planetary government down with as little bloodshed as possible. The Omegans had now officially joined the ranks of the rebels.

*

SPACE DOCK, TATOCHI

Bishop Franklin Jones watched his Pleiadian corsair approach Space Dock over Tatochin. Looking out at the large rotating wheel of the space station, he saw the emerald glow of the planet in the background. The moons, Capach and Wechen, were both visible off the port bow. The corsair was like an ark in space, bound for the Trilateral Conferences.

Jones watched as an Omegan saucer landed in a cargo bay in a section below the passenger Corsairs. The breeze of premonition grazed his awareness. He worried about Pope Hurus on Salvington. We worried about Bodono.

Where is that crazy Italian! The Proclamation of Freedom! Oy! He plays for high stakes!

The herenow buzz of the Corporation's defeat on Navidrrr had dominated conversation and holoscans. It had set a serious tone. Now, the information had disappeared from all mainstream media, excepting the techno-geek sub-pathways.

A chorus of groans from the passengers in his corsair, met the announcement of a delay for disembarking. The partially fabricated reason was assigned to a planetary upgrade in security in preparation for the Trilateral Conferences.

With much less delay than anticipated, the corsair was docked, and the passengers began their exit. The local and planetary media, without missing a beat, began bombarding the passengers from every quadrant.

Awestruck, Jones observed: *The Corporation! They waste no time spreading their subliminal programming, from the moment that we came under their jurisdiction!*

*

COLONIAL CORPORATION HQ

Gentain Carbone monitored the alert from Colonial Corporation headquarters. Renjinn, and his Belfars had escaped, but were being tracked on the grid. They were heading for Landfall. He did not want a downtown chase scene so he began working on a different plan. *Too many nosy tourists and off-world media around!*

"I want the terminal clear in twenty," he barked to a security Belfar on a holo before him.

Metropol was five minutes behind them. He flipped from station to station barking his orders like a bulldog on a short leash. "Back off, no sirens. We will get them at Landfall. Let them come. We will surround them."

He was setting up the intercept at Landfall. Flipping to the main terminal, he watched the evacuation. The spaceport was bustling with activity. He swiveled around and keyed up Astronav in the adjoining bubble.

"Detain the passengers until things clear up down below. Just tell them that heightened security is creating delays. Tell them nothing else, or I will have you ground up and fed to a slag wallow," Carbone muttered.

He swiveled in the COM and pressed several buttons on his arm console. Landfall popped up like Razzle Berry Mosh Tarts. He watched his orders being carried out on the flashing holos arrayed before him.

A banta of Troopers in auto-armor was still ten minutes away from Landfall. Another Banta of Landfall security guards were moving into an intercept position near where the Tadole fugitives would have to breach. Two Banta of security troops were setting up secured positions at all entrances and exits. Three Colonial Interceptors would not reach position in the atmosphere for almost 20 minutes.

A score of Metropol flitters were closing the gap on the Katofar and his Belfars as they pulled up in front of the spaceport. The hover-cab came to a halt about 100 yards before the entrance to Landfall. They did not fall into the trap the Troopers had set.

Instead, they scuttled the transport. Leaving the hover-cab running, the nullfield rudders kicked up a plume of fine red dust. The dust swirled and drifted in a soft wind over the Mollimix composite tarmac.

Rivo, Renjinn, and a half dozen Tadole Belfars burst out of its doors, opened the trunk, and armed themselves with the arsenal Rivo had prepared. They grabbed various portable explosives, lasers, charge cartridges, and a formidable, and portable, Kelson Laser cannon!

They bolted from the cab using the swirling dust to obscure their movements. Before they reached the entrance, they headed toward a utility fence beyond a stand of ornamental foliage. Already, they had secured an advantageous field position on the enemy.

Renjinn's orders were methodical. The Belfars anticipated his every command. They did not have the time to consider whether the evil Tharrr had possessed their commanding officer. It was clear to all of them that if they did not escape, they would become bog fodder by sundown. The Tadole understood war. Renjinn was the best. Rivo had planned well.

Unbeknownst to the Belfars with Renjinn, through merging with the Tharrr, the Tadole of Navidrrr had taken a evolutionary step of great consequence. The circle was beginning to grow.

Gentain Carbone cursed under his breath. *A half a dozen Tadole soldiers are an even match for a hundred Troopers! Tadole! Best fighters in the colonies! Not enough time, damn it! They will get away!*

Watching the holos around Landfall was like viewing a holofeel action-adventure story. The burly Gentain, with spaghetti sauce on his uniform privately lamented.

Renjinn and the other Tadole fighters scattered into a field of high brush that led to the fenced landing field behind the entryway to the empty terminal. The red pulse of the laser cannon shot out from the field, and took out the navigational and surveillance tower. The holos blinked off.

"Damn them, they knew just where to target us."

Gentain Carbone addressed Trigo-nav. "Send a pulse fax to Kaitain Majaiya and inform her of these actions".

Smoke and fire rose from the tower overlooking the terminal. All around the spaceport holos blinked out. Portions of the terminal lost power. Alarms sounded in a cacophonous jumble of discordant tones.

The crowds of evacuating travelers had been shuffled out of the terminal but they had not left the area. The sirens and alarms spooked them. Soon they became a panicked mob seeking safety in all the wrong places. Although no announcement was made. The Tadole sought escape rather than confrontation, yet, weapons fire echoed throughout the large area around the terminal. The revolution had essentially begun.

SPACE DOCK

Minutes before the Kelson cannon blast, the Omegan saucer touched down in the cargo bay along the vast rim of the enormous Space Dock. The Delaney Corsairs were lined up on the vast staging area dedicated to intergalactic shipping. Important events were happening with greater intensity, as an energetic matrix of interdimensional connectivity expanded.

Soon after the saucer landed, Space Dock had went on red alert. Smith and Chandri monitored the transmissions from the transport saucer. "It is not us they are after. However, they are not allowing any disembarkment", Smith said, as they loaded and locked their laser rifles.

"I think we should wait and see what is happening. They are alert and aroused. We will have greater difficulty now. We should wait." Chandri said, as she flipped through the Space Dock computer core.

Suddenly, she had Landfall on line. "What's this...code 5...that's multiple armed assaults! This is it!"

"Can you call up a holo?"

"I think so."

The holos jumped up from the rotating projector ports built into the floating floor. Chandri's hands danced across the keyboard as different views of Landfall shot up like tarot cards. Concentric circles of images revealed the herenow of illvibe panic. It was a war zone. Within seconds, they had an overview of the situation.

Donning virtual gloves, she moved screens in the electronic field before them with the panache of a musical conductor. Suddenly, she gasped. "It's Renjinn!"

As they watched, Renjinn was pointing at the control bubble outside Landfall. From the camera mounted on the main tower, you could see six heavily armed Tadole warriors with their dorsal fins fully raised. The tips tinged with scarlet. One was pointing a Kelson laser cannon directly toward the holo recorder. They had taken positions just inside a mangled fence.

"He's going to fire," Heidi said.

The laser burst ripped through the air. An angry red stain slowly grew from the center of the holo-projection as the laser-excited plasma hurled toward the tower. It blotted out the entire image. The Tadole had struck with deadly accuracy. The holo blinked off with a large snapping sound.

"I don't understand?" Heidi said. The Gaian Sentient Life rights observer was clear that she had a job to do. "The Katofar is the Corporation's man, no?"

Chandri turned to the holo field and moved around several projections in the virtual field. A shot of a burning tower stood pixilating upon the holo-projector. She turned to Heidi and looked her in the eyes.

"When I came to you, Renjinn had already been arrested. He is Tadole. All Navidrrr ex-pats, civilian or military, were arrested after the Corporation's defeat to the Tadole. As far as Renjinn and his staff go, their loyalties seem clear. It looks like they have brought their revolution here to Tatochin," she explained.

"They are trying to come to Space Dock", Chandri said.

"I agree they will come to us. Escape is their only option," Smith said.

"This could be a good diversion, then we can make our move", Chandri said.

Smith had wanted to move like lightning. He felt vulnerable in the tiny saucer with no armor or weaponry. Yet, Chandri was right. "Okay, we wait," Smith said.

Chandri put down her laser rifle and continued to work at the COM-station in the saucer. Her hands danced over the buttons like a mad genie. She began to broadcast a coded message.

Where is that Bodono!

*

LANDFALL

The laser cannon that had destroyed the surveillance bubble had an unexpected effect on Renjinn. He began to wake from a monumental dream. He memlocked his apartment. *Something inside me?*

He felt different. Instinctually he reached his hand down toward his sexual organ, it felt different. *By the blighted bogs of Terristrrr!*

It was gone! He panicked as a jumble of memlocks combined. A deep loss of his male Tadole organ of pleasure and reproduction vied for ascendancy with the greater ramifications of his new status. *Vichillia be merciful, I've got the other sexual organ! I am a female! No! No! No!*

More memlocks assailed his awareness as the Tharrr within sought to navigate the integration of consciousness. This was the Dance of Life to the Tharrr. To Renjinn it felt like he was losing control.

More memlocks flowed into his awareness. *Time is short; you have much to accomplish. We need the Tadole warrior now. You must remember.*

Renjinn saw it all in a flash. They had seared a path of destruction freeing the Tadole Belfars. They had plowed through fences, burning buildings, and security barriers. They had survived a high-speed chase through Ecksol to Landfall. He looked up and saw the ruined tower. It still smoldered and sparked with tangles of equipment spitting and coughing up nasty electrical fires in the wake of the direct hit. *My orders? Well done…I think?*

Pieces started to fit together. The Tharrr was integrating her identity into Renjinn. *I am not in control, by the blighted bog*!

His great golden eyes rose and embraced a moment of shear terror as he observed the apparitions that floated around his quivering dorsal fin. *Tharrr!*

Renjinn hissed, exposing primal levels of response. Suddenly, a smattering of a highly corrosive enzyme spurted from his frontal fin. The very rock he had taken shelter behind sizzled as it began to melt into something that resembled super-heated lava.

A corner of his brain, that had not yet integrated, roiled and churned like panicking snakes within his skull. His body was an activated chemical factory. He was morphing into the female of his species as he accepted the Tharrr symbiont in a mating ritual.

Rivo escaped from the Korum. He is the Tharrr Father now! He is…and I am? Rivo! By the Bog, he….then, he…NOOOOOOOO!

The Tharrr had joined to hundreds of different life forms through time. It was never the same twice. Each cellular transformation brought about by the powerful but rare mating, was its own story. This version starred Renjinn and he/she did not appreciate it at all. Then the Tharrr 'became' him, and the turmoil vanished. Information piled into his awareness. *Mother…of a circle! I need a cigar!*

The Tharrr reached into his pocket, slid a large Salvington cigar into his maw, and lit it. *I lit it?*

Integration had begun on a consciousness level. The new Renjinn slowly began to emerge. It would be a bumpy ride for some time. He looked at the Oblionese refuge. *Who is he?*

In a flash of memlock it was all there. Rivo's journey as a Tharrr/Oblionese was part of the collective awareness the Tharrr gave him. He saw all of these events as a series of interconnected strings. His mind had a quantum dimension that had been dormant. It was a part of the unconscious mind, driven by super conscious desires.

Rivo had been a Tharrr/Oblionese living off world. He was one of the few that ever left Oblion. Once Oblion had been destroyed, he had been captured by the Korum, and then offered protection. The Korum had unwittingly given refuge to the Tharrr!

Also an expert at surveillance, Rivo had been monitoring Renjinn for years in the employment of the Korum. His association with the Korum had given Rivo the inspiration to hope for the future flourishing of the great circle of the Tharrr. He had devotedly gathered knowledge of the soon-to-be Mother.

Renjinn's throat bellows inflated and deflated making loud farting noises. *Rivo...Father?*

Rivo purred with delight, upon Renjinn's musings into self-awareness. Rivo, the Tharrr, stood lightly panting. Fuzzy unformed light, in rainbow hues, whirled above and around his peculiar three-lobed skull. The Tharrr could mimic and manipulate holographic imagery. When not being consciously directed, it became a wonderland of visual phenomena.

The complex shift into the Tharrr mating ritual continued. The rapid biochemical energies activated during the primary process, impressed the personality and emotional body of the Tharrr. Though only a spore in its original physical manifestation, once joined with its host, a cacophony of changes occurred on many different frequencies.

To Rivo's right, Ostinglink and the rest of the Belfars, crouched behind the collapsed light tower that had fallen when the Kelson Laser hit the traffic control building. As they observed the Tharrr, the powder-coated mollimix stanchion still bubbled from the excoriating heat.

The military mind of Renjinn became dominant. The Katofar assessed the situation and became determined to lead his Belfars to glorious victory. The Tharrr enhanced the pure undiluted power of the Tadole warrior.

His senses registered all the data of his immediate environment with lightning speed. They were just short of the tarmac. A sub-light shuttle looked usable. A command summation was reached. All of these mental shifts within Renjinn occurred in just a few seconds.

The sound of laser weapons fire brought him out of the quantum nexus of revelation into the herenow in maximode. Landfall's security force was approaching. He knew it was only the beginning. Speed was their advantage.

Renjinn looked down the tarmac, marking the distance. He had not been out in the field for several cycles and realized that he missed the battlefield. Now, he had a new and vastly more important mission. He had entered the revolution totally. The Orion sector would become his battleground. First, he had to get to his home world.

He ordered a series of commands befitting a seasoned Tadole fighter. The Belfars responded with the expected efficiency. One of his Belfars did reconnaissance on a shuttle parked at the edge of the nearest landing pad. He waved an all-clear. The Belfars, Rivo, and Renjinn headed toward the shuttle.

Renjinn was calm. *The Tharrr need us and Navidrrr needs the Tharrr. The new Circle must survive!*

The first real opposition began to stream out of cargo ports onto the landing field. The white uniforms of Colonial Troopers started to mingle behind the standard blue of Landfall security. Several miles down the shuttle port, hover assault tanks were honing in on Renjinn's position. The Kelson lasers, their primary weapon, could derail escape. Time was of the essence. They would be in range in only a few short minutes.

With the Tharrr, he found himself processing all the information coming to him very rapidly. Even though he was out in a field, about to steal a spacecraft, he was able to experience the thrill of awareness, as if he was ensconced in his electronic COM-chair back at the Corporation. Now, it was available to him through the collective aspect of the Tharrr. *I suspect Gentain Carbone is at the COM, they are too well organized for it to be anyone else.*

"Katofar, what next?" Ostinglink stared at his boss, struggling with the urge to smear him into the eternal bog. His dorsal fin wobbled wildly showing multiple colors. *Is he Tharrr?*

"We take a shuttle to Space Dock and seek a plus light Corsair. We are going home!"

As Tadole, he knew his men would rally to the cause of their home world, Tharrr, or otherwise. Navidrrr was the top priority.

Renjinn no longer inhibited by the yoke of Colonial Trooper command and the need to be Corporate Conformed, rallied his Belfars in the Tadole warrior way. The deep drone of his throat baffles were the songs to summon war. The other Tadole joined in. Renjinn knew that the spores lodged within his lung cavity were ejected. The Belfars then became impregnated with the Tharrr symbiont. Gestation would leave Ostinglink, and the other Belfars, to their own wits for a while yet.

Renjinn growled to himself and sucked the acrid smoke of a cigar deep into his massive lungs. The Tharrr did not understand the cigar. For now, it was clear that the burning plant gave Renjinn some kind of chemically attractive sensation.

Renjinn noted the appearance of more uniformed security. "Let us go before the auto-armor arrives. Ostinglink, you slagwallow, pass out fresh charge packs by Vichillia's deep shadow!"

Oddly enough, Ostinglink's distress was pacified by Renjinn's demanding tone. It sounded like his boss. He had no interest in sitting in a Corporation jail, especially now. At least for now he trusted Renjinn to navigate them to freedom. *Navidrrr must be protected!*

Renjinn shot a volley of laser bursts into a gaggle of Metropol peace officers, as they emerged like ants from the terminal garages. He focused on the white uniforms, killing the troopers he had previously commanded. He felt no remorse.

"Long live Navidrrr!" he croaked.

The Belfars all inflated their throat bellows and chanted the ancient battle songs. Renjinn saw the all-clear sign by the Belfar who went ahead to access commandeering the shuttle. They rolled.

All opposition was slaughtered. The urge to return to their home world unified them. Their tactical firing rhythms were the stuff of legend in military circles. They reached an armored military shuttle and immediately dispersed to tend to various tasks.

Meanwhile, Colonial Troopers landed a dozen small tactical saucers on the tarmac. The heavy plus light interceptors were still descending from Space Dock. The hover-tanks would arrive any moment. Upon the stolen shuttle, a Belfar operated the front mounted laser. It ripped throughout the ranks of ground resistance holding them all at bay.

It was quickly turning into a pitched battle. The front mounted laser picked up the attack and a second flitter burst into flaming Mollimix. Fiery gobs of melted metal rained down on the bruised tarmac. The last shuttle landed. A dozen Troopers in auto-armor began to emerge from the carrier, but they were too late.

They rely on strength and numbers rather than a warrior's training. The fools! See how quickly we change the odds!

Everyone was on board with no casualties.

The distinct feeling that Rivo was fawning over him put him off. *Protecting the unborn horde within me? By the blood of the bog... Mother!*

Just then, a hover-tank crashed through the burning wreckage of the cargo vehicle barely missing the stolen shuttle as it lurched from the ground. The laser cannon fired but the blast rushed under the shuttle just missing it.

Renjinn stood in the open hatch holding two laser rifles that he depleted and then threw to the ground before closing the hatch. The shuttle's atmospheric afterburners lit, and they took off in a sharply ascending spiral toward Space Dock.

They entered the vacuum of space in low orbit. Space Dock was visible. The Interceptors were only several minutes behind them. They surged toward the spiraling wheel of the Space Dock with its lights giving it a jewel-like appearance. They landed on the space station with no interference.

*

CHAPTER FORTY-TWO

HIGH MOUNTAIN BASE
"That Which Can Spring From Fire"

I have eyes in a fire,
I weep and nourish in the water
I am a pillow to rest in the land
I feel everything in the air
I dwell in a universe of love
I am Shelila, the mother of all you see.

From: The Archives of Keltori

The faces of the rebels that gathered around the huge bonfire revealed an ocean of contained emotion. As he had so many times, Enro stood with a few friends among the ancient Ashwoods at Skull Rock. In his earlier life, he stood before Tritons of Colonial Troopers. Now, it was evolutionary forces of intergalactic dimension! In his gut, he knew he stood with the Pleiadians, the Elders, and Orville Parker.

Enro had memlocked many campfire meetings. It was his trademark. The fire was soothing and disturbing at the same time. It often had preceded violence and the loss of life in Enro's experience.

How often the campfire talks had been the preemptory inspiration calling the people to put their lives on the line. Often an inner voice seemed to indicate which of his comrades-in-arms would fall. It was something he would never get used to.

Gazing at glowing embers of a campfire had a leveling effect. Dangers, fears, and pains could be divided, and joys multiplied, in a group of friends. Some invisible force forged a bond in the collective focus upon a central flame.

Was it not also true of the Central Sun? Orville had once asked Enro that very question. Deep in his heart, Enro yearned for something different. That urge that struck most humans had hit Enro late. The flame had become externalized. *Shimtach. I have always wanted to be with her, ever since I came back to my planet.*

The time of Rahi was indeed far more than an ancient ritual. A pang of loneliness stabbed at his heart as he saw love blooming all around him. *So what if war was on the horizon! It didn't stop others. Why had it stopped me? Shimtach has been patient.*

The information Father Bodono had given all of them was extremely useful. Tactical information about sensitive locations, security code overrides, and the subtleties of the Centaurian surveillance systems, fueled the demand for action. Orville, Cleo, Enro, Tango, and Lesha, rose to the occasion diving into multiple and intense planning sessions.

Bodono's knowledge of the Centaurian technology that was pouring into the colonies was pivotal. It required a quantum leap in understanding bi-polar artificial intelligence, and system inter-link codes. Orville was in his element.

Cleo had been successful in translating her meeting with the Elders into a better focus. She explained that liberty is about self-governance. Organizing a system needs to be subservient to that liberty in order to align with the Elders' teaching. Concrete plans allowed pieces to fall into place. It was easy to experience the Elders' plan in a world of action. Philosophy would come later. For now, events crashed upon the beach of life like high tide.

Orville looked up at Enro, his ebony skin shining by the light of the primordial flames. His long twisted locks giving him a mane like a huge male Lecad. He felt the heat of Cleo's body next to him and imagined that it was the heat of the Central Sun itself. He snuggled closer to her and wrapped his arm around her side. They looked into each other's eyes.

Cleo said, "It's his job to infuse these people with a broader view of the events they find themselves embarking on."

Enro raised his arms and the crowd quieted down. He paced around the circle of flames with words on the edge of his lips. He would speak from his heart. There were no rehearsals and no script to follow in evolution. He planted his feet and took a deep breath of the cool evening air.

"The Corporation must go down."

The entire encampment stood and erupted in cheers and hoots that echoed off the cave walls.

"He's so good at this," Cleo said.

His arms rose again. "First, we will try diplomacy. However, we will not yield for anything less than home rule."

Again, everyone was on their feet cheering and hooting. "It hasn't been a straight road but we have had a lot of help along the way. We have friends, and that's important." Enro paused, making contact with the eyes of his listeners. They rested on Orville's for a long moment. A voice called from the crowd.

"I love you, Enro," a gruff baritone laced with a little Tatochin wine bellowed out. Wild applause filled the cave, tweaking a few stalagmites that hummed like tuning forks.

"I am going to ask you to expand your awareness beyond what is happening here on Tatochin. A revolution has begun. Right here on Tatochin, a group of Tadole, including our old friend Katofar Renjinn, have broken out of jail. Renjinn is Tadole. Navidrrr is his home world. The Corporation went to Navidrrr and the people rose up and destroyed the invaders. They said "NO" to the Corporation." Enro paused, letting the information sink in.

"Now, it gets even more interesting. Forces of great power and influence gather on Tatochin. We have been contacted and asked to join the greater cause that is our cause. I want to throw the Corporation out! I say "NO" to the Corporation. What say you?"

The crowd in the cave went wild. This had been what they were waiting to hear. After a long pause for hooting and hollering, Enro continued.

"The friends who brought me to you ten years ago, the friends, who said, go home your people need you, are now here to aid us in our moment of action. Some of them seem to wear the clothes of the enemy. Some of them you thought you knew. All of them are here for a common cause. We must stand united."

The people cheered. The meeting went on. Orville and Cleo came out to rousing applause. Tango came out with Lesha to hissing. They recounted the horror of the Lynch Cafe. Once they heard the truth, they turned the crowd around. The sole survivors!

"They survived the Lynch Cafe Massacre", buzzed through the assembled group like a jab to the collective gut. The Cafe was on the way to becoming an icon of the revolution on Tatochin. "Memlock the Lynch!"

Father Bodono came out with his red burnt face and tourist clothes. When Enro announced him as an Omegan liaison to a faction of the Omegans backed by Pope Hurus, the whole camp had erupted in laughter. It took a while for the rebels of Tatochin to be convinced of the Omegan priest's sincerity. It was a formidable task even for someone as trusted in the ranks as the mighty Kaitain Enro, the second-born leader of the revolution.

Humor could be empowering. Some time during the hilarious inquisition, the rebels embraced Father Bodono. One very drunk voice in the crowd kept yelling, "Show us your scar again, Bodono!" This was followed by intense laughter.

New wood was thrown on the fire and bottles of wine were opened. From that point on, the meeting was a formality. They were ready for action. Enro saw that this was an army unlike any he had ever commanded. The force of the Elders' will was a palpable reality.

Yoshen was tired as she approached the Kaitain's tent. The lamp was still burning and the flaps were open. He was deep in conversation with the Omegan priest, Bodono, and Orville Parker, the guy that was 450 years old. An open bottle of wine sat on a small table between them.

"Yoshen, things are heating up. You should be here. We may be waking the entire camp soon."

Enro turned to Orville and Bodono. "The escape Renjinn made at Landfall is now continuing at Space dock. The Delaney Corsairs are in the space station. The Trilateral Conferences could be in jeopardy. There is no word from Flex. We intercepted a plus fax, its some kind of code. Enro read the coded transmission:

MOON GODDESS SEEKS ITALIAN STALLION.
CLOSE TO BIG D'S CORSAIRS NEED DIRECTION.
OTHER PROBLEMS WITH PARTY CRASHERS.

"Does this make any sense to you?" Enro handed the paper to Bodono.

Bodono took the page. He stood up in a rush as he read the first word. "Its Chandri, she is close to the Corsairs. We have a Father Smith who is with us."

Enro stroked his hair. "Hmmm, party crashers?"

Orville jumped in, "Renjinn and his Belfars are the party crashers!"

"Right", Bodono exclaimed. "We have got to help Chandri!" Bodono said.

Orville looked deeply into the Omegan priest's eyes. He saw that the man's heart was connected deeply to the Elders. *He is a natural!*

Orville was delighted and simultaneously recognized the need for more data. "We need to make several plans. Father, tell us where to insert teams. We need to coordinate on several fronts." Bodono called up detailed schematics of the Royal Orion.

Yoshen picked up the wine and took a long pull straight from the bottle before she exited the tent. "I am going to get the rest of our team leaders assembled."

*

Tango and Lesha had discovered the most romantic spot at High Mountain Base. The area around the cave's hidden mountainside entrance had been landscaped. It had become the lovers lane for the rebels. The lip of the cave offered a breathtaking view of the highest peaks of the Tshini Mountains.

As the twin moons grew closer in their orbits, their lips found each other. Though Lesha and Tango were off-worlders, they felt the power of Rahi building. They walked slowly back toward the center of the camp in silence.

The trills and gurgles of the crystal clear stream was the dominant sound. The muffled voices of late night celebrants could still be heard off in the distance around the large fire. As they approached the edge of the light from the fire near a tent, a voice startled them in the dark.

"Arafad Tango X, you don't fool me."

A glaring light blinded Lesha and Tango, momentarily. They both nearly went into attack mode when a familiar evil laugh issued forth, and a cloud of blue, skunk-smelling smoke curled like a mirthful tide across the beam of the light.

"Vinny! I oughta shoot your tires out. What are you doing here?"

"The heat came down after the Cafe Lynch, Tango. Shit, I thought you had bought it. The question really is: where have you been?"

"Off world. It was too dangerous to contact you, Vin."

Vinny was a bottom line kind of guy. He had no need for long descriptions of events. "I'm glad you were thinking of me, cousin."

"Vinny, this is Lesha. Lesha, this is my cousin Vinny."

"You're taking your life in your hands hooking up with this guy. But, he's cool. He's my homey. Hey, it's a pleasure." Vinny turned back to Tango.

"I escaped, you know in the tunnel. Oh, they came after me soon after the Lynch went down. The fucking brain police! So, I blew up the warehouses. Sorry about your place, but I got them back good for the Lynch Cafe. I was pissed. I was sure you were vaporized when that one came down."

Vinny paused to take a long inhalation of one of his Menthol Rastas. "So I enlisted in the cause. Shit, I sold them most of the crap they got here. Tango, I modified an I-Wing for a certain wheel-chaired pilot!"

Tango felt Lesha tense. *"There is somebody listening in the dark!"*

"That is true, there is."

Shaso's telepathic skills had allowed her to read Lesha's projected thoughts. She came out of the shadows in her black leotard like a Lecad prowling in the night. She stood by Vinny, her hand meaningfully resting on his shoulder.

"They don't know she is a Dragon Fem", Vinny supplied.

"I am not a Dragon Fem anymore. Thanks to Vinny." Shaso smiled. It wasn't a big smile, but it was an honest one. She was aware that the gesture was a new thing. The flesh on her face was not used to moving that way.

Tango looked at Vinny and grinned giving him a soft punch on the shoulder. "Your secret is good with us," Lesha finished.

At that moment, Yoshen came up to them all in a huff. "Orville and Enro are meeting in the Kaitain's tent. There is a fight at Space Dock. We are going to intercede."

"Space Dock! That probably means us," Vinny said to Shaso.

"Tango, we got ourselves a two-seated combat I Wing. Its perfect for the two of us. Its older but its been modified. An Uton hyper-drive! You name it! Shaso and I will hear you on your com. I got my own squad, Tango! Who would have ever thought?"

Tango inwardly smiled. His cousin had survived great suffering. Now he has found love. He thought of Lesha. Talk about an Uton hyper-drive, Lesha, I love you.

*

Space Dock

The saucer Smith had commandeered from Tatochin slipped by security alerts in the chaos that Renjinn and his Belfars were creating one floor below them.

"Renjinn's flitter already landed before they ever got out of the launch bay. If there will be any diversion, it will be right here."

"I say we go while we can," Smith said from behind her.

"The timing will be delicate," Chandri noted.

Smith opened the airlock to the saucer and they slipped down the ladder on to the bay floor. Several of Smith's pilots made it to three of the Corsairs. They neutralized the guards posted on each ship before the trouble started. Securing the other three Corsairs would not be as easy. Chandri informed the deployed teams that Renjinn was making a move in the cargo bay below them. She had no idea what their objective would be.

*

Renjinn's tactical flitter landed below the tier where the Corsairs were parked. He was pleased. Though they were built for cargo, they had many weapons upgrades. Alot of firepower for a cargo Corsair.

The gangway to the flitter opened. Renjinn and Rivo conjured up the apparitions that would fool their enemy. They now looked like the enemy they sought to overpower. Colonial Troopers exited the flitter with lasers blazing.

The holographic Troopers confounded the actual Colonial Troopers. They were confused and unwilling to fire upon their own men. All around the flitter, bodies dropped boiling with the heat of the laser bursts. They believed that they had been trapped in a friendly fire event; their own men were shooting them!

"Why are they shooting at each other?" Smith asked.

Colonial Troopers seemed to be teeming through the entrance but something was wrong. Some of the Colonial Troopers began to return fire. The Belfars stayed well covered.

"They shoot at their own soldiers", Heidi commented.

"Look, the laser bursts pass through them! Apparitions! They are Tharrr," Smith said.

A charge from a laser cannon cleared the entryway to the ramp that led down to the Corsairs. Cargo of all types scattered everywhere.

"That was definitely not an apparition!" one of Smith's postulants said.

Now it seemed that hundreds of Tadole warriors were pouring through the opening.

"Where the hell did they come from," Smith bellowed in frustration.

Holographic apparitions were difficult to discern in the heat of combat. When one of Renjinn's fighters that had joined with the Tharrr was hit, the apparitions summarily evaporated back into the ethereal manifestation that had been called forth. Laser bursts increased as a pitched battle had began in the Cargo bay.

Among them, Chandri recognized Katofar Renjinn with a long, glowing Salvington cigar protruding from his lips. The Tadole cleared the ramp, and were on the floor where the Corsairs stood on their large landing struts. Laser bursts erupted with greater intensity in the chaotic skirmish.

Smith directed a portable sensor in his hand toward them. "According to this, only eight life forms are in front of us."

"They are heading for our position. They seek the same Corsairs we are trying to get. Now what? Shall we help?" Chandri asked. *The enemy of my enemy is my ally. I heard that somewhere.*

*

High Mountain Base

High Mountain Base had shifted into high gear. A dozen I-Wing fighters were being prepared for combat. Missiles were being loaded and fuel being pumped. On the sides of the fuselage, the rainbow colored rays representing the colonies, surrounded a brilliant star, still sticky with fresh paint. They would provide escort once the six Corsairs were secured.

They had just received intelligence that Renjinn was also trying to gain access to the large vessels at Space Dock.

Orville and Cleo had stated it clearly to Enro and the group. Orville stared at the holo-screens as he spoke. "Those Corsairs will give us the ability to begin to export the revolution to the colonies. I would say the Tadole are our friends at the moment."

Cleo chimed in when Orville returned his attention to the holos. "Renjinn and the rebels are on the same path. We must liberate those ships. It's now, or never."

*

SPACE DOCK

Wheelchair Vinny zoomed around in his chair answering questions and sending workers scurrying with last minute preparations. His own modified, wheelchair friendly, I-wing had been ready for days. Shaso stayed in the sanctuary and helped with the surveillance. It seemed best for her to keep a low profile. Dragon Fems were feared. Until the combat begins.

Orville and Cleo studied the Trigo-navigational layout of the Space Dock above Landfall. Tango and Lesha outfitted Bodono with a Relocator. Nimro, Sally, and Yaark, who had come from Mirror with advanced Relocator knowledge prepped Bodono, Nimro, and Sally for insertion.

They strapped on the Relocators and reviewed the details of the plan with them. Armed with pulse lasers, Centaurian disrupters, an array of timed explosive charges, and concussion grenades, the two teams were soon ready.

Sally got their attention. "All weapons on deep stun. Enro wants zero casualties. We want zero problems. Aim well!"

"Remember the cleaner this goes the less likely it will be that we disrupt the Trilateral Conferences," Orville said.

The portal was bathed in intense blue light, as the teams discorporated into sub-molecular, inter-dimensional goulash, bound for Space Dock.

Cleo and Orville stayed behind. Soon they would descend to the Royal Orion. They didn't need relocators to travel anymore.

*

TATOCHIN
Space Dock

The cargo bay bloomed into a thick webbing of crisscrossing laser fire. Chandri and Smith's group held positions around the outside of the three Corsairs that they had captured. The battle for possession of the remaining three Corsairs raged on.

Chandri grabbed Heidi's shoulder. "Come on, let's get on of those ships, now." She looked up getting Smith's attention. "You are one pilot short. If need be, I am a pilot."

"We will take care of the other two first," Smith said.

The Omegan Dame dropped into the pilot seat, and called up several command holos. She familiarized herself with the controls. *Quite a bit of firepower for a cargo carrier!*

Actual Colonial Troopers teemed through several entrances, and took up secure positions behind cargo that had been off-loaded. Renjinn and Rivo had led the Tadole Belfars to the Corsairs in a combined effort of confounding apparitions. Relentlessly, they expended deadly laser fire, as they fought their way to the plus-light space vehicles. Apparitions of cargo that was not there, offered false cover for Troopers who had just entered the bay. As cargo cover evaporated, a blood bath ensued.

I-wing fighters had launched from the military area of the dock. They buzzed about outside the cargo bay, like angry wasps around a jostled nest. The Colonial Troopers were caught off guard. In spite of that, if the Corsairs launched under the current conditions, they would be vulnerable.

Chandri closed her eyes and sent a strong suggestion toward Renjinn. *"Friends...Its Chandri... we have three Corsairs."*

Chandri felt the contact and recoiled. *Tharrr! A circle? Renjinn! My God.*

The Tharrr had received the message. Rivo and Renjinn directed the Belfars. With one flank covered, they started to make progress toward the ship that Chandri and Heidi occupied.

Suddenly, a dozen brilliant blue tapers of light materialized into the forms of the rebels from High Mountain Base. Lesha, Tango, and ten others bolted for the closest Corsair. Yaark, Sally, Bodono, and the rest of their team took cover with Smith and his postulants.

"We've got these four now. Chandri's inside that one," Smith yelled above the fray.

Bodono heard the exchange on the COM. When he heard Chandri's name he looked up to figure out, which Corsair held his beloved moon goddess. A laser burst slammed into his shoulder.

"Bodono is down," Sally sent.

"Is he dead?" Orville asked. He was monitoring the situation from High Mountain base. The terseness of his question startled him.

"No, he got hit in the shoulder, but he is a mess," Yaark said.

Orville exhaled. Things were happening fast. They were depending on the Omegan priest to enact their daring plan, but he realized in that nano-second that he had grown fond of the skeletal priest. "We need him conscious to make this plan work. Any chance of that?"

Bodono's head rolled toward them as if he was about to hear a confession. He grimaced with pain. "I'm alright...sort of..."

Tango took command of the situation, as laser fire crisscrossed the transport bay above his head. "Smith, Nimro, Sally, take him into the Corsair and we'll work on getting off this hunk of metal", Tango vocalized into the COM units they all wore. "Smith, you will pilot that one, ok?"

"Which one?"

"The one we are going to take now!"

Having given those orders Tango turned toward the battle on the bay floor of the space station. They ran shooting as they moved. To his left flank, he saw Renjinn, Ostinglink, and the other Tadole, burst into the Corsair occupied by Chandri and Heidi.

"I guess they are with us ", Tango uttered to Lesha. As they secured the Corsair.

They watched Smith help Bodono get to the Corsair. Blood streamed down his mangled shoulder. Tango continued to command.

"Sally! Plug him up and give him some juice to take the pain away, and keep him up. We will relocate him back to the sanctuary as soon as he opens the cargo bay. He is the only one who knows how to over-ride the system."

Tango looked at the portable radar sensor scrolling through several views. The device essentially hacked into Space Dock's liquid core matrix and pilfered the needed data. "The I-wings from High Mountain are on approach. It looks like it's gonna be a thick ship-to-ship dogfight outside the cargo bay soon," Tango said.

He discarded a spent power cartridge and reloaded his laser rifle for emphasis. "We got the best pilot in the galaxy coming with the cavalry from High Mountain Base. The sooner we take off the better." *You go Vinny, you go boy!*

*

Gentain Carbone reviewed the surveillance holos of the theft of the Corsairs from Space Dock. Intelligence had shown that besides Renjinn and his Belfars, rebels from Tatochin had stolen the rest of the armored plus-light Cargo Corsairs. He looked at his staff barely containing his seething rage.

Those fighters materialized from thin air! A transport device. We knew they existed but now…

The rebels of Tatochin had just become a hundred times more dangerous than he had ever expected. He felt a pain in his chest.

*

A REBEL SAFE HOUSE

South of Sobash St.

The trick with good makeup was blending with a large and soft brush. Flex chose colors that he intuitively knew would play off the lighting scheme of the Casbah. Tonight required something special.

Many Korum visitors would crowd the decidedly neo-Ottoman decor of the gaudy nightclub. Tonight he would transform himself into Topaz, the anachronistic harem dancer. Francine needed a rest. If there were watchers who witnessed previous contact, he did not want to set off a memlock of a suspicious pattern.

He strutted down the street with his usual erotic sashay. His thoughts buzzed with the effervescent herenow as the adrenaline pumped through his system and the twin moons of Tatochin neared their destined conjunction of Rahi.

As he approached the entrance to the Casbah, he noticed that the brain police were crawling all over the place. Something was going on. He had caught a holo-bulletin while the vactube transported him along the shore of Lake Wechen toward the resort at the mouth of the Remorah River. Landfall was shut down. Nobody knew why.

The remaining rebels at Skull rock had migrated through the catacombs to various safe houses throughout Ecksol. Everything was coming to a head. Flex felt the impending violence. His blood twitched with the ancient pull of Rahi. The attraction he felt cross-dressing as the sensual Topaz had put him into a giddy mood. Nimro would be shocked if he knew.

I am a rebel…almost like him.

He approached the crowded entryway to the Casbah. He ignored the line and strutted to the entrance.

Topaz doesn't wait. She creates!

Topaz approached the door with all her feminine charms swaying in the lake-cooled night air. She was admitted into the club that was packed. The wall of music, the smell of perfumes, exotic smoke, hungry eyes, and sexual tension permeated his awareness. Flex sensed that danger was close like a cool blade thrust into the heated fat of a roasted slagwallow.

Topaz surveyed the scene looking for the Gaian ambassador at the pharmo bar. His eyes went crazy. A woman stood in a black rubber dress tailored to reveal an intricate pattern of tattoos around her shoulder, waist, and hips. He was impressed; she looked amazing. He slowly approached, socializing to prevent any suspicion.

The music was a hyper-tech retro mix from Ganymede called, "Virtual Scan Lust". The lyrics seemed to sharpen the blade of danger that tweaked the jewel in Flex's navel like a tuning fork.

"Flippin synapses flyin sly.
sippin sexoid sacred thighs.
Cyborged ultra charged
chronic grinding.
Tumblin fever
in zero gee winding.
Gelled in slippery contours
Gyrating in grand glory,
laser licking feeling horny."

Flex reviewed the first meeting he had with Martha Fox. It had been brief. She was preaching restraint. "The UGC may intercede making any violence unnecessary," she had said.

I underestimated this woman's abilities…delightful!

Martha was distracted by the sheer lust the crowd exuded. *Maybe this Rahi is more than just a secular holiday! They say it is a time for celebration from ancient times. Hmmm, on Earth it was those ancient celebrations that were linked to the movement of planets, that laid a foundation for establishing religious holidays.*

She thought of her time on Tatochin. She feared for her friend Heidi's life. She was so impulsive. *Going off with errant Omegans to join the rebels!* How would she explain her absence to the UGC? How had she ended up at this nightclub in this ridiculous outfit?

The slinky black rubber dress left too much of her upper body exposed. She was a long way from home, and now she was all bloated as her moon cycle was approaching. *Damn those twin moons! I feel like the Pacific Ocean in here!*

The high heels she wore were the fashion. She could not imagine a more foolish idea. *If the Gaians could see me now!*

A beautiful harem dancer approached her, as she stood at the pharmo-bar.

*

Colonial Corporation HQ

Gentain Carbone crumbled the pulse-fax as he watched the view of Space Dock from his COM-chair. The coded message was from Korgon. Delaney was dead.

He squeezed the flimsy fax hoping to milk some dark satisfaction from the assassination. Korgon might take years to complete the rest of his mission. The charred remains of a Matter Relocator rescued from the warehouse in downtown Ecksol had been passed to corporate techno-geeks. It had been severely damaged.

The discovery of Quantum particles was of extreme interest to the most covert intelligence within the Corporation. Gentain Carbone held a secret post within Monarch. He had tasked the Korgon to find more evidence.

"Find the owner of this broken device and you will retire to whatever destiny you desire with all the credits you will ever need," Carbone had offered.

The situation at Space Dock was puzzling. Renjinn sought escape. That made sense, but other fighters were apparently involved. *They are way more organized than we suspected!* He was jolted back to the herenow when the Trigo-nav operator buzzed him.

"We have a dozen I-wings coming around the Northern hemisphere of Tatochin toward Space Dock."

"Is it Maijaya?"

"No, sir, they are unidentified."

"What do you mean unidentified!" Carbone sliced through the holos with his virtual glove moving various data fields until the I-wing fighters from High Mountain base popped up on the rotating ring of screens. *The latest models! Armed to the teeth! Space Dock is under siege!*

His thoughts turned to the Intergalactic Corsairs that had just arrived with over a thousand delegates and participants eager to attend the Trilateral Conference. He had held off on disembarkation for an hour already. If those I-wings arrived soon, a space battle would be a fiasco. The integrity of the entire conference was uncertain. The old warrior in him groaned. He had been defeated.

Politics!

"Pull back our people. Let them get away, he said.

"Sir?" The Belfar who sat nearest the Gentain looked up from his screens. All around Carbone the staff all looked at him for further confirmation. They were in shock.

"I said stand down. Broadcast the recall on all frequencies. We don't want any space battle going on outside Space Dock with all those people arriving! Let's set up some tracking on them.

Double the security at the Orion but keep it low profile. Don't spook the guests. Make sure the areas near the cargo bays are off limits. I don't want those visitors from off world to know anything about what happened in the cargo bay. Is that clear? Let those cargo Corsairs go. We will deal with them in other ways."

*

SPACE DOCK

Suddenly the rest of the Colonial Troopers exited the cargo bay. The rebels let out a tentative cheer. Bodies and cargo were strewn across the bay floor.

"They are pulling back", Smith said.

"It looks like they don't want a confrontation," Sally said. "Come on, lets get Bodono to safety. We gotta get out of here fast!"

Tango and Lesha carried the lanky injured priest into the vessel. Bodono was strapped into the Corsair's control station. Sally put compression on the wound. The injured priest turned his attention to the ships COM system. With his good arm, he deftly manipulated several holo-screens and hacked into the Corporation's surveillance systems. He bypassed every security protocol in the liquid core matrix.

Suddenly, the system in the cargo bay began to respond to Bodono's dictates. Blinking amber lights rotated, and bells sounded throughout the cargo bay.

Bodono looked up from his console as Lesha and Tango piloted the Corsair, "I can't get Chandri or Renjinn for that matter. They are not responding. Landfall is also dark. Do we have anything happening at the spacedock?

All the cargo corsairs had been taken over. Father Smith and his people piloted three of them. Tango and Lesha had one; Sally and Yaark another. The sixth had Chandri, Heidi, and Katofar Renjinn and his Tadole Belfars.

Enro directed his next orders to Bodono. "Can you get in?"

"I am trying but they have turned off some of the systems. It must be Renjinn. Nobody else would be able to do that. He is the only one who knows these systems well enough to block me unless it's the Centaurians."

Suddenly, Orville cut into Bodono and Enro's conversation from High Mountain base. "It must be the Centaurians. Renjinn would not protect the Corporation at this point. The Elders showed us that the Tadole were a part of a greater plan. Cleo confirmed this. This may involve the Tharrr, I am not sure."

At Space Dock, the cargo bay was devoid of life on the floor of the hangar. A metallic robotic voice droned on the loudspeakers. "Decompression in two minutes, please exit the cargo bay."

Tango and Lesha prepared the Corsair for flight. On the floor of the Space Dock the warning was repeated in three other languages. The conventional magnetic pulse engines of the Corsairs slowly built up power as the space doors opened to the vastness of stars. In all, six Delaney Corsairs departed the cargo bay. The bodies of Troopers and cargo floated out into the vacuum as the six ships departed.

Bodono's fingers danced across the console. He ignored the throbbing pain of his wound. "I got them". The exterior view of the Delaney Corsairs loomed up on the holo-projector.

Enro's voice floated across all the wired rebels. "They are letting us go. Stand down weapons. Let's leave quietly. The day has just begun. We do not want to spook the guests either. They are playing into our plan perfectly."

Enro gave thanks to the Elders for the reprise from all out combat.

*

A dozen rebel I-wing fighters joined the large cargo transports as soon as they cleared the orbital Space Dock. No sooner did the small rebel fleet consolidate, when one of the Corsairs activated its plus light engines and disappeared into the field of stars.

The Delaney Corsair with Renjinn and his Tadole warriors had left the planetary system of Tatochin with Dame Chandri and Heidi Roth, the sentient rights representative for the UGC, on board. The Tharrr had escaped the control net of the Colonial Corporation completely. The rest of the Corsairs dispersed with escorts to begin the transport of rebels to strategic locations.

Father Bodono watched the holo and gasped, "My Chandri where are you going!"

*

COLONIAL CORPORATION HQ

Gentain Carbone watched the Corsairs departure with a deep frown. "Release all the passengers in bay six. Close the north passage and direct them to the downtown military base in Ecksol. Landfall is closed."

His excuses though plausible were not the real reason for the closure of Landfall. The mess would take several hours to sort out. A secondary tower was almost operational. His intelligence staff was working feverishly with media to misinform the public properly. His head was spinning.

Perhaps we will announce a civilian accident at Landfall. He made a call to his media contacts within the corporate offices. They would see to the details.

Now we will escape. The Centaurian vessel was cleared to land on a hidden frequency communicator given to him by the Dravithian Lord Karnad. He sighed with displeasure. *The rebels have made a fool of me!*

Gentain Carbone had seen enough to make an assessment. The rebels were an army. He was sure that some unknown technology had been involved. With Renjinn and Bodono among the ranks of the rebels, his only hope was Majaiya. It was a slim hope at best. He started to make plans for the Corporation evacuation.

*

TOPAZ

The Casbah was filled with visitors bound for the Trilateral Conferences. It was also a interplanetary mélange of life forms. The dance floor was sea of diversity with the chaotic combination of visual stimuli including jiggling arms, wobbling eyestalks, all manner of tentacles, exoskeleton insects, as well as, humanoid life forms.

Languages of many types created a droning chitter of strange sounds that mingled with popular music from across Orion. Bowel wrenching woofers pumped out low frequency bass combined with soaring high-pitched frequencies. This was the fashion in what was anachronistically referred to as, a disco.

Within all the chaos and visual virulence, a pearl of beauty ignited the crowded room. Topaz had cleverly chosen a spot that was well lit. Martha could hardly believe her eyes. *This Flex is one weird cat!*

Topaz laughed, as he approached Martha. She smiled seductively at the line of attractive males that opened a cordon through the gesticulating alien crowd. Though he was immersed in his role-playing, he was not lost in his devotion to being Topaz. Flex was intent on making an important contact for the rebels.

With little further indulgence directed toward Martha, Flex put her at ease, without ever departing from his persona as Topaz. "I prefer to hide in plain sight. It has always worked for me. It allows me to express other sides of my personality. I assure you, Ambassador, I represent the rebels of Tatochin. I am here for that reason, and that reason only."

Martha relaxed. She wasn't sure that Flex's motives were all business but it appeared to be working. It was comforting. Taking his cue, she relayed her most important message to the glowing goddess.

"The UGC is willing to recognize the freedom fighters as a separate and legitimate group. The Corporation wouldn't dare make a move against the UGC."

Topaz flipped her hair, "The Corporation, they may not act openly. In my world much happens in stealth." Topaz's jewelry jingled as she sipped her drink.

Flex didn't see it coming. A Centaurian disruptor froze his motor operations as the drink spilled down his fake cleavage.

Black seemed to materialize out of the fog of freakily attired patrons. Several priests dressed as customers caught Flex as he began to tumble.

"Give her some air, she will be fine," Black said.

The priests quickly hustled the rebel to a flitter that waited outside. Black turned to Martha who was still recovering. One of the so-called priests restrained her.

"So the Gaian Ambassador enjoys the night life of Ecksol? I suppose keeping the company of terrorist murdering scum is part of your job? Is that what you will say? Really, I am surprised."

Martha had gotten a good jolt from the disruptor's field. Feeling painfully returned as her scrambled nerves settled down.

"I don't know what you are talking about." Martha managed.

"I should have you turned into compost, you dirt-loving ecology slag", Cardinal Black sneered.

He looked around at the crowded nightclub. A large crowd of regulars and off-worlders gathered around the Gaian and the unconscious Topaz. "Thank you for leading us to the notorious Tshauna Flexington. He has been wanted by the Corporation for a long time." *Fuck the evacuation. I will get some vengeance before I depart this dam abortion!*

Black's eyes rested on the attractive Gaian for a long moment. With a flourish he glanced at his people, signaled the Omegan priests, and they departed with Flex.

*

A CORSAIR IN PLUS-LIGHT SPACE

On the ship with Chandri and Heidi, the Tadole Belfars had immediately assumed command positions in the plus-light Pleiadian designed ship. With a combination of awe and fear, Heidi and Chandri watched the Katofar Renjinn chew on the tip of a bright blue cigar. Apparitions swirled about his dorsal fin just like the Oblionese refugee, Rivo, who sat in the pilot's chair.

Heidi turned to Chandri, "The one from Oblion I can understand, but now Renjinn is one of them."

Chandri hissed in a low voice, "it means they are spreading, and jumping species."

"I know, I know," Heidi whispered back to her in urgent tones.

The idea of possession evoked primal fears. Heidi's professional commitment as a sentient life rights observer was the only thing that dammed up the fear, and allowed her to remain objective. She had learned to compartmentalize difficult memlocks in a crisis.

Chandri had spoken to Bodono just after he had decoded the cargo doors. The Troopers had pulled back from the fight in the cargo bay.

"What about the Tharrr. Now, what will happen?"

"I don't know, but I am not being given any choice. I am going with them to Navidrrr. I love you!"

Bodono felt the contact fade. He also sensed the thoughts of myriad life forms. It was something large and expansive. He was worried that it might be the Tharrr.

*

HIGH MOUNTAIN BASE

High Mountain Base was in a froth of action. Whether it was Rahi, the Goddess Shelila's blessing, the Elders, or the strange man, Orville Parker, with his flyaway hair and diverse cohorts, the world would never be the same again. Everyone was in maximode. The nearnow loomed largely in their collective awareness.

Enro watched a lone Corsair break from the pack and jump to light speed disappearing from the screen.

"The coordinates suggest a standard pattern for Navidrrr," the rebel who monitored the Trigo-navigational display said with finality.

Orville looked up to see Cleo standing in the shadow of holos in the sanctuary. Cleo stared at the blank spot where the holo-image had been. Her eyes, like a large luminescent question marks, looked up at Enro and Orville.

"Chandri and Heidi Roth, the Gaian Ambassador were on that Corsair."

*

CHAPTER FORTY-THREE

RAHI
TATOCHIN

"Human beings thrive on mythologies.
They are often occupied with their
own personal retrostory with such fervor,
that they have little energy for anything
besides propagation and livelihood.
It is our job to provide a greater context
based on consciousness. If this is not done
with utter honesty it will return to haunt us.
With the truth this awareness will grow more
rapidly and peacefully".

Cardinal Fellini: Address to the council of Cardinals. 2345

From above the planet, Bodono watched the approaching conjunction of the moons, Wechen and Capach, as they glowed brightly above of the Tatochin's landscape. Several I-wing fighter escorts took up positions that flanked the cargo Corsairs that had been reassigned hastily as rebel transports. His thoughts phased like the heterodyne electric pulses of alternating current between Chandri's fate and the coming assault.

His shoulder felt pretty good. It was a little tender and itchy where the proto-skin covered the worst of the laser blast. He phased back to the last hour. First, he had been shot in the cargo area of Space Dock just before he could reunite with Chandri. He had been relocated, and with expert triage, he stayed on his feet.

Tactical saucers were delivering rebels to several Corsairs in stationary orbit. It was time to act and move. Stealth and secrecy were not important anymore. The final assault on the Corporation was in full swing. The use of the Relocator technology gave them an edge in rapid deployment unlike anything the Corporation could muster. Kaitain Enro's plan was complex. Strategic locations had been chosen to retake the entire infrastructure of the Corporation.

"When we relocate to Ecksol and the Orion, I want you with us. Are you physically up to it?" Enro had asked.

"Yes, of course I am", Bodono lied. He had consciously been suppressing the pain and weariness he felt from the moment of being wounded. He had to go.

Bodono thought of Jones. *There has been no contact possible! Hopefully, that will come soon.*

He phased to Chandri, calling up the image of her face in an instant. If the Tharrr had possessed Renjinn, what would happen to Chandri? He tried to put the grim thought aside. He loved her and feared for her safety.

*

Tango and Lesha joined him in the passenger quarters. "Enro says the show will start in twenty minutes. Once we are fully deployed at Space Dock, we will relocate to the COM room at the Royal Orion." Lesha reported.

"Smith will precede us with a Banta of Omegan postulants and fighters from Mirror. While they secure the Colonial Corporation building we will take the COM room at the Orion. Then we will summon you to the control room." Tango said.

"I can assist in securing the Colonial Corporation building much better from the COM room at the Orion. Renjinn had insisted that there be overrides. I programmed them myself. The sooner I'm in the chair the better."

"Cleo says your injury is more serious than you let on. Is that true?" Tango asked.

He looked at the two of them and sighed. "I'm able to handle the COM, but don't count on me for any fighting."

They looked at each other. "Okay", Lesha said, "You stay with us."

Bodono took the Matter Relocator that Lesha offered him and began to strap on the forearm controller. His shoulder protested.

"Here let me help you with it," Tango said.

Kaitain Enro was just finishing some instruction somewhere. "Father Bodono. How is your injury?"

"Much better. Damn sunburn is still itchy though."

Bodono scratched for emphasis. Enro of course couldn't see that. He was on some flitter speeding toward Ecksol at that moment.

Enro let out a short laugh. "You stay with Tango and Lesha."

Addressing Tango and Lesha he said, "It's hard to gauge the timing with Nimro in Ecksol. As soon as possible, let's get the good father to his COM chair."

Yoshen's voice from High Mountain Base came through in all their earpieces. "We have taken over Space Dock. We are sending any passengers to the military space-port near down-town Ecksol. Oh, and its ten minutes to Rahi."

Everything in Enro's plans was designed to achieve a balance of two goals. The first goal was to achieve the tactical objective. Second goal was to create as little damage and loss of life as possible for friend and foe. Success with no mess had been his mantra.

*

Bodono phased back to the herenow buzz. Whether it was pure adrenaline or the movement of the moons, the bodies of the rebels tingled with the powerful energies impregnating the atmosphere.

Bodono suddenly remembered Cardinal Black. "Enro!"

"Yes, Father."

"Get a message to Smith. Cardinal Black is in charge of the Colonial Troopers. He is a dangerous psychic. He will know we are coming."

Enro spoke into his microphone. "Did you get that Smith?"

Bodono heard Enro in his earpiece as well.

"Yes, I did Enro."

"Thank you, Father Bodono."

*

"The King and Queen of the Ball"

Out in a quiet garden area, two tapers of white light materialized into two strangely garbed partygoers.

Cleo felt fairly naked in the outfit Orville had picked. It was the way he sniggered along with his refusal to explain. *What does Fredrick's of Hollywood mean anyway.*

They easily mingled with the other guests dressed as they were as a merry widow and a hairy gorilla. They fit in perfectly.

*

ROYAL ORION
"The Chocolate bars"

Gentain Carbone had made his required appearance at the reception. He had tried to avoid any meaningful contact. Visitors had been outwardly polite. He had felt the flush of embarrassment and heard the whispers of gossip as he shook the various hands, and mandibles, that were required of him.

Prince Kalimafar cavorted about the room laughing too loudly and saying too much. His corrosive tongue fueled by some local plum wine. His long list of cheeky innuendos caused Carbone to momentarily phase to lethal and poisonous thoughts.

They were never far from the surface for him anyway. With Delaney, he had handled his betrayal in the usual manner. Korgon was reliable. The shape-shifting assassin had performed his function as was required.

He fantasized that given the opportunity he would relish personally overseeing Kalimafar's session on a torture ring. *The bastard is too dangerous to kill though. King Fezam would not rest until it was avenged.* He phased to his meeting with Kalimafar earlier. *Infuriating!*

The obscene Korum bad boy had approached with women lewdly hanging on his shoulder like accessories. One was a vicious looking Dragon Fem. *How dare he!*

Kalimafar had barely hidden his delight as he observed Carbone's scowling face. Carbone felt his head heat up with anger. *Just because this event is sponsored by the UGC he thinks he can ignore protocols. Arrogant!"*

"Sorry to hear about Space Dock," Kalimafar chirped.

Several heads had turned. Space Dock was classified information! Technically, he was not even supposed to know about it.

Carbone shook with anger momentarily. *His techno-geeks would easily hack into that shit!*

"Perhaps, the Prince has had too much to drink?" An overstuffed sheik from the Korum delegation had intervened.

Kalimafar introduced Sheik Abbas. Carbone recognized the name. *He's not part of any delegation. This is a known smuggler. How did he get in here?* He silently recalled that Renjinn had him under surveillance as a weapons black market trader.

Carbone was demoralized. Everything was falling apart. The Corporation had failed. Sheik Abbas milked the moment for all it was worth. It was clear to Carbone that he was being minimized by virtue of recent events. *He hides beneath the carrion wings of the Korum.*

Kalimafar moved on to his next quarry. Gentain Carbone exited the UGC reception with twisted thoughts of strangling Kalimafar. He retreated to the back hallways that led to the COM room. An area with vending machines was his immediate target. He sought some small form of solace by destroying several food-dispensing machines with his Mollimix tipped boots. He shamelessly looted one for chocolate bars that he stuffed in his pockets and maw, carelessly.

The acute aspects of his rage spent. Carbone entered the COM room. Something felt different. The hairs stood up on the back of his neck. He felt as if someone was in the room. It was like the calling card of a Dravithian to appear in astral form. His body tensed. *It feels different.*

A sudden wisp of cool air seemed to graze his chocolate smeared cheek. He turned and surveyed the spherical room with its secondary bubbles. Then sat in the COM chair and watched the reception from the holoscans that surrounded him. He alternately muttered curses in languages that spanned galaxies and voraciously consumed the rest of the chocolate bars.

The holos still tracked Kalimafar's movements in the midst of the crowded reception. He was introducing his special dancers. Two voluptuous naked women undulated into position beneath the argon lights. They had huge, engineered, cleavage that commanded significant reconsideration.

They stood still in readiness. One was completely red and one blue. They began to move with the music of droning pipes, whistles, and strings combined with soft drums, and dramatic light sequences. Shifting shadows played upon their naked forms. They erotically enveloped each other, demonstrating amazing control and suppleness in a full contact dance. Ample folds of oiled pigmented flesh undulated into sapphic eddies of lust and arousing display. The juxtaposition of quivering blue flesh, and jiggling red flesh, was an artistic expression of the conjunction of Rahi. The orgasmic moment hovering over the hearnow.

Gentain Carbone looked around the surveillance room. One of the last of the chocolate bars had melted in his mouth during the performance. Many of the holo stations of his team were lit up with energetic display of the powerful and beautiful forces conjoining at the time of Rahi. He stuffed the last chocolate bar into his salivating mouth.

*

Farooq Masad glanced at the holo centrally placed in his suite. The holo-caster chirped on like a great and ugly parrot in corporate speak. Selling the entertainment provided by the Korum, a naked, writhing women promised an experience that would razzle-dazzle a zombite.

Not what King Fezam would prefer: Prince Kalimafar flirts on the edge of scandal, but I suppose on this planet with this Rahi business, it must be tolerated. The crowd does seem to be enjoying it...

Farooq still had concerns about what the impact of the prince's clandestine arming of the rebels might yield. He privately admitted to himself that anything that might clip the fetid wings of the carrion-eater, Corporation, might benefit the whole.

*

Martha was looking forward to the evening's festivities. She had successfully contacted rebel elements and delivered her message, in spite of Flex's unfortunate capture. Though it was upsetting, she was looking forward to being in the Korum Ambassador's company. She knew it would be politically wise, however she was genuinely enamored in the great man's presence. She wore her witch costume, embellishing the dress she had worn at the Casbah. *I like this man. He is sexy. This Rahi thing is affecting me!*

Martha wore a semi-transparent black rubber dress that clung to her hourglass body. It had lashed openings on her shoulder, ribs, and hips. Cleverly crafted to display the delicate tattoos that were so popular on Earth. She regarded her outfit in a mirror. It was very sexy. She had some concern that the Ambassador might be put off by such a display. Then she smiled and joined him in the hall.

Farooq Masad wore a stylized Bedouin robe with multi-hued metallic thread. The plumed mask gave him the look of an exotic demi-god.

He placed his arm around hers as they approached the Gala. A small vactube opened up to a private VIP room just off a grand stairway down to the main floor. From there, Farooq and Martha could see the crowded ballroom of the Royal Orion.

"You see," Martha said, "You will fit in. You look very handsome."

The touch of her body on his hand sent forbidden tremors of pleasure to dusty synapses that screamed with excitation. *I should do this more often! She evokes such warmth in me.*

In spite of Martha's immersion in the spirit of the evening, she retained some rationality. She realized that the ambassador was challenged by her physical energy. The attraction was palatable. *Is it Rahi? I am feeling very juicy!*

A higher understanding of reality was his only safe harbor. As a public figure, he often found himself caught in such conundrums. In the current situation, it was not the politics of the Korum, or the evil of the Corporation, rather it was his personal life.

Martha looked up at the peacock-masked man from whom she had learned many things. She respected him greatly. *He battles with his feelings. By the Goddess, I think I must have him!*

Farooq Masad was considered a champion of the Gaian movement because of his writings. He had been compared to Gandhi. That he should look upon her with such adoration impressed her deeply. *Later, we will make love.*

Together they watched Kalimafar's dancers. Farooq Masad groaned. *That Prince Kalimafar is a dirty dog!*

Casually, they left the safety of the observation deck and mingled with the crowd.

*

THE ROYAL ORION

Bishop Jones found himself surrounded by the many guests attending the festive affair. His face was hidden beneath a cheap mask that he had hastily purchased at a gift store in the lobby of the resort. It made his nose itch causing him to sneeze. *A sneezing Demigod! That's just what I don't need.*

With Bodono and Chandri gone, he had to put together bits and pieces from postulants and functionaries loyal to Hurus. The entire Omegan safe house near Landfall had been destroyed by saucer drones. Smith and all the postulants had disappeared.

Cardinal Black was no help at all. Carbone had been almost feral! Jones was happy though. His intelligence, though sketchy, pointed in a satisfying direction. So, he watched as waves of colorful faces paraded about celebrating Rahi.

Jones spotted the Gaian Ambassador who Chandri had been charged to watch. *She had contact with Chandri before she disappeared!*

He changed course and navigated through the sea of bodies toward her. On a nearby stage a singer hugged the microphone and sang the song especially created for Rahi!

*

"The land tremors with your shadow play,
Lets dance the night away.
The tides do swell expressing
the yearning of my lonely heart.
Blue knight's sword casts his shadow
on the Red Goddess's glowing cave.
Perched on the bosom of Shelila.
Rahi's come like a midnight sun
Let's dance the night away".

Jones was startled by the heat and mood of the crowd. This planet with its twin moons put expanded meaning to the word lunacy. People laughed and wept with total abandon. Many were in a trance state. He found himself moving in the rhythmic manner of those dancing just to navigate toward his destination.

He felt the crush of a woman's breast, a hip here, a buttock, and a tail waved before his eyes. A hand slid across his crotch, giving him a squeeze as it slipped back into the nameless mass of people. Inside he felt his blood boiling with feelings that had been dormant his whole life.

His experience went beyond sexual attraction, it was community bonding. His body tremored with tribal and almost savage waves of energy. Finally, he stood before the Gaian ambassador and groaned. *This Rahi appears to be the real deal!*

The Gaian ambassador had captivated Jones thoroughly. "Ambassador Fox, allow me to introduce myself, I am Bishop Jones."

"Glad to finally meet you. You look a bit flushed are you okay?"

"Hmmm, yes, I am unaccustomed to such gatherings."

"Indeed, so am I…Do you know Farooq Masad?"

"It is my pleasure. Your reputation precedes you."

Farooq had heard of Bishop Jones. "I had occasion to meet with Cardinal Fellini several times before his passing. He mentioned you."

"He also told me of your meetings. I have followed your work. As you might know, there are many of us, including Pope Hurus, who oppose the Corporation."

Farooq Masad was not in the mood to be an ambassador, however, habit and duty prevailed. He leaned toward Jones and whispered.

"Only now, when blood is shed and forces gather for war, do you come forward. This would not have been Fellini's way."

Jones reaction was swift. Fellini's death had etched deep grooves into Jones' soul. He knew on another level that Farooq Masad would receive a more valuable memlock.

"Hurus, the Grand dame, and I were at his side when Fellini died." Jones stepped back and his voice took on a softer tone. "He asked to be propped up in his bed and to be turned to the North. He asked Hurus to take the popular position so that he could become Pope."

"So, Hurus sided with the faction that wanted the liaison with the Corporation. This was the only way to keep a wedge in the plans of the Corporation. We have sought to keep his ideas of a healthy and decent Omegan path alive. Only now has the balance of power shifted so we can openly oppose. It's not a moment too soon! The shift has come from the people themselves. Please do not judge us all for a few."

Farooq was silent.

"The Grand Dame Taylor will be here tonight. Ask her yourself. I also have some issue with the Korum. I find your view of the Omegan's endeavors curious in light of our very detailed intelligence concerning the arming of rebels through your illustrious Prince Kalimafar."

"I do not believe for one moment that you had anything personally to do with it. However, I think it is fair to say that we all have dirty laundry. This would not happen without King Fezam's knowledge."

Martha was keenly aware that she stood between two men who took their work very seriously. Masad grunted with acknowledgement.

"Your group of heretical Omegans is not the only faction opposed to the status quo. Herenow unrest arises in many of the colonies in proximity to the Corporation."

"So, okay let's kiss and make up." She said while striking a pose that would melt any man's resolve.

The two men looked up with their ridiculous masks, and Martha burst out laughing. The two men shook hands and laughed too.

"Bishop Jones, I suppose you would like to ask me about Father Bodono and Chandri."

*

Orville and Cleo sipped Andarian Fizz and watched the dancers conclude their improvised contact ballet. The air of the reception was taut with the sexual tension it was meant to evoke. The double lunar conjunction of Rahi approached.

"Orville, I am just fine but really… I am not accustomed so such display."

"You know Rahi is actually an old ritual to sanctify marriages. It has become, alas, little more than a public display of sensual sexual behavior.

"Living on Mirror is really not like any place else. When we have our honeymoon perhaps we will visit Mychronitia, the Pleiadian home-world. Boy, that place will shift some energy! For now, let's just observe the fruits of many years of planning."

Cleo smiled and placed her hands on her hips. In the merry widow underwear, she looked sultry to Orville but he didn't react."

What is a honeymoon?", Cleo asked in demure tones.

"It's a special time when people get married. They go away together or spend time together in a new home."

"Okay, you can take me," Cleo giggled and began to tickle the giant brown gorilla that escorted her. In the atmosphere of Rahi it didn't even raise an eyebrow.

"*We must be careful but act carefree, my love, let us pay attention to our primary task. We need to make contact with Tremador and Ziola.*"

Seeking stability through concentrating on their task, while appearing carefree and playful, they observed various groupings of dignitaries, ambassadors, and trade reps, as the festivities continued. The harmonics that collectively issued from the crowded room seemed to be slowly but surely reaching a crescendo as midnight approached. Orville spotted two familiar faces that sought and found his eyes.

"Tremador and Ziola!" Orville said to Cleo.

Cleo was distracted by the sudden presence of Alphonse in spirit form, just as they had noticed the couple. The Elder who had been the spiritual guardian of Tatochin spoke from his realm directly to Cleo.

"*You are to go with them. A place has been prepared.*"

Orville registered the communication between Alphonse and Cleo, while he observed Farooq Masad, Bishop Jones, and Martha Fox. Orville looked at Cleo.

"*So we have other allies in our midst!*"

"*Yes, visible and invisible!*"

Cleo dressed in her merry widow and Orville in his gorilla suit joined Ziola and Tremador. Together they approached Farooq Masad, Bishop Jones, and Martha Fox. After a few choice words, they resolved to take their conversation into more quiet surroundings.

They all intuitively understood that while they were present at a festive gathering and an intergalactic conference, beyond the walls of the resort a revolution was fomenting. Large forces had gathered in a nexus of transformation that could easily explode into chaos. The group began to depart the room.

*

Carbone quickly sent a pulse Fax to Maijaya and a Centaurian vessel cloaked in an outer orbit. *We can do our evacuation at Landfall.*

He turned his attention to the central ballroom of the opening reception and watched the gathering with sudden interest.

Farooq Masad and Bishop Jones! This does not look good. Who is that stunning woman in the slit dress? The Gaian Ambassador! Friends with that sentient life rights bitch!

Carbone began to key the auditory controls. Just then the Control room monitors filled with static. The hairs on the back of his neck once again stood up, as his body registered what his eyes had not yet seen.

"What the…"

Dozens of tapers of light brilliantly lit the COM room, as the forms of Tango and Lesha and the team, from the orbiting Delaney corsair, materialized before the Gentain. The particle beam laser in Tango's hand was trained on Carbone. The room was full of armed rebels.

They stunned the rest of Carbone's surveillance crew with Centaurian disrupters. The room was secured and rebels were stationed at the lone entryway to prevent any surprises. Lesha spoke to her link.

"Okay, bring him in, the Orion COM is secure."

Moments later, Carbone's eyes widened as Father Bodono appeared before him. The purpose that glowed in Bodono's eyes combined with the absurd tourist garb of the former Omegan unnerved the defeated Carbone. His vicious, feral nature showed.

"You will pay for this, Bodono!"

"Gag him, he has a big and distracting mouth." Bodono said.

He slid into the COM chair and let his fingers dance across the twin keypads in the rotating chair. Moments later, he had taken over Space Dock, and the entire Colonial Corporation planetary net with deft precision. The face of Yoshen and Enro appeared on holos before them. Bodono had a glow about him.

"Greetings Kaitain, and welcome to Rahi at the Orion."

"Well done, Father. Good work all of you. We are sending Smith and our people into the building now.

"Look, there is Orville and Cleo", Tango said, pointing to the holo-cluster of surveillance windows covering the midnight festivities of Rahi.

Bodono manipulated the scanners and watched them depart. "They will be here in a few moments. Tell our guards with the costumes, I don't want any accidents."

Gentain Carbone stared, fascinated and vexed. He had just noticed that very grouping before the rebels had arrived. Even more unnerving was the face that had appeared on the holo moments before.

The Kaitain lives! He is the rebel leader!

He was stunned with the revelation. He knew right then he was doomed to defeat. His disgrace was complete. *Only the Centaurians can help us now. They will be reluctant.*

*

Colonial Corporation Building

The lunar shadows mingled with the objects and bodies that roamed Shelila's skin. Sexual pheromones mingled with the energies of festive cheer, and deadly revolutionary resolve. A hushed but meaningful message began to circulate on the streets.

The area around the white monolith of the Colonial Corporation building was surrounded by a colorful array of costumed rebels. They had wandered away from the main festivities with a casualness that only coalesced into a strike force moments before the action was to begin. Pieces of costume that hid their weaponized war gear fell to the tarmac as they approached the target.

The flames of passion roused by the full conjunction of Capach and Wechen cast its violet shadow across all that passed upon Shelila's ardently vibrating skin. The rest of the grand parade of costumed marchers wove down the street while hordes of onlookers hooted and hollered. It was a perfect diversion for Enro's plan to take Tatochin back from the Corporation.

Five blocks down from the parade, Nimro stood with twin-laser assault rifles and about eight other deadly weapons. On his signal, Nimro's ground troops dropped all sense of Rahi and produced an extensive array of light weaponry. Four groups began assembling several portable Kelson lasers that would breach the entrance for the ground assault.

"We are in position", Nimro vocalized into his link.

The entire rebel strike force heard the voice of Enro. "Okay. Now remember, we only want to soften them. Good luck and bless you."

Wheelchair Vinny had modified his I-wing fighter with several spy drones. He manipulated a separate console from a low stationary position above Ecksol.

"Come down low and give me a position in downtown by the building. I need to see what's going on in front of the Colonial Corporation," Enro said.

"My old neighborhood, what about that," said Vinny.

Yoshen had established command at Space dock. Once the government fell they would coordinate a takeover of all civilian services.

The Corsairs had landed and disgorged the fighters from High Mountain Base. Several nearby urban parks and a soccer stadium had become improvised landing sites.

"Enro, I'm going to look for Flex".

"Nimro, be careful. Let Sally and Durga cover for you".

"I've already briefed them." Nimro said in his usual terse manner.

"Wait for my signal. Smith is making his move." With that, Enro's link went silent.

*

COLONIAL CORPORATION HQ

Smith and his team relocated to The COM room. It was empty. His team stood in the empty spherical chambers. The rest of the Corporation headquarters was still occupied, but the big brass had vanished.

"Is it a trap? Test for explosives."

"All clear," One of Smith's postulants announced.

Bodono lifted the bypass off the system from his position at the Royal Orion. The COM-room surged to life. Holos popped from the scan-projectors.

At Smith's nod, Kalak jumped into the chair and felt out the controls. "I've got High Mountain Base." Moments later, holos of Enro and Yoshen appeared before them.

Smith wasted no time. "Nobody is here. We have checked for explosives. Nothing! I think we scared them off."

Enro was wary.

Yes, they have left. Less bloodshed is good, but it means they knew what was coming and that isn't so good.

"I've sent Nimro, Sally, and Durga in," said Enro. "If you feel an explosion, that will be Nimro's team opening the front of the building. Hold on." Enro nodded to someone off scan.

Sally cut in on audio, the zing and pop of laser bursts was prominent in the background. "We're going in. There is heavy weapons fire."

Smith and his team felt the monolithic tower shake as the Kelson Lasers fired.

*

SKULL ROCK

Enro had heard enough to make an assessment. The Corporation had accepted defeat some time ago. They were cutting their losses.

They have left a skeleton crew behind, only the most expendable. How will they escape, we have Space Dock locked down?

His mind leapt to the Royal Orion. Gentain Carbone was there. They would not resist for very long. The officers and core command were already seeking their escape. This quiet secession was buying some time.

Carbone must feel that he is invulnerable. He will not run. I must also deal with Majaiya. I wonder if Orville knew that my supposed death would also lead to a resurrection. I will become even more famous now. Geez!

The plan was shifting. His ability to see a developing situation and respond with lightning accuracy and success to contingency, upon contingency was infectious.

"Yoshen, I am going to relocate to the Orion."

Enro paused and adjusted his link.

"Vinny once the Corsairs land and discharge our troops, regroup and take your I-Wings to Landfall. I got a hunch. Let's do the submarine move we discussed, okay? No communications until then! Call me when you're in position."

*

INDUSTRIAL WATERFRONT ECKSOL

The I-wing squadron descended to the shore of Lake Wechen near the piers. They hovered over Lake Wechen and slowly sank beneath the waves.

"Okay now, single file through the channel to Landfall."

The chatter began.

"Can we do this?

"We are airtight where it counts."

"Any time for fishing? Just kidding."

"Is the rest of the I wing waterproof?

"Yeah, but how about the other parts, like the frigging motor."

Vinny had no time for arguments he already had lost. "Radio silence. Geez! The Pleiadian designers say we cannot only do this but we can end up with a shiny clean body. Now let's get our butts wet. Now!"

The modified I-wing fighters had become submarines closing in on Landfall in complete stealth.

*

Rahi

Wechen embraced Capach. The grand spirits merged in a union only understood in the language of the stars themselves. Shelila, their mentor looked on.

"My children tremble with the love attendant on this occasion."

Every cell, vibrating atom, DNA strand, Neutrino, Lifetron, Mayatron, rock, water, flower, and creatures, large and small, living on any astral levels had gone through a shift. The power of love is a relentless and all-powerful source.

*

THE ROYAL ORION

Cleo called these moments into her multi-dimensional awareness as they approached the time of a critical meeting. She was aware that Orville was with her in his thoughts. Though it was new for him to co-exist on many planes of reality simultaneously, she was pleased to see that his blood pressure was not going up. He looked at her as she phased through that enriched herenow.

"Whew! This is one big Taco." Orville said.

Martha Fox let out a short little laugh.

*

CHAPTER FORTY-FOUR

"RECEPTIVE RECEPTION"

The laser light display that danced upon the night sky at the Royal Orion Resort was visible from Ecksol. Despite the trouble at Landfall and Space Dock, the Corporation had been able to suppress the spread of news. The local media buzz had been the opening gala of the Trilateral Conferences.

*

ON ROUTE TO NAVIDRRR

Voices whispered in Chandri's ear. That was not unusual. Her psychic ability had opened her to many experiences. It was the sense that one voice represented many voices that distinguished itself from her usual experience.

The power that was evident and increasingly strong had become a tendril of an unknown quality that seemed to have attached to her very soul. With a growing horror, she realized that, like Renjinn, she had been taken by the Tharrr.

Oddly, her body did not react with any perceived repulsion. That worried her. She looked over at Heidi Roth. The gutsy sentient life rights monitor was a reflection of the fear that she felt.

Heidi turned to her. "Have you been infected?"

Chandri silently nodded. The whispering continued. They were a community of souls that all had access to each other, in a personal and intimate way. She felt pressure. It was a struggle to be in control. The symbiont pulled back when it reached a crisis. In a strange way, it was nurturing and caring.

It knows my thoughts!

The Tadole crew had gathered in the front of the Corsair. Renjinn spoke to them in a voice they had never heard before. Ostinglink, and the six other Tadole Belfars, had recently experienced the transformation Chandri was just beginning. She had sensed the conflict when they had first been thrust together back at Space Dock.

Now they have become Tharrr!

The new Circle had been born. The individual souls of the Tadoles had joined the united souls of the Tharrr. Rivo the Father, looked on as Renjinn, the Mother, shared her "Jafem."

When Chandri wondered what Jafem meant she heard a voice within her.

It is the essence of the distilled wisdom of the individual soul of Renjinn and the Tharrr within.

Renjinn spoke with authority. Gone were the idiosyncrasies of Renjinn the cigar smoking swaggering Tadole of Tatochin. "We go forth from our bondage to our great home-world, Navidrrr. We come in the wake of their triumph over the Colonial Corporation. We will bestow the Tharrr upon our planet. A great circle will be born."

Without any rancor or protest, they returned to their various tasks for the journey through several parsecs of space.

Chandri had experienced the meeting as if she had been present in the same room. Her prescience delivered her the herenow buzz. She heard herself say, "Heidi, we have decided to take you with us to bear witness to our coming together with Navidrrr."

Another aspect of her un-integrated self screamed for the apparent loss of individuality.

Where is my Bodono, I need you!

The hatch behind Chandri and Heidi opened to reveal Renjinn. He waddled up to the pair. "We must decide whether we will confront Majaiya, or go straight to Navidrrr. Either way you will accompany us. We are all rebels now!"

Heidi watched and witnessed Chandri's struggle. They had bonded deeply in the brief time they had been thrown together. Their moon cycles had already synchronized. The twin moons had provided large reminders. They were both richly and passionately aware of the power of their womanly connection.

Heidi gathered her courage. Her vocation in life was her passion as well. It was true that her core instinctual program screamed out in horror at the notion of a life-form occupying another being. That program of fear was the product of evolutionary forces from a largely isolated pre-contact Earth.

The idea of a symbiotic life-form attaching itself to a previously sovereign being was regarded as invasive. As she was beginning to understand, the Tharrr were life affirming, and protective. They were a creation meant to join other life forms. It was, according to the Elders, natural.

The Tharrr are sentient. What does this mean? If it is their way, should I consider their rights as well?

Another part of her raged in anger at the violation of it. Her friend Chandri; was she gone? She did not want to lose her. She loved her. *I will face this, and by the Goddess, I will get through it.*

Renjinn stood before the two women. "We are approaching Maijaya's fleet of Corsairs. They are badly damaged. We are assessing the weaponry status of the Corsair in the herenow." Renjinn paused and drew in on his cigar. He let out a cloud of smoke that curled into little flowing eddies.

Heidi watched his great golden eyes. She had never met Renjinn before he was taken over by the Tharrr.

"Do you speak for the Tharrr?"

Renjinn's laugh came from deep in the baffled chamber of his inflatable throat. It sounded like a chorus of farting bean-eaters to the human ear. It was sacred song to Tadole.

"I like someone who can think on their feet," Renjinn said. His dorsal rose and the apparitional glowing lights around them brightened and swirled in a variegated series of patterns.

A language!

Renjinn spoke to Heidi's unspoken thoughts. "To speak for all Tharrr requires development I have not achieved as a unit. However, I can speak to you of the Tharrr. I can also tell you what we are doing right now."

Telepathy as well!

She realized there was some hierarchical structure in play. "Why do you go to Navidrrr?" Heidi blurted out the question that tugged at her awareness. *Will it spread?*

Chandri spoke up. Her hand squeezed Heidi's as she struggled with the transformation that was going on inside her. "Renjinn is the Mother of a new circle."

Chandri managed to steer the conversation to where it would help her friend the most. "They are going to spread throughout Navidrrr. I know this sounds crazy but I think it is a good thing."

Rivo joined the three who sat in the passenger section behind the bridge area. His blending into the conversation, as if he had been participating all along, demonstrated an aspect of having the Tharrr within. "I am the Father of the new circle, Rivo of Oblion. I was part of the previous circle that was almost destroyed at Oblion. We go to a new home world but our destiny includes many worlds."

Heidi did not visibly register her newest revelation. *Destiny; they believe in higher spiritual orders!*

She decided to take a risk: "You are new to this area of the galaxy, are you aware of the fear we have of you?"

Rivo raised his hand and scratched his flat triangular head. "Yes, Of course we are. We have a dilemma because our evolutionary path is judged immoral by your kind. We, however, are not wrong. Oblion was our home for many cycles. We lived in peace and harmony. We were as one. It was the Corporation that destroyed Oblion. We have many reasons to fear you. We have learned the hard way, but are adapting to your ways. We are not some evil force bent on endless vengeance for the genocide committed on Oblion. We are of the light. Our wish is to align with many civilizations. Your Elders are ours. Your Enro, one of our greatest heroes." *Renjinn, they know we fight a greater enemy!*

Heidi was amazed at Rivo's conviction. In spite of her misgivings, she sensed a great spiritual presence.

Rivo looked up suddenly. The apparitions about him dramatically shifted. Renjinn's dorsal seemed to rise like a periscope above his personal sea of swirling light.

"We come upon Maijaya and her fleet. They will never reach Tatochin!" Rivo hissed.

Renjinn chewed on his cigar furiously. "We will continue this later. Ostinglink! Station."

The Katofar waddled off to the COM chair. Rivo followed and plopped down in the pilot's chair.

Chandri wept in Heidi's arms. "I miss Bodono...How could he accept me now?"

Heidi followed her instincts and reached out to her Gaian sister. "You still seem to be Chandri to me, sweetheart. I won't leave you."

Chandri felt the Tharrr within her. It felt expansive and wise. When Heidi soothed her racing thoughts the calmness that followed allowed her to examine other perceptions. *The Tharrr, they/ we need Heidi, for the Elders wish us to join the new Earth. My goddess! The new Earth!*

*

Colonial Corporation HQ

Cardinal Black stood before the control panel of a Centaurian Alpha Probe. He worked a knob on the console that evoked an involuntary scream from Flex's nerve wracked body. He hung suspended from a torture ring. There was hardly anyone in the building to hear him scream. Black turned to see the Korgon, Carbone's creature.

"My master is pissed. You may be the next one up there, Omegan!"

"Shut up, you mutant verder." The flair of anger pushed Black's hand further on the dial. *I cannot get him to talk. He would rather die!*

Flex moaned. The Centaurian device was truly a horrible contraption. Flex managed to pick up his head. *They probably want me alive for now.* His head dropped and he lost consciousness.

The Korgon reveled in the whirlpool of pain and chaos that torturing a victim precipitated.

"Well Blackie, don't we want to have some fun at the reception, too?"

"You keep your hands off him!" Black sneered, "I need him alive."

"I need him alive!" The Korgon repeated Black's previous comment as his face shifted into a caricature of Black. After a moment, he morphed back to a face similar to the one before his outburst. The Korgon continued to laugh at Cardinal Black.

"What do you want him for? He dresses kind of kinky, are you looking for some ass, Blackie? You can have what's left of him. I could not care less about your pathetic chain of command." He wagged his finger derisively. "Oh, and don't try any of those psychic powers on me, Omegan. I have a polarizing disrupter that can turn your feeble mind into quaziflems!"

Cardinal Black inwardly cringed. The miserable device the Korgon held was as nefarious a weapon as the torture ring and Alpha probe he utilized. Such weapons had been outlawed on most worlds. They were a favorite among black market traders. The Centaurians were feared because of such intrusive and brain damaging devices.

*

CHAPTER FORTY-FIVE

"AFTER MIDNIGHT"
"Limping along in the space lanes of Orion"

Within each form a spirit lives
Which to its kin it yearns.
Self illumined each atom glows,
Casting shadows on the nearnow
Like seeds expanding the soul.

Alfred Tron
Poetry Collection Vol. 3
Mychronitia 2362

Maijaya pushed an errant lock of her robust red hair to the side. Her long and angular face was twisted in a tight scowl as she assessed the tactical situation. Half of her controls were destroyed. Several technicians with burning knuckles were swiftly soldering bypasses to keep her ship operating. She had been alerted to the approaching Cargo Corsair.

They know we are here! They seek us!

Maijaya's battle Corsair, The Sharari, was only capable of sub-light speed. The surprise attack at Navidrrr had caught her entire fleet unawares.

We were arrogant! Too full of ourselves!

The Tadole had used small vessels, each carrying one large missile. They were correct in noting that the smaller vessels were not watched very carefully by Colonial Trooper security. What appeared to be routine planetary commerce had exacted a deadly expense upon Maijaya's entire fleet as it arrived in high orbit above the swampy home-world of Navidrrr.

The Tadole mounted a coordinated assault. A full legion of Tadole warriors had secretly assembled within the Space Dock and turned the weapons of the Corporation on their own ships. The entire population had quietly mobilized once the knowledge of her fleet's imminent arrival had leaked. It had been a blood bath.

We underestimated them!

A large cataract of tortured metal caused by laser fire, had shredded the Pleiadian plus-light engine of the Sharari. Maijaya's face was in a rictus of tension. Her temples pounded. *Disabled with our own weapons. Outrageous!*

Not a single Corsair in the remnant of Maijaya's fleet was capable of plus-light speed. Six were damaged severely and forced to make emergency landings on the planet. They had been quickly defeated in battle by ground forces of Tadole militia.

The dock itself was littered with the wreckage of her fleet. The remaining three Corsairs including the Sharari, Maijaya's command vessel, slowly approached Tatochin, the closest Colonial Troopers base.

Maijaya's knuckles turned white as she thought with disgust of the botched mission. *Gentain Carbone must give me command of the invasion fleet leaving Salvington High World. He must!*

"Status on the cargo Corsair?"

"It's within hailing range, Kaitain."

"Do we have any weapons that work at all?"

"We have one short range Kelson Laser, three operational I-wings, but we have no more missiles. Only one has operational plasma lasers."

We are basically defenseless. I wonder how much fire power that corsair is packing.

"Go on red alert."

"Please establish a holo-link with the Corsair."

"Sending."

"Well?"

"They are not responding. Wait, there is something."

The holo-screen captured the pulse of a particle beam laser as it seared its way across the vacuum toward the Sharari.

"Brace for impact, weapons activated."

A particle beam laser slammed into the Corsair to Maijaya's right. It burst into flame and exploded. When the shock wave had passed, the holo in front of Maijaya's command COM lit up with the large featured face of the Katofar Renjinn. His dorsal fin stood erect with whirling apparitions pulsing around his cranium.

"Kaitain Maijaya, I would have never guessed that you would be the target of my weapons."

"Renjinn!"

He laughed inflating his throat sacks and producing a chorus of flatulent decompressions. Maijaya was at a loss for words. She witnessed the telltale apparitions that the Tharrr could produce around his dorsal fin. *How did he get here! Those apparitions...The Tharrr!*

"My God!"

Renjinn's dorsal fin rose to even a greater height as he spoke. "Prepare to fight Kaitain. I take great honor in doing battle with my former commander."

The Tadole Corsair banked sharply preparing for its next attack. Maijaya controlled her anger. *Some day I will have my revenge but not today.*

She decided to abandon her ship. "Take the COM." Maijaya barked to her first officer. "I am going to commandeer an I-wing. Once I launch take that overstuffed toad out!"

"With what?" the sullen first officer said. He knew in that one tragic moment that he had just been put on top of list of the expendable.

*

CHAPTER FORTY-SIX

"LOSS AND RECOVERY"

Aboard the Delaney Corsair, Heidi Roth and Dame Chandri were aware of the increased activity. Chandri closed her eyes and regulated her breath. She reached out with her mind to discover what was going on. Right away she knew that the Tadole, or the Tharrr, she was not sure which, had met up with the Colonial Corporation survivors coming from Navidrrr.

Heidi turned and was startled to see glowing apparitions swirling about her friend's head. "Chandri, are you all right?" she asked feeling like the question was superfluous.

Chandri's eyes opened. The answer was written on her face and in her red, tear-stained eyes. "No, my friend, everything feels very wrong."

A second flash of light and subsequent lurch caused by the explosion of a second Corsair punctuated the moment. Then, shortly, a third explosion finished off the Sharari.

"The returning fleet from Navidrrr has been destroyed. Tatochin is safe," Chandri said. She heard herself talking, but it was as if it was somebody else. She gripped Heidi's arm and looked into her eyes.

In that moment, she realized that the Tharrr within her was looking through her eyes. She took a deep breath and made contact with the Tharrr within her.

"Can I talk to you?"

"Yes, and I have much to say, dear Chandri."

Heidi watched her friend's gaze turn inward as Chandri tightly gripped her arm. She didn't know what to expect.

"Chandri, are you okay?"

"Yes, everything is fine now", Chandri said.

The Tharrr!

Heidi was unsure whom she was talking too.

*

The plume of white heat from Renjinn's Corsair entering plus-light speeds toward Navidrrr, dissipated. A single I-wing fighter floated in the debris field where the Sharari once existed. It powered up its engine. Maijaya had survived.

The Sharari is no more. What will become of me now? I must be given a chance to redeem myself!

The Kaitain pondered her fate as she closed the distance to Tatochin. She dwelled in a dark place where only vengeance and retaliation lived. Not a single thought of remorse crossed her mind, for the thousands of Troopers and officers that perished in the lost battles.

*

COLONIAL CORPORATION HQ

Nimro disabled a door that served as a service entrance. He slipped into an empty hall with the echo of battle in the distance. His quiet entry coincided with the beginning of the siege.

Durga and Sally commanded the frontal assault. The rebels slowly gained ground in the main lobby of the Colonial Corporation entrance while lances of laser weaponry scorched its opulent décor.

Fireworks lit up the sky as the midnight celebration of Rahi continued. They completely masked the urban assault that was less than ten blocks away.

Nimro moved down the argon lit corridor that served as a service access for deliveries. The sound of battle became muffled, then absent, as he used a service lift tube to the central levels. He knew the military offices and detention centers would be there. His hope that Flex was okay kept him acutely aware of his surroundings.

Cardinal Black did not need any communicators or surveillance intelligence to know Nimro was coming. He had sensed his dangerous thoughts through his extensive training and abilities.

Black was on his way to his escape saucer waiting in a bay on the detention floor. It was normally used to bring in prisoners. Now it would secure his escape. Landfall was the only route off world that the rebels hadn't closed.

Korgon was with him. He was un-nerved by the shape-shifter. *I don't trust any creature who lives among the Centaurians!*

"Korgon, a rebel called Nimro seeks the rebel Flex. He is just above us."

"He is dead, is he not?" The shape-shifter asked.

"Near death. I left him on the torture ring. He could be. I was unable to get much from him. I didn't have time or interest once we got the order to evacuate.

"Not dead? Are you going soft Blackie?"

"I haven't got time for your bluster, Korgon."

Black was in a hurry to leave. The Korgon assassin was extraneous baggage to him.

"He may have the device that you seek, this Nimro."

The Korgon knew that Black was trying to lose him. He did not care nor was he bothered. Nevertheless, he saw it as an opportunity.

"I will stay behind and see what..."

"He comes," hissed Black.

As Black ducked behind a pillar, a disruptor hit Korgon directly in the center of his chest. Black scurried to escape and psychically diverted Nimro's attention from any further pursuit by amplifying his concern for his friend, Flex. Inwardly, he reveled in being rid of the assassin.

Nimro continued down the corridor towards the detention center with greater caution, passing by a dozen cells. All of the prisoners were dead. The smell of blood and boiled flesh sickened him, and his anxiety for his friend grew.

As he entered the interrogation room, the smell of old blood washed over him. A large vertically mounted metallic hoop dominated the middle of the space. A bundle of insulated cables ran into a console that operated the multi-functional torture ring.

Flex hung on the bindings around his legs and arms. Pieces of prosthetic hips and breast that had been part of his disguise as a belly dancer still clung to his beaten body. It looked hideous as it combined with large slashes of crisped flesh and blood blisters from lasers.

Labored breath escaped him as blood oozed from deeper wounds and swollen, bruised flesh. His head hung to one side. He was barely conscious.

Nimro suppressed the urge to run to his side and swiftly found the switch to turn off the gravity field. Urgently he surveyed the machinery seeking the best way to detach his friend from his tortuous position. He gently called out his name.

Flex gasped, as the pain in his body returned with his awakening. The wig he had been wearing dressed as Topaz, fell to the ground exposing his blue and yellow hair.

"Nimro?" His voice was just a gasp. Drool leaked from his torn and bruised lips.

Before he could reply, the forms of a dozen rebels armed to the teeth materialized in the torture chamber. Bodono and Yoshen had scrambled together another back-up team from High Mountain Base. The team recognized Nimro immediately.

"You two. Hold him. I've turned the gravity field off." They lowered Flex's ravaged body to the floor. A Pleiadian medic immediately bent over him and injected him with something. His medical scanner whirred to life.

"Fit him with a Relocator. I want to bring him to High Mountain Base." the doctor said.

A moment later, a voice was heard within the wired fighters and diplomats. Orville Parker had used a Pleiadian broadcast device that came to life. Everyone in the torture room heard the voice of Enro.

"Good work, Nimro...Doctor, is he going to make it?"

"If I can get him to surgery, possibly. His nervous system has severe electrical damage. I have seen worse recover and less be fatal. I need better conditions to do much."

"I want to go with him."

"Sure, Nimro, stay with him. Let me know as soon as you know how he's doing."

*

The Royal Orion

Orville looked at the glowing form of Alphonse with his astral vision. To Cleo he whispered, "What did he do?"

"Just play along. He is filled with Shakti. He can channel this from a very rare level. We all can feel it. He is also fond of making dramatic entrances."

Orville noticed that the power in the presence of Alphonse, purified and charged the room with awareness and clarity. The very fabric of the universe upgraded to a finer frequency of manifestation.

The sounds of the celebration of Rahi faded in the distance as the door to the room closed. Pieces of costume, and a large gorilla suit, were placed on a table thoughtfully provided.

Orville noticed Martha Fox standing by the chairs around the table. Orville regarded the voluptuous women with swiftly blinking eyes and some heavy breathing to get his thoughts in order.

Fortunately, Martha Fox has not removed any of her costume below her head; otherwise, we wouldn't get anything accomplished. She is just dazzling!

Cleo had not removed any part of her costume. She was already uncomfortable with how much it revealed. She playfully jabbed her elbow in his ribs. "That's enough Rahi energy! We have work to do."

"Hey, I'm just being multidimensional."

"Orville, we are not alone in our multi-dimensionality," Cleo indicated the four Pleiadians who quietly chatted.

Orville poked her in a ticklish spot he had discovered. She jumped and giggled. Her hand went to her mouth, as she struggled to gain control. The spell of Rahi was upon the couple from Mirror once again.

I just want to kiss his face all over. Geez this Rahi energy is making me…wet. Oh God, did I think that!

Yes, you did. I want to touch you all over, my delicious Cleo!

Just then, Tremador wagged a finger at the squirming couple.

"Right on cue," Orville gasped as he struggled to gain control.

"Orville, we are being discussed. Try to act your age."

"Me! You got invisible friends floating around, and I'm the one who has to act my age?"

"Orville, stop it."

They giggled some more. "Oh, okay."

Suddenly, the room ignited in a soft but brilliant light. Ten points of light clarified along a vertical axis. From within the nimbus of growing light, the form of Alphonse appeared in three-dimensional reality.

Orville was reflective. *Pleiadians just love ceremony. Wow, ten points of light!*

Cleo glided over to the glowing Elder, with Orville in tow. She gave her friend a hug, and introduced Orville. The Pleiadians, each in turn, greeted the Elder with the slightest bow.

Bishop Jones and Farooq Masad's jaws dangled as they beheld what was to them a total miracle. Scholars sought to interpret such miraculous manifestations of spiritual power as allegorical stories meant to convey a teaching. Alphonse's glowing appearance shattered that interpretation into pulp.

Orville reflected as he looked on. *Some day they will learn how the Dravithians were behind the suppression of these universal and reconciling experiences. We lost hundreds of years of real progress because the greedy assholes wanted profit over progress!*

Martha Fox had joined the line of Pleiadians greeting Alphonse. Unlike the Korum Ambassador and the Omegan Bishop, she had been born to a family of Gaians. The knowledge of Ascended Masters was common and studied broadly. As she looked into the unfathomable eyes of Alphonse, he seemed to shimmer and become another being. Tears leaped into her eyes. A memlock of a visitation she had experienced as a child had moved her deeply. She had composed an affirmation to retain the precious memlock.

I am a worthy daughter of Gaia! I always have been.

Farooq Masad and Bishop Jones joined the line. It was taking some time for them to integrate the powerful wave of realization and greater awareness they had to quickly process in order to maintain their roles in the confluence of beings surrounding them.

Alphonse was in essence a manifestation of answered prayers. Tangible proof that humanity, as well as all life forms, are guided from realms of spiritual evolution far beyond the veil of mortality and a limited view of reality. Each moment that transpired in his presence would ripple outward through the fabric of life and create a shift.

It was a step into a larger universe. The reward of such moments could be measured. It wasn't so much about attaining perfection, but more about perfecting the essence of being itself.

Alphonse looked at Orville Parker standing on the edge of eternity. *If only he saw himself as I see him.*

"Orville Parker. I believe you have important news to impart to this most auspicious gathering. It is your place to introduce yourself to those gathered."

Orville blushed. He had always insulated himself from public exposure in his vast travels. Many experiences had laced his long life. He had a fleeting thought about excusing himself and buying a taco from some street vendor.

Tremador sniggered then cleared his throat. Orville followed his example and cleared his throat. He knew it was true. He knew it in his gut. His mind was in such personal paradox. *I really have no idea of what I am doing!* He leapt into a non-linear relationship to the herenow: *Oh well, I just open my mouth.*

"Tonight at midnight the people of Tatochin have taken their government back from the Colonial Corporation. The patriots known as rebels, as they were known to the outside galaxy, now have control of the Corporation headquarters, the planetary Space Dock, and the Royal Orion Resort. Gentain Carbone is in the rebels' custody.

Many of you have heard of the Kaitain Enro. You may memlock his passing on Oblion. Well, what you don't know is that he is alive. And it is Kaitain Enro who is the leader of the rebels of Tatochin."

He paused as several people gasped at this news. "As some of you may know, he is also a native of Tatochin. Yes, he is alive. It is his destiny to lead the people of Tatochin to liberation from the clutches of the Corporation. This is the herenow in maximode."

"The Kaitain is alive?" exclaimed Jones.

"Yes. He left the Corporation years ago during the Siege of Oblion to return to his native planet. I helped him to do that. Your Father Bodono helped the rebels accomplish the takeover. He authored the Proclamation of Freedom, and sits in the COM-chair right here at the Orion.

"Good", Jones said.

The bishop's smile and simple answer eased Orville's mind. Orville turned his attention to the Korum ambassador. "Farooq Masad, I have followed your life for many years. You know my dearest friend. Arafad Tango X has been my comrade for many years. It was I who suggested that he become involved with the Korum."

The room was silent. Orville realized that for Jones, Fox, and Masad, every fiber of their being was impacted by what he shared. This information would require them to adjust and expand in ways they had never dreamed.

On another level, Orville realized that the souls gathered in the room were here, because they could receive what he was saying. Orville's awareness expanded as he fully reconciled any conflicting feelings.

The awareness of Alphonse, Cleo, and the Pleiadians were suddenly available to him, energetically. Empowerment flowed towards him on the cool clear wings of spiritual love and attunement. His body relaxed. He felt light and clear.

"I have the great honor of being among the first humans to carry on the work of our Pleiadian benefactors. Through my association with them, I have come to be involved in the work of aiding in the evolutionary process of humankind, and other sentient life-forms in a similar position."

"A long time ago, I also worked for the Colonial Corporation. I left that because I did not like what was happening. We have brought you here so that the Trilateral Conferences could be spared the chaos. Kaitain Enro will join us as soon as he is able to turn over command. He will assume planetary leadership during the transition of power."

"I have only one request. What we have hoped for by having this meeting is to have your organizations, or governments, recognize the rebels as the rightful rulers of their own world."

"I have studied Tatochin's ways. They are in greater remembrance of the truth of things than Earth ever was. Kaitain Enro is a native of Tatochin. His Grandfather was Cardinal Fellini, his Grandmother, the Grand Dame Taylor. He has a credibility that the UGC would recognize especially with your blessing."

Orville had finished. He looked over at Cleo. Her Mona Lisa smile was pregnant with the deep love they shared.

Martha Fox spoke first. She wore her long raven hair down. With the lunar conjunction of Rahi her appearance even challenged the Pleiadians who were in attendance. The energetic vibration of the room swelled with sexual tension that the male gender memlocked gazing upon the Gaian representative of Earth.

Martha was completely aware of the effect her energy was having on the room. She felt enlivened. Between her experience of Alphonse and her new experience of becoming the primordial Aphrodite, she found her center. She had begun to integrate the quickening of spirit offered to her.

"The Gaian government has been working closely with the Pleiadian government from Mychronitia. We have already petitioned the United Galactic Consortium for sanctions against the Corporation for sentient life rights violations. This is a fortunate turn of events, as far as we are concerned."

Alphonse took her hand, "Thank you for that."

The Elder's touch penetrated to the core of Martha's being, sending trilling sparks of healing holiness to rare and new dimensions awakening within her soul. She, more than the other leaders, was ready to embrace the expansion of consciousness into multi-dimensional frequencies. She found her awareness travel within the landscape of his reality as he spoke.

Some of Martha's experience would become permanently available to her. Other realizations would come in time. In her innermost awareness, she rejoiced recognizing that she was experiencing the quickening that had been foretold.

*

COLONIAL CORPORATION HQ

Enro continued to direct the mop up at the Colonial Corporation. Minutes later his command flitter landed on the roof. Smith and Kalak watched the rebels accept the surrender from the remnants of the Troopers who had been cornered in the lobby below.

Within the Colonial Corporation building, the rebels busily took over the entire grid that had subjugated Tatochin electronically. Unaccounted for pockets of resistance, Metropol and loyalists, were still a liability. Enro directed the rebels to remain in stealth mode.

Outside the building, off in the distance, you could hear the festivities of Rahi continuing on the street. Many of the celebrants had no idea that in the wake of Rahi the morning would bestow its light on a completely different government. They had been given back their home world. The disease that had been the Corporation would be purged.

*

CHAPTER FORTY-SEVEN

ROYAL ORION SURVEILLANCE HUB
"As above so below"

"When the children of the heart's path disperse past the warmth of their own sun, the Dravithians will come forth from their banishment. In that time the power of the righteous ones will draw the Elders, their benefactors, to aid in the quickening. False walls will eventually fall into ruin."

Seeress Aubrey of the Keltori

Father Bodono had cobbled together a working staff of rebels to operate the COM-room. "I think it's amazing what Enro has accomplished. Those Relocators give us a tactical advantage that is just amazing," Bodono said.

Tango reached out to Lesha as he answered the former Omegan priest. "I know. That is why Orville guards its use so carefully."

Lesha slid into Tango's grasp. "How do you think the people will respond to the takeover?" Lesha asked. She gently pulled on his braided ponytail.

"Tango, are you all right?" Lesha stroked his stubble.

"You need a shave."

"I do?"

Bodono watched the couple flirt. The power of Rahi was still upon them. He felt the pull but all his emotions swirled about with worrisome virulence. *Chandri, I hope you are safe.*

Tango grew silent. His senses told him something was happening. A cold wind of prescience had blown through his soul. Upon the ethers, dark energy coalesced into a carbuncle of virulent dark power. He tried to discount it. But, there it was: a feeling unformed that came from outside of him. It wasn't the wellvibe of Rahi, rather, it was something sinister.

"Tango, you're a million light years away."

"Lesha, I'm sorry I have this feeling of danger."

"Tell me about it."

"It feels like something is coming our way.

Let's double check everything. I sense an etheric energy surge," Tango said.

"Etheric?"

"Yes, I can't place it", Tango said.

Bodono rotated the COM toward the Gentain Carbone who sat cuffed and gagged. "Your greatest Kaitain comes back to haunt you, Carbone."

A tremor seemed to ripple through the room. It was not visible manifestation but everyone felt it. A collective primordial experience activated the fires of the body. A general gathering of energy, in the way that precedes intense action, descended like a spell over everyone in the Orion surveillance bubble.

As the Gentain watched Bodono's craven face with a backdrop of blinking lights, he felt a touch all too familiar. A cold and unforgiving force penetrated his shivering soul. Everything around him seemed separated by a wall.

Another life-form had occupied his body. He knew that a Dravithian Lord had taken possession of his body. He had experienced it before. Eyes not his own seemed to peer out at the situation in the COM room. In his mind, he heard the voice of the Dravithian, Lord Karnad.

"Carbone, you have done miserably. I should leave you here like fodder for a slagwallow, but I have need of you."

*

The meeting in the conference room was going well. Farooq Masad and Bishop Jones were full of questions both being philosophical in their manner. It was an equivalent of a first contact at a higher frequency.

Cleo was distracted by a sudden presence. A cold and malevolent energy seemed to pass through the room like a curtain that dampens the light. Orville grasped Cleo's hand and they exchanged a glance filled with urgency. Eyes contacted each other, as the question of what was going on was telepathically ruminated.

"The Dravithians! I thought they were banished for a thousand years, or something," Orville hissed. Alphonse stood. Cleo silently nodded.

"The unknown or the unforeseen can surprise even the Elders," Alphonse said. "It seems we have an unwelcome visitor. I must go tend to this. Cleo represents the Elders, as well as I. I will explain later."

Alphonse slowly became transparent, and then, in a flash of violet light, vanished from the room. Cleo comforted those that witnessed the departure.

*

ROYAL ORION COM ROOM

In the COM room, a foreboding had seized them all. Bodono felt the touch of a maleficent mind.

Carbone had experienced the Dravithian signature. He had become accustomed to the feeling, but was unable to establish contact.

Tango checked the charge on his assault laser.

"If you fire that thing in here you will fry the circuits," Bodono said.

"I fear our problem comes from another realm," Tango hissed.

The room grew cold. A smell of ozone burned the nostrils. A rush of icy wind thrust into the room. Tango had been correct in his estimation.

Bodono was lifted up off his COM chair by an unseen force and sent flying across the room.

Tango was at his side immediately. "Are you all right?

"No, I hit on my shoulder. I think it's bleeding again."

Another cold gust of wind lanced through the room, as if there were no walls. Holos screeched with static. Flecks of a dark form seemed to flash in and out of visibility like broken colored glass in a cyclone.

A nightmarish presence filled the room. The air seemed to depart from unseen openings. The entire fabric of space was torn asunder. A constriction in the heart choked the life out of Tango, Lesha, Bodono, and the rest of the COM room staff.

Suddenly, the room itself was gone. Like a holographic shift, it also included all aspects of material matter. Instead of the smooth curved metallic walls and banks of advanced Centaurian circuitry, a nether world of storm and lightning replaced it.

Purple and gray clouds screwed into whirlpools of shifting dark plasma enveloped the sky. Jutting structures of biomorphic matter festooned the landscape like malignant tumors.

Sulfuric air, whipped by the tangled wind, bit at the senses. Keening, discordant, high-pitched sounds created vertigo among the assembled rebel team.

A sickly yellow light appeared in the visible distance. From within the nimbus, a Dravithian Lord floated in the cancerous firmament. He was dressed in ornate silver armor. He wore a black iridescent single body suit beneath a dragon scale chest piece, with sculpted intricate patterns that reflected his family and rank, according to their dark conjured retrostory. The maliciously glowing yellow light throbbed with churning plasma.

Tango sensed the ethereal attack. His energy was being sucked from him. He practiced every technique of psychic defense he knew, but the power he faced was inexorable. He screamed out his frustration. Lesha's eyes told him of her distress.

You could hear the laugh of the Gentain Carbone as his bonds burst apart. He drifted to the side of the dark Lord. Visible beams of arcane energy held Tango, Bodono, and Lesha in a grip of pure and lethal power. Bodono struggled to maintain consciousness as the dark lord sought to drain the life force from his already ravaged body.

Several rebels opened fire with particle beam lasers and projectile weapons. The hot beams and glowing bursts passed through the spectral lord with no effect. Several bio-circuits shorted as they struck the surveillance bubble super-imposed on the nightmarish landscape.

Lord Karnad, lifted his hands and arms with deadly anticipatory intention. A twisted smile of morbid lethal intensity was pasted on his face. He waved his hand and an invisible energy sent the rebels flying against the tortured metal floor. They were no match for the power of a Dravithian killer.

Suddenly, the dark and stormy firmament burst open in a gleaming violet and white eruption, devouring the darkened orb. A sound of incredible purity accompanied the sudden illumination.

The Dravithian lord loosened his grip on the rebels. Carbone disappeared in a recoil of the disrupted firmament. The form of Alphonse coalesced in a field of lambent, brilliant light.

Alphonse's expression was serious, to say the least. He commanded the Presence of Being to defeat anything the Dravithians might be able to conjure up.

"Karnad, you are banished from this place." Alphonse's auric field seemed to swell and contract like a lung of light.

"Banished? Then, how is it that I am here, Phonsie?" The lord spat.

Alphonse sensed the linkage to other Lords. They had joined minds in a room filled with Centaurian Psychic amplifiers. In this way, Karnad could penetrate the seal the Elders had placed upon them. The collective minds combined to amplify Karnad's power. It was a hellish mechanism. It did, however, have its limits.

Tango, Lesha, Bodono, and the other rebels, looked on helplessly as the two ascended beings, Lord Karnad and Alphonse, crossed metaphysical swords.

"I am surprised so many Dravithians can work together toward a common cause. Usually, you are all too busy stabbing each other in the back."

The Dravithian Lord answered by sending forth a powerful bolt of arcane force that appeared in the astral landscape as a miniature comet directed toward Alphonse. It struck the nimbus of light surrounding Alphonse and dissolved into nothingness.

Alphonse raised his right hand. As he did, the place that Karnad occupied erupted into light. You could hear a roar of frustration as the lord vanished, returning to the place of darkness.

Alphonse glowed with an unearthly light that slowly dissipated as his face became relaxed and a slight smile replaced the grim resolve. He turned his attention towards Tango, Lesha, Bodono, and the other rebels. They were all unconscious around the ruined COM room.

He took a breath and a pink light suffused them. They slowly regained consciousness, awakening to the Com room at the Orion; not the eerie, and confusing, astral landscape. As they picked up their heads, he smiled at them with kindness in his eyes.

"I have sent the Dravithian back." Alphonse said. "Now if you will tend to those electrical fires on the wall we may perhaps not burn the place down." He smiled as several rebels made quick work of extinguishing the fires.

Alphonse was usually a light-hearted soul with a penchant to make small jokes, even in times of stress. His face turned very serious and his voice emerged from a deep place that at one time was called channeling. In the herenow, it was a communion with the Elders.

"For some of us the Seal of Eldera is just a small deterrent. The Battle magic you have witnessed is as old as stories of the Bitherin's from the fourth universe with their Dragon awareness. Memlock these arcane examples of such power. They are still loose in creation."

Alphonse took a deep breath. In a dismissive voice he said, "Now, that was something, huh?"

"Where is the Gentain," Tango managed to say as he choked on the smoke of some sizzling electronics.

"He is a minion of the Dravithian lord. He is with the Centaurians and under their protection. They have been secret allies for some time."

Alphonse raised his hand. "Go back to your people now. Much needs to be done! Those that were with you need comforting. They are alive and will recover. I wish you wellvibe. By the way, Tango. Congratulations."

*

CHAPTER FORTY-EIGHT

LANDFALL

Cardinal Black had arrived at Landfall. Some smoke still poured out of the ruined control tower. Smoldering ash still glowed with heat from the destroyed tactical saucers on the tarmac. He counted himself fortunate to have found refuge with the solitary Centaurians.

Black watched the last of the elite families of Colonial Corporation officers board the enormous Centaurian battle cruiser. He pondered the way they always managed to use their great wealth to buy their way out of any crisis.

They managed to survive after all!

It was still dark. Off to the west, the hint of dawn outlined the Tshini Mountains. Wechen and Capach glowed in the sky. Capach was still partially eclipsing Wechen. Weird red and blue shadows crossed the littered tarmac at Landfall. The charred remains of several hover-tanks and a plus-light command flitter, dotted the immediate landscape.

Several Rishma stood like metallic statues on either side of the lift tube that was under the tremendous saucer-shaped vessel. Black was repulsed, and at the same time, fascinated by the Centaurians' spawned mutant Rishma.

The cloaking device had allowed the intergalactic vessel to land undetected by any known system. They had agreed to give the Corporation safe passage. He walked into the bowels of the tremendous saucer.

Suddenly, he was before a Centaurian. It stood a full eight feet tall. The pale metallic purple exo-skeleton creature made his hair stand on end. His psychic ability had no effect. It was his sense of smell that had been aroused by an unidentifiable stench.

Their thoughts are completely sealed off to me.

Cardinal Black was stunned. He cleared his thoughts of all distractions and focused. Calling up all his years of training as a powerful psychic weapon, he sought entry to its thoughts.

Suddenly, he gasped. Beneath the insectoid exterior was a creature of great intelligence.

His momentary connection was brutally snapped by a jolt that created a headache he would feel for several days.

The Centaurian Legate, who greeted the soft human, had triggered a nerve scrambling device. It was a psychic stun gun that rendered Softs mentally impaired for several minutes. Once a semblance of consciousness returned to Black, he realized that the Centaurians had read his thoughts or something.

A device sensed my psychic attack. Though I was subtle, it still triggered the alert. My God, he's wired ...a technoid bug!

He staggered to a passenger area and downed several strong drinks. Fear and paranoia played ping pong in his scrambled mind. He thought about how the giant insects looked at humans.

They call us softs. They regard our need for clothing as a crude and degrading way to cover up the meat and flesh that mask the bones. Fascinating, they are just as judgmental as we are! Dangerous!

He wondered about the invasion force preparing to engage the Tadole at Navidrrr. Where were the Omegans in all this? Had Pope Hurus shifted his support toward the UGC and the Gaians? With the fall of Tatochin, would the invasion include this planet as well? Would the UGC intervene? Would the Centaurians?

The Centaurians. Hmmm. I was told that the insectoid Centaurians genetically altered the Rishma. A genetically created insect army controlled by command level Centaurian bug, like that legate with the nerve scrambler! All created by the Centaurians? Could it be? So in the end, are they bugs?

The image of changing robes to a more popular color phased across his racing mind. His eyes widened, as Gentain Carbone walked out of the Centaurian Saucer to greet Black.

What of Gentain Carbone? How did he just walk out of the Centaurian saucer? By what agency or power could that have happen?

Black strolled over to the field COM to listen in on the herenow. Gentain Carbone nodded to Black and returned his attention to his COM-1ink.

"Remnants from Space Dock. The rebels have control of that, too." Carbone spoke as Black came up to him.

"Is there any pursuit?" Black asked.

Just then, Vinny's I-wings group rose out of the canal. Black froze on the spot, his gaze glued to the rebel I-wing Fighters that had just appeared. The frown that was etched permanently on his face tightened with unspent rage.

"It really doesn't matter", Carbone uttered.

Wheelchair Vinny and his squadron of I-wing fighters regrouped and entered the airspace at Landfall. He called Enro, as agreed. "Your hunch was correct Kaitain. A Centaurian saucer is loading the Corporation brass."

"Do what you can. We can't afford to send in ground troops from the Corsairs."

Vinny took control. "Attack pattern, three on my mark. Enro was right! The worms are crawling into that giant clam. Let's make chowder out of them. Two heat seekers each. Target the saucer," said Vinny.

They launched their missiles as a protective field was deployed around the Centaurian saucer. It easily repelled the missiles. Large panels began to open on various points on the upper surface of the saucer. A bristling array of weapons rose on the shell.

"Holy shit, we didn't touch the thing," one of the rebel pilots said.

The chatter on the COM continued as the I-wings re-grouped in the stratosphere.

"Hey, guys. I think we are chum for a bigger fish."

"Hey, Vinny, that saucer's showing some serious voodoo."

"I see lots more surface to air lighting up, Vin".

"Shit, those are laser cannons…big ones… the verders! That seafood is showing some lethal force. We only have so many decoys!"

Vinny knew it was hopeless. "We are no match for the Centaurians," he informed Enro.

"Let them go", Enro told him.

Vinny sighed. He didn't like retreating. "Scatter pattern X, on my mark. Let them get close enough so we confuse the guidance systems. On one, we fire our own rear heat seekers. On two, we hit the afterburners. On three, we sail. We will regroup downtown in the old neighborhood, the waterfront south of Sobash Ave."

*

On the ground, the hum of laser canons powering up hurt Black's ears. The canons fired. Two rebel I-wings exploded moments later. The remaining rebel fighters launched their own weapons directed at the incoming Centaurian counterattack. The sky exploded in myriad bursts as missiles hit missiles. The rebels, cued on the detonation, scattered in four directions and disappeared into the sunrise.

Black and Carbone walked past several Rishma warriors. They stood silently as sentinals on either side of the ramp.

Black sheltered his eyes from the blazing sun and stared into the sky. *The Centaurians are not to be trifled with!*

*

CHAPTER FORTY-NINE

THE ROYAL ORION

Only a few moments had passed since the battle between the Elder, Alphonse, and the Dravithian Lord Karnad had ended. Tango held Lesha who was still lying on the floor groaning. One of the rebels tended to the angry wound on Bodono's shoulder that had begun to bleed again.

Suddenly, Kaitain Enro appeared at the entrance to the partially destroyed surveillance room. "What in the nether beast of hell..."

"Kaitain Enro, thank the brightest star! You don't know how well that fits," Bodono said. He groaned from the floor. "Help me up, please."

Several rebel guards helped him up.

"Father, be careful," Tango said, from where he tended Lesha.

"I am alright. The other guy got blasted by that Elder. Whew." Bodono pushed a few buttons on the arm console that he was using to obtain some balance. Kalak's face appeared on a holo.

"Bodono what is going on? Did Enro arrive?"

"I am here, Kalak, the COM room was attacked". Enro slipped into the COM after helping Bodono to a chair. Tango helped Lesha to her feet. She was shaking. He held her close to him, soothing her.

"He was sucking the life out of me, and I couldn't stop him. And, and ...", she convulsed with sobs and began to wretch.

Tango looked up at Enro. "Can we get a doctor to relocate here?"

"I'm all right. I'll be okay", Lesha said. Immediately after she spoke, she began vomiting.

"Honey, you don't look alright to me. You're puking your guts out," Tango said with weariness and concern. "A psychic attack like that can have far-reaching effects."

"It's not the attack," Lesha whimpered as she held her stomach. She tried to continue speaking but her vomiting had advanced to a round of projectile vomit, cleverly aimed toward the recycling unit.

"What is it, then," Tango asked.

"I'm bruuuuuuuuuughaaaaaaaa!

"What? It's okay just breathe!"

"I'm bruuuuuuuughaaaa!

"Lesha we will call in a medic!"

"No, its just aaaaaaccccckkk."

"My God!"

With a supreme effort Lesha took a deep breath and then giggled. At this point Tango was at a loss, and just stared in disbelief. Lesha took his hand.

"It's really ok...I'm pregnant!"

"WHAT!" Tango, Enro, and Bodono said at the same time.

"I'd offer you one of Renjinn's cigars but he took them all," Bodono said as he clapped Tango on the back.

"Pregnant... How?" Tango was stunned.

"He's looking a little pale." Enro observed.

"Tango, what kind of question is that? The usual way!" Lesha looked up from the primary target site that had been inundated with Cleo's health drink and bile.

"Pregnant?" Tango whispered.

"Yes, with our baby. Is their something wrong with that? brrrrrruuuuuuuuugh."

After the last bit of the contents of her stomach unceremoniously departed, Lesha began to recover her strength. She was always very strong. She watched different emotions play across Tango's face, all his defenses dissolved away.

"Baby," he mumbled. He had gone over the edge of some barrier within himself.

For so long I have been a spy, living with the enemy. I have always been on alert, always keeping up a persona for the cause of freedom, and in service to the Elders.

I made friends with those enemies. Some of them were decent people. Always, I felt alone. I had accepted that my life was about that and nothing else. I had to improvise, and respond to the moment; and I have always done that well.

Then Lesha comes along. Now, I am going to be a father! I don't know what to do?

Bodono intruded into Tango's thoughts. *Give your lady a hug, you'll figure out the rest.*

"A baby...Lesha that's great." Tango took Lesha in his arms and held her close.

"Congratulations, both of you", Enro said.

"I'm going to be a father, ha, ha!" Tango said. The couple sat side-by-side gazing into each other's eyes.

Enro turned his attention to the COM. "Okay we got a revolution to finish. Vinny is headed toward Ecksol. Orville and Cleo are waiting for me at the meeting."

Enro sat in the chair. "Vinny?"

"Yes, Enro."

"Position."

"About five minutes west of Ecksol."

"Vinny, before you go back to High Mountain Base soften the secondary targets you asked me to consider."

"It's my pleasure to serve," said Vinny as he turned up the volume on some current music. Just then, a tremendous sonic boom sounded across the land as the behemoth Centaurian saucer invisibly departed Tatochin.

"Father, are you well enough to take the COM?" Enro regarded the wounded Omegan.

"Sure, Enro, I'll be fine". Just then, several doctors arrived in the Royal Orion COM room to tend the injured staff.

"Tango, tell me what happened." Enro brushed his dreadlocks away from his forehead, the white of his eyes dramatically contrasting his chocolate brown complexion.

"A Dravithian lord. Never met one before. I thought they were banished. They got Carbone. An Elder, called Alphonse, appeared and drove him away. That Dravithian was sucking us to death. If Alphonse hadn't shown up, we would have been killed."

Enro listened with one ear to Tango's description of the encounter. The other ear focused on his thoughts that were rising to the surface.

This explains many things. The Centaurian rescue vessel, the endless weapons, all Centaurian. We play the game they wish us to play. They have no loyalties. Now though, with the Dravithians, we might have the most unholy alliance!

"Thank the Elders for showing up when they did. When this is over, we will have to discuss dealing with the Centaurians. They are in attendance at the Trilateral Conferences. They are senior members."

"Understood. Anything else before you go to the meeting?" Tango asked.

"Yes! Send the word to High Mountain Base, Space Dock, and the Corporation headquarters we have done it. Victory is ours!" With that, Enro departed.

Enro strode through the remnants of the Rahi festivities that had taken place at the Orion. A few revelers were still standing. The reception ended long ago. As he approached the door where Orville and the rest were meeting, he observed that an entourage of concubines was carrying Prince Kalimafar from the main hall where the reception had been. He chattered inanely in Arabic.

When Enro arrived at the meeting, Alphonse was giving his account of the attack of the Dravithian Lord, Karnad. Enro sat down beside Orville and listened. Alphonse smiled and then concluded. "I will make myself available for any questions later, but now I would like to hear from Enro."

Orville stepped up and introduced the tall and striking kaitain first to the Pleiadian ambassadors, Ziola and Tremador. Then onto the Korum ambassador Farooq Masad, the Omegan, Bishop Jones, and Martha Fox who represented the Gaians.

Enro cleared his throat and unceremoniously began. "Tatochin has been restored to its people. It will take time for re-adjustments, but it is the people's wish to be under the protection of the United Galactic Consortium."

There was a knock on the door.

"There is someone knocking on the door...it's a polite knock, I seriously doubt it is a Dravithian Lord", said Alphonse, with a conspiratorial smile.

It was apparent that he knew more than he was telling. Everyone in the room had a good chuckle as Cleo opened the door. In walked the Grand Dame Taylor. Enro's grandmother.

"Where is my grandson? Oh there you are. Enro, why haven't you called me? I have been worried sick. I'm your grandmother, after all."

"Grandma, I have been busy."

"I'll say you have."

The sight of seeing the great Kaitain Enro reduced to the status of a grandmother's grandson was too much for Orville. He broke out in great gushes of laughter.

The grand dame placed her hands on her hips and regarded Orville. "What is wrong with him, is he feeble minded?"

Most of the room had been politely sniggering already. Orville's extrapolation broke the floodgates. The irony of the situation was not lost to the Grand Dame. Though her age was great, she had walked among the greatest and most powerful people in her life. She had been married to Cardinal Fellini who was known to be the most loved and respected Omegan that ever lived. She was as sharp as a knife, her wits intact. She shifted gears at just the right moment.

"I couldn't sleep a wink last night with all this carousing about Rahi! It was on all the holoscans this morning. All kinds of nonsense. They said you were alive! Don't usually watch the infernal thing. I knew you were somewhere around here making a speech or some such thing. Doesn't he make good speeches?"

"Grandmother!"

"Don't just stand there, give me a kiss."

The meeting went on. It was decided that Enro would be the temporary leader of the government while a Pleiadian structured government was formed. He would also make a formal announcement during the opening moment of the Trilateral Conferences.

The Grand Dame Taylor offered to assist her son. The Zemplars, Ziola and Tremador, also volunteered to assist in the transition. Yoshen would manage the rebel forces as they transitioned into a security force.

It had been a long night. When Enro's head finally rested on a pillow in a suite at the Orion, he thanked the Elders that the loss of life had been minimal.

Shimtach had appeared in his room as he showered. He enjoyed the amenities he had missed for so many years living in the wilds of the rebel encampments. He slept well.

*

Bodono tossed in his bed, with all he had gone through over the past four days. Thoughts of Chandri his beloved moon Goddess, trapped on a corsair somewhere between Tatochin and Navidrrr tortured his mind. *I will go to Navidrrr!* Though his shoulder still throbbed from a laser blast, he slipped into a fitful sleep.

*

The sun had cleared the Tshini Mountains. The Remorah River flowed out of the mountains through the ashwood forest of the Planetary Park. It then poured into Lake Wechen on the doorstep of the Royal Orion resort.

Across the vast plains that spread west to the shores of the Capach Ocean, fields of mosh swayed in Shelila's breeze. The Corporation had set up partially automated farms, but many traditional native farms still existed. Farmers were tending the fields. There may have been a revolution last night but it was the right time to harvest mosh and that was more important.

In downtown Ecksol, the food processing plants that poisoned the food with hypnotic drugs, and addictive compounds were burning. As ordered, Vinny had destroyed the secondary targets. The burning of the processing plants would serve as a symbol of the vast changes in store for the now free citizens of Tatochin. The fire department watched them burn and successfully kept the fire from spreading to the Moorhead Brewery that had been mysteriously spared.

Amazingly, civil order was maintained. Small post Rahi gatherings and street parties were being reported. The name of Kaitain Enro became public knowledge. He had been a legend and now a resurrected leader that Tatochin accepted. The rebels were ecstatic with relief.

Cleo lay in bed and watched the light come in the window. Orville was nestled onto her breast softly snoring, a wisp of his untamable hair lifting with each outbreath. She felt her awareness spread encompassing Shelila's entire realm. The verdant planet had been restored to its people without too much damage to her ecosystem.

She thought about the long retrostory of Earth. They had suffered under the worst form of slavery for so long.

Soul slavery! We became willing participants. How could we have gotten into such a hole? Never again!

Her awareness spread like a gossamer rainbow through seven dimensions to the Central Sun itself. Tugs and pulls of energy gathered at points in a grand procession. Everything was vibrating with life. She felt her cells tingling, and stardust gathering to form a new star, as two equally accessible experiences.

Cleo would move through this universe to where, or to what, she knew not. She could hardly wait for the next breeze of life to caress her cheek. Running her finger through-Orville's hair brushing it from his face, she curled herself around him and drifted off to sleep.

*

CHAPTER FIFTY

"INVITED TO A FIRE"

Enro stood on top of the Corporation headquarters in the morning sun. As a rebel he was most comfortable outside. Yoshen sought him out. She looked at the kaitain and burst into tears. Enro was alarmed. Yoshen was not usually the demonstrative type.

"What's the matter? What's going on?"

"Flex was captured and tortured. Nimro blasted his way past Black and the assassin, Korgon. Stopped the Korgon dead in his tracks. Grace was with him to jump the gun on that treacherous minion."

"Black disappeared. Nimro made his way to the detention center, and found Flex barely alive. He took him to Mirror. Not sure if he will survive."

Cleo and Orville joined them on the roof. They had just heard about the Korgon and Nimro's fortune. Enro came to face the couple. He put his large hand on Orville's shoulder.

"When you brought me here, five years ago, they were an unruly pair. Couldn't keep Flex out of the city or get Nimro near one. Yet they were the best of friends." Enro's voice cracked with emotion. He looked out along the horizon.

He thought of the Intergalactic Diaspora and the billions of souls that had departed Mother Earth over the past four hundred years. All of them with a timeline back.

We build the safe harbor here restoring the bridge to peace through Grace and Love.

Cleo guided Orville to Enro's side. She took his large calloused hand and encouraged the two men to face her. She lifted her hands and they formed a small circle on the rooftop of the conquered enemies' castle. They all instantly felt an electrical charge that grew as they connected their very beings into a master frequency that matched the power of the Central Sun itself.

Astral planes of existence co-mingled in a higher more refined manifestation of the hologram known as creation. It was the power of the Elders, focused at this gathering of rare and precious people, that transformed the environment into a nexus charged with a greater essence.

Cleo spoke with the power of many voices. "A long time ago when humanity was young, the Dravithians contributed to the evolution of your worlds. The fear of death and soul damnation was installed in your cultures by these slavers. They installed beliefs and altered the genetics as well. Your DNA was shut down. As a result, religions, thought processes, and desire bodies, evolved on the path of fear."

"Over great lengths of time, these seed thoughts evolved with a life of their own. A basic fear of the power within you has deep underpinnings. As we evolve, this is surfacing and beginning to break down." Cleo paused and removed some tears that formed around her almond shaped eyes.

Orville looked on, absorbing the deep textured feelings as his beloved spoke from a higher state of awareness. She continued after making silent contact with Enro.

"Our relief at the bypassing of the spectre of death is a misplaced focus. Death is perfectly safe. Death does not separate us from each other permanently. We come back, and continue, or go on, and participate from other realms. That which ultimately binds us together is not of the flesh. It is eternal, and in truth, we are already there."

Cleo's gift was an ability to illuminate related experiences to all that heard her words. As she spoke past life memlocks, the faces of Elders, and many soul-shaping experiences, scrolled through all of their awareness. Locks to previously inaccessible parts of being that had lain dormant began to open up. Integration of those useful memlocks would fill their days with wonder.

"Accept your role as leaders. Perhaps the safe harbor that you seek to build is found in the wisdom of your true self. The vastness of living in a more spiritual herenow is the challenge you have been offered. Life does not wait. As you will soon see." Cleo closed her eyes and took a deep breath.

The ability to conjure had grown in Cleo from the ascended realms in which she had dwelled. The images of Tharrr holographic symbols revealed its spark of life within the local orb of their reckoning. It arrived as a premonition for the nearnow. Like a momentary flash of illumination, it pulsed through them all and vanished back into more rarefied realms of dimensional expression.

Enro, Orville, and Cleo stood on the roof-top holding hands as the intense energy subsided. Like King, Queen, and Champion, they formed a triad that was a pinnacle of creation. They were shepherds leading the way back to the spiritual realms whence we had all come.

Some time passed as the three of them digested the amazing experience they had just shared. They dropped their hands after a time.

Collectively, they knew that the details of the day would soon take them far from the space they had just encountered. They each knew that they had been forever changed by the moment they had shared.

*

EPILOGUE

THE PENDULUM OF PHENOMENA

They gathered at Enro's offices to share lunch with Father Jones, Farooq Masad, Martha Fox, Orville and Cleo. Orville had arranged to have tacos for lunch. Before they sat down to eat, Enro's assistant, Cedrai, handed him a note. Enro eyes darted across the page. He looked at Cedrai with a questioning look.

"It came in from the Lunar Space Dock, all communication is out land-side," she quickly said.

Enro handed the note to the Gaian ambassador, as Jones, Orville, and Cleo looked on.

The face of the Gaian ambassador shifted as the words were read. "My Goddess. Oh, my Goddess!" She stood in shock. Martha ominously handed the note back to Enro.

"There has been a catastrophe on Earth. It has tilted on its axis. No one has been able to make contact. This pulse fax came via one of the orbital space docks in the asteroid fields of Melona near Jupiter. It originated from the Lunar Dock near Earth."

Enro excused himself and followed Cedrai to the COM room. Farooq Masad encouraged the ambassador to a chair. He held her hand and let her absorb the news.

Orville recognized that a critical moment had begun. He knew the Earth was destined to go through this change. He had memlocked detailed prophetic dreams hundreds of years ago on Mirror. He wondered about what had occurred on Tatochin and what was now happening on Navidrrr. Earth was included in this transition.

Now she has shifted orbit! What of the Tharrr? What of Cleo?

Orville felt a deep tremor that resonated in every cell of his 24 strand DNA rarified flesh.

It is cellular memlocks! Amazing!

The emotional intensity and compassion for the loss of life was poignant. But all the recent experiences with Cleo, and the Pleiadians, had pushed his awareness into new and amazing places. The scientist in him was roused. A native of Earth, he had not fully realized the bond to his home world.

Cleo held his hand. She recalled her meeting with the Elders. *Had they known of this potentiality then?*

Cleo knew Orville was handling everything quite well. Her own parents had revered old Earth, and told her many tales of ancient Gaia.

They looked into each others eyes. Orville took a deep cleansing breath. "It has always been a part of Earth's retrostory. Inside, we have always known it would come. We wondered if we would survive as a species in the twenty-first century. Earth did well in that regard. I am standing here with all of you and say this is proof," Orville said. "Now it comes to me. The Earth is re-emerging. I think it's the sixth time."

Maybe the Earth itself can be a part of my exploding life form club!

Human beings from the planet Earth had migrated into the galaxy for almost four hundred and fifty years. The worlds they had discovered, the lessons that they had learned, the vast variations on what being human meant, had expanded to immense proportions. Earth had become the stuff of myth and lore. Now time itself was laying down its burden of a dream of immense proportion. It was becoming a singularity. Space itself was now the dreamscape.

Orville's ability to appear at will in any place, was growing. He understood that it would soon be the herenow trend in maximode. He sighed. *"Wow!"* was all he could think.

The vibration was dense with transformation and very intense change. Among the Pleiadians hope reigned. They whispered among themselves about the Zentalissa. They would tend to the Earth as they had many times before. Human beings from Earth were still digesting the vastness of the expanse that had grown from miles to light years, in a very short time. Orville trusted them. They would oversee the great transitions. He was comforted.

Everyone was beside themselves with concern. Though lunch had been served events had disrupted everything including appetites. The cold tacos went uneaten as the day passed.

*

EARTH: THE SIX EMERGENCE

Gaia was pleased that her children had spread far and wide across the vastness of space. They too would witness the re-birth of the motherland. She accepted gladly and fearlessly the new changes in her evolutionary journey. Storms, winds, and fire raged as vast transformations were occurring within her body. Great arcs of electrical energy coursed around the planet.

Swirling clouds twisted in tight screws as the elements of her physical body were in a froth. Earthquakes and other movement within Earth Gaia's body collapsed lands creating new valleys and lakes. Land masses thrust upward forming new mountains. The very continents shifted as the great plates moved. All the great oceans frothed with giant waves as Gaia trembled with change.

There was much physical death. She drew the many souls that had passed beyond the veil of three-dimensional life to her side. From an ethereal heaven, they attuned themselves to the Great Spirit's vibration.

When the Earth had stabilized she spoke. "You see, my children, I have made the world new once more. There is nothing to mourn. You have earned the opportunity to continue to live upon my breast."

It was time for renewal. The old structure had been swept away rapidly and completely. This allowed for new patterns, fractals, and mutation. She knew that life would continue. She would nurture that life both old and new.

The ending found in a new beginning.

Printed in the United States
By Bookmasters